Generation Nemesis

Generation Nemesis
Sean McMullen

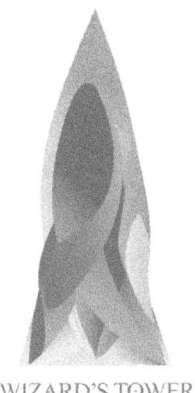

WIZARD'S TOWER

Wizard's Tower Press
Rhydaman, Sir Gaerfyrddin,
Cymru

Generation Nemesis

First edition, published in the UK November 2022
by Wizard's Tower Press

Paperback ISBN: 978-1-913892-44-9

Cover illustration and design by Ben Baldwin
Car image by Feòrag NicBhrìde
Editing by Betsy Mitchell
Design by Cheryl Morgan

http://wizardstowerpress.com/
https://seanmcmullen.net.au/

CONTENTS

Praise for Sean McMullen   8

Prologue Day   10

Day 1: Arrival   15

Day 2: Central Heating   43

Day 3: Recreational Gasoline Vehicle   66

Day 4: Three Hundred and Seventy Flights   96

Day 5: Sixteen Pound Cat   115

Day 6: Climatically Incorrect Child   129

Day 7: Deconstructing a Motorcycle   144

Day 8: Burning Wood   164

Day 9: Riding to the Fireworks   183

Day 10: Recreational Train by Proxy   195

Day 11: Retirement Fund   219

Day 12: Doctor, Doctor   228

Day 13: Not Eextreme Enough   243

Day 14: Squander by Inaction   276

Day 14: - Continued   298

Day 15: Sentence   305

Epilogue Day   343

Acknowledgments   349

About the Author   350

SEAN MCMULLEN

For Svante Arrhenius, who linked the burning of fossil fuels to global warming back in 1896. Are we paying attention yet?

PRAISE FOR
SEAN MCMULLEN

"... one of Australia's best SF writers." — *Interzone*

"McMullen has a gift worthy of the best mainstream authors for creating memorable, finely nuanced characters ..." — *Booklist*

"Sean McMullen has a passion for using alternate technologies, a tremendous talent for storytelling ..." — *SFRevu*

\#

Generation Nemesis is based on the novelette "The Precedent", first published in *The Magazine of Fantasy and Science Fiction.*

'Sean McMullen's novelette "The Precedent" ... begins, "Even when the climate crime is so serious that death is not punishment enough, one still gets an audit." — *New York Review of Science Fiction*

'... tribunals in the future pass judgment on "tippers," the wastrels whose giant carbon footprints led the world over the edge to disaster.' — *The Smithsonian Magazine*

SEAN MCMULLEN

'Set in a future that feels very plausible... The story is chilling, both for the vision of the planet that it describes, and for the callousness of the legal system that this has created.' — *Locus*

'As bleakly intense a take on climate change and its consequences as you'll find. ... The stuff of nightmares.' — *Unbound Worlds Library*

PROLOGUE DAY

When did it start to go so terribly wrong? Perhaps the catastrophe began when Thomas Newcomen invented his steam engine in 1712, or when a descendent of that engine was installed in a railway locomotive in 1804. There is certainly a case for declaring that early cars began transporting us along the road to ruin around 1900, and that the aircraft that soon followed them led to a global transport industry that flew us to disaster ten times faster. All those inventions took carbon out of the ground and dumped it into the atmosphere, all of them were tools for squander. Now squandering attracts the death penalty, and the methods of execution are very inventive.

#

I shall start my story on a desert road, in the intense heat of a clear summer afternoon, greatly enhanced by greenhouse warming. Teams of people born before the new millennium were harnessed to wagons, and I was one of them. Those wagons were SUVs stripped of their engines, bonnets and seats, and loaded with water, food and desiccated bodies. The road was not well maintained, but that was deliberate.

We were being taught the hard way just how much energy was required to move a vehicle, and how much of that energy had been squandered moving billions of those vehicles for a century and a half. Each of the SUVs was painted with words declaring NO FUEL RESOURCES ARE BEING CONSUMED ON THIS JOURNEY.

We were tippers on our way to be audited, and the process was supposed to be fair. Even when your climate crime was so serious that death was not sufficient punishment, you still got an audit. We were being taken into the desert to Audit Camp 71, where passably affluent people with European backgrounds were audited for climate crimes by their Generation Victim peers. A third of us had already died.

None of the wardens who guarded us were older than forty-five, and all were volunteers. They carried assault rifles and did not hesitate to shoot when provoked, yet they treated us more humanely than they probably thought we deserved. There was no sense of superiority in Generation Victim, although they had a right to feel outrage. They walked beside us, shared the water equally, and ate the same food as we did, yet they would help make an example of us at the end of the journey. We were a message to the future, in case anyone was again tempted to chew up the world, then excrete into the oceans and belch into the air.

The bodies of those who died along the way were cut open and staked by the roadside to dry out. This had to be done before they rotted, because decaying flesh releases greenhouse gases. Part of our job was also to collect the desiccated bodies left by earlier caravans, and these we loaded onto the roof racks of the SUVs. At the end of our journey they would be buried in deep, abandoned mineshafts, removing their dried flesh from the carbon cycle like coal mining in reverse.

GENERATION NEMESIS

In death the people of Generation Tipper would not pollute the atmosphere as they had in life.

#

At dusk our SUV caravan stopped. The wagons were left on the road, because there was no other traffic in either direction. It never ceased to amaze me that the wardens did not treat us with the brutality that even I thought we deserved, but the journey was not entirely free from payback. We were only allowed to rest while the sun was below the horizon because our generation had turned it loose upon the world. Thus we slept well, but worked in a furnace.

The evening meal did not take long, everyone just wanted to rest in the cooling air. We tippers slept on the roadside sand, under the blankets that had been our sun cloaks during the day. I was wearing only the remains of a flannel shirt, fraying jeans and improvised sandals.

For those who could no longer walk, the hours of darkness held new terrors. The wardens allowed them to ride on the wagons, but this meant harder work for those who were still in harness and doing the pulling. Every night there were muffled screams and cries for help as groups of vigilante tippers made sure that the infirm passengers did not survive until morning. As long as the bodies were staked out to dry before we moved on, the wardens asked no questions.

The wardens were all fit, well trained and disciplined. They wore red shirts, bamboo fabric jeans, conical wicker hats, and sandals with hinged wooden soles. Their assault rifles all had bayonets, because shooting a tipper was considered to be a waste of resources unless it was an emergency. Warden Olivia had just been rotated to my SUV team as overseer, and when she walked past on inspection I was already lying under my blanket with an arm over my eyes.

"How ya doing, Mr Hall?" she asked cheerily as she shone her solar powered torch down on me.

"Not dead yet, and it's Doctor Hall," I replied, anxious to get on with the urgent business of resting for the next day.

"You're really Dr Fitness. You made it to the mine."

It was clear that she wanted to talk, so I could not ignore her. I sat up, slowly and with the stiffness of someone who had been helping to tow a two ton wagon along badly maintained roads for the past fourteen hours. Our journey had taken a month so far.

"Not there yet," I said, gesturing about at the desert.

"It's only ten miles more, we should make it in time for lunch tomorrow," Olivia said, turning and pointing down the road. "You can see the old crane towers from here when it's light."

"I'll take your word for it."

"Cheer up. You'll make it."

"You talk like that's good."

"What's wrong with being alive?"

"People keep trying to kill me."

"Now who would want to do that?"

"The people who put me on the longest trek to any of the six dozen audit camps on the continent. The people who want me audited by such a strict Auditor General that she had her own parents and three brothers executed for climate crimes."

All along the road a long line of old people was settling down for the night. It was the year 2045 and vengeance was upon us. Everyone born before the year 2000 was considered guilty of climate crimes, and the penalty was death for all of them. We were called Generation Tipper and we were tough and fit. The weak, frail, sick or disabled had not lasted long when the health services collapse and famines joined disease as everyday realities.

"This is my fifth tour of duty," Olivia said. "Most wardens just do three, but I like it. You get to meet a lot of people at the audits."

"And kill them," I replied, past caring whether or not I was causing offence.

"Not always. Some tippers go onto the backlog as borderlines, and they can stay there for years. The lucky ones fall off the perch before the Auditor General gets back to them."

"You call that lucky? Roasting in the middle of a desert while facing a death sentence?"

"You don't know anything, Dr Fitness. Life at Audit Camp 71 can be one long party if you don't step out of line."

She walked on, and I settled down under my blanket again. *What sort of party can one have in a death camp?* I wondered.

#

DAY 1: ARRIVAL

At first light, an hour before the sun actually appeared, we were roused by the whistles of the wardens, and there was an inspection to determine who had not survived the night. After a minimal, climatically correct breakfast of solar distilled water and vat grown protein slush, we staked out those who had died or been murdered, then bundled their clothes and blankets into the wagons. It was a depressing task, but we were meant to be depressed. We tippers had once discarded clothes merely because they were unfashionable, and had done much the same with our cars, houses, appliances, pets and just about everything else.

We were already moving along the road by the time the sun appeared on the horizon. This was my favorite time of day, because it was still cool and I was rested. In theory we could have done all of our traveling during the night, guided by solar battery torches, but that was not the point of the journey. Generation Tipper had heated up the world and now we were being forced to experience the consequences.

It took the entire morning to travel to the audit camp, and a few more tippers died on the way. Their bodies were carried on the wagons, to be staked out to dry in the camp itself. For the last five miles the road was flanked by stripped out SUVs. I counted five hundred to either side as we passed them. They were parked ten rows deep, so this added up to ten thousand. The SUVs of our caravan would soon be added to the automotive graveyard.

The audit camp itself was ringed by a wall of SUVs piled five cars high and five miles in circumference. These were wrapped in chainlink and topped with coils of razor wire. There were also watchtower pyramids of SUVs piled fifteen high. We entered, dragging our ghosts of a dead transport system through an arch of SUV bodies. The camp was a vast collection of tents, fences and prison pens on red sand, built on the site of an abandoned mine. We paused at the perimeter arch while the concierge warden checked the ID chips in our arms with a reader, then a security team with metal detectors and sniffer dogs scanned us for weapons and contraband.

Warden Olivia pointed out the main features of the camp once we were moving again.

"Now that open area near the fence with nothing on it is a minefield, not a great place for a picnic. Over on the left is Farm Field, that's where we grow the vat food. Further along on the right is Dormitory Field, no prizes for guessing that's where you sleep."

"But there are no tents or buildings there," wheezed someone.

"All you need is a trench and a blanket, and you got blankets already."

"But it might rain."

"Hasn't rained in twenty years, thanks to Generation Tipper. Anyone from Generation Tipper here?"

Nobody bothered to answer.

"Just past that is Refectory Field, it's another big favorite because you eat there."

"It's only got a couple of tents," said the woman beside me.

"The seats are planks on mounds of sand, or plain sand if you prefer something softer. Look left, and you see an arena. That's the Audit Arena, it's where you get audited. You may think that's a worry, but it's almost as popular as Entertainment Field - which is way over on the right, you can just see the stands."

"Where do we get killed?" the woman asked.

"The carbon reclamation fields are dead ahead." Olivia paused, but nobody laughed. "Hey, lighten up, you gotta admit that was just a teeny bit funny. Class One executions happen under those two old mining towers. Way over to the left is Solar Field, where we get most of our power."

"It's all so flat," I said.

"Yeah, that's true, but why build up when there's so much free space?"

There were a lot of signs: names of fields, where to go, where not to go, and electronic screens displaying schedules for various work groups. There were very few substantial structures. The Audit Arena and Entertainment Field's stands stood out, but most other buildings were only large, low sheds built from salvaged concrete slabs. Mostly it was all tents, solar cells and fabrication vats. This made sense, because it never rained and there was little wind, so it was only a matter of keeping cool during the day and surviving the chill of the desert night.

"So even the Auditor General sleeps in a tent?" I asked.

"Yeah, all the auditors and wardens do," replied Olivia.

I looked across to Farm Field, but it was like any other farm, just a mosaic of rectangular vats where sunlight converted carbon dioxide, water and a few minerals into protein or vegetable slurry. It was tended by prisoners who shuffled about slowly because they were all old and the temperature

was already over 40 Centigrade. There was no corporal punishment in Audit Camp 71, yet these people were definitely
being punished. Those who showed real defiance were audited the next day, and that meant they would be dead by noon.

As we drew closer to Dormitory Field I saw that it was just
red sand, shallow trenches and marker posts. Sand is quite
good insulation, so one just dug in while it was warm from
the day, and covered oneself with a blanket. There were
thousands of marker posts, but by now it was late morning
and nobody was ever allowed to sleep in. The few people that
I could see there were digging out the bodies of those who
had died during the night.

The layout of the camp was scrappy but functional. The
Audit Arena in the center reminded me of the open air
theatres built by the ancient Greeks and Romans. Its gallery
had been constructed from the carcasses of cars and rubbish
from the old mine, and most likely it was meant to last only
until everyone from Generation Tipper had been audited.
The administration and armory buildings were substantial
concrete slab structures, and Administration was the real hub
of the camp. It was a very desirable place to work, because it
actually had air conditioning for the computer and communications equipment.

We finally stopped at Staging Field and dragged our SUV
wagons into neat rows. While borderlines from the camp
did the unloading, we newly arrived tippers sat or lay in the
hot sand where we had stopped. Beside Staging Field were
the execution fields, although the wardens referred to the
ultimate punishment as 'reclaiming carbon.' I watched as
a man with BORDERLINE 270 on his headband hurried up to
the caravan warden. He was probably in his late forties, and
unlucky enough to be born just a year or two on the wrong
side of Year 2000.

"You're late," he said, his voice full of authority and
self-importance.

"Live with it," replied the warden, who knew that he had no authority.

"It's almost noon. The morning audits have already finished."

"Lots of deaths on this run, and they all had to be staked out to dry."

"Yeah? That's good. More deaths mean less audits."

"True, but less audits mean less climate justice. Over to you."

Borderline 270 climbed onto the roof of an SUV at the middle of the caravan and held his hands high. Warden Olivia blew her whistle for attention.

"Gather round, ladies and gentlemen, gather round," he called. "Don't be shy. That's it. I'm Borderline 270."

We tippers got up stiffly and shuffled into a semicircle around the SUV, all holding our blankets up as sunshades and looking like a crowd of ragged walking tents.

"Welcome to Audit Camp 71," he declared. "Does anyone know what the National Audit is?"

"We all do," croaked a man from my SUV's team.

"Okay, silly question, but can someone provide a bit more detail than that?"

"It's the legal arm of the National Forced Democracy League," I called, when it became clear that nobody else was going to answer.

"And what does the NFDL do?"

"It forces people to think before they vote," I said.

"You got it. When people think, they start asking questions and questions need answers. This camp is part of the Australian National Audit, and it audits folk who are climate criminals. There are audit camps for pretty well all ethnic and racial groups. Audit Camp 71 is for affluent folk of European background, people who should have known better when they squandered, displayed, denied, or screwed the climate with acts of greed. The good news is that we get audited by people of our own background. The bad news is that nobody has ever been pardoned. Now I'm a borderline. Borderlines are tippers with difficult audits. Because of us, there's a backlog of climate criminals who need their carbon reclaimed."

The borderline gestured to a gallows away to the left. Some tippers smiled, others looked uneasy.

"So, we borderlines gotta wait, and while we wait, we work. There are twelve thousand people in this camp, and we have to be self-sustaining."

"What about if we get sick?" called the woman who had been in the harness beside mine.

"You get audited right away, then go to one of those six fields behind me to have your carbon reclaimed."

"You mean killed."

"Think of it as being removed from the planet's carbon cycle."

"By being killed."

"The climate criminal's death is part of the carbon reclamation process."

No more than three hundred people had survived the month-long journey to the camp. Most had been chosen by lottery, but there was one volunteer. Me. Nearly all could expect to have easy audits. The whole world knew that "easy audit" meant the hearing lasted only a minute or so at Audit Camp 71, and that the sentence was always death. Difficult audits were adjourned after about fifteen minutes, and the tipper became a borderline. One could remain a borderline for years if one behaved, and there was every chance that one might die of natural causes. This was not an ideal situation for us, but it was an improvement on being dead.

"Now I know what you're thinking," continued Borderline 270. "You reckon it's all doom, gloom, hard work and death sentences out here, but that's not true."

"Just mostly," croaked another borderline.

"We're allowed to have fun, and there's plenty of entertainment available. As a matter of fact, the morning's entertainment is approaching right now. You lucky tippers have arrived just in time to watch the day's carbon reclaimings. Okay, speech over. Back to you, wardens."

He climbed down off the SUV's roof, then the wardens herded us into a straight line to merge with what turned out to be the daily audit procession.

#

The audit procession was led by the Auditor General, who had the hood of her cloak raised and was flanked by two wardens with assault rifles. She was attended by the Clerk of the Bench, whose assistant was pushing a writing desk on wheels. Behind them were the Advocate and Retributor, who wore white and black top hats respectively, and behind these were eight men and women, designated as auditors by their green bowler hats. A lone bagpiper followed, playing an adaptation of Purcell's "Funeral March for Queen Mary."

Next came the condemned tippers, interspersed with borderlines and wardens. The tippers had their hands bound, and each was being escorted by a personal warden. The wardens from the caravan told us to merge into the procession, and it was not long before one of the borderlines drifted over to me. He looked to be in his late forties, and had an oddly self-assured manner.

"You from the morning's caravan?" he asked.

That was obvious, because I did not yet have a headband with a number. Still, how else to start a conversation?

"Just arrived," I replied.

"What climate crimes are you charged with?"

"Everything."

"Yeah? Bummer! Me, I got greed. The Retributor went for Class Two Death, no mercy, but I got borderlined. Name's Chaz."

"I'm Jason. So, we're allowed to use names here?"

"Yeah. Why not?"

"The borderline who welcomed us said he was Borderline 270."

"Oh him! Alf's a wanker, he's in the First Thousand Club and he wants everyone to know it."

"As in first thousand to arrive at the camp?"

"You got it. There's only six of them left, they've been waiting years for a second audit."

"I'm going to apply for auditing tomorrow."

Chaz whistled.

"Priority audit? Don't you like being alive?"

A condemned man was walking in front of us. He was designated condemned by the red cheesecloth neckband he wore, which also indicated what was about to happen to him. His hands were tied behind his back with red cord, symbolizing that the blood of seven billion people was on them. A warden walked beside him, holding him firmly by one arm. He turned back to us.

"I got Class Six Death for denial, squandering and greed," he said, as if eager to impress us.

"What was your line?" I asked.

"Meteorites."

This was a surprise.

"As in bits of rock that fall from the sky?"

"Yeah, I hunted them for a living and sold them through mail order. I knew all the tricks, like how to get 'eyes on' in the desert, then to look for the 'pop-out'."

"Pop-out?"

"That's when the dark brown meteorites start jumping out at you against the red sand."

"How does a meteorite hunter get convicted for denial, squandering and greed?" I asked.

"I drove an SUV to reach the best spots."

If there was an SUV in your past, you were in a lot of trouble unless you really needed one to earn a living. This tipper was not a scientist, he had just serviced a novelty market. That meant he had burned fossil fuels to do work that was not vital to the survival of the planet, and that was definitely a climate crime. Although he was being marched to his death, he was actually smiling as he turned away from us.

"You hear that sort of spiel pretty often," whispered Chaz.

"What do you mean?" I asked.

"Some tippers try to pass on their skills, like how to tune a V8, ways to score in nightclubs, tricks to beat the share market, even how to arrange Christmas lights."

"That makes sense. The old lifestylers probably want to keep their legacies' memory alive."

"Right on," said Chaz after thinking for a moment. "Never thought of it that way."

The actual lifestyles were being executed as well as ourselves. Owning a V8 would get you lynched, nightclubs were not what they used to be, shares were illegal, and Christmas lights were a request for the death penalty.

#

The procession stopped at what Chaz told me was the Tipping Point Gallows, and the wardens herded the prisoners into a neat line beside it. The gallows was built of timber and scrap iron from the old mine. It consisted of a beam with a noose, and beneath this was a raised see-saw with one end weighted down by a barrel filled with lumps of coal. The other end was directly beneath the noose.

The Auditor General held up her hand for silence, and the background of murmurs and whispers faded away to nothing. She was wearing a black cloak, hood and sunglasses, only her gloves were red. I knew her face better than anyone else in the entire world. The other auditors were fanned out behind her, all wearing olive green cloaks matching their bowler hats. The Retributor wore a black top hat and cloak to look confronting and intimidating to those being audited, and he certainly managed that. The Advocate was a woman of about twenty, dressed identically, but in white. Somehow she did not convey the same authority as the Retributor, and this was probably intentional as well.

The bagpiper turned out to be the Executioner. He handed his pipes to a warden, pulled on a red balaclava, and completed his change of uniform with a red bowler hat. He led the first prisoner up the steps beside the tipping plank and put the noose around his neck. The man happened to be the meteorite hunter I had just been talking to. A warden stood with him beside the tipping point plank, holding him by the arm. The Auditor General addressed him.

"James Francis Harrington, you have been found guilty of denial, squandering and greed. For this you are sentenced to Class Six Death, with mercy."

"Mercy means the rope is placed to snap his neck, not strangle him slowly," Chaz whispered to me.

SEAN MCMULLEN

"As you did take from the Earth, so now you must give back," the Auditor General continued. "Have you any last words?"

"I love the wilderness, I really do," called the tipper, either by way of apology or to make a last bid to stay alive.

"You poisoned the wilderness with fumes from your recreation vehicle and tore up the delicate ecology of the desert with its wheels. Executioner, reclaim his carbon."

The warden remained beside Harrington while the Executioner led a procession of wardens who filed past the barrel of coal holding down the other end of the tipping plank. Each took a lump of coal from the barrel and dropped it into a basket beside the plank. The plank began to teeter. Harrington started to scream as the tipping point approached, then the barrel was spilled as the tipping point was reached. Harrington dropped, the gallows creaked, and the wardens applauded.

The Executioner singled me out, handed me the basket and pointed at the spilled coals on the sand. He pushed Chaz after me. Together we gathered up the spilled coals and put them back in the barrel while two wardens took the body down.

"Damn fine kill," said Chaz as we worked. "Nice and clean."

"I heard his neck snap," I said, shuddering.

"And only for driving an SUV."

"Him and a couple of billion others."

I poured my basket of coal back into the barrel on the tipping point plank. An elderly woman who was also wearing a red cheesecloth scarf began to shriek and struggle when told she was next. The warden who was escorting her to the Executioner was only about seventeen.

"Pull yourself together, you're embarrassing me," muttered the girl sternly.

The woman continued to struggle and shriek.

"Quartermaster!" called the Executioner.

A warden wearing a backpack produced a spare red scarf and gagged the tipper with it.

"Sara Jennifer Robbins, you have been found guilty of squander, specifically, gratuitous holidaying on the proceeds of your superannuation payout, and display for building a fourteen room mansion for entertainment," said the Auditor General. "For this you are sentenced to Class Six Death, without mercy. Clerk of the Bench, you will note her last words as *Incoherent Screaming*."

This time the knot of the noose was placed behind the woman's neck. The wardens commenced their deadly procession again, slowly emptying the barrel of coal until the tipping point was reached. Robbins dropped, then squirmed for about a minute while the rope choked her. To me, and doubtless to Sara Robbins, it seemed more like hours. Once again Chaz and I gathered up the spilled coals.

#

Each execution lasted about five minutes, which Chaz said was roughly what it took to do most audits. The fifty executions were over by mid afternoon, and by then one of those waiting had collapsed and died of heatstroke.

"Gallows day is always a long haul," said Chaz as we gathered the coals from the final execution. "Eighty-five is the record, but every one of those was with mercy so it was all just snap, no struggle."

"You mean the other types of executions are not as common?"

"It varies. Greenhouse, Rising Sea Level and Finite Resources take longer, but are just as quick to set up. The Auditor General attends every one of them, declares the charges and records the last words."

"Why? Does she enjoy killing people?"

"Nah, it's National Audit regulations. Each execution for climate crimes must be a ceremony, and all those executed must be treated as people, not things."

By now the auditors, wardens and tippers had left. A woman of about seventy arrived, pushing a cart and wearing a backpack where a collection of healthy, living plants was growing.

"Hi Chelsea," Chaz called.

"Greetings and Rebirth, Charles," the woman replied. "Are they finished with the coal yet?"

"Yeah, you can haul it away and lock it up for tomorrow."

"Has the sun finally got to me, or do I see a woman wearing a garden?" I asked.

"Nah, it's meant to be a forest."

At this point Warden Olivia joined us.

"Come along, Dr Fitness, time to make you a happy camper - Hey Chaz! Is that really you?"

"Good to see you back, Livi," said Chaz.

"How are ya doing? Still dodging those auditors?"

"My agenda's to die old, in mid-orgasm."

"I'm always ready to help."

"You need a mentor for this new tipper?"

"Sure. Come along."

I was astounded that they could be so cheerful after fifty executions, but deaths in Audit Camp 71 were just part of the daily routine.

"Who was the woman with the plants on her back?" I asked as we walked.

"That's Chelsea, she's a Greenhand. They worship -"

"I know what Greenhands are. Why is she wearing a garden in the middle of the desert?"

"Because the Green Man needs to live in a forest."

"I once thought about joining the Greenhands, but didn't."

"Too weird?"

"Too tame."

"What did you think of the carbon reclaimings, Dr Fitness?" Olivia asked.

"Depressing," I sighed.

"Hey there, lighten up. You'll soon get a chance to be the star of the show."

The woman had the most confronting brand of gallows humor I had ever encountered, yet in a way this made sense. Serious, self-righteous people with psychotic conditions were banned from becoming wardens, because the National Audit was absolutely meticulous about not crossing the line between judicial execution and murder on an industrial scale.

"I really like the Tipping Point Gallows," said Chaz. "It's quick and clean. The Carbon Dioxide Mask can last twenty minutes, and death by Greenhouse Tent can drag out for a couple of days."

"The Carbon Dioxide Mask is Class Five Death," said Olivia, as cheery as ever. "You suffocate on your own breath, so it's painless."

"I can't believe you actually volunteered to come here," I said to her, more to change the subject than because I was interested.

"Hey, it's just one big working holiday. Everyone wants to off a few climate criminals, but you gotta be special to be a warden. There's the psych tests, three months of training with weapons, physical conditioning, then the trek all the way out to the audit camps. Takes commitment to get through all that."

"I suppose we should be flattered that you took the trouble," I replied.

"So what were you, Dr Fitness?" she asked.

"I was a climatologist."

"A climate change *denialist*?" she gasped. "I didn't think any of them were still alive."

I heard this sort of thing a lot, so I had my snappy, five second explanation ready.

"No, I was a weather scientist. I spent my whole life trying to warn people about climate change, way before it was obvious."

"Yeah? So why are you being audited?"

"Because everyone born before 2000 is a tipper, and every tipper gets audited."

This was a fundamental flaw in the National Audit's job statement. Was any tipper truly innocent? Were all the people in from Generation Victim innocent just because they were born after 31st December 1999? Practically everyone had squandered at least some of the Earth's resources for recreation or greed - or even to make a living, like meteor man.

"So you were a tipper who tried to make a difference?" she asked.

"Yes, but the National Audit thinks I didn't try hard enough."

"Don't worry. Sounds like you're gonna have a hard audit, so you'll soon be made another borderline."

"I hope not, I want a full audit and sentence."

"But those who get as far as sentencing always score death in AC 71."

"I know. I was in a backlist occupation but I volunteered to be audited."

That was a real conversation stopper, and it even silenced Olivia for a moment.

"Er, like, why?" she asked. "If you want to go out with suicide, there's easier ways."

"I think a better benchmark standard for climate guilt is needed. Just where is the boundary between a well meaning tipper and a climate criminal? Being born before the first day of the new millennium is too arbitrary, and guilt on a planet-wide, generational scale is something the law has never encountered before."

"I dunno, it all sounds a bit intellectual."

"So what was your line?"

"Name's Olivia, wanna do some climatically correct recreational sex?"

Chaz laughed, and I managed a smirk as well.

"I meant your job, before you became a warden."

"Computers, systems admin. Then I got audited."

She stopped, lowered her jeans and showed us the brand on one thigh: "S" for squandering. Chaz bent down for a closer look. I noticed that her underwear was as plain as that worn by men. Lace and frills were classed as marginal squander, and were as extinct as the tyrannosaurus rex.

"It hurt like hell, but I deserved it," she said as she pulled her jeans up again.

"To me that's squandering a mighty fine leg," said Chaz.

"I'm impressed," I said. "I thought no tipper had ever beaten the Audit here."

"I'm not a tipper. I was born this century."

Her age had not been easy to pick because she was so lean and heavily tanned.

"Ah, Generation Victim," I replied. "Then why were you audited?"

"I was two-ninety pounds at the time. Can you believe it?"

"Gluttony?"

"Yeah, I was living on Coke, turkey stuffing and fries. Got Class Six Branding in AC 37, but I was lucky. The Retributor wanted me to get Class One Service for life."

#

The chill of the air conditioning in Administration actually set my teeth chattering, and Olivia said it was thirty degrees cooler than outside. The clerk at the induction desk said that I was late, and that he had nearly put out an escape alert for me. Warden Olivia told him that an escape alert could not be issued without signoff from the escapee's overseer warden, and that was her. Faced with the prospect of his unimportant status being challenged, he quickly backed down.

"Jason Andrew Hall, climatologist, aged 85," he read from his screen. "Fifteen *pages* of climate crimes!"

"All of them invalid," I added.

"Most people only have only a couple of dozen crimes."

"Important people with hidden agendas want to make sure that I'm convicted and executed. That's also why I was assigned to the most remote audit camp for Anglos on the continent, with a perfect record for convictions."

"But the trek didn't kill him because he's Dr Fitness," added Warden Olivia.

"Do you want me to read the charges out?" asked the clerk.

"All fifteen pages? Don't bother."

"It says here that you volunteered for an audit."

31

"Yes, they got that right."

"Why?"

"Because I have an agenda. I want to beat the audit and save millions of lives."

"Now *that* would make you celeb of the century."

"That's not why I'm doing it."

"Then why?"

"For the same reason I spent my life studying the climate and trying to fix it. To do good."

"Weird! Well, there's no apprehension category to cover volunteering, except under the Religious and Ethnic Borderlines Amendment. You are entitled to indefinite adjournment of your audit by claiming membership of a religious, racial or ethnic group that has suffered genocide since 1900. Do you claim to be of Jewish, Cambodian, Rwandan, First Nation or any other such background?"

"No. And don't those people have their own audit camps?"

"They do, but there's a tiny bit of overlap. A while back I caught a paid up member of some neo-Nazi crowd trying to pass himself off as genetically Jewish but an atheist."

"Was he?"

"Descended from Jewish ancestors? Nah. Faked his DNA records, but we spotted the hack."

"Awesome," said Olivia. "What was his climate crime?"

"Off-road laser tag war games in SUVs."

"I reckon his audit will last about ten seconds, and he'll get Greenhouse Tent, without mercy."

"More like Finite Resources, without mercy," said the clerk.

"Like to bet your day's coffee ration on that?"

"You're on."

"What about my induction?" I asked.

"Oh, yeah. I'll have to message the Auditor General about creating a special category for you. Any preference for audit priority?"

"Tomorrow?"

"Totally awesome! First time I ever put 1 as the priority. There you go, tomorrow morning."

"I'm looking forward to it."

The clerk stared at his screen and swiped several fields.

"No history of mental illness in your family. That can't be right, but it's none of my business. Your code number is 78749, it's on this headband."

He tossed me a strip of white cloth with my code written on it in charcoal. White for the sun, charcoal for the carbon dioxide in the atmosphere. Like practically everything else in Audit Camp 71, it could be washed clean and used again.

Nearly eighty thousand of we old people had entered the camp since it first opened, but just eleven thousand were still alive. Roughly one in seven had survived as borderlines. That was not a cheering statistic.

"You are entitled to wash your clothes and blanket every fortnight, but I don't suppose you'll last that long. The five digits on your headband's inner lining are your sleeping trench's position in Dormitory Field. Do you have a mentor assigned?"

"A what?"

"A mentor. Someone to explain the duties, rules and routines to you."

"Give him Chaz, 5713," said Olivia. "They've already met."

"Then we're done. Jason Hall, Welcome to Audit Camp 71."

#

GENERATION NEMESIS

For the rest of the afternoon I did what I had been doing all the way out to Audit Camp 71: hauling a stripped-out SUV across the desert. Now that the supplies and dried bodies had been unloaded in Staging Field, we dragged the improvised wagon back the way we had come - between Farm and Dormitory Fields, through the arch in the perimeter wall, and past the five miles of car corpses. After that the tires were hacked off, and we carried the pieces of rubber back to the camp's recycling field on stretchers.

The sun was on the horizon by the time we had emptied the rubber into the enzyme processor vats. Sunset meant that work was over for the day, and the camp had a bugler to announce it. Chaz told me he always marked sunrise by playing a few bars of "The Party's Over," and sunset by "Goodnight Irene." The evening meal followed, but the food was much the same as we had been given on the long journey across the desert: rehydrated protein slurry, seaweed biscuits, fiber powder and distilled water.

I missed what was being staged in Entertainment Field that evening because Warden Olivia was finishing my induction. She said it was some sort of sporting event.

"Who has the energy left for sports?" I asked as cheering erupted in the distance.

"You'd be surprised. Tonight it's a wheelchair chariot race reenactment."

"You just lost me."

"Ever see that old movie, "Ben Hur"?"

"Yes, it was the first of the big-time epics."

"Well they're doing the race scene with wheelchairs and people instead of chariots and horses."

That was as much as I could get my mind around, so I did not ask any more questions. Sleeping spaces in Dormitory Field were strictly allocated, and Olivia showed me where to dig a shallow trench to sleep in, using my bowl. The sand was still warm from the day, and the idea was to pile it onto your blanket after settling down. I wore the bowl on my head as I slept to keep the sand out of my hair. Dormitory Field was lit by solar powered LED lights that glowed a dim but harsh blue. The wardens patrolled continually, watching for anyone trying to do anything except visit the privy pits or each other.

I lay on my back under my blanket, looking up at the stars. Those around me were asleep, and none were snoring yet. I had learned on the journey to the camp that those who snored were often found dead the following morning. In the distance the crowds continued to cheer the improvised chariots.

#

Audit Camps like this one were scattered across the continent, and were a direct result of the Climate War. It had not been a real war, more a verification of the old saying that western civilization is only three days from chaos if the supermarkets close. As droughts and accelerated global warming ravaged crops across entire continents, supermarkets, open air markets, and even emergency ration distribution centers did indeed close.

When angry and desperate citizens marched on the grain silos and warehouses, they learned the same lesson that both sides had been taught in the fields of France during World War One: machine guns are very effective at stopping large crowds of people, and they kill at a distance that transforms those people from humans into targets. That makes killing way easier. Only nine nuclear bombs were detonated during the chaos, but each of them destroyed a city. It is said that there were three sides in the Climate War: the starving, the heavily armed, and the climate itself. The climate was the real winner.

The leaders who had not survived had faced revolts by their own armed forces, police, and personal guards. They had forgotten that the people behind the riot shields, tear gas launchers and machine guns had families too, and were bright enough to know that they would be next to miss out. Naturally the leaders who were still alive had made a point of dressing in shabby clothes, keeping thin and eating the same rations as the rest of the population. Some people with pioneer lifestyle fantasies fled to the national parks and wilderness reserves to live off the land, but the Generation Victim wardens caught up with them very quickly.

The Climate War itself was over in just weeks, but the killings continued. Someone had to be blamed, and if culprits were being punished then voters would be happier with whoever was running what was left of civilization. After watching their children starve while those in retirement condos had obscenely large carbon footprints and well stocked pantries, the young fell upon the old like wolves in a pen of geriatric sheep. Rich survivalists were particularly popular targets for the warden ranger squads, because they had stockpiled food and weapons, and they tended to be loners or small family groups.

Punishing the guilty turned out to be an exceedingly popular political platform in Australia, and was guaranteed to generate voter support for any government. It was quick, cheap, and made good Cloudcast screentime - in contrast with fixing the climate, which was difficult, expensive, and would take longer than the life of any politician, let alone government. Eventually the meager food supply was able to keep up with demand, but people still wanted to see the climate criminals punished.

Governments clung to power by running the distribution centers, and this meant that anyone who did not support climatic justice missed out. However voter support depended on entertainment value as well as the food supply, and the Australian climate crime audits were very popular entertainment worldwide. Politicians love popularity, and so the International Audit Movement was becoming very powerful. That meant there was every chance that the entire world would adopt Australia's audit model, but that would be catastrophic for the climate as far as I was concerned. How many others shared my belief? None, as far as I could tell. All I could do to quite literally save the world was to volunteer to be audited, then try to survive twelve audits.

#

Footsteps approached, and stopped beside me. I thought it was a patrolling warden, so I sat up. Sand cascaded from my blanket, and I shivered in the chill night air.

"I'm new, I arrived today," I said. "Have I done something wrong?"

"How should I know?" asked a female voice. "You have not been audited yet."

"Who are you?"

She pushed back her cowl, and by the dim, blue light of the security lamps I saw the face of the Auditor General. As I said, I knew this face better than any other in the entire world.

"Who would you like me to be?" she asked. "A woman worried about the future? The Auditor General? The most terrifying mass murderer that this continent has ever known? Your granddaughter?"

I put a hand to my eyes.

"Oh crap, I can do without this."

"Hello granddad."

"Hello Renny."

"How very important we have become."

"You're important. I'm just a tipper."

"Not so, you're the most important tipper of all. I've followed your career on the web for the past three decades."

"And only sent me a one-liner birthday text once a year."

"That is more than anyone else got from me."

"Hardly surprising, you had the rest of our family executed."

"They were legally audited climate criminals. Anyway, you only sent me emailed birthday cards."

"Cards that I drew myself and scanned."

"You did?"

"Yes, all thirty. You deleted them, didn't you?"

"I - yes. I'm sorry. If I had known ..."

"You would have kept them? Ask one of your audit assistants to hack my account on the WorldCloud, I kept the scans. Oh, and before I forget, I've been following your career as well."

"Granddad, can we be a little less toxic with each other? The whole planet will be watching the World Cloudcast when you get your audit tomorrow."

"Bullshit, the shepherds will watch, not the sheep. Only National Audit spin doctors care what I say in case it causes political embarrassment."

"Bullshit is climatically incorrect, and the word will cause offence if you use it at the audit."

This was climate culture on steroids. The world's cattle had once produced vast amounts of methane, but now there were only a couple of thousand left, roaming wild in wilderness reserves and culled only by tigers, lions and other large predators.

"Is Generation Victim trying to save the world by killing words?" I asked.

"I'm being serious. You devoted your life to warning the world about climate change before it was an obvious problem. Tomorrow the world will be listening at last, so mind what you say and don't give offence."

I shook my head in disbelief.

"I suppose you're going to lecture me about neglecting your father while I tried to save the Earth."

"No way. Dad was a lazy pratt, I convicted him of gluttony and squandering last month."

"I noticed. You killed my son, your father, your daughter's grandfather! Anyone else would have at least had the decency to send him to Audit Camp 72."

"Even there he would have got Greenhousing, without mercy. I gave him Tipping Point Gallows, with mercy. Believe it or not I was being humane, even though he did not deserve it."

I had definitely been assigned to Audit Camp 71 because the presiding auditor general was not above executing members of her own family. This was not at all easy to come to terms with. After wishing that we could see more of each other for the past thirty years and writing as much in my birthday cards, I now just wished that she would go away.

"I thought meeting accused tippers out of session was forbidden in a court of law," I pointed out.

"It is an audit, not a court. Many rules and procedures are common to both, but not all."

"I'll put it another way. Piss off, you're really upsetting me."

"I'm just telling you not to expect special treatment tomorrow for being my grandfather."

"Point made, now leave."

"Is that all you have to say?"

"Yes."

"These may be our last private moments together."

"You mean you care?"

"Of course."

"So I'm to die?" I sighed.

"The odds against you suggest it."

"I don't suppose it matters. I'm old, and this is the end of the world."

"It's not the end of the world, just your world."

"Never thought of it as my world. So many others said they had a right to everything."

"And now I am auditing their claims."

"Is it gratifying work, killing the rich, the slobs and the airhead celebs?"

"Yes."

"You're murdering an entire generation!"

"That generation is not innocent!" she retorted, and very sharply. "Its leaders were once willing to wipe out humanity with a thermonuclear war. At the height of the madness Generation Tipper leaders had thirty thousand nuclear warheads ready to unleash because people didn't like each other's economic models. Remember the snappy one-liners? *Mutual Assured Destruction*? *Better dead than red*? Members of the Twentieth Century generations very nearly handed the planet over to the cockroaches. Nothing that Generation Victim is doing now can even come close to that."

"We managed to force policy changes and stop the nuclear madness."

"And then tipped the world into the climatic fireplace to support unsupportable lifestyles. Do you deny that?"

"Many from Generation Tipper fought against climate change."

"But few fought very hard."

40

"True," I sighed.

Now the climate crimes of everyone from Generation Tipper were being audited, and Death was the auditor. Death was also my granddaughter.

"So, no clever comeback?" Renny prompted. "You will have to do better than that in front of the audit bench."

"Why not drag me off to the tipping point gallows and murder me now?"

"Because everyone gets an audit. Good night, granddad, and good luck tomorrow. Remember, a worldwide audience will be watching."

"Why such popularity?"

"Because you volunteered for this, and that gives you credibility. Check the Cloudcast access stats for your audit as they come in. People believe in you, many more than you think."

"You don't."

"I do, actually, but that will not influence the decision I make."

She left. I shook my head, then scooped the spilled sand out of my trench bed and lay down again, although my thoughts were racing. For most of my life I had tried to make myself a climatically viable model for affluent, middle class people, those who were causing the most damage to the biosphere.

I was living proof that one could live well while not taking more than the Earth could give, yet I had been ignored. Why? Affluent people had preferred to enjoy all the advantages of being affluent without thinking about the consequences. Now the Earth was presenting its bill, and everyone had to pay.

Rich, poor, disadvantaged, entitled, all had their audit camps. If you had been able to afford your own home, you were considered to be somewhere between low level affluent and filthy rich. That qualified you for Audit Camp 71, which was a mercy-free zone.

Somewhere in the distance someone was snoring quite loudly. Soon there was a scuffle, followed by muffled cries, then silence. I sat up in time to see several figures hurrying away, hunched over.

"Some newbe from your caravan," said a voice from the trench next to mine. "So you're the AG's grandfather?"

"That's me."

"Awesome. I was at your son's audit. He -"

"Give it a rest!" cried someone nearby.

He fell silent. Clearly it was dangerous to keep people awake unless you were the Auditor General.

#

DAY 2: CENTRAL HEATING

Natural light was looked upon as a resource that was not to be squandered, so the breakfast bell woke us as the first traces of halflight glowed from the eastern horizon. I sat up, shook the sand out of my beard and blanket, then sat waiting to be told what to do next. Chaz arrived just as a body was being dug out of a sleeping trench not far away.

"Was he snoring?" he asked.

"Yes, but not for very long."

Refectory Field was beside Dormitory, but first we joined the queue for the privy pits. There was another queue for breakfast.

"It always creeps me out to think that what we just dropped off will soon be on the menu," said Chaz.

"Spare a thought for the microbes who have to eat it first," I replied.

"Yeah, it's not a good job statement. They spend their lives eating shit, then get eaten. How do you reckon you'll go at the audit?"

"Everyone thinks I won't be here for lunch."

"Dunno. I've met quite a few tippers over the years, and you got that special something in your attitude. I reckon you'll be such a tough case that the Retributor won't have you nailed down in fifteen minutes."

"I'm counting on that."

"You'll be okay. The Auditor General will give you an adjournment option, and you can choose to become a borderline. Borderlines got a one in three chance of natural causes knocking them off the perch before they get audited again."

"But I can request a continuation audit for the next day."

"Jason, my man, trust me on this one: you don't want to do that."

"I do. Seriously."

"But the default sentence gets worse automatically."

"I know. I've done my homework."

Breakfast was a ladle of something that looked like corn flakes and smelled like seaweed, but was probably neither. Still, nobody was choosy in a world that was being ravaged by climatic fever. Chaz lent me a comb carved out of plastic packaging for some long forgotten product, and I combed my hair and beard to look at least halfway presentable. With my blanket over my shoulders and my bowl and spoon dangling from my belt, I rubbed my teeth clean with my headband.

"Why go to so much trouble?" asked Chaz. "The auditors won't care how you look."

"I want them to know that I haven't been broken," I replied. "Good grooming shows that."

#

The bugler played "The Party's Over" as the sun rose clear of the horizon.

The planet-wide party that had been the industrial revolution was well and truly over. Parties are very messy

SEAN MCMULLEN

things, and if you clean up as you go along, they are not as much fun. Thus broken glass and crisps get trodden into the carpet and spilled drinks are not mopped up. The plates of artistically arranged party food soon get scoffed, and as more guests arrive the hosts have to send for takeaway pizzas. These get washed down with the host's expensive whiskey and liquors because all the cheap stuff is gone by then.

Around midnight the auditory nerves of the party people have been numbed by alcohol, so they are collectively a little deaf. They start shouting to make themselves heard above all the other people shouting to make themselves heard, and the stereo gets turned up louder and louder until the neighbors complain and call the police - unless the hosts took the precaution of inviting the neighbors. People are vomiting in the bathroom, and some are incapable of aiming at the toilet, even when kneeling in front of it with a hand on either side of the bowl.

Dawn arrives, and the realization that the party really is over sets in - along with the hangovers. Coffee and water become the drinks of popular choice for a house full of seriously distressed people. The stereo has been unplugged, but a few people are shouting at each other about what they did with other people's partners.

Now it was dawn at Audit Camp 71, and for the dominant species on planet Earth it was time to clean up. The tippers scheduled for auditing were listed on the public notice screens, but the wardens already had us herded together and arranged in order of appearance. Warden Olivia had decided that I was a celebrity, and being something of a groupie she decided to be my escort warden for the audit.

The Audit Arena was a walled, semi-circular space, built from the rusting bodies of cars that were now superfluous to the needs of their former owners. They were piled up in tiers so that off-duty borderlines could sit on them, watching climate justice being dispensed.

Standing there and looking about, I was struck by just how fit all the old people were. That was, of course, because the sick, frail and infirm had died on the journey through the desert. For those who were left, the food was nutritious and well balanced, even though it was boring and there was less of it than people wanted. Continual work to support the camp contributed to people's good health, exercising joints, keeping muscles strong, and giving everyone a daily aerobic workout. Getting sick or incapacitated was a sure way to have your audit given high priority, and the only way to remain alive was to stay in the borderline backlog with a low priority.

The Auditor General, eight auditors, Retributor, Advocate, Clerk of the Bench and Executioner paraded into the Audit Arena. The Auditor General was carrying a length of iron pipe that was her judicial mace, and she seated herself at a raised desk. The eight Auditors sat along a bench in front of her, each shaded by an umbrella held by a borderline. A dozen borderlines pedaled bicycle generators, providing electricity for the laptops used by the auditors. There was no need for the generators, Solar Field provided more than enough electricity for the entire camp, but the auditors wanted Generation Tipper people to be reminded that electricity did not just appear by magic.

There was seating for a thousand tippers and borderlines in the Audit Arena's gallery, with the tippers on the inner circle and the borderlines on those above. They were all in rags, and holding their blankets up as sunshades. The accused stood on a low dais that was actually an oil barrel cut in half. The Clerk of the Bench had a wheeled table, chair and laptop. The Retributor and Advocate sat at opposite ends of the audit bench.

The gallery had nine tiers for the nine circles of hell and nine degrees of warming that were predicted by 2100 unless we could build a lot more carbon dioxide extraction farms. There was a daily quota of audits, so only a few minutes were

46

given to any individual tipper. Unless the Tipping Point Gallows was the sentence, the executions took longer to set up than the audits, so the number of audits was limited by the time it would take to execute the tippers that same day.

The Auditor General banged her mace on the desk to signal that the bench was now in session. The first audit turned out not to be mine. Andrew Archer was brought forward by a warden and he stepped onto the dais. He was about seventy, stooped, and he walked with a cane. The cane was probably a prop, to get sympathy. Nobody who needed a cane to walk could have made it across the six hundred miles to Audit Camp 71, although a few in wheelchairs somehow got through that ordeal.

"Audit of Andrew Archer, sales representative," called the Clerk of the Bench.

"Charged with using oil burning central heating in his house, while living in an area where six forms of heating from renewable energy sources were available," said the Retributor. "Archer also bought a recreational boat worth $45,000 while using the oil burning central heating, clearly demonstrating that he had the financial means to upgrade to better insulation and heating based on renewable energy."

"Andrew Archer, do you deny the charge?" asked the Auditor General.

"Er, no, but -"

"Honorable victims, who audits guilty?"

All the auditors on the bench raised their hands.

"Guilty as charged. Andrew Archer, I sentence you to Class Three Death, without mercy."

"But my furnace had a three star energy rating!" Archer shouted, sounding genuinely shocked.

"It burned fossil fuels and produced greenhouse gases. You had the financial means to install insulation and solar heating instead. Next audit?"

Archer was dragged away by the wardens, screaming for justice, his rights and his lawyer. His audit left me apprehensive, to say the least.

"Audit of Jason Hall, climatologist," declared the Clerk of the Bench.

Warden Olivia walked me to the dais, holding me firmly by one arm. The Auditor General's face was turned in my direction, but her expression was blank and sunshades hid her eyes.

"Retributor?" she said.

"Multiple charges, mainly squandering and display."

"We shall hear a specific charge of your choice, Retributor. Declare the charge."

"I have records showing that between May 2010 and July 2014 the accused lived in a house with oil central heating."

This was a sensible sort of choice. Archer had just been sentenced to death for the very same climate crime, and his audit had lasted mere seconds.

"Dr Hall, do you deny the charge?" asked my granddaughter.

"Yes. The audit's records should also show that the central heating was never turned on while I lived in that house," I replied.

"You still lived there, and you had the financial means to have it replaced," said the Retributor.

"It was not my house. It was provided by the university as part of my contract."

"Just living in a house with oil central heating available provided a bad example."

"I refer the audit to my Facebook photo, posted 10 May 2010."

"Clerk of the Bench, call it up," said the Auditor General.

"I have it, your honor. Transferring to the screens."

On the laptop screens and on the general display screen behind the Auditor General the photo of a front door appeared. Pinned to the door was a sign reading:

THE OIL CENTRAL HEATING IS TURNED OFF IN THIS HOUSE. CLIMATE CHANGE IS REAL. GET YOUR ACT TOGETHER.

The Auditor General nodded. "I accept the defense of the accused. Honorable victims, who agrees?"

Six auditors raised their hands. That flagged to me that two auditors were really hard core, but I had beaten the charge! None of the auditors showed any reaction or emotion whatsoever, but I knew that they were trained to look absolutely impassive - except for the Retributor and Advocate, who were expected to show passion. I had my back to the gallery, but I could hear applause behind me. The display of support was a surprise, and very gratifying.

At that very moment one of the tippers pedaling to generate power toppled sideways and lay still. A gaunt, cadaverous looking man with thinning hair and either long stubble or a short beard was escorted from the gallery by one of the wardens. He was wearing what seemed to be a white canvas laboratory coat, and looked as if he had not slept enough for months. Kneeling in the sand, he checked the fallen man's pulse.

"He has surrendered his carbon, your honor," he reported.

"Thank you, Dr Gibson," said the Auditor General. "Wardens, remove the body."

She turned back to the Retributor.

"Retributor, do you have further charges against Dr Hall?"

"I do, your honor."

"Dr Hall, I can grant you borderline status. You will have to work in support of Audit Camp 71 until another audit can be scheduled, and that may be quite some time."

"Borderline status is a tacit admission of climate crime guilt, your honor," I replied. "I wish my audit to continue."

"Do you realize that the severity of your sentence will be upgraded because you may be squandering the resources of this audit bench?"

"I accept that, your honor. I am confident that I can prove my innocence and will not require sentencing."

All at once there was an outburst of cheering behind me. It was unheard of for anyone to refuse borderline status. The Auditor General banged the mace on her desk and called for order.

"I declare the audit of Jason Hall, climatologist, adjourned, to continue tomorrow. The minimum sentence applicable will be Tipping Point Gallows, without mercy. Clerk of the Bench, schedule Dr Hall's audit to continue tomorrow morning."

"Point of order, your honor," said the Advocate.

"Yes?"

"What is Dr Hall's status?"

"Clerk?"

"At the discretion of the Auditor General, Dr Hall has borderline status, while not actually being a borderline. He has the option of pleading guilty at any time and not squandering the resources of the planet any further."

"Dr Hall?" said the Auditor General.

"I still choose not to plead guilty or become a borderline."

"Very well. By way of clarification, Dr Hall has been declared to be a tipper with borderline status. Until the continuation of your audit, Dr Hall, you will work as a borderline because you too consume the resources of Audit Camp 71, and must help support it. Warden, assign him to the vacant generator."

She was making a point by making me work, but there was renewed applause and cheering from the gallery as Olivia led me over to the generator, tracked by the Cloudcast camera drone.

"Our Cloudcast is trending over nine hundred K followers," she said as we walked.

The Auditor General again struck her mace against her desk and called for order as I climbed onto the seat and started pedaling.

"Clerk of the Bench, who is next?" she asked.

"Audit of Professor Kieran Harley, who owned and operated a jet ski."

I knew Harley. He was eighty and walked with a stick, which was sure to be for show. He took longer to shuffle to the dais than Archer's entire audit. It was an act, but it would do him no good.

"He was Dean of Environmental Science at my university," I said to the borderline on the pedal generator next to mine. "He used to be my boss."

"Save your breath," the man wheezed back.

"Was the jet ski used for recreation at any time?" asked the Auditor General.

"Yes, but -"

"Honorable victims, who audits guilty?"

All auditors on the bench raised their hands.

"Guilty as charged. Kieran Harly, I sentence you to Class Three Death, with mercy."

"But I haven't been allowed to defend myself!" shouted the former professor.

"The charge against you is indefensible. Wardens, carry him back to his seat, we are falling behind schedule. Next audit?"

The audits had well defined rules and protocols. Using oil heating when there was absolutely no alternative was a possible defense. Using oil heating while having the money to buy recreational vehicles or investment properties, or to go on overseas holidays, attracted the death sentence. If you could have afforded to get rid of it, you should have done so. As soon as a viable alternative became available, you were expected to have installed it before buying luxuries. The list of items considered to be luxuries was very long indeed. Central heating had survived in the few countries where winter was still actually cold, but was powered by hydrogen from renewable sources.

I had been saved by my years of working in a freezing cold house, wearing many layers of clothes and buying carbon credits for when I did turn on my portable electric heater. The Retributor had been careless and overconfident when he chose his first charge. He would not make that mistake again.

#

Although I was quite famous in my own field, I was never a celebrity until now. It was true that people had once invited me to speak at conferences, sit on committees, collaborate on papers and appear as a talking head on television documentaries, but I had never been mobbed by fans or confronted by young women wearing only bathrobes outside my hotel room door at 3 am. Suddenly I was the tipper who was facing off against the National Audit, and I had actually won the first round.

All through the rest of the morning's audits I was aware that more eyes were watching me than were focused on the Auditor General, Retributor and other tippers being audited. When the audits were finally over I really was mobbed by well wishers. My pedal generator was surrounded by cheering tippers and borderlines, ranging in age from their late forties to those who had celebrated over a hundred birthdays. After being lifted from the seat and carried shoulder high from the Audit Arena, I was smothered with kisses, had my hand shaken until it ached, and was groped so many times that I lost count.

There was a lunch break, but those facing execution did not get any food because that was regarded as squandering resources. The rest of us were given ten minutes to eat a thing resembling a green muesli bar that tasted like cabbage and dry hummus. The stuff could only be swallowed if you had water to wash the mouthfuls down. When I ran out of water, an anonymous hand offered me another bowl. I drank, and very nearly choked.

"Moonshine," laughed someone as the bowl vanished back into the crowd surrounding me.

Some borderline had done the impossible, and managed to ferment something and distill spirits without the wardens noticing. The contents of that bowl would have been worth the equivalent of a thousand neo dollars a bottle. By now I knew that in Audit Camp 71 that would have been a month's worth of vat-grown coffee rations or maybe five Viagra coupons. I was flattered to think that someone was honoring me with even a sip.

"Smooth," I wheezed, and those who were surrounding me laughed.

If the tippers and borderlines thought I was as sexy as a bodybuilder on Viagra, the wardens thought I needed a bit of perspective. While the auditors, tippers and observers from the morning session set off to witness the carbon reclaimings, I was put to work shoveling out the privy pits and hauling the contents across to Farm Field. Oddly enough, I quite enjoyed this work because it gave me alone time.

The following four hours allowed me to sort out my thoughts and impressions of the camp. I had to keep reminding myself that the audits were the reason that I was in Audit Camp 71, facing down death. Too many people were dying, but once a system is in place, it is very hard to change. Nevertheless, if I could get a large worldwide Cloudcast audience I might change popular opinion about what to do with members of Generation Tipper. Nobody born before 2000 still had the vote, so I would have to appeal to Generation Victim when delivering my message if I wanted to make a difference. The down side was that many in my audience would only be watching because they wanted to see me dead.

#

Shoveling out the privy pits entitled me to have a bath. When I say bath, I mean I was given a large saucepan half full of water smelling of disinfectant, and a piece of toweling about the area of my hand. By the time I was finished I was passably clean and smelled of whatever germ killer was in the water. There was enough water left to rinse out my clothes, but the water that I wrung back into the saucepan was a sort of burgundy color so I decided not to use it on my blanket as well.

The carbon reclaimings were still going on, so I found myself with nothing to do. I sat in the sun, wearing my wet clothes and steaming them dry. A borderline arrived to take the saucepan away.

"Does my dirt get recycled as well?" I asked.

"Yeah, it will get evaporated down to a paste and sold as body paint."

"You're joking!"

"Not me. You're famous, so it should be worth more than moonshine whiskey."

I continued to sit there, slowly drying off. By now I had grasped the basics of living and staying alive in Audit Camp 71, and I also had the measure of the audit bench. The Auditor General did not like the Retributor, and both of them despised the Advocate, who seemed well meaning but insecure. The Clerk of the Bench prided himself on being absolutely impartial, so he was quite a useful resource.

What people had already noticed was that my audit was powerful and compelling theatre. The other audits were more like the ancient Roman Coliseum spectacles than the dramas of Shakespeare, and even death loses its shock value after a while. My audit was changing that. Lion eats Christian? Boring. Christian eats lion? Hey, where can I buy tickets?

Everyone wanted more of what I was providing, I was sure of that. The members of the audit were being given a chance to be characters, and this was after years of being like lions pitted against people who were merely unwilling to burn incense to Roman gods. If I gave her good enough defenses against the charges, I was fairly sure that the Auditor General would continue to adjourn my audit, and that fitted right in with my strategic plan.

I was not given anything else to do for the rest of the afternoon. This was because most people who were assigned to the privy pits took twice as long to shovel them out, so nobody had expected me to be finished so quickly. I was fit and hard working in spite of being old, and once given duties I took them very seriously.

Tippers and borderlines kept visiting me as they hurried from one task to another. I dried out, which was good. My blanket was stolen, which was annoying. My blanket was returned, wet and clean, by a woman who explained that the water used to wash and rinse it was worth a lot of trade goods. She asked me what I would like in return, and I said having a clean blanket was sufficient. That was not good enough for her.

"Then what about a little comb?" I asked.

An hour later a man arrived with a comb that he had carved out of a plastic beer mat that had been decades old. His face was decorated with red paste, which he said cost him thirty neo dollars. Neo dollars did not exist, they were just value attached to trade goods that were actually paid for with coffee rations, Viagra coupons and suchlike. Thirty of them for some paste was very impressive, it was coffee for a day.

Finally Chaz returned from flaying bodies and staking them out in Desiccation Field. We had dinner together, and he told me about the executions of the day. He also told me that my audit had been the topic of nearly every conversation he had overheard. I pretended to be surprised, but I was well aware of how much interest was being taken in myself.

"I can't remember the last time we had someone famous in Audit Camp 71 who lasted more than one night," he said.

"Should I be worried?"

"You don't understand. Usually the big-time tippers are former CEOs or politicians, and they often get lynched by the borderlines as soon as the wardens look the other way. *You* are actually a hero for us. You tried to warn Generation Tipper about the climate catastrophe when it was early enough to do something constructive, instead of bleating about economic growth negativity and GDP shortfall."

SEAN MCMULLEN

This was a surprise, because I had never even had fantasies about being a popular hero. One tends to remember the abuse, trolling and death threats rather than the applause.

"Oh. So what should I do now?"

"We'd better get you to Entertainment Field tonight, to let people see you. You defied the audit bench and won, so you're a good news story. Good news is in short supply here, as you may have noticed."

#

Entertainment Field came to life straight after dinner. Chaz and I arrived early, and we watched as a humming chorus rehearsed the theme music from various Twentieth and Twenty-First Century television series. Chaz told me that some borderlines had also memorized their favorite movies and television shows, word for word. He said that episodes of *Cheers, Star Trek, Buffy, Neighbors, Seinfeld, Game of Thrones* and *Westworld* were acted out at dusk, or when there was moonlight.

I had expected life in the camp to be all fear and despair, but I was now seeing that the borderlines and tippers had an incredibly strong sense of community, and even fun. Faced with death at worst, and life imprisonment as the only alternative, they maintained a strange, ragged simulation of the second half of the Twentieth Century, and to me it seemed that they were happier than they might have been in retirement villages, nursing homes or lonely units in high rise apartment blocks. More than anything else, they reminded me of rebellious, disrespectful teenagers.

There was a queue of people wanting my autograph, a handshake, a hug, or just a few words with me as we sat waiting. I was asked to sign the breasts or buttocks of several women, and some of the better built men wanted their biceps or pectorals autographed. Chaz explained that there were tattooists in the camp who would make my signatures permanent. Offers of sex were not in short supply, but with a thirty day desert trek completed only thirty-two hours earlier, I would not have been up to it even had I been sixty-five years younger. I was invited to say a few words before the show began, but I decided that it might not be a good idea. When your life hangs by a thread, you do not do acrobatics.

On this night there was a quarter moon in a clear sky, so an abridged performance of "The Rocky Horror Picture Show" was possible. In the opening scene, the actors were pushed in on two wheelchairs tied together to act as a car, and people threw sand to mimic rain. The performances were stiff and arthritic, the props minimal, and the music was hummed and whistled by an aged orchestra, but it somehow held together and was actually convincing.

At the centre of the stage space were the actors, while others played the parts of chairs, tables, doors and a bed. Flanking them was a chorus of singers to the right and an orchestra of hummers to the left. Surrounding the stage area was the participating audience, whose members sang, danced, and called responses at the actors. They were wearing costumes made of plastic rubbish, and had fishnet stockings and suspenders painted on their legs.

About half an hour into the show, and without any hint of a warning, the audience participators charged the wardens, shouting lines from the show, hurling rocks and waving walking sticks. Everyone else jumped from the stands and flattened themselves against the sand as the wardens opened fire with their assault rifles.

"Don't move," called Chaz, who was lying beside me.

"Who's moving?" I replied.

"Only the kamikazes."

"Who are they?"

"They're tippers facing death without mercy. A bullet is way better."

One of the kamikazes stumbled over my legs, dropping her walking stick before staggering on into a burst from an assault rifle. The stick had the neck of a broken bottle tied to the tip. Although definitely a weapon, it was just as definitely not an effective weapon. If anything, it was just a declaration that she was armed, and that she wanted to be a target. The firing died down to an occasional shot, but still nobody moved.

"That's the Inspector of Wardens, finishing off kamikazes with a Smith and Wesson 1006," said the man on to my right. "Beautiful gun, a real classic."

"I'll take your word for it," I whispered.

"Now those wardens, you see what they got?"

"Assault rifles?" I guessed without raising my head.

"Chinese copies of AK-47s."

"Which are Russian."

"Yeah, you got it. Real old design. Even the M16 could shoot faster and further."

"Then why use them?"

"The old AK can take real rough treatment and still do the job. They're also cheap to build and easy to maintain."

The wardens were still methodically checking that all the audience participation performers were dead. There was a burst of automatic fire as a wounded performer suddenly lurched to his feet and charged a warden, waving a sharpened walking stick.

"And effective," I whispered as the man fell.

"Yeah, but with guns you need the best. That gives you an edge."

"Not so. Guns are like the modern world. These days everything just needs to be good enough. Slightly better at twice the cost is no advantage."

"But if good enough was really good enough, we'd still be using flintlocks."

"The firing squads in some camps use flintlocks," said Chaz softly. "They have a small carbon footprint."

"Good enough is perfect," I added.

"You guys just don't appreciate a good gun."

We fell silent as a warden approached, kicking at armed corpses to check for signs of life. She stopped as she spotted the glass tipped walking stick

"Who owns this joke?" she demanded, nudging it with her foot.

"It's better than your pathetic AK-" began the gun fancier, but a short burst from her assault rifle pulverized his head. She snatched up the weaponized walking stick and moved on.

"Some people just don't appreciate a good gun," murmured Chaz.

In the distance the Inspector of Wardens blew his whistle.

"All stand!" he shouted.

Chaz and I were assigned to a stretcher team, and we carried the corpse of the gun fancier away to Desiccation Field.

"Want some friendly advice?" asked Chaz as we staked out the body in the moonlight.

"If it involves staying alive, yes."

"Steer clear of people like the gun nut."

"But I like discussing things with people I don't agree with. It helps me sort out my own thoughts and ideas."

"If that warden had heard all your talk about guns, she might have thought you two were planning another attack."

"It doesn't seem fair. I thought everyone gets an audit."

"This is Audit Camp 71, fair is not in the job statement."

Chaz rummaged in the pockets of the trousers we had just taken from the corpse.

"Amazing!" he exclaimed softly.

"Takes a lot to amaze me these days."

"He's got a handful of 22 caliber LRs."

"You mean little bullets?"

"They're little, but Long Rifle cartridges are mean suckers. You can bore them out into hollow points so they'll have the stopping power of a 38."

He rummaged about in the dead man's other pockets, but did not find a gun to go with the bullets.

"Makes sense," he said. "The wardens look for gun shapes in clothes, not bullets."

"I hope you're going to hand them in."

"Will you tell anyone if I don't?"

"I saw nothing," seemed like a safe reply.

"He's got a gun, that's for sure. I wonder where he's hidden it?"

"Why do you want a gun?"

"To have an edge."

"Against hundreds of wardens with assault rifles? I'll stick to beating the audit."

"Trust me, the odds against that are way worse."

#

By the time I got to my bed trench the moon was setting behind the perimeter wall, its light shining through the spaces between SUV carcasses. After the terrors of the Rocky

Horror massacre I thought I would be up all night with post traumatic stress, but after a minute or two I was already drowsy. Footsteps approached, then stopped beside me. I opened my eyes to blackness studded with stars, and the distinctive figure of the Auditor General standing over me. I sat up, and sand hissed softly as it cascaded off my blanket. In the distance, wardens patrolled in the faint blue light.

"You're back," I said.

"I'm back," she replied in a voice that no longer had an edge.

"Is this a social visit, or am I still being audited?"

"Social."

"I'm all out of candles, cashews, and chilled chardonnay."

"I'll do without. May I ask a personal question, grand-daughter to grandfather?"

"Will my answer be used in evidence against me?"

"You never know."

"Ask anyway."

"You were working in climatology, which is a backlist occupation for tippers."

"Easier work than breaking up old oil refineries by hand."

"Your audit priority was so far down the lottery list that you would have been a hundred and thirty before it was heard."

"That's right. I volunteered to be audited."

"No other tipper has ever volunteered for an audit."

"Maybe they don't like the climate here."

"Was that a joke?"

"Yes."

"It was in poor taste. So why volunteer - and please, no more comedy. Are you looking for fame?"

"No."

"You were acting like a celeb in Entertainment Field."

"Everyone else was acting as if I were a celeb. I just did hugs and autographs."

"Maybe you want a reputation as a martyr?"

"I already have a reputation, and martyrs are fools."

"Then why volunteer for the audit?"

Why did she even need to ask that question? I symbolized the fact that some members of Generation Tipper had tried to make a difference before it was too late. If I were found to be innocent, the criteria for judging my generation would have to change. That was why I had been forced to trek six hundred miles to this camp, face fifteen pages of charges, and be audited by the notoriously strict Auditor General Renny Hall.

"I want to save lives," compressed all that into five words.

"Explain?" she asked, this time with genuine curiosity in her tone.

I remembered a moment thirty-five years earlier, when she had asked me if the end of the world were coming. Back then I had explained that we humans had been too greedy, and would soon have to live with a lot less. As far as greedy people were concerned, that was indeed the end of the world. She had clapped and laughed, then told me that she did not like greedy people. This was another such moment.

"The Nazi Holocaust against the Jews was indiscriminate; so was the genocide of the Hutus against the Tutsis in Rwanda. Back in the 1790s the French revolutionaries guillotined aristocrats just for being aristocrats. Am I right so far?"

"In general terms, yes."

"So how is the National Audit different? Everyone born before 2000 is a tipper, and every tipper is considered guilty."

"But every tipper gets a fair audit, and remember what happened in other countries? Mass lynchings of older people in Brazil, the United States and Canada, and bounty hunters outnumbering police in the European Union and Russia. People want climate justice, and Australia's system delivers that. No other audit camp is as big as this one, and the National Audit accounted for only seventy thousand carbon reclaimings last year. There are millions of tippers in the queue to be audited, but most will die of natural causes before that happens. Still, the public wants to at least see some climate justice handed out, granddad, so the audits continue."

"Don't talk bullshit, Renny, it's climatically incorrect, remember? Retributors want tippers to get Class Two Death without mercy for buying their kid a battery powered Darth Vader toy. That looks ridiculous, so those audits get adjourned and the tipper become a borderline."

"True enough."

"And now there are thousands of borderlines in Australia. There will be millions if our audit model is adopted worldwide."

"Also true. They are quite a burden on the audit system."

"Precisely. Borderlines are prisoners, and many have skills that could help heal the world, yet you keep them in audit camps, shoveling shit and burying bodies. You need a precedent. If there were a precedent, many borderlines could be pardoned, branded, or at least given a fixed sentence of service."

"But we have no precedent."

"Well, I want to be the precedent. Tippers of good will should live what remains of their lives in freedom, pardoned, healing the Earth."

"Not an option. Generation Victim wants to see justice handed out. Cloudcasts of the Australian climate audits are watched by millions, and many countries are joining the International Audit Movement and adopting the Australian model. It's better than lynchings and bounty hunters."

"Better but not good enough. At the very least they should be allowed to help heal the planet. They are a genuine resource that the Earth needs."

She appeared to have no answer to this, and it was some time before she replied.

"You are a hard act to follow, granddad," was what she finally said.

"What do you mean?"

"Ask those who follow you."

#

DAY 3: RECREATIONAL GASOLINE VEHICLE

The breakfast bell clanged out at first light. Actually it was not really a bell, just a length of iron pipe suspended in a wooden frame. Still, when struck with another pipe it sounded like a bell, so why squander resources by casting a real bell? All around me the tippers and borderlines sat up, like a vast field of vampires rising from their coffins. Dr Gibson went about with little flags on sticks, checking for pulses and marking those whose beds had become temporary graves. Pushcarts would call past later to collect the bodies.

Refectory Field contained a couple of dozen tubs of bubbling protein slurry heated by solar batteries. I shook the sand out of my bowl as I stood in a queue, then collected my ration and sat in the sand to eat. Sand actually makes quite effective furniture, it moulds itself to whatever body shape is sitting on it. It is also a good cleaning material. After a minimal rinse we all scoured our bowls with a handful of sand and brushed it into one of the many recycling pushcarts. The muck was later offloaded at the solar distillery arrays, where the moisture was extracted. The dry residue was either buried to return the carbon to the Earth or used as fertilizer in Farm Field.

Our bowls became sun hats as dawn glowed on the horizon. I was herded into the group to be audited and taken to the Audit Arena. The audit bench procession was late, and arrived as the sun's disk made its first appearance. The bugler was playing "The Party's Over" as we marched behind them into the Audit Arena. This time the crowd in the gallery was overflowing, and the clapping and cheering could only have been for me. They obviously hoped to see a Christian eat a second lion. I was selected to be first to stand before the audit bench.

#

"First audit of the day is the second hearing of Jason Hall, climatologist," declared the Clerk of the Bench.

"Retributor, what is your next charge? said the Auditor General.

"I have records to show that between May 2003 and July 2007 the accused owned and operated a recreational gasoline vehicle. Specifically, a 350 cc motorcycle."

"Dr Hall, do you deny the charge?"

"I do deny it. Not all motorcycles are recreational, just as not all innocent people are retributors."

This drew laughter from the gallery, and I was caught by surprise. There was very little to laugh about in 2045.

"Order!" called the Auditor General, and I could see the furrows of a frown on her forehead. "The accused will refrain from making irrelevant insults."

"My apologies, your honor. I was just emphasizing the point by using a simple example."

"Objection!" called the Retributor. "The accused has implied that I am an idiot."

"Objection overruled. I shall be inclined to agree with Dr Hall if I hear any more objections as trivial as that. The accused may proceed."

"My motorcycle was a road bike. I used it to commute between the university where I taught and a field station where I was doing research."

"350 cc is a very big motorcycle."

"350 cc is the optimum size for solo commuting. Any smaller and the parts wear out too quickly, squandering resources on repairs."

"Ah, so 350 cc is the optimum size?" said the Retributor.

"350 to 500. The National Audit has made a pronouncement on this matter, I can provide the references."

"In that case how do you justify owning and operating a 750 cc motorcycle for seven years between 2007 and 2014?"

"I commuted on it with my girlfriend of the time, who was another scientist. Two people, one 750 cc vehicle, and half of 750 is 375."

"You should have used bicycles."

"We tried bicycles. Because of the distance involved, we found we were spending five hours per day commuting. That was squandering time that should have gone into climate research."

"You should have lived closer to your workplace."

"We were working at a research station in a national park, studying transpiration in the vegetation. There were no living quarters where we worked."

The Auditor General glanced at her watch.

"Honorable victims, who votes that the defense of the accused is valid?"

Five hands were raised.

"Dr Hall, your defense is accepted. Retributor, do you have further charges?"

"Multiple charges, your honor."

"Dr Hall, your audit will continue tomorrow unless you wish to accept the status of a borderline and not squander the resources of the audit bench further. Your default sentence will be increased to the CO2 mask with mercy if you insist on proceeding."

"I believe that continuing will be in the interests of the greater good."

"The greater good? Can you explain why squandering the resources of the audit bench is for the greater good?"

A scatter of applause came from those in the gallery. Apparently they approved of squandering the resources of the audit bench.

"I represent a very large number of people of good will who can make a substantial contribution to healing the damage done to the planet by the fossil fuel releases over the past three centuries. A desire for revenge against those who committed climate crimes should not come before efforts to heal the world."

"But if climate crimes go unpunished, it will encourage future generations to commit more climate crimes. Would you pardon a murderer because he gave a lot of money to charity?"

"Of course not, but many members of Generation Victim are no more innocent or guilty than those of Generation Tipper. By all means audit everyone from Generation Tipper, but accept that not all of them deserve a death sentence merely because they are old."

"Very well, Dr Hall, your clarification is noted and you may stand down. Next audit, Clerk of the Bench?"

"Harold McIver, former president of the Drag Racing Association of -"

"Honorable victims, who audits guilty?" asked the Auditor General.

All the auditors raised their hands. McIver was a strong, fit looking man in his fifties. He had not even reached the dais.

"Guilty of whatever he is charged with," declared the Auditor General.

"You can't do this!" McIver screamed. "I have rights!"

"Yes I can, and no you don't. I sentence you to Class Four Death, with mercy. Next audit?"

McIver screamed with fear and anger, and tried to rush at the audit bench. He was tackled and brought down by the wardens. Olivia led me to a gallery seat while he was held down and bound.

#

On this, my third day at the camp, I was assigned to Greenhouse Field after the morning audits. This was the Class Four Death area, for causing the greenhouse effect. Tippers got roasted slowly in their own little greenhouses. I was one of a dozen prisoners harnessed to a stripped out SUV, and we were made to tow it to an area the size of a football field. The field was filled with little A-frame greenhouses about two yards long. Each contained a body, staked down and unmoving, although the occasional faint groan told me that not all were dead. Our SUV was loaded with glass panels.

We followed the auditors as they led the prisoners to the places of execution. The Auditor General declared the sentences for six tippers, then the auditors moved on to executions in another field. I watched as Harold McIver was forced to the ground by the wardens. He was stripped, spread eagled on his back and chained to wooden stakes.

"I've got rights!" he kept screaming.

"You contributed to the greenhouse effect," responded the supervising warden. "We've got the right to greenhouse you."

"I demand a retrial."

"Waste of the Earth's resources."

"I've got the right of appeal."

"No tipper has the right of appeal."

"I want a proper lawyer."

"So do I. We like greenhousing lawyers."

"Your turn will come! This is a concentration camp."

"You helped run a concentration camp called the global economy, and you kept Mother Earth and the Green Man in there until they were living skeletons. Now we're nursing them back to health by greenhousing you."

The wardens took two large glass panels and clamped them over the tipper in a tent shape. I watched with my SUV team as they put a funnel in McIver's mouth, and he was force fed sump oil from some long-dead car. Finally they fitted glass triangles over the open ends. The man harnessed beside me nudged me in the ribs. His headband declared him to be Victim 395. He was the first of the Generation Victim prisoners I had met. Unlike those of my generation, he would eventually be released.

"You're the celeb, aren't you?" he asked.

"So I'm told."

"In that case welcome to hell. That guy got Class Four Death with mercy. It's meant to be merciful because it's quicker."

"It's still appalling," I replied.

"I reckon it's humane."

"Humane?"

"Yeah, if they gag on the oil and choke, it puts them out of their misery."

"All done, move on!" called the supervising warden.

I was very relieved to get away from McIver's greenhouse tent. He had survived being force fed the oil, and was hoarsely screaming defiance. We stopped while a second tipper was greenhoused. I looked away, but perhaps that was a mistake. All around us were glass tents containing the bodies of people who had stayed alive long enough to become sunburned while they were being roasted. Only a few had vomited their motor oil and choked. I had to remind myself that these were the lucky ones.

"What a nightmare," I said, more or less to myself. Victim 395 nodded.

"You got it. The unlucky ones last until evening, get to cool down at night, then have to face a second day. Nobody ever survives the second day."

It seemed to take forever to greenhouse the remaining four tippers, then we set off through the rows of glass tents that had already been set up. Most were marked with red flags to indicate death. We stopped where a pair of borderlines were slicing open the skin of someone recently executed, and two of our team collected the glass plates of that greenhouse tent.

"Why mutilate them?" asked the woman behind me, who had arrived with that morning's caravan. "Everyone who dies gets cut open. Why take revenge on the dead?"

I was amazed. She had walked six hundred miles across the desert without once asking that question. Perhaps she had been too frightened.

"The cuts are to dry out their bodily fluids faster, before the bodies rot," I explained. "Rotting produces greenhouse gases like carbon dioxide and methane."

Suddenly I realized that I had become a hardened old-timer of Audit Camp 71 by my third day. I was part of the establishment, explaining to a tipper how climate crimes were punished. Would I be making jokes about it by tomorrow? It was so very easy to fit into the status quo, and I was a celeb with a great deal of status. At any time I could let myself be classified as a borderline and live out my remaining years in comfortable slavery. I had to keep reminding myself why I was there.

There would, of course, be a cutoff point for my audit. Regulations would not allow the audit bench to squander a quarter hour per day on me for fifteen pages of charges. Already I had been given time that could have been spent auditing a dozen other tippers, declaring them to be borderlines or marking them down for unpleasant and vengeful deaths. The Retributor had hundreds of charges prepared, but I would not be given hundreds of adjournments.

On the other hand, I was already granting a few extra days of life to some tippers by squandering the audit bench's time. Strategically, I was also establishing precedents that might keep other tippers of good will alive by turning them into borderlines. I needed to keep remembering that, because my nerves were beginning to fray. The Retributor only had to beat me on one charge, but I had to beat him every time.

Thus, while I was not a young, beautiful woman like Scheherazade, I was in her situation. One dud performance and I would be killed, yet every time I survived my fame grew. The very fact of my survival was making my audit's Cloudcast figures go viral and I had passed a million followers. Soon the entire world might be watching, and that was definitely part of my agenda.

#

73

After visiting twenty more flagged greenhouses, we took our load of glass plates to a maintenance yard for cleaning. After this we returned to Greenhouse Field and loaded the bodies into the SUV. They were quite stiff, as if carved out of wood.

"Do you have a real name?" I asked Victim 395 as we worked.

"Not any more. I decided to leave my name and old life behind me."

"How long have you been here?"

"Since the start. I got Class Two Service. Fifteen years to go."

"Fifteen years of this?"

"It's job security. I'll be sixty when I'm released, then it's back to work."

"Work? What was your work?"

"Landscape gardening."

"And for that you got Class Two Service?"

"I carried my gear in a big off roader. I got it free, so it seemed like a good deal back then."

"When was that?"

"Just after the tipping point year."

"That was a bad time to own an off roader."

"Yeah, but I was young and stupid. Should have rigged up a solar hybrid."

"You were lucky to just get Service."

"Yeah. Not many people who drove off roaders get less than death, even GVs."

"What saved you?"

"I never drove mine recreationally."

"More people like you and the world could have been pulled back from the edge."

He smiled self-consciously. Praise was obviously as scarce as mercy in Audit Camp 71.

"How about you?" he asked. "Why all the fuss about your audit?"

"I was one of those predicting what would happen while most others were stoking up the greenhouse."

"That won't be enough to save you. Nobody ever gets anything except death, or adjournment as a borderline."

"The Auditor General seems to think I'm special."

"Well, you've survived two audit charges. I'm honored to have met you."

He shook my hand, then several other borderlines took that as the signal to come over to congratulate me.

"I hope you spoil the Retributor's perfect record on convictions," said a woman about twenty years younger than me, and with considerable venom.

"I'm still guilty until proved worthy of pardoning."

"We're all guilty of something," she replied, "but the crimes we're being accused of were not crimes when we did those things. I once flew to Port Douglas, just to relax by a swimming pool in a bikini and drink cocktails. It was legal back then, and I only did it once, but now it's a climate crime."

"You were lucky to only get borderlined," said Victim 395. "I thought the Auditor General would have given you the carbon dioxide mask."

"I won the trip in a competition, and I worked for a wind farm company. That meant I could demonstrate good intentions. That Retributor bastard was so sure he had me that he didn't prepare backup charges. The auditors couldn't decide whether or not my holiday cancelled out my work on renewable energy, so I was borderlined."

"You really were lucky," I said.

"You said it! These days if the audit bench can prove you even farted you get charged with adding to the greenhouse effect. My name's Silvy. I've watched both your audits, Dr Hall. Now I'm a big fan of yours."

"Thank you, and I'm fine with Jason."

She shook my hand, then hugged me. She had looked after herself and was very attractive, like some top model trying to keep her grooming and clothes halfway decent on some reality-adventure television show. People like her had taken some of the load off the Earth back in the days before Forced Democracy, the National Audit and the terrors of accelerated greenhouse warming and global famines. She should have been given honors, so why should she be borderlined while Victim 395 escaped death just because he was born on the right side of 31st December 1999? True, he did seem to be a person of good will who left a responsibly small carbon footprint upon the world, but Silvy had helped build power generators that had kept megatons of carbon out of the atmosphere.

"What are your feelings about the Anthrophobes?" she asked, suddenly switching the conversation in a radically different direction. "They don't think anyone is truly innocent, and they think humans should be wiped out."

"I think human stupidity can be controlled by human good will."

The Anthrophobe terrorist sect made even the National Audit look benevolent. Its members were doing their best to drive the human race to extinction by just killing everyone, whether Generation Tipper or Generation Victim. Quite apart from bombings and gas attacks, they were also inclined to attack the carbon extraction farms.

SEAN MCMULLEN

"Do you know much about them?" Silvy asked.

"I made a study of the Anthrophobes after one tried to recruit me when I was working in Antarctica. When I showed no enthusiasm he made a very credible attempt on my life."

"And you survived? I hear they are very good at killing."

"I can look after myself. I've spent a lifetime dealing with people who follow up on their death threats."

"An Anthrophobe got caught in this camp and audited last year, I was in the galley for it. He said the Anthrophobes were part of the medieval Cathar religion, which taught that there were two gods, one of light and the other of darkness. The material world was the realm of the dark god, so humans were encouraged to have no children, and ultimately to wipe the human presence from the Earth. Is that what you learned?"

"More or less, but I don't believe the Cathar connection. The Anthrophobes have the same functional objective, the extinction of humanity, so they just call themselves Cathars. Unlike the Cathars, they believe that the biosphere is truly beautiful and sacred, and that only humans are evil."

"So what do you believe?"

"I think humanity is worth saving, but that we citizens of the mid-Twenty-First Century need to tread a very narrow path between human stupidity and human thirst for revenge. What degree of genuine innocence should earn a pardon for a member of Generation Tipper? Sorting the well intentioned from the slobs is more constructive than killing everyone."

"Are you religious? Like, there are not many people who have ever heard of the Cathars."

"I've got some sympathy for the Greenhands."

"What?" she laughed. "They claim to be followers of the Green Man, a sort of European woodland sprite who symbolized rebirth and renewal."

"Yes, and there's archeological evidence that they date back to the last ice age."

"How can a scientist believe in an eleven thousand year old cult?"

"I said I sympathized, I didn't say I believed."

"So you're an atheist?"

"No, I don't have enough faith to be an atheist."

Silvy laughed again. We loaded the last of the bodies onto the SUV, then got back into our harnesses and hauled it along the sandy track. Silvy had strapped in beside me.

"Do you watch those strange nostalgia shows?" I asked her.

"Like that Rocky Horror massacre?"

"Yes."

"I attend, but not often."

"Don't you like them?"

"No way. They're a celebration of what screwed the world in the first place."

That reassured me. Silvy and I did seem to have a lot in common, and she had genuine allure.

"You must find this place depressing."

"Yes and no. The camp has a solar cell field for power, and I've got skills in renewable energy tech. I'm a fully qualified electrical engineer, in case you were wondering. Personally, I think it's a waste of resources, keeping a pro engineer here, I ought to be in one of the really big solar farms that are extracting carbon dioxide from the atmosphere. "

Again, the National Audit was putting punishment for past climate crimes ahead of repairing the damage from those crimes. I did not need to point that out, however.

"Last night's Rocky Horror Show was pretty bizarre," I said, steering the conversation back toward the surreal.

"Did you clap?"

"I didn't get a chance to. The audience participators charged the wardens before the end, so the massacre stopped the show."

"You might have dodged a bullet by not clapping."

"You're joking!"

"I'm dead serious. Want a word of advice?"

"I'm listening."

"Go along at least once a week, but look bored. If you don't go, the vigilante borderlines will kill you."

"For not being one of them?"

"You got it, but remember not to clap too hard. The wardens are always watching, and they report happy clappers to the Retributor."

"I don't follow. What's wrong with clapping?"

"Hard clapping lets the Retributor charge you with being unrepentant about lifestyle abuse. You know what that means?"

"Death, Class-something-bad?"

"Wrong, it's the mine. That's way worse than dying."

"But lots of people were clapping, and they looked really happy."

"Borderlines can clap. They have adjourned audits, and will probably die before the audit bench gets back to them. They can do what they like."

"Thanks, Silvy. I owe you one."

"We should all be thanking you, Jason. You put the National Audit on trial, and thanks to the Cloudcast there's over a million people in the gallery."

"That's stretching my importance a bit."

"Don't try to be modest. There's loads of qualified and experienced people who really did try to make a difference. Making us haul SUV wagons instead of doing work to repair the atmosphere is bare-arsed squandering. I was on the original project to turn atmospheric carbon dioxide into oxygen and a pile of carbon bricks using solar farm converters. As soon as the first converters went operational, I was marked for audit and balloted in."

"Lunacy," I sighed.

"Yeah, and I know the jealous bitch who did it. If ever I get out of here I'll slap a squandering charge on her."

Our next stop was at one of the mineshafts. I never found out what had been mined there, but the two shafts went down vertically beneath the crane towers. Wardens guarded the shafts, which had heavy hatch covers that were normally locked down. They removed the padlocks on one cover and winched it open. Cries that were human yet lacked humanity echoed up from below.

"There are people down there!" I gasped.

"That's stretching the definition of people tight enough to play a tune on it," said Silvy. "They live off meat from the dried bodies, and artesian water that seeps into some tunnels. Their job is to carry the dried bodies deeper into the mines, so that the carbon returns to the earth and stays there."

I did not want to know any more. We carried the first body over and heaved it into the pit. By estimating how long it took the body to hit the bottom, I worked out that the shaft was maybe three hundred feet deep. The sounds that came up from the darkness are beyond my powers of description.

#

The conspiracy theorist cornered me over lunch.

"Dr Hall, my name's Taylor, Tim Taylor," he said, flopping down beside me without even asking if I minded him joining me. "Have you ever thought about the carbon dioxide extraction farms?"

"I did some of the modeling that went into their design," seemed a fairly safe sort of reply.

"Ah, but were you aware of the agenda behind building them?"

"It's science, not politics. Burying the bodies of dead tippers does return a little carbon to the Earth, but industrial-scale carbon removal by highly specialized extraction farms is what is going to really take the pressure off the planet."

"I bet you don't know how they really work."

"There's nothing complicated about them, they're enormous but simple. Take an huge tray of genetically optimized algae, add water, and bubble in air. Powered by sunlight, it becomes a biological engine that takes six carbon dioxide molecules and six water molecules, and uses the energy from sunlight to convert them into a sugar and six oxygen molecules."

"Why not just use solar cells and catalytic converters to break down carbon dioxide?" asked the woman sitting opposite us, who turned out to be a former schoolteacher named Lisa.

"The difficulty with carbon dioxide is that it's a highly stable molecule, and needs a lot of energy to split it into carbon and oxygen," I replied. "It makes more sense to just let sunlight and plant life do the work. Just like the giant power stations and automobile industries once sucked fossil fuels out of the Earth and poured carbon dioxide into the atmosphere, farms that cover hundreds of square miles are now removing that carbon."

"But it's a very expensive industry that produces no useful products," babbled Taylor. "Doesn't that make you suspicious?"

"That's not the point. The extraction farms repair some of the damage done to the atmosphere by former lifestyles."

"They are fully automated, no humans work in them. Don't you realize what that means?"

"It means you have never been to an extraction farm," said Lisa. "I did, before I was sent here, and there were hundreds of us, all human. The work could have been automated, but robots with sufficiently advanced AI are needed for the more important work like the lunar fabrication plants and the Antarctic kelp farms. It's tippers who operate the pumps and compressors, and drive the electric trucks and tractors that cart the sugar residues away and bury them."

All of that was common knowledge. Like the burying of the dried corpses, the extraction farms were coal mines and oil wells in reverse. The carbon was being put where it was out of temptation's way. Those who worked the extraction farms were tippers waiting to be audited, but after the audit process none of those people were returned to the extraction farms, even if they were borderlined. Generation Victim wanted climate justice, and political stability depended on the government providing it.

"Were you happy there, Lisa?" I asked.

"Yeah. It was a bit boring, but I had a sense of repairing the world after a life running a car when I didn't really need one."

"Don't listen to her!" Taylor interjected his eyes wide and his expression manically eager. "Can't you tell? She's an agent of the National Audit climate conspiracy."

"The National Audit does some pretty appalling things, but it's not secretive about them."

SEAN MCMULLEN

"Oh this is far worse than just killing tippers. Don't you think it's suspicious that the extraction farms are all on the coast? I've done some calculations, and they prove that the farms are really breaking seawater into hydrogen and oxygen. The hydrogen rises to the top of the atmosphere and is blown away by the solar wind, but the oxygen stays. The National Audit is secretly increasing the oxygen and carbon dioxide in the atmosphere to make the world like it was a hundred million years ago."

"That's shit on steroids," said Lisa.

"I suppose you're going to tell us that aliens are responsible?" I asked.
"No, no, this is serious science. Look, we all know that dinosaurs were the most successful species ever, right?"

"I thought that was roaches," said Lisa.

"The National Audit has a long term plan to modify human DNA to make us more like dinosaurs, so that -"

"Mr Taylor, leave and leave now!" I said firmly. "If you do not, I shall report you to the wardens for climatic treason."

"There's no such crime."

"Let's find out tomorrow morning, in front of the Auditor General. Interested?"

Taylor left without another word.

"There goes one of the most dangerous people in Audit Camp 71," I added.

"Why so?" asked Lisa. "He's just a harmless nut."

"Think so? I volunteered to be audited so tippers like you could be returned to the extraction farms where you can do some good. Just imagine if I survive my audit, and tipper policy is changed. Thousands of tippers go back to the farms, but maybe a dozen will believe the dinosaur DNA theory. How much damage could they do?"

"Point taken," said Lisa

83

People like Taylor made me furious. They invented their ludicrous theories to gain fame and power, and in fact they were guilty of display. Worse, they kept approaching me, because I would give them credibility.

The idea of climate justice was all that was holding our frail and brittle government together, and this restricted the useful deployment of tippers and borderlines in the restoration programs. If even a handful committed acts of sabotage, everything that I was working to achieve could be undone by one nut with a loud mouth. That was a very depressing thought.

#

Now that we were in the camp, we were permitted to rest when temperatures exceeded 50 degrees Celsius. If too many died before being audited, the voting public would not see enough climate justice being done. Being a celeb as well as a new arrival, I was selected to give a sort of TED talk to borderlines and tippers during an extreme temperature break.

The Audit Arena was not in use, so a couple of hundred people came along and rigged their blankets up on poles as sunshades. We had just been given lunch, so some of those in the audience were asleep before I even started speaking. I was introduced by the supervising warden, then left to speak about whatever took my fancy. Silvy acted as host, and in the front row were three savants with astounding powers of recall. Their role was to remember everything that I said, and to repeat it to other audiences in Audit Camp 71. I had planned it as a lecture, but it soon became a question and answer event.

"This might be a good time and temperature to talk about Antarctica," I began, attempting humor, and I actually got laughs and a scatter of applause. "I worked there for two years, as a consultant. Temperatures in parts of Antarctica are now pretty moderate due to global warming, so it has become feasible to establish farms. Now when I say farms, they're not open fields full of crops and GM ultra-chickens. Because cold snaps and blizzards can brew up in a couple of minutes and kill everything in the open, most crops are under glass."

"Are the farms carbon neutral?" someone called.

"By law, all industrial and agricultural operations must be carbon neutral or even carbon negative. If not, the owners and staff are shipped here."

That got a lot more laughs.

"Naturally, the competition to work in Antarctica or on the supply ships is pretty intense. The ships are the wind powered rotor types, and they transport all the produce and materials. There are also undersea farms off the Antarctic coast, growing various types of seaweed. Some bits of green stuff floating in our meals probably came from there."

"Are there cities in Antarctica now?" called a man who I recognized as Dr Gibson.

"There are maybe fifty thousand people living there, total. Only farmers, maintenance engineers, researchers and militia wardens are allowed."

"Why militias?" asked Gibson.

"Piracy. There are plenty of groups eager to dash in, steal a load of produce and make a run for it. Any refugees who make it there are shipped here and charged with squandering. We can't afford to waste agricultural land on towns, so the population is being kept to a minimum. The buildings are all made from compressed organic fiber, to tie up as much carbon as possible. I was a climate consultant when they were being planned."

"Do you think they have a future?" asked Silvy.

"I'm optimistic. During the Cretaceous Period the carbon dioxide levels were up to four times higher than they are now, and the polar icecaps had melted entirely. The dinosaurs thought it was great. Some of them even lived at the poles."

"If the dinosaurs didn't have a problem, why is greenhouse warming such an issue for us today?"

"The average raptor only had to worry about where its next stegosaurus was coming from. We have a huge global population that depends on an industrial economy. As long as the population of vegetarian dinos did not outstrip the supply of cycads, things were fine. If not, the neighborhood allosaurus would step in and eat some of that population. Computer modeling has shown that without our fabrication machines and protein factories, a Cretaceous-type climate could only support maybe a hundred thousand humans. The National Audit puts the number of people who have made it through the famines, heat waves and wars of the past couple of decades at less than a billion. Without technology, most of them would go down the toilet within weeks."

"Dr Hall, what the folk in Audit Camp 71 really want to know about is you," said Gibson. "How did you manage to develop such a carbon-responsible lifestyle and outlook decades ago, before climate change became a visible issue?"

"How did my lifestyle evolve? Well, perhaps I have my parents to thank for that. I was eight years old when I decided to not accept anything other than food, clothes and education from them - you don't want to know why. That meant I had to deliver newspapers and wash cars to earn my own recreational money. Luxuries like color television dropped off my radar, and by the time I realized that First-World lifestyles were killing the Earth, I already had a pretty small carbon footprint.

"Use less of everything and waste nothing, and you reduce your cost of living dramatically. Repair things like bicycles and washing machines instead of tossing them and buying the latest model, and you save even more. I like to think that I developed the first carbon credits system, because from 1980 onwards, whenever I had to drive or fly anywhere, I would buy a load of coal and dump it into landfill, returning it to the Earth before it could be burned and put into the atmosphere as carbon dioxide. Whenever I spoke about this in climate research conferences I got laughed at, but that just trained me to ignore ridicule, so all good."

"But the world was geared up to force people to have a big carbon footprint back then," said Gibson. "How did you resist the temptation to do what everyone else was doing?"

"Beef cattle fart out loads of methane, so I stopped eating beef. I measured which appliances still drew a little power, even when the off button was pressed, and by turning off all my appliances at the wall socket I dropped my energy consumption by 25%. I even adjusted my sleeping patterns so that I was always awake when the sun was above the horizon, so I could read and work by natural light. I visited and studied nomad societies, checking whether they had anything to teach us about carbon-responsible lifestyles and attitudes. Even so, it was 1982 before I could honestly say that my own urban lifestyle was in balance with what the Earth could support."

"By the late 1980s the rest of the world began to catch up with you," said Gibson. "Did you start feeling optimistic then?"

"At first, yes. Some experimental environmentalists learned to live with an even smaller carbon footprint than mine. In 1987 George Turner's science fiction novel "The Drowning Towers" confronted the world with greenhouse warming and rising sea levels, and even won awards and prizes. I thought at the time that people had finally woken up to the problem, but I was wrong. Most people will not leave the comfort of their armchair until their house is on fire."

"How much of a role did you play in establishing the National Audit? Like, your granddaughter was one of the founding auditors."

"Hard to tell. Because I spent so much time providing free child care for my granddaughter, I was able to teach her a great deal about the plight of the climate. I also told her all about historical events such as the Little Ice Age, and how some children's stories like "Hansel and Gretel" might have had their origins in the famines caused by that medieval catastrophe.

"Unlike the more politically correct grandparents, I told Renny that the climatic change that was already under way just might trigger a new outbreak of witch hunts, because witches had been blamed for the medieval climate catastrophe. I still remember our discussions on the subject. She said it would never happen, because everyone was to blame for climate change. I told her that everyone might indeed get blamed, and that young people who were not responsible for our crappy lifestyle had already started pointing the finger. Worldwide, there were about eleven hundred lawsuits involving climate change."

"You're joking!" exclaimed Silvy. "When was that?"

"The Overshoot Year. Runaway greenhouse heating went on to kill billions, and young people started a new type of witch hunt against all old people. You must know what used to happen to witches."

"You mean getting burned at the stake?"

"Yes. I told Renny it was not climatically correct to burn people and release carbon dioxide, so she should just hang us wrinklies. Back then I meant it as a joke."

"That was a very early use of the term 'climatically correct.' Did you invent it?"

"Maybe. I asked Renny whether she would make an exception for her dad, mum and brothers? She said they could swing, because they were carbon farters."

"No wonder she became an auditor general," said Silvy, eyes wide with astonishment and head shaking.

"Well, I like to think that I laid the foundations of her outlook. We were very close until she turned sixteen, more like friendly scientific colleagues than grandfather and granddaughter. Then she went to university and fell in with people who were way more radical than me. Being in my fifties I was probably an embarrassment to her, so communications dropped away to text messages on birthdays and not much more. Until I arrived here I'd not seen her face-to-face for thirty years, which is a bit sad."

From the expressions on the faces of those who were still awake, I could tell that my story was not an uncommon one.

"Dr Hall, can you tell our audience how long it is since governments have known about global warming?"

"In 1965 an American science advisory committee reported that the carbon dioxide levels in the atmosphere were rising, and that fossil fuels were the only recent source. It also said that effects on the climate might be visible by the year 2000, and that those effects could be bad for humans. Any humans here?"

"So they knew that we were on the road to hell eighty years ago?"

"They certainly did. Actually, it was back in 1896 that the Swedish scientist Svante Arrhenius first suggested that burning fossil fuels might lead to global warming."

"So the science has been out there for a century and a half?"

"Yes, but it was an inconvenient truth back then, so it was ignored."

"This may be a good time to finish, the temperature is edging down," said Silvy. "One last question, anyone?"

Several hands were raised. Silvy chose one and the man got to his feet.

"When I was a boy, the sorts of things that have happened to the world would have been called science fiction," he said. "Did science fiction predict stuff like climate change when you were a child, and did it influence you?"

"Yes and yes. I was a precocious little wretch, and I was seven years old when I discovered science fiction. In that year I read Neville Shute's "On the Beach" and Harry Harrison's "Make Room! Make Room!" The first novel was about nuclear annihilation, the other about annihilation by overpopulation. The contraceptive pill seemed to provide a solution to overpopulation, so as a teenager I just marched in anti-nuclear protests. Then came 1973, and the movie version of Harrison's book was released. It was "Soylent Green", and for the first time I heard the term greenhouse effect.

"I was thirteen by then, and I did some research in the library. I concluded that the nuclear apocalypse would probably not happen, because everyone had everything to lose. Climate change was *already* happening, however. Our lifestyles, the very foundations of our civilization, were driving it. When I got to university I tried to raise consciousness about climate change among other students, but nobody wanted to know. They could be against nuclear weapons and not have to give up anything, but if they truly believed that carbon dioxide drove climate change, they could not borrow dad's V8 to go on dates.

"Because I was a hyper-bright kid I got into university only a year after seeing "Soylent Green". I went into climate research and meteorology, and it was an exciting time for weather science. Early computer models for weather and climate prediction were being developed, so I also studied computing. My PhD research modeled the behavior of the Earth's atmosphere according to how much fossil fuel was being dumped into it. In 1980 I became Dr Hall, and I began my sixty-five year battle to convince people that the climate apocalypse was already under way. Very few wanted to know."

A whistle sounded in the distance, signaling that the temperature had dipped low enough for us to return to work. Two of the audience did not get up again after my talk, but nobody made jokes about them being bored to death.

#

It may sound unlikely, but there was an environmental movement among the borderlines of Audit Camp 71. Silvy hung about on the edges of the crowd of admirers surrounding me during dinner, then came over as we scoured out our bowls.

"Will you be going to Entertainment Field tonight?" she asked.

"If I have to. What's the performance?"

"*Game of Thrones*, 'Battle of the Bastards' episode."

"With real deaths?"

"Of course."

"Do I have a choice?"

"Yes. There's also the Dating Field."

This stopped the conversation for a rather long and awkward moment.

"Dating, as in flowers, chocolates and holding hands?" I asked.

"More like seaweed biscuits and sex, but the wardens and vigilante borderlines will leave us alone. Want to check it out?"

"If it's sex you're proposing, I'm feeling a bit ragged just now."

"Whatever, but I need to talk to you in private about what can be done to save the world."

"What's there to say? Qualified people like us should not be squandered out here, facing death for being born in the wrong century. That's why I volunteered to be audited."

"And some of us want to help you. Come on, let's talk."

Dating Field was just a hundred acres of undulating sand where couples could lie between their blankets and do whatever they were capable of doing, with or without chemical help. Wardens patrolled the place, so it was not of much use to those in search of privacy to build weapons, deal drugs or trade contraband. Silvy and I stripped down to our bare bodies at the perimeter gate, left our clothes with the concierge warden and walked on, wearing just our blankets. She turned out to be way less scrawny than me, and she said she had a hormone replacement implant, a type designed to last for decades. It would still be functional when she died, even if she dodged the Retributor's attentions until she was over a hundred.

"This spot looks pretty well out of earshot," she said when we reached a clear stretch of sand.

We sat down together. There were about a dozen other couples in Dating Field, but out of a total population of eleven thousand borderlines and tippers, this was quite a small number. Perhaps there would be more once the show in Entertainment Field was over.

"So this is what passes for privacy in Audit Camp 71?" I asked.

"There's no absolute privacy, you never know when a sand drone is listening."

"Sand drone?"

"They look like rocks or bits or rubbish, but they have cameras and microphones. Say the wrong words near one of them, and the next morning the Retributor will be playing the recording back to you in front of the audit bench and the Auditor General will be sentencing you to Class Six Death."

"Is what you want to say climatically incorrect?"

"Jason, *everything* you say must *always* be climatically correct or you will not last long. You are spending a lot of time in front of drone cameras that are Cloudcasting to the world. Trending algorithms predict that three million people are going to be hearing whatever you say tomorrow."

"Don't tell me, you have a message you want me to slip into one of my audits."

"Nothing so obvious. There are fifteen highly qualified environmental engineers and scientists in Audit Camp 71. They call themselves the Owl Academy because they're bright and they only meet after dark. There are seventy-two audit camps on the continent."

"That means maybe thirteen hundred similarly skilled people are being wasted as borderlines, and all of them for absolutely trivial climate crimes," I said after a moment's calculation. "You people should be free, and working to make a difference. If I beat the audit and get a pardon, they can be re-audited and pardoned under my precedent."

"Now *that* is what the world needs to hear."

"Let's crunch some figures. Thirteen hundred experts with maybe fifteen years life remaining to them could develop tech that removes maybe a thousand tons of carbon from the atmosphere per head of population, per year."

"This is intense, our thought processes are practically identical," she said, squeezing my hand. "We really must work together."

"I'm willing to work with anyone who genuinely cares about the planet."

"So let's get to work, Jason. The word *squandering* is the key. You're squandering the audit bench's time, but the audit is squandering our time as well. The audit removes a few pounds of carbon with every tipper they execute, but each of my borderline experts could remove thousands of times more than that. By anyone's definition, that's squandering by the auditors."

She fell silent as two wardens sauntered past on patrol.

"Celebs like you can do a lot better than her," said a female voice.

Her companion snickered, then they were gone. Silvy sat silent and unmoving. I had a fairly good idea of what she was thinking and how she felt.

"They're jerks, ignore them," I said.

"Sometimes, just sometimes, I feel like giving up and letting Generation V and what's left of the world go straight to hell," she muttered.

"I know, but we have to save a few jerks so that all the deserving people survive."

"Do you think any of the GVs are worth saving after what they are doing to us?"

"Take a look at the junkyard we left to them and you have your answer," I said. "Nobody's blameless."

"So now what? What is your strategic plan?"

"Help me strike back by embarrassing the audit bench with a squandering charge."

Just then we heard distant gunfire from the direction of Entertainment Field. It went on for quite some time.

"We'd better lie out flat," said Silvy. "Stray bullets."

"I don't remember wardens with assault rifles being in *Game of Thrones*," I said as I lay absolutely still.

"Historical revisionism," she replied.

"What should we do?"

"Stay here and don't move until the wardens give us the all clear whistle. You're a very valuable asset, Jason, you need to be kept safe."

Silvy's idea of keeping me safe from stray bullets was to lie on top of me. Between us we had lived nearly a century and a half, and my hormones were not exactly raging, yet it had been twenty years since I had been in that sort of contact with a naked woman. Whatever we did could hardly cause a scandal, so in spite of warnings from my better judgment, I let the inevitable happen.

Judging from the stars, it was after midnight by the time we were allowed to leave Dating Field. By then I had learned a lot more about the audit process from Silvy than I ever could have through Chaz or official channels.

#

DAY 4: THREE HUNDRED AND SEVENTY FLIGHTS

I had a lot of trouble getting myself out of my sleeping trench and functioning after the breakfast bell jangled. I was not getting enough sleep, but there was not much I could do about that. Warden Olivia met up with me in Refectory Field.

"Dr Fitness, I hear you had a big date last night."

"Nothing climatically incorrect about that."

"Why didn't you give *me* a wave?"

"You're a warden."

"Fraternization's okay."

"Look, Silvy and I were discussing scientific things. Leave it at that."

"What sort of scientific things?"

"Like, will the oxygen released by the carbon dioxide extraction farms have an unforeseen effect on the climate?"

"Shit! Hadn't thought of that. Will it?"

"Nobody knows, that's why we were discussing it."

"In Dating Field?"

"Where else can we get the privacy to discuss issues the Retributor might try to use against me?"

"I think Silvy's trouble, Dr Fitness. There's lots of perks for anyone who gets intel out of a celeb tipper being audited."

"I have no intel or secrets."

"So what did she get out of you?"

"Sex! Once! Okay?"

"Yeah, yeah, don't get emo. All I'm trying to say is that you're becoming a celeb, and it's real easy to charge celebs with display. If you stretch out with every fan who makes a move on you, the Retributor can say you're only challenging the National Audit to attract attention."

"But you keep saying you're available."

"I'm not being audited, so I'm safer."

Sensible advice about sex was not what I expected from Warden Olivia, yet I could not fault what she said. I decided to tell Silvy that my body was off limits while I was being audited, because the Retributor could use that sort of activity against me. How to explain my single lapse if he raised the matter before the audit bench? Perhaps I could say that I was demonstrating my commitment to carbon-neutral recreation. Whatever happened, I was going to have to be celibate from now on if I did not want to be audited for display and squander.

"Calling Doc Fitness, anyone home?" said Olivia, waving a hand in front of my face.

"Sorry, lots on my mind."

"Stars must have been lined up for big-time news last night, the whole camp's been working the goss machine."

"I haven't heard a thing?"

"You kidding? Doctor Fitness screwing Psycho Silvy is number one."

"Can we move onto number two?"

"Remember that borderline, Tim Taylor?"

"The conspiracy theory nut? What about him?"

"He was found in a nutritional yeast vat an hour ago."

"Accident?" I asked, fearing the worst.

"Only if he managed to cut his own throat, then hide the knife before jumping into the vat."

"That's terrible."

"Nah, a bit of blood is just extra protein in the yeast."

I had called him the most dangerous nut case in Audit Camp 71, and said that his lunatic theories were a threat to the future of the planet. Someone nearby had heeded my words. Apparently the opinion of Dr Jason Hall was being taken more seriously than I had realized. *I'll have to be more careful about my opinions as well as my sex life*, I thought guiltily.

"I'm sure the guys in flying saucers will be relieved when they hear he's been pushed off the perch," I said, trying to gloss over my role in his death. "What was the third news item?"

"Big escape last night."

"Escape from here? How?"

"Easy, once you know the paths through the minefields, but not many people bother. It's a bad way to die."

"How did they get out?"

"They just walked, during the *Game of Thrones* show. There were fewer wardens on perimeter patrol."

"I suppose there will be a hunt for them."

"Why bother? That would be squandering."

"So anyone is free to escape?"

"Anyone is free to die, Dr Fitness."

\#

The escape of three tippers was headline news on the public address speakers and announcement screens while we were having breakfast. In spite of what Warden Olivia told me, I assumed that a pursuit would be organized, and that the escapees would be back in the camp by lunchtime. That was not the way escapes were dealt with in Audit Camp 71.

The Refectory Field screen switched to the view from a monitor drone hovering five hundred feet above the three escapees. They must have been very fit, because overnight they had actually made it twenty-five miles south of the camp. The infrared camera of the drone showed them as brightly glowing humanoid shapes against the much cooler surface of the desert in morning halflight. The leader appeared to be wearing a headpiece, probably night vision goggles. They were still keeping up a brisk pace, and the man taking up the rear was trailing something behind them to cover their tracks.

"If they got any sense they'll stop for the day," said a voice behind me. "The temperature will probably get up around fifty-five Celsius."

It was Dr Gibson.

"On the journey here we had to keep walking at fifty-five," I replied.

"Yes, but they were trying to kill a few of you. I'd say the escapees only arrived recently."

"Why is that?"

"Nobody who knows this camp would be crazy enough to make a break."

"Because the drones will guide the patrols to them?"

"No, because the patrols will be directed away from them."

"You're losing me."

"Dr Hall, how much water you think those men can carry?"

"Maybe twenty pounds each, max."

"Food?"

"Another twenty?"

"Forty pounds, that's not much if you want to cross six hundred miles of scorching hot desert."

"A pint of water per day, that gives twenty days," I estimated. "If they're tough, they probably reckon they could get four hundred miles. Maybe they could stretch it to six hundred if they're hyper-tough."

"Six hundred miles on starvation rations? Medically impossible. Give them ten days and they'll be doing less than a dozen miles per day. In twenty they will be maybe two hundred miles away, out of water and - to use a very Nineties phrase - rubber ducked."

"But they walked here, we all did. They must have known what they were up against."

"Perhaps one of them did a camping holiday hereabouts, maybe thirty years ago. The temperature was a lot lower, and there was game. If you knew your bush craft you could collect water and hunt."

I thought about that. On the trip out to Audit Camp 71 we had brought a lot more water than that per person in our wagons. I remembered seeing no game at all, and virtually no plant life that was still alive. There was not a trace of surface water, so unless you were a particularly tough insect, there was no living off the land. Why had the escapees ignored what was before their eyes? It did not make sense, but then they had probably ignored the signs and warnings about climate change for years, so perhaps it made sense after all.

"So they're dead, Dr Gibson?"

"We're all dead, Dr Hall."

#

Because of some scheduling problem, my audit was not the first of the day.

"Cameron Andrews, accused of squander and sloth," announced the Clerk of the Bench as a brilliant speck of light appeared on the eastern horizon and the bugler played in the distance.

Andrews was a Generation Victim and was in his mid-thirties. He looked a lot younger than most people brought before the Audit.

"I have video evidence that the accused owned and used a leaf blower powered by a two stroke engine," said the Retributor.

"Cameron Andrews, I am appalled," said the Auditor General. "A Generation Victim like yourself should have been setting an example by using a broom."

Andrews looked frightened, but without actually being terrified. After all, he was GV, and was by definition innocent.

"It was a wedding present from my parents," Andrews said. "Like, it wasn't very practical."

"You operated it past the Tipping Point Year," said the Retributor. "I have a date stamped YouTube video of you chasing your pet dog with the device."

"The accused chased a dog with a petrol powered leaf blower *after* the Tipping Point Year?" exclaimed the Auditor General.

"Yes, your honor."

"Clerk of the Bench, play the video."

I could not bring myself to watch the images that condemned Andrews to death, but I could hear the dog's barking above the sound of the engine. I had counted to 125 by the time the video ended. Two minutes and five seconds of pouring carbon dioxide into the atmosphere when he could have just tossed a ball for his dog to fetch.

"Stupidity and insensitivity on this scale cannot be tolerated, even when the accused is Generation Victim," said the Auditor General. "Honorable victims, who audits guilty?"

All the auditors raised their hands.

"Cameron Andrews, I sentence you to Class Four Death, without mercy."

Andrews was visibly astounded. Because he was GV, he probably expected to just get a decade of Service.

"You can't do this, I'm a victim, like you!" he shouted.

"And because you *are* Generation Victim, you should have known better."

"You're mass murderers!"

"Your stupidity contributed to the deaths of seven *billion* people from famines, pandemics and heat stress. Granted, many of the dead also contributed to their own deaths, but the audit bench exists to catch survivors. Hothouse Earth is the greatest catastrophe ever to afflict the human race and the planet itself. It will not go unpunished."

Andrews lost all trace of self control, soiling his trousers, collapsing to the sand, screaming incoherently and thrashing about. He was bound to a pole by his wrists and ankles, then carried from the Audit Arena while the tippers and borderlines in the gallery clapped, cheered and whistled their approval. A GV had been brought low. They liked that.

"Next audit?" called the Auditor General.

"Jason Hall, the climatologist," said the Clerk of the Bench, this time sounding a little bored. There were two other Jason Halls in the camp, so climatologist was appended to my name whenever I was called.

102

By now Warden Olivia did not have to show me where to go to face the auditors. She just walked beside me because regulations said that I had to be escorted. That boosted my celeb status, and made me feel a little more in control. The gallery crowd cheered, and packets of coffee rations, sun hats and even occasional items of female underwear showered down as I walked. The Auditor General banged her mace for order, but without real enthusiasm.

"I have records to show that the accused made no less than three hundred and seventy international flights totaling two million, five hundred and ninety thousand miles of distance traveled," said the Retributor. "Statistically, all usage models show that some of them must have been recreational."

"Dr Hall, do you deny this charge?" asked the Auditor General.

"I do deny it. Every one of those flights was to deliver and install environmental monitoring equipment, give lectures, attend conferences or appear before parliamentary hearings, pre-COVID. All were in defense of the Earth."

"Are you seriously claiming that none of those flights were recreational?" demanded the Retributor.

"I documented them all on a database and posted it on my blog. I can give you the link if you like."

"Why didn't you teleconference to those events instead of appearing live?"

"I did teleconference, whenever I could, but it's hard to install equipment at remote locations by teleconferencing."

"You should have bought carbon credits for your flights."

"I did, when the system became available, and I paid out of my own money. I also bought retrospective carbon credits for the earlier flights, or bought coal and buried it in landfill."

"Ridiculous! That would have cost a fortune."

"It did, but I was well paid. Because I lived a simple and responsible lifestyle, I could and did afford it."

"Clerk of the Bench?" asked the Auditor General.

"Checking, your honor... verified! He never took a single recreational flight."

"What?" exclaimed the Retributor. "All three hundred and seventy flights were connected with saving the planet?"

"Yes."

"I can't believe that you didn't take at least one of those flights for pleasure."

"Objection," called the Advocate. "My honorable colleague must prove or disprove whether squandering for pleasure took place. His personal opinion is not relevant."

By now I was losing patience with the Retributor in particular and the audit in general. Perhaps the Retributor had been trying to provoke me into doing something foolish. After all, he was very good at skirting the edges of the rules when trying to antagonize tippers. At the very last moment I convinced myself not to shout, which quite possibly saved my life.

"I took pleasure in trying to save the Earth, but I don't hear the Retributor talking about -"

"Order!" called the Auditor General. "Dr Hall, this Audit is not a forum for personal exchanges and abuse. You will observe our protocols or be found guilty of contempt and find yourself on a conventional gallows."

"I apologize, your honor."

She waited for any qualifications that I might make, but I had decided that a simple apology might imply that my outburst had been due to goading by the Retributor.

"The Advocate's objection is sustained," she continued. "Retributor, you will refrain from idle speculation. If the

Clerk of the Bench makes a pronouncement, you must accept it."

"Yes, your honor. Please accept my apology."

"You will remove your sunglasses for the rest of Dr Hall's hearings, to remind you to confine yourself to facts in his audit."

Slowly, and with obvious reluctance, the Retributor removed his sunglasses and handed them to his attending warden.

"I find that the charge against Dr Hall has not been substantiated," the Auditor General continued. "Honorable victims, do you agree?"

All eight auditors raised their hands. Perhaps the rebuke given to the Retributor had rattled them a little.

"Retributor, do you have further charges?"

"I do, your honor," he replied, but in a much less assertive tone.

Without his sunglasses he was not able to present the blank, implacable face of some god of justice. The sight of a retributor being humiliated must have been delighting GT people worldwide.

"The audit of Jason Hall is adjourned until tomorrow. Clerk of the Bench, upgrade Dr Hall's default sentence appropriately, unless he has changed his mind about becoming a borderline."

"Dr Hall?" called the Clerk.

"I choose to upgrade," I responded.

"Then you face Carbon Dioxide Mask, without mercy," said the Auditor General.

Strangely enough, the Carbon Dioxide Mask, without mercy, meant that I had the option of keeping myself alive for a bit longer, rather than just fading out in a painless fog after a few minutes. I would be given a hand cranked pump, and as long as I could pump air from outside through a pinhead sized hole, I could add a little oxygen and stay alive. Protein soup was available through a tube, but the longer I stopped to drink or rest, the more carbon dioxide built up in my little reserve of air. It was meant to demonstrate that one must give oxygen back if one uses it. Tippers could last for days by learning to sleep for very short stretches, but in the long run they always died.

There were enthusiastic cheers as I was escorted back to my seat, and the Auditor General banged her mace on her desk and called for order.

"Next audit, Clerk of the Bench?" she asked once the commotion had died down.

"Melissa Lind."

"Retributor, you may wear your sunglasses again. What is the charge?"

"She is accused of squandering and display. Specifically, flying to Thailand for cheap plastic surgery."

"Could the work have been done in this country?"

"Yes."

"But the flight saved me thousands!" Lind protested.

"Order!" called the Auditor General. "You could have traveled to a local clinic on a commuter train, and thus kept a lot more carbon dioxide out of the atmosphere. Honorable victims, who votes guilty?"

All eight hands were raised.

"I sentence you to Class Five Death, with mercy. Next audit, Clerk?"

#

Andrews put up a frantic struggle when faced with his Class Four execution. After being untied from his carrying pole he rushed back at the auditors, knocked the Retributor's top hat off and jumped up and down on it before the wardens dragged him off. Before he was tied down he managed to kick the Executioner in the groin and bite Warden Olivia's neck.

Is it worse to watch someone being put to death like a bewildered sheep, or desperately struggling for a few seconds more life? For me, his was the most upsetting execution so far.

"He was hoping for a bullet," said Chaz as we hauled our SUV along to collect more bodies from the greenhouse tents. "I've seen it happen before."

"You mean he wanted to be shot?"

"Yeah, that would have been quick and clean, but the wardens are trained to handle that sort of thing."

#

That night Entertainment Field offered something less crass than usual but more confronting: an episode of the crime scene pathology show *Silent Witness*. It was set in a nursing home where inmates were being murdered, and sure enough when it came to the re-enactment of post-mortems on the elderly victims, all of the bodies were real, as was the team of equally elderly pathologists - headed by Dr Gibson. Actually, the script diverged from the original quite substantially.

I watched as the pathologists dissected three corpses of those who had died in Dormitory Field the night before. Two had died by being smothered, and the third had been sent into whatever afterlife did or did not exist by blunt force trauma to the head. Interviews were conducted with those who had been nearby, and it turned out that two of the victims were notorious for snoring. The other had a flatulence condition that had been putting more than his share of methane into the atmosphere.

I suddenly realized that this was meant to be more of a reality show than a scripted drama. One of the dead men was in his early sixties, and had been the strongest borderline in the camp. He had survived three earlier attempts to smother him, killing one of his attackers in the process. The other two bodies had ante-mortem bruising from being held down, along with the distress to minor facial blood vessels that smothering causes. The big man had died from a single blow.

Further dissection suggested that two of the victims probably had snored, and there was enough post-mortem flatus released from the lower intestine of the farter to establish beyond doubt what had pushed his attackers to commit homicide. A length of pipe with traces of blood and hair had been found, and the fingerprints on this were matched to one of the borderlines who had been sleeping nearby. He was handed over to the wardens.

Interviews with neighbors, scratches on suspects, the sizes of handprint bruises and fibers detected on the two smothering victims identified three other vigilantes. What astounded me was the improvised medical equipment. A trestle from Refectory Field was used as the post-mortem table; scalpels, pins and clips had been made by just grinding down scrap metal; the microscope consisted of cardboard tubes holding lenses that had been salvaged from discarded mining laboratory instruments.

I had half expected that the wardens would execute the prisoners at the end of the show. Sure enough, a portable gallows was rigged up, and this was carried out and put where the post-mortems had been conducted. One by one, the guilty were hanged, with the rope placed to snap the neck.

"I've never seen a show quite like that before," I said to Dr Gibson as we left the field.

"Everyone knew who they were, they were well known for taking vigilante action a bit too far," he explained.

"So it's nothing to do with climate justice?" I said.

"More like a law-of-the-jungle way of cancelling out annoying behavior."

#

I was sitting up on my blanket when Warden Olivia walked past on patrol. She stopped and trained her solar torch on my face.

"Hey there, it's Dr Fitness," she said. "How are you doing?"

"Staying alive."

"That's got everyone surprised."

"I saw you get bitten at the executions today."

"Oh yeah, that Andrews fella just didn't want to give up his carbon."

"Hurt much?"

She trained her torch on the teeth marks in her neck.

"I've done worse to fellas, but it's been during rec sex, you know?"

"I can imagine."

"You know, executions really are a bit like sex."

"You can't be serious!"

"It's true, they're totally intense and physical."

"Intense, yes, physical, certainly, but I have doubts about the sex."

"You gotta do it to understand it. Offing tippers makes me horny as a rabbit on Viagra. I'm off duty in an hour. Want me to cruise past?"

"Thank you, but no."

"I'm serious. Hey, I bet I could give you a more intense blast than that Silvy gal. You might even get a heart attack."

"And as you warned me, I might get charged with display if the Retributor finds out. Thank you anyway."

A cloaked figure was approaching. Warden Olivia raised her assault rifle and thumbed on the targeting laser.

"Halt! Who goes there during curfew hours?"

"The Auditor General."

"Advance and be recognized."

My granddaughter walked forward, and her face was lit up by Warden Olivia's torch. The warden shouldered her weapon and saluted.

"Pass, your honor."

"I have private business with this prisoner, warden. Leave."

"Yes, your honor."

Warden Olivia hurried away. The Auditor General stood over me.

"You beat the Retributor again," she said. "Nobody has ever beaten him on their airline flight records."

"So?"

"So you really are defying death."

"That means I'm defying you."

"What do you mean?"

"The tippers and borderlines say that *you* are Death."

For some reason she seemed to find that confronting. Perhaps it was because she thought of herself as an extension

110

of the National Audit, and had a poorly developed self image. She looked down and scuffed at the sand with a foot.

"That's silly of them, I just want to see climate justice done."

It was a climatically correct reply, she was hiding behind her authority. I decided to attack that authority.

"You call the National Audit justice?"

"Yes. Do you?"

"No!" I snapped, genuinely angry.

"Why not?"

"It's a parody of justice as it used to be."

"Justice as it used to be was not good for the planet. The old system of justice allowed seven billion deaths."

We were silent for a moment. She looked over to where Warden Olivia had stopped to speak with someone else.

"She propositioned me just now," I said.

"She likes to do it with men she is scheduled to execute. I can't decide whether she likes giving them a pleasant send-off, or if she's a closet serial killer."

"Does it make any difference?"

"Yes. If she likes killing, she becomes a murderer. The penalty for that is death."

"I'm surprised. Human life has become so very cheap."

"Did you accept Olivia's offer?"

"No."

"Yet you spent recreation time in Dating Field with Silvy Rossica last night."

"Yes."

"Why?"

"I like her. I like sex, too."

"She's a born rebel. She was once in the Forced Democracy League, then she turned against us after the National Audit was formed."

"She might have done that because the National Audit went too far."

"She's also a spy. That trip to Port Douglas was a rigged prize, it was just cover for her to spy on a meeting of CEOs for political reasons that were never disclosed, even to me. I was going to give her Class Three Death, but I was ordered not to."

"So someone important is protecting her?"

"Someone important is *employing* her. If some tipper needs to be killed before saying something embarrassing in front of the audit bench, that tipper may die the night before. She's an assassin, granddad, I am not the only person who make the decisions about life and death in this camp."

"So she has she killed already?"

"Five times, that I know of. She runs the Owl Academy, but that has to be a front. I know her type, and her type does their real work in shadows."

"And her people are interested in me? I'm flattered."

"You should be frightened."

"I'm frightened too, but everyone frightens me, including you."

"Take this seriously, granddad."

"Beware of those who never laugh, granddaughter."

For a time neither of us said anything.

"Don't say I did not try to warn you," she said at last. "Take the Audit seriously. You're important."

"Me? Important? My life's work was predicting a climatic catastrophe. In case you hadn't noticed, nobody listened until it was too late. Most of China, Australia and Africa got turned into searing deserts. The US and Europe were snap frozen because the Gulf Stream got screwed, then it got hotter and now they're deserts too."

"You forgot accelerated polar melting, sea level up two feet, and Category Seven hurricanes every week."

"Silly me, but that proves I'm unimportant."

"Not so. You are important because you threaten important people."

"Me, threatening? Get a life."

"I get a great many lives. Do you know how very rich people used to become rich?"

That question was straight out of left field. I had to stop and think.

"By third level greed and second level squandering?" I asked.

"Not so. They just became good at gathering money. They did not have to earn money, just accumulate it."

"Bullshit."

"Please, remember that the word is climatically offensive. Wealth and growth are now unfashionable, thanks to lateralist economics, yet there are still rich people. Position, power and reputation have become wealth in Generation Victim society."

"Same flies, different shit."

"Believe it or not, you have a reputation and you are very powerful. The Retributor values his reputation, and you threaten it. He has a perfect record at getting death or borderline verdicts for tippers. Not a single pardon."

"Yet I threaten him?"

"Yes. He's the new type of rich man, and the rich like to hold on to their riches."

"Do I threaten you?"

"No. I only care about justice and the planet."

"Then we have a lot in common, Renny. Maybe it's genetic."

"Perhaps. Were I born four months earlier, I too would have had to face the Audit. I keep wondering if I would have had your courage. Good luck tomorrow, and watch out for Silvy."

#

SEAN MCMULLEN

DAY 5: SIXTEEN POUND CAT

On the morning of my fourth audit I attracted a substantial crowd in Refectory Field. Most of them acted like the fans of the old-style celebs, but some just wanted to be seen to be near me because I was cool, and apparently cool rubs off. I was bombarded with questions that seemed to span every subject in Unipedia, and as always I had to choose every word that I spoke in reply with meticulous care.

Live as a celeb and you will also be targeted by people who want to make celebs of themselves by dragging you down. You very quickly learn to smile a lot while saying very little, preferably answering questions with questions. This was why Chaz was so useful: he fielded questions meant for me. He was only known for being my friend, so nobody could be bothered baiting him.

Oscar Wilde once wrote that youth is wasted on the young. Had he lived a bit longer he might have also written that fame is wasted on the old. I was eighty-five, so I was definitely old, no arguments with that. I was now also famous, after a lifetime of merely being an important authority. That

115

meant people wanted to buy a bit of my fame and influence, but what could they offer in return?

Money had lost its clout as a motivator. If someone gave you a trillion retro-dollars, what could you do with them? Buy a big mansion on a large estate and throw lots of wild parties? That gets you charged with squander and display, and attracts a sentence of Class One Death. Buy an executive jet and fly around the world, visiting all those places you've always wanted to see? *Guilty of squander and display* would be the verdict, and Class One Death would be the sentence. Invest it, to make two trillion? Guilty of greed and neglect, and you get sentenced to Class Two Death, if you are lucky.

Sex is generally waved at anyone with some degree of fame, and it was certainly waved at me. Remember my age, eighty-five? While my sex drive was still operational, at eighty-five it was no longer a strong influence on my behavior. My predilections are heterosexual and boringly conventional, which further narrowed the scope of what could be offered to me. The idea of doing it with warden girls a quarter of my age made me feel humiliated, because I had a fair idea of what their unspoken thoughts about me would be. Women closer to my age tend to be about as enthusiastic as, well, myself, so any interest shown in my scrawny body was bound to be an act. That left those maybe twenty or thirty years younger, generally with a hormone replacement implant. After what Renny told me about Silvy the night before, this seemed a dangerous option. Had what I had done with Silvy in Dating Field been a bad idea? Knowing what I now knew about her, definitely. Was it worth taking the same chance with anyone else? Definitely not.

How about drugs? They would mess with my mind, and give the Retributor an edge. Gourmet food? How gourmet can dried seaweed and vat grown protein be? Alcohol? Same deal. Fast cars? Illegal and extinct. Clothes? Rags are worn by everyone born before 2000, and are admirably suited to living in the desert's searing heat.

That left power, and it was indeed on offer. Every group of borderlines that I met wanted to have me as their figurehead leader, chief, president, captain, elder, chairman or director. Only the Greenhands did not try to make me their leader, but this was probably because they had no supreme leader.

Power was the one currency that had survived unchanged from Generation Tipper. The auditor generals were exceedingly powerful, but they had to follow the rules and guidelines laid down by their own tele-congresses. Those rules were meant to guide humans toward a lifestyle that was in balance with the Earth's biosphere, and they were not negotiable. Besides, I was being audited, so by definition I had no power.

Thus it was strangely liberating to be in my position. I did not want or need anything, so I could not be bribed with possessions, power or privilege. Even better, everyone else had been dragged down to my own rather Spartan standards by climate change. I could not help comparing myself to a character in Terry Pratchett's *Discworld* novels, Cohen the Barbarian. He was eighty-seven, yet still living the life of a barbarian adventurer. Unlike Cohen, I did not have piles or a bad back, and I still had most of my teeth, but otherwise our situations had a lot in common. We were both old, able, alone, but still fighting. Unlike Cohen, I had spent my life fighting for a specific cause.

#

Again Warden Olivia just walked beside me as we entered the Audit Arena. As usual, the Retributor frowned at the marginal breach of protocol, but that was probably posturing for the five million watchers behind the Cloudcast camera.

His top hat had been repaired, but it would never be the same again. Getting a new one made would attract charges of display and squander.

"First audit of the day is the next hearing for Jason Hall, climatologist," said the Clerk of the Bench.

"Sunshades, Retributor," said the Auditor General, and he sneered at me as he removed them. "Declare charges."

"The accused possessed an oversized pet, specifically a cat weighing sixteen pounds. This type of animal can be statistically demonstrated to have a bigger carbon footprint than a small car over its lifetime. The maintenance of this animal amounts to blatant squandering."

"Do you have a response, Dr Hall?" said the Auditor General.

"Firstly, Titania was a university pet, she was merely registered in my name. Secondly, she was fed on vermin shot in the Antarctic national parks, and on protein donated from staff rations. Thirdly, she was an excellent mouser, and was thus a form of biological pest control. Because of her we never needed to put down traps or use poisons in and around the laboratories."

"Who is looking after Titania now?" asked the Auditor General.

"She died of old age last year, her heart just stopped while she was lying on my bed. She was a hard working member of the research staff, and a very loyal companion."

"Did her death have anything to do with you volunteering to be audited?"

"No."

"Could you expand on that?"

"She died a week before my eighty-fifth birthday. When I turned eighty-five I began to wonder what I could do with the rest of my life, and I decided that someone ought to make a stand against the mistakes of the National Audit."

"Even though that might involve you dying horribly."

"Yes, but it still seemed like the right thing to do."

"Surely this is evidence of squandering," interjected the Retributor.

"Why?" I asked.

"If you believed that it was important to the Earth for you be audited, then you should not have postponed volunteering for the sake of a pet."

"My reason for volunteering for an audit might have been triggered by the death of Titania, but I would have volunteered eventually. She was very popular with the other climate research staff, so there were other people to look after her. I volunteered because I genuinely believe that borderlines and tippers of good will working in reserved occupations should be freed from the perpetual threat of an audit."

"The maintenance of a cat is still squander."

"Titania was also employed as a member of the research staff as a relaxation therapy assistant, I can give you the link. Cats have been proven to be more effective than most psychotherapists at relieving tension in severely stressed and overworked people."

"Clerk of the bench, please check that on Unipedia," said the Auditor General.

"Checking ... confirmed."

"You had a duty to volunteer earlier," began the Retributor.

"Objection!" called the Advocate. "The accused has answered that question already."

"Objection sustained. Retributor, try to stay more focused. If you have nothing else to say, I must conclude that the charge has not been substantiated."

The breath hissed between the Retributor's teeth, but he bowed to the Auditor General and said nothing.

"Honorable victims, who votes against the charge?"

Seven hands were raised.

"Do you have any further charges, Retributor?"

"I have, your honor."

"Then prepare one for tomorrow. Do you wish to continue tomorrow, Dr Hall?"

"I choose to continue, your honor."

"Then we shall see you at dawn. Next case?"

"Peggy-Anne Smith," said the Clerk.

I returned to the gallery benches amid the usual applause and cheers, but there seemed slightly less enthusiasm in the voices. By now I was considered to be a champion, and champions were expected to win as a matter of routine.

#

Peggy-Anne Smith was led in by another warden. She looked to be only half my age, but that was sure to be due to hormone replacement implants. She also managed to seem stylishly dressed, even while wearing rags. What caught my attention was that she was distinctly stiff in her movements, which was odd for someone who looked so young. I estimated that she was probably older than me.

"The accused is charged with gluttony, squander and display," said the Retributor.

Cries of "Meow! Meow!" erupted from the gallery, and I suspected that the Retributor would never live down his attempt to use Titania against me.

"Order!" shouted the Auditor General, banging her mace. "One more outburst like that and I shall have the gallery cleared. Continue, Retributor."

"I have records, receipts and photographs to prove that the accused spent seven million retro-dollars on cosmetic surgery and implants for mere vanity. The Audit has images in support of the charges."

"Let me see," said the Auditor General.

She stared at the screen of her laptop, then looked to the prisoner.

"Remarkable. You look about forty or fifty, but you were born in 1945."

"I look after myself, victim people," declared Peggy-Anne, with a hand on her hip.

"The accused was a well known socialite who inherited a large amount of money," continued the Retributor.

"Now listen, sonny, I'll have you know that I earned a pile more with some very well managed divorce settlements."

"Order," called the Auditor General.

"I have records proving that the accused organized two thousand three hundred and eighty-seven extravagant parties over a period of ninety years," the Retributor concluded. "The first was for her tenth birthday."

"So you are saying that a lot of resources were gratuitously squandered?"

"Yes, your honor. My estimates are based partly on records and partly on standard party consumption models. Do you wish them to be read out?"

"Of course. This is quite an unusual case."

"Forty-six tons of food types now classed as exotic or frivolous. One third of that was vomited by guests or later discarded, going on standard models of waste for the period and social class."

"What else?" asked the Auditor General.

"Twenty-five thousand bottles of wine, champagne and spirits were consumed. I also have estimates on resources squandered on decorations, lighting, heating, and status presents that were bought only to be seen being given, then discarded unused."

"Do you have the total value, in retro-dollars?"

"In excess of twenty million retro-dollars, your honor. She also bought a large quantity of party clothing and costumes, as well as a town house, seaside estate and yacht, all to stage parties. Her party apparel was typically worn once, then discarded."

The Auditor General shook her head.

"Hundreds of times more waste than a petrol-fetish motorist with a collection of touring cars," she sighed. "Honorable victims, who audits guilty?"

All the auditors raised their hands.

"Guilty as charged. Peggy-Anne Smith, as you clearly show no remorse for your long life of squandering, I sentence you to Class Six Death, without mercy."

"Well, I'm glad I never wasted an invitation on any of you lot," said Peggy-Anne, rolling a hip in the direction of the audit bench.

This caused an eruption of cheers and clapping, along with a shower of coffee rations, improvised high heels, underwear and Viagra coupons. The Auditor General banged her mace on the desk until the edge splintered.

"Rest assured, Madame, that if anyone on the audit bench had voluntarily attended even one of your parties, they too would be audited," she declared once the outburst had died away.

"I'd name names if I could see faces," said Peggy-Anne.

My granddaughter slowly removed her sunshades. The rest of the auditors did so as well, and they were followed by the Advocate and Clerk of the Bench. The Retributor removed his sunshades last of all. Peggy-Anne stared at him.

"Aren't you the Worthingtons' kid?" she asked.

"My parents were Adrian and Anita Worthington."

"Thought so, you have your father's face. I remember your folks coming to my Global Financial Crisis party back in 2008. They brought their little boy along, and they only had one kid, so that must be you."

"My parents took me to a great number of parties, but I did not attend any of them voluntarily. After the age of fourteen I attended no parties at all."

"Bet it was because you got no invitations. How are Addy and Anni doing?"

"Their carbon was reclaimed last year."

"Pity, your father was a good screw."

The Retributor's face contorted for a moment, and there were titters of laughter and calls of "Meow! Meow!" from the tippers and borderlines in the gallery.

"Order," said the Auditor General with a hand over her mouth, probably to hide a smirk.

She put her sunshades back on. All the other auditors took this as a cue to replace their own optical armor against the glare.

"Have you anything else to tell the Audit?" she asked.

"You GV people still have parties, and a lot more orgies than in my day. Why are GVs innocent and I'm not?"

"Our dances have live bands with no amplifiers, and the lighting is from the moon or solar charge batteries," said the Auditor General. "As for orgies, recreational sex does not consume resources or increase the population, so it is encouraged as climatically correct entertainment."

"So if I'd staged sex orgies instead, would I have still got death?"

"That would depend on the catering. Next audit?"

Peggy-Anne sauntered across to the gallery to louder cheers than I had received. She took the seat next to mine.

"Hi there, Dr Hall, what did you think of my audit?" she asked.

"Astonishing," I replied, and that was absolutely true.

"I'm starring in an execution in maybe an hour. You're invited."

"Thank you. I'll be sure to volunteer for witness duty."

"No champagne, sorry about that."

"I'm sure someone will pass around a flask of something," I assured her.

"Chaz told me all about you last night. Wish I could have got to know you better."

"Me? Why?"

"You're a celeb. I like celebs."

"I'm quite boring."

She reached across and groped my crotch.

"You're cute," she said. "If the rope breaks, call over and see me tonight."

#

True to my promise, I volunteered to attend Peggy-Anne's execution by the tipping point gallows. Four of the five of the tippers sentenced to the gallows that day chose "Meow! Meow!" as their last words.

Peggy-Anne was a hundred years old! Killing old people had once been abhorrent, but now it was climatically correct. The Earth had gone to the pack, and the victim generations

124

wanted revenge on those who had turned the pack loose. She was undeniably one of them.

I watched as Peggy-Anne was escorted onto the tipping point gallows. She had slit her ragged skirt right up to her hip, painted fishnet stockings and suspenders on her legs, and improvised high heels out of scrap plastic. She had also tied the bottom of her blouse to improvise a push-up bra, and was showing a lot of synthetic cleavage. A noose was placed around her neck.

"Is this thing safe?" she asked the Executioner.

He shrugged, then returned to the coal tub at the other end of the tipping point gallows, leaving a warden holding Peggy-Anne by the arm and keeping the noose steady at the back of her neck for a slow choke. The Auditor General began her declaration of carbon reclaiming.

"Peggy-Anne Smith, you have -"

Peggy-Anne stamped a high heel into the top of the warden's foot. As he released her arm and doubled over with pain, she drove her hip into him, knocking him off the platform. She then gave a flick of her head, moving the knot of the noose to the side of her neck.

"Next time you can't find a good party, don't come crying to me!" she shouted.

Peggy-Anne jumped off the tipping point gallows, and there was a snap as her neck broke. I sagged with relief. The Executioner climbed up and checked for a pulse.

"Dead, your honor," he reported.

"Peggy-Anne Smith has been found guilty of gluttony, squandering and display," continued the Auditor General. "For this she was sentenced to Class Six Death, without mercy. As she did take from the Earth, so now she has given back what carbon remained to her."

"And silicone," called a voice from the crowd of tippers and borderlines, sparking some laughter and meows.

The Auditor General walked over to the Executioner.

"Executioner, you will have the access platform extended all the way around the tipping point plank so that such an incident cannot happen again. How long will that take?"

"No more than one hour, your honor."

"All executions by tipping point gallows are suspended for one hour. Executions by Carbon Dioxide Mask and Rising Sea Level will be brought forward. Inspector of Wardens, take charge."

Peggy-Anne Smith had actually beaten the system in a minor yet spectacular way, and everyone was talking about her as we stood about, waiting for new work schedules to be organized. It was what she had wanted, being stage center as she went out.

#

A nightclub was scheduled for Entertainment Field once dinner had been served and eaten. Try to imagine several thousand elderly revelers with perhaps half a million years of life between them jumping up and down and singing that they were too sexy for their car, led by two dozen drummers beating on old barrels to provide a pounding bass, and the usual choruses of hummers and singers.

To my absolute astonishment, Peggy-Anne's body was wheeled in, seated in a wheelchair that had been streamlined with cardboard packaging with PORSCHE written on the sides. She was wearing the Retributor's stolen sunshades and top hat, and the party gear that she had been executed in. She had not yet been slashed open in the desiccation field, the cuts to dry out her fluids had just been painted on so that

126

they could be cleaned off for her final party. She definitely looked too sexy for her car.

The music for the next dance was "Rah Rah Rasputin," with the choruses screamed rather than sung. Due to rigor mortis, Peggy-Anne's body was frozen in a seated position, but this did not stop a bearded borderline dressed as Rasputin lifting the corpse from the wheelchair and dancing about with it in his arms. I was given another sip of Audit Camp 71 moonshine, but I did not join in the dancing - on Silvy's advice. I did help carry two bodies away from the dance area during a break in the music. There were always deaths during high exertion entertainments, and Dr Gibson had set up a temporary morgue.

"Only two so far?" he said as we stretchered the second body in. "Quiet night."

"What do you do if they're still alive?" I asked.

"I try to make sure they stay alive. I am a doctor, after all."

"But aren't they trying to dance themselves to death?"

"They are trying to die accidentally, Dr Hall. Big difference."

"Why bother treating them?"

"It's my way of reminding Generation Victim that life is important. In case you had not noticed, the entire generation is having a memory lapse."

"Sorry. With so much death in this place, I'm having trouble remembering too."

Peggy-Anne's body was slashed open later that night, but it would be a couple of days before rigor mortis relaxed its grip on her muscles and she could be stretched out in Desiccation Field. All the while I felt guilty for admiring her because she had defied the National Audit. I am a defiant person too, but unlike myself, she had never once spared a thought for the climate or environment.

GENERATION NEMESIS

She was a member of Generation Tipper who would never have changed or made concessions, so why did I go to her nightclub wake, even as a volunteer paramedic? That is a very good question. Perhaps I wanted to be part of history, because when the camp's bugler played "The Party's Over" the next morning, it would literally be true. We were figureheads of the opposing sides, and although she was magnificent, she was dead. I was still standing.

#

DAY 6: CLIMATICALLY INCORRECT CHILD

The morning of my fifth audit did not start with the routine of all the others. The nightclub in Entertainment Field had not just killed people, it had left a lot more tippers than usual suffering from strained muscles, torn tendons, hangovers, and general exhaustion. As I was escorted into the Audit Arena I noticed that there were actually a few seats vacant in the gallery.

Once the audit bench was seated, the Clerk of the Bench announced that I was the first audit of the day. The Auditor General reminded me that I was facing Class Four Death - which was Greenhouse Field, with mercy.

"I am aware of that, your honor," I replied. "It's a particularly depressing prospect, but I am confident that the risk is worth it."

"Nobody has ever reached a fifth audit, so we need to establish protocols. Do you wish to be reminded about your default sentence for each adjournment?"

"I don't much care either way."

"Clerk of the Bench, make a note that any tipper who goes on to a second audit must be reminded of their default sentence at the commencement of proceedings."

"Done, your honor," said the Clerk after a moment.

The Retributor scowled. Clearly he did not like the idea of anyone surviving so many of his charges. At a gesture from the Auditor General he removed his sunshades and held up his pad.

"The accused is charged with raising a child with climatically irresponsible attitudes," he declared.

This charge was a complete surprise, because I had never seen it used in all the studies I had done of National Audit proceedings. Ever since my son had left school, he had rebelled against his upbringing - which had been climatically correct, even though the term did not exist back then. That had been a source of grief for me, and I had agonized for years about what I might have done wrong. I could not have provided Albert with a better example of how to live responsibly, but perhaps my example had been too good.

He was bright, and got a job in a company dealing in shares. He made a lot of money very quickly, and began to spend up big on everything that would pour carbon dioxide into the atmosphere. That had hurt me at a very personal level. He drove a restored 1960s V8 and built an enormous house for his five children. Each had their own television room and en suite, and the entire place had central heating and air-conditioning. He bought each of them a car when they turned eighteen. Renny's car was still in the garage of the abandoned house, and had not been driven since the day it had been delivered.

"I cannot account for what my son thought, and what he did," I told the audit bench. "It is possible that he just rebelled against the way I was raising him."

"Why would he do that?" asked the Auditor General.

130

"We were living in an indulgent and materialistic society, but I was preventing him from enjoying the same pleasures as his friends."

"So you accept responsibility?" asked the Retributor.

"No. It is the nature of children to rebel, to a greater or lesser extent. Albert Hall's youngest daughter in turn rebelled against the environment in which *she* was raised. Albert, his wife and three of his sons died here in Audit Camp 71, sentenced to death by Renelda Kylie Hall."

"Myself," said the Auditor General.

"His other daughter died when she crashed her V8."

This was all material that the Retributor would have seen, yet he was showing signs of nervousness. Perhaps he sensed that his case was collapsing, but was not sure why.

"My own son has not rebelled against my beliefs and way of life," he declared.

"Your son is eleven years old," I countered, because I too do my homework and I had researched everyone on Audit Camp 71's audit bench well enough to write detailed biographies of them. "When your child reaches the age at which teenagers rebel, he may not do so openly because he fears for his life."

"Objection!" exclaimed the Retributor. "The accused is making idle and unfounded speculations about my son."

"Objection overruled," said the Auditor General. "The accused was making a general statement. You made it specific to your family, and he replied to your assertion. Dr Hall, would you mind telling the audit bench more about your son? Whose fault was it that he lived so very differently to yourself?"

She was talking about her father, the man whose death sentence she had pronounced. As a teenager she had often told me that she hated him and wished he were dead, but that sort of talk is common among teenagers. She had followed through with those words, however. Now she wanted my opinion on why he had turned out the way he did, and I had to deliver that opinion in an audit being Cloudcast to the entire world - unrehearsed. Did she want justification for executing him?

"As I have already said, I blame the society in which Albert was raised, your honor. To be out of fashion is to be out of this world, and when he was growing up it was not at all fashionable to worry about greenhouse warming or resource depletion. The superpowers of the time were threatening each other with hydrogen bombs that could have annihilated humanity, along with all forms of life more complex than bacteria."

"Could you be a little more specific?"

"Quite a lot of people lived as if the world would be destroyed in their lifetime. The sexual excesses and rampant materialism of the 1960s, 70s and 80s may have been a symptom of that. Something as slow, subtle, and far into the future as climate change was not regarded as important."

"Retributor, the National Audit is now holding those Twentieth Century generations to account," said the Auditor General. "Do you deny that?"

"No, your honor."

"Both of us know that there is nothing quite so distressing as being alone in a crowd. You and I were lucky enough to be born into an age of responsibility, but Dr Hall was not. I am satisfied that the choices of the accused's son were not within the control of the accused, and that this charge has been answered. Remember, in common law parents cannot be held liable for the actions of children over the age of eighteen. Fellow victims, can I have a show of hands for my assessment?"

Six hands were raised.

"Retributor, do you have any further charges?"

"I do, your honor."

"Dr Hall, are you willing to resume the audit tomorrow, with the default sentence increased in severity to Greenhouse Field, without mercy?"

"I am, your honor."

"Audit adjourned until tomorrow."

#

There was only lethargic applause for me as I walked to the gallery, but I knew I was no less popular. The effects of the night before were plainly visible on the faces of everyone watching.

"Clerk of the Bench, who is next to be audited?" asked the Auditor General.

"Audit of Shihan Antony Tyler, master karate instructor," the Clerk of the Bench announced.

"Charges, Retributor?" asked the Auditor General.

"I charge the accused with neglect, and maintain that he had knowledge of the plight of the Earth, yet refrained from actively working to prevent the catastrophe that took place."

"Objection, your honor!" called the Advocate. "On that criterion, members of hunter gather tribes throughout the world could be charged with neglect. Precedent has already been established that hunter gatherers preserved lifestyles in balance with pre-agricultural ecosystems, and have provided us with valuable examples of sustainable living."

"Right of reply, Retributor?" said the Auditor General.

"The accused is not from a hunter gatherer tribe. Although he had a very small carbon footprint, the students who came to his property to study martial arts squandered considerable resources in terms of jet fuel and other travel overheads."

"Objection overruled. Proceed."

"While the accused did not encourage students to visit him, Mr Tyler did not discourage them either."

"The accused's title is Shihan, Retributor," said the Auditor General.

"I apologize, your honor. I am not familiar with all subtleties of martial arts titles."

"It is in your brief for this case."

"Yes, of course. My apologies."

What is happening here? I wondered. *Is she reminding him that his authority is limited, or forcing him to tighten his act and take me more seriously next time?*

"Shihan Tyler, do you have an answer to the charge?" the Auditor General asked.

The karate master displayed no real interest in the proceedings, and was certainly not in fear of the audit bench. He stared calmly at the Retributor for a moment, then turned to the Auditor General.

"I believe there is no charge to answer, your honor," he declared.

"If there is no challenge to the Retributor's charge, then I shall have to put it to a vote and pass sentence."

This was more than I could stand.

"Your honor, I wish to speak for the accused!" I called.

I had memorized the rules of procedure for audits, and I knew that observers could declare themselves to be expert witnesses. The trick was to be accepted as an expert.

"Your CV does not list you as being qualified in martial arts, Dr Hall," said the Auditor General.

"My expertise includes professional travel commitments and teaching, your honor. I refer the audit bench to my second and third audits, regarding motorcycle and airline travel."

"Accepted. Please proceed."

"I suggest that Shihan Tyler was following good travel practice. Only very advanced students would have taken the trouble to travel to the master's home. These would then return to their own schools of karate and teach other students."

"Why was this any better or worse than Shihan Tyler traveling to where his students lived?"

"If the master offered to make the journey himself, everyone would have been willing to have him travel to local martial arts schools and learn from him, squandering more transport fuel. Because he did not travel at all, only those teachers who were truly dedicated would have taken the trouble to travel to his residence and learn from him. The total carbon footprint would have been smaller."

"Objection, your honor!" said the Retributor. "The witness cannot prove that."

"Dr Hall?"

"Your honor, the Retributor cannot prove otherwise. It is my professional opinion, as an expert and teacher in the sciences, that a smaller carbon footprint will be generated by students having to travel to a master."

"He should have used video links for teaching people in other countries," said the Retributor.

"Martial arts involve a lot of physical activity and bodily contact," I said, now resorting to guesswork. "One might as well ask someone to learn about sex by watching pornographic videos."

"Many people do," said the Retributor smugly.

"And they often develop sociopathic behaviors, which then have to be treated. This is classed as squandering."

I had realized by now that the Retributor was distinctly uneasy about accusations of climate crimes against himself. Although I had not mentioned him by name, he was quite obviously in my crosshairs.

"Order," said the Auditor General, coming to his rescue. "Dr Hall, the discussion is starting to drift away from the Retributor's charge. I cannot accept your argument, but neither can I accept that the Retributor has refuted it. Shihan Tyler, your audit is proving to be difficult. Are you willing to accept an increase in sentence severity for your next audit, and to become a borderline?"

"I do not wish to plead either way, I shall accept whatever is best for the planet," he said, showing no emotion, or even interest.

"In that case, my decision is to give you borderline status and increase your default sentence from Carbon Dioxide Mask with mercy to Carbon Dioxide Mask without mercy. In favor? Against? Carried! Next case, Clerk of the Bench?"

Why had I intervened? I really can't say. Perhaps it was because Shihan Tyler had been leading a more climatically blameless life than practically anyone else in Audit Camp 71, wardens, auditors and even myself included. I had come to the place to challenge the National Audit and get some real justice into the audit process. Tyler's case demanded that he be given real justice.

His escort warden brought him to the seat next to mine.

"Why did you speak for me?" he asked softly.

"The charge against you was flawed, and the Advocate was not doing her job," I replied.

"But I am a stranger to you."

"Is the duty of every martial artist to stand between danger and those who are helpless?"

"Yes."

"Well, you were helpless, and in danger."

He considered this carefully for some seconds.

"People like you should be in charge of the auditing process, Dr Hall."

#

Fashion was rarely thought of as a contributing cause of the climatic apocalypse, yet like all the bricks that combine to make a house, it played a part. Mark Porter had arrived with the day's caravan, and was greeted by a large and excited crowd, mainly composed of women. How did they know he was coming? How did the security breach take place? Silvy provided the answer, almost casually. Someone in the previous caravan to leave the Torrens staging camp had recognized him in a queue.

"I bet the wardens are seriously worried about the breach," I said when she told me.

"Their job is to worry."

"He won't last long. Do you know what he did?"

"Yes. He invented dash fash, the online system for fashion clothing delivery. If you chose an outfit and entered your body profile, a fabrication depot ran up the clothes and a drone dropped a package on your doorstep half an hour later. It allowed people to do a fashion makeover every day, and in some cases several times a day."

"Very good, Jason. Now he's to be audited for grand squander."

"Let me guess, that's worse than squander."

"Don't be cute."

GENERATION NEMESIS

There was no reason for me to meet with Porter, but a meeting was inevitable. Celebs are meant to meet other celebs so that their fans can watch the confrontation. Why confrontation? Because celebs are walking, talking reality shows, shows are entertainment, and confrontation entertains.

\#

It was during the evening meal that Porter and I were brought together. He was actually from Generation Victim, born in the early years of the new millennium.

"So you're the mad scientist who started the fuss about climate change?"

I turned around and stood. Porter and his entourage of ragged fashionistas had come up behind me, and in spite of the horrors and hardships of the trek across the desert, he had managed to keep himself looking passably sharp. His opener was the gauntlet flung down by a knight at the feet of a rival knight. He was unlikely to survive his audit the following day, and he wanted a chance to sneer at his executioners. I was surviving, so he had decided that I shared many of their values. This was a good reason to attack me, as far as he was concerned.

"Mad as in deranged, or just angry as all hell with people like you?" I asked.

"Don't get smart with me! I pioneered waste reduction in the clothing industry, and now your friends want to murder me."

"You opened the floodgates to a whole new level of waste *production*, you poured petrol on the fire that's burning the world," I countered. "Why didn't you think your concept through?"

"I eliminated the possibility of unsold clothes."

Suddenly I realized that he never answered a question directly. I knew the type.

"You invented the idea of changing fashions four or five times a day - and tossing clothes in recycling instead of the washing basket."

I had him. He had to give a straight answer.

"Consumers wanted that."

"I'm sure consumers also wanted weekly shopping sprees in Paris and London, but that would have dumped the planet straight into the fireplace if everyone did it."

"Nerds and geeks like you are always going to be jealous of jet setters. I've brightened up the lives of millions."

"Who invented the jet?" I countered. "Some jet setter who swanned around at cocktail parties?"

Again, I had him.

"Rolls Royce, wasn't it?" he managed, guessing that it might be a classy company.

"Actually it was a German physicist named Hans von Ohain, and he was not a great party animal. Speaking of parties, would you invite John Logie Baird, the engineer who invented television? How about Alan Turing, the mathematician who invented electronic computing?"

"Well? Just because a pilot flies me somewhere, should I have him to dinner?"

"So you never invited anyone who knew about climate change?"

"People like you sold climate change as a load of hype, that's why important people ignored you."

"So did you ignore red lights when you drove a car, because you thought you were too important to stop?"

"I was important enough to have someone else drive me."

The exchange was beginning to irritate me, partly because I just wanted to get on with my dinner. I was about to reach for one of my seaweed biscuits when a tall, lissome and decidedly elegant woman walked between Porter and me. Like all the rest of us, she wore rags, but they were tasteful rags and she somehow contrived to wear them with flair. She would have been somewhere between fifty and ninety, it was impossible to tell from the way she walked and dressed. She probably paid a lot of attention to her physical fitness without being a fanatical exerciser, and had probably paid a lot of money for her hormone replacement and nanotech therapy implants decades earlier.

"Alette Borden," prompted someone behind me.

While she was not as well known as Mark Porter, even I knew about the woman whose reality television shows had included *Dressing for the Climate*, *Op Shop Elegance* and *Timeless Fashion*.

"Dr Hall, we meet at last," she said, her voice as understated yet compelling as her appearance. "You once wrote that I did more to save the planet than a solar cell mega-factory. Thank you for that."

I shook her hand. This was one celeb who I really did respect.

"You read one of my articles?" I said. "I'm flattered. Actually, I'm surprised."

"Why? Because you think all fashion authorities are like *that*?"

She gestured to Porter. He bristled, but was too intimidated to reply.

"Sorry, I've not had any contact with fashion authorities," was what I said.

"What a pity, you should have invited us to your parties. We're generally bright and intelligent. Many of us would have taken you seriously."

"I've never thrown a party, at least not one that involved more than red wine in coffee mugs and a plate of crisps. Scientists are more about talk than cuisine."

"Well, never too late to start. I'm having a party tomorrow, in Recycling Tent 15, after dinner. Do come along. You too, Mark, if you're still alive."

And with that she turned away and strode off through the crowd of onlookers that had gathered around Porter and myself.

"My apologies, I need to finish dinner so I can get a good seat in Entertainment Field, Mr Porter," I declared to my celeb rival. "See you at the audits."

#

Shows that featured older characters like Walter White from *Breaking Bad* were particularly popular in Audit Camp 71. In White's case it was probably because he was doing illegal things under the very noses of the authorities. I was actually aware that I was being turned into a real-world Walter White because I was dodging every attempt by the auditors to nail me down.

On this night the Entertainment Field featured a heavily edited version of "The Lord of the Rings". This was another popular choice, because if you read the text carefully, most of the characters are middle-aged, exceedingly old, or even immortal. I paid little attention to the performance because I was thinking about its symbolism. Sauron and Gandalf had particular relevance, because they represented Generation Tipper. Sauron was everything destructive about GT, and could no longer be tolerated in Middle Earth. Gandalf had an immense amount to offer, yet like Sauron, he was old. Who would be foolish enough to condemn Gandalf merely because he was very old, like Sauron?

141

Many of those in the camp were Gandalf look-alikes, but without the staff or hat. Their skills and experience could be so very valuable in the fight to drag the world back out of the furnace, but they had been born into the age of neglect, greed, display and squander. That was not their fault, but it gave them the look and feel of the enemy for Generation Victim people.

"So, can we save the world by living like hobbits?" asked Silvy as the audience streamed out.

"Only if hobbits practice contraception, don't aspire to luxury goods and reject planned obsolescence. Could you stand to live in the Shire?"

"For a while, yes, but I think that I'm one of those who would become stir crazy and go off looking for adventures."

"Antarctica was cozy and secure, yet here I am, in Mordor."

"If only our problems could be solved by just tossing a ring into a volcano," she sighed.

"If only everyone could leave their old lifestyles and values in the landfill bin of history."

"I suspect that it's rather like dieting."

"Dieting?" I said. "You really will have to explain that one."

"Spoken like someone who never had a problem with weight gain," said Silvy. "If you're a few pounds over ideal, you spend months eating less and exercising more until you're ideal. Then you allow yourself an extra chocolate, and skip a gym session because there's more to life than exercise. A month goes past, and by then you're hogging down a half a box of chocolates every night, there's almost always a good excuse to skip the gym, and the extra pounds are back."

"Are you saying that in a few hundred years we will have our planet out of intensive care but be driving back to hell in SUVs with V8 engines?" I asked.

"The temptation is always going to be there, Jason. Speaking of temptation. How about spending an hour in Dating Field?"

"Nice thought, but it could be dangerous."

"Dangerous? You didn't get a heart attack last time."

"I meant that if the audit goes against me, all my associates could get dragged down as well."

"Jason, how sweet!" she exclaimed, then she kissed me on the cheek. "I can't remember the last time someone was worried about me."

"Maybe we can celebrate with a night there if I beat the audit."

"Not if, Jason, when."

That was a massive relief for me. I had half expected her to be furious and accuse me of dumping her for someone else, but she had taken what I said at face value. Strangely, my excuse was the truth. Well, not the entire truth, but she did not need to know that.

#

DAY 7: DECONSTRUCTING A MOTORCYCLE

By the morning of my sixth audit the borderlines had re-covered somewhat from Peggy-Anne's memorial night-club, the gallery seats were again packed in the Audit Arena, and there were even people sitting on the steps. Nobody had ever survived five audits, and by now it was clear to the Retributor that I had followed a lifestyle that most members of Generation Victim would have been hard put to match. Better still, I had done it in a society that was generally un-sympathetic, even hostile, to my beliefs. That gave me a lot more credibility with the auditors. The Retributor not going to catch me out with any of his standard, dependable charges because I had pioneered the very standards he was using. He would need something subtle, something that would make me look bad while taking me by surprise.

"The accused is charged with supporting the petroleum vehicle industry in the disposal of his motorcycle," he said once the formalities of the morning had been attended.

Did I breathe a sigh of relief? Quite possibly, but nobody seemed to notice. During my sixty-five years as a scientist and activist I had published over five thousand documents of one sort or another dealing with resources, recycling, and keeping fossil carbon out of the atmosphere. Quite a few of them were not online, or even indexed in online databases. Apparently the Retributor did all his research online.

"May I ask which specific motorcycle you are referring to?" I asked.

"A 350cc Honda."

"No part of that bike contributed to the continued support of the petroleum industry."

"Even trading a bike in for a more fuel efficient vehicle meant that your previous vehicle would continue to pollute the atmosphere in the hands of a new owner."

"What evidence do you have that it was traded in?"

"I don't need to present any such evidence. You must prove that you disposed of it responsibly."

How does one prove that one disposed of an irresponsible item responsibly? The Auditor General had done so by never accepting or even touching the car that her father - my son - had bought her. That even counted in her favor, being a car owner who had neither touched her brand-new car nor allowed anyone else to drive it. I was born earlier than 1st January 2000, however, so I would have to work a lot harder. Fortunately, I had never been afraid of hard work.

"Firstly, I removed the oil and petrol, for use in my new bike, then -"

"Before you traded it in?" exclaimed the Retributor.

"I did not trade it in. Next, I disassembled the old bike into its component parts, and there were hundreds of them. Small items such as spokes, bearings, levers, pistons and the chain were bundled up in waste plastic and sent to landfill. Larger items, like the forks, frame, seat and exhaust pipe had to be pulverized with a sledge hammer or cut up with a hacksaw."

"Ridiculous. Parts like the engine block would have been too hard to smash, and too big to cut up with a saw."

"It was not necessary, I just damaged the block and gearbox casing so badly that they could not be used as spare parts for any other bike. I actually damaged all the individual components so that they could no longer be used, and they all went into landfill. My old motorbike was completely removed from the petroleum transport system."

This was more than the Retributor could cope with.

"Your honor, fellow victims, this has to be a flight of the wildest fancy," he said, addressing the audit bench. "Such an operation would have taken months. Even if the accused did what he claims to have done, such an effort should have been written up and published. Not to do so would have been an act of squander."

"Dr Hall?" asked the Auditor General.

"I did publish an account of what I did, in an underground, hardcopy magazine called *Ethical Extremes*, Volume 2, number 6."

"Your honor, this will have to be verified."

"Clerk of the Bench, do a Unipedia search and issue a crowdsearch call for this article," said the Auditor General. "While we wait, Dr Hall's audit will be suspended rather than adjourned. What is the next case?"

#

The next audit was for my fellow celeb.

"Mark Porter, fashion designer," said the Clerk of the Audit.

"Retributor?" asked the Auditor General.

"The charges are numerous, and cover all four main categories," said the Retributor.

"Choose one."

"Specifically and primarily, he invented and promoted the concept of dash fash, which generated a statistically significant amount of greenhouse gas and squandered a vast amount of resources for no better motive than the accumulation of money."

There were some moments of silence as the Auditor General sat staring at Porter. He stared back.

"Before the audit bench votes on your guilt, do you have anything to say for yourself?" she asked.

"Dash fash was meant as an environmentally responsible innovation," he declared, although he could not possibly have believed his own words. "Clothes would only be run up as they were needed, and there would be no more unsold items to be sent away and shredded. Unanticipated demand was what turned the scheme into a squander monster."

"Mr Porter, if I thought that were true, I would be inclined to give you the option of borderline status. The problem is that your concept was called dash fash from the very start, and according to my screen you promoted it as 'All the style you can handle as often as you can handle it'. Excess was built into the very structure of your concept as far as I am concerned, but the audit bench has the final say. Honorable victims, who votes guilty?"

Eight hands were raised.

"And that's it?" exclaimed Porter. "Eight dorks in cloaks and bowler hats think I should die just because I have a bit of flair and style?"

"No, Alette Borden has style, and she got the option of borderline. Actually she has wonderful style, even I go to her for fashion advice. You caused tens of thousands of tons of cloth to be squandered, and your carbon footprint looks like that of a forest fire. You are sentenced to Class One Death, with mercy."

I expected hysterics, but Porter just sneered, then allowed himself to be led away.

#

"Next audit, Clerk of the Bench?" asked the Auditor General.

"Robert Grant, charged with squander."

I put his date of birth at after 2000. That meant the Retributor might not push for the ultimate penalty, in any of its twelve forms. I turned out to be wrong.

"While the accused is Generation Victim, the charge is one of gratuitous squander," he said, pretending to sound relaxed, even a little bored. "The accused was a tagger, someone who sprayed graffiti tags on walls and vehicles."

When the accused was GV, such people generally got between ten and fifteen years of service for this sort of charge. Thus Grant looked confident, even a little smug. He fancied himself as a rebel, antagonizing members of the establishment. He did not seem to realize that gratuitous squander carried a mandatory death penalty. The Retributor did.

"The accused deliberately targeted the walls, fences and vehicles of those who were known to scrub the tags off or paint them over within a few hours. He would then tag them again at the earliest opportunity. I have audited calculations to show that he caused at least twenty times more squander than a typical tagger because he was deliberately provoking responses."

"Any comment, Mr Grant?" asked the Auditor General.

"I just did a few tags to brighten up the place."

"Let me put it another way. Gratuitous squander attracts the ultimate penalty."

"What? But I'm Generation Victim."

SEAN MCMULLEN

"A Generation Victim climate criminal who shows every sign of re-offending, and so damaging the biosphere further. The only cure for that is reclaiming your carbon."

"Er, that means death, doesn't it?"

"Yes."

Grant's expression instantly became one of dismay.

"But, like, the big-time graffiti artists used way more paint than me for their artworks. Lots of GT artists just got border-lining."

"Graffiti is a difficult area," sighed the Auditor General. "Some of it is genuine art, some is protest or rebellion, and then there was just plain vandalism. I do concede that some vandalism can be considered protest, for example when wood chipping machinery was smashed by protesters. Why were you vandalizing walls and trucks?"

Grant decided to say what he thought the audit bench wanted to hear.

"The owners were cli-crim pigs."

Like a leopard pretending to be a spotty bush while a particularly stupid gazelle wandered ever closer, the Retributor had been lying in wait. Now he sprang.

"The owners of a great many walls and trucks could be described that way in the period when you were active. You specifically chose people you could antagonize, and who would repeatedly spray over or scrub off your tags. My squander app estimates that you caused between eight hundred and a thousand cans of paint to be squandered to spray over your tags, even though you may have only squandered a few dozen directly. Your honor, fellow victims, I can provide similar figures for water and cleaning fluid, power for sand and water blasting equipment, and so on."

"Members of the audit bench, who finds the accused guilty?" asked the Auditor General.

149

Eight hands were raised.

"I find the accused guilty of gratuitous squander," she said, shaking her head. "Robert Grant, I sentence you to Class Six Death, with mercy."

"No, no, I'm GV!" shouted Grant. "I max at Class 6 Service, with branding."

"No you do not."

"You can't do this!" he screamed. "Didn't you hear? I'm GV."

"That is why you will be hanged so that your neck is snapped, killing you instantly."

Not instantly, I thought. *There will be a very worrying fraction of a second during which you will be alive and falling, Grant.*

Grant had to be gagged as well as bound before he was carried away. The focus returned to me.

"Clerk of the Bench, have you found Dr Hall's article?"

"Still working the crowds, your honor."

"Next audit?"

#

Elver Lyn was an astronomer, but there was more to her audit than that. She had been engaged in climate research, which counted in her favor. The climate she had studied was that of Mars, however, and to the climatically correct auditors of Generation Victim, that was sure to sound a lot like squander.

"I charge the accused with blatant squandering," said the Retributor, with just a trace of mania in his voice - probably because I was likely to beat him again, and Elver was a fellow scientist. "The study of other planets has no relevance to the damage suffered by the Earth's climate, and her research consumed valuable resources at a time when climate change was already known to be a serious threat."

I knew Elver professionally, and was all too aware that she was incapable of conducting her own defense. I was surprised that she had even survived the trek through the desert. The Advocate had no answer to the charge, but part of her job statement seemed to be having no answer to most of what the Retributor said.

"Your honor?" I said, raising my hand.

"Dr Hall, you have a point to make?" said the Auditor General.

"I do indeed. Does the audit bench agree that human-induced climate change does not play a role in the atmosphere of Mars?"

"This is reasonable," she replied, but a trifle suspiciously.

"Do you accept this proposition, Retributor?"

"Yes, but only in principle," he said, also suspicious.

"Go on, Dr Hall," prompted the Auditor General.

"If the climate of Mars changes in parallel with that of Earth, then climate change must be due to variations in solar radiation, because that is the only influence that the two planets have in common."

"In other words, changes in the sun's heat could be the only possible influence?" asked the Auditor General.

"Yes."

"Accepted. Go on."

"But if the climate of Mars were found to be stable while that of Earth changes, the influence of humans on the climate of Earth looks more likely."

By now the Retributor had realized that the innocent looking pile of leaves that he had just stepped on contained a noose and a spring release, and that he was hanging upside down, suspended by one leg.

"Objection!" he barked.

"On what grounds?" asked the Auditor General.

"In my opinion that is a flimsy excuse for the indulgent squandering of resources in the name of scientific research!" he declared angrily.

"Your opinion is noted, but your objection is overruled," said the Auditor General. "Professor Lyn, do you have anything to contribute to the discussion?"

"Well, there are a number of parameters to consider when assessing climate variability in planetary atmospheres. The more elliptical nature of the Martian orbit, for example. This subjects the planet to quite substantial variations in solar radiation. Earth's orbit is elliptical as well, but to a far lesser degree. In addition, the Martian atmosphere is not influenced by oceans, which are subject to a number of phenomena such as rotational storms, which function as thermal engines."

This was a disaster in the making. Elver was on track for missing my cue and admitting that her work had nothing to do with climate change. Even if it did, nobody but me would be able to follow the science, at least not the way she explained it.

"Professor Lyn, did you find any evidence for climate change on Mars?" I interjected. "Please answer yes or no."

As a scientist she found this seriously confronting. There was a lengthy pause while she thought about the evidence for the two alternatives.

"I can't answer the question so simply," she said, putting her life in serious danger without realizing it. "The eleven-year sunspot cycle varies the amount of heat produced by the sun, and this does influence the climate on Mars."

Fortunately the science was so far above what the Retributor could follow that he risked looking stupid if he so much as opened his mouth.

"Let me put it another way," I continued. "Factoring out variations due to the sunspot cycle, does Mars show the same sort of evidence for climate change as does the Earth?"

I could see that she would have given anything for a coffee machine, a whiteboard and another four or five hours of discussion. My question had only two answers, however.

"No," she said, although clearly unhappy about being backed into a corner.

"Your honor, I put it to you that Professor Lyn has shown that the atmosphere of Mars can act as a valuable baseline for human-induced climate change in the atmosphere of Earth," I declared, hoping that I did not sound too smug.

"Your honor, objection!" exclaimed the Retributor. "Only Professor Lyn and Dr Hall are qualified to comment on the science being discussed here."

That was a very good observation, and it was the only weakness in the case I was building.

"Objection sustained, Retributor," sighed the Auditor General. "Professor Lyn, the audit bench does not have the hours or perhaps days that it will take to assess whether you are a climate criminal or a hero. Not for quite some time, anyway. Will you accept borderline status in return for a more severe sentence if you are convicted later?"

"I'm not sure I understand."

"Trust me and say yes," I suggested.

"Order!" shouted the Auditor General, banging her mace on her desk. "Wardens, if Dr Hall says anything else before the audit bench returns to his audit, escort him out of the Audit Arena and put him to work in the privy pits until he is called back. Professor Lyn?"

"Er, yes, I suppose," said the scientist.

The Retributor was not smiling. I had torpedoed his case and saved another life, at least long enough for her to die of natural causes.

#

"Clerk of the Audit, have you located Dr Hall's evidence as yet?" asked the Auditor General.

"I have, your honor. Text only, twelve hundred words, three tables."

"Your honor, that article is no sort of proof," said the Retributor. "He could easily have dumped his bike into a river and written the article to pretend he went to all that trouble."

"Your honor, may I call a reliable witness?" I asked.

"You may, Dr Hall, but do take care."

"I call upon the Auditor General, who watched and helped for two weeks as I disassembled my motorcycle and disposed of it in landfill."

"Audit bench, you will pardon me for remaining seated, the bench does need a presiding officer," she declared. "Go ahead, Dr Hall."

"You were on school holidays at the time, and I was providing free child care while on recreation leave, as I recall. Can you verify what I said about the disposal of my motorcycle?"

"It is indeed true."

The Retributor's face contorted, probably with anger, possibly with hatred as well, and definitely with frustration. Again, he had walked straight into my trap. Those in the gallery cheered, laughed and meowed. The Auditor General called for order, then called on the auditors to vote. All eight of them were sufficiently impressed to vote in my favor.

"I find that the charge has not been substantiated, Retributor. Dr Hall, unless you wish to become a borderline, you will face a seventh audit tomorrow, this time with a potential sentence of Rising Sea Levels, with mercy."

"I choose the audit, your honor."

I was now halfway through the number of audits allowed under climate crime legislation. The cheering was so loud as I was escorted back to my seat that I could not hear the Auditor General banging the mace on her desk and shouting for order.

#

I did not attend Porter's carbon reclaiming out of any sense of triumph. If anything, I had the odd notion that he needed the company of other celebs in his final moments. Alette was there as well, and with her were several other men and women whose dress standards were subtly superior to the norm in Audit Camp 71.

This execution was Mines, with mercy. Porter's ankles were bound, then he was suspended upside down over the mine shaft while the cover was unlocked and pulled back. The Executioner held the end of the rope that released the slip-knot supporting Porter.

"Mark Porter, you have been found guilty of squander, greed and display," said the Auditor General. "Do you have any last words before your carbon is reclaimed?"

"The world will be an uglier place when I am gone," he said, defiant even though he was suspended upside down above certain death. I had to admire him for that.

"The world is already an uglier place because of your life. Executioner, reclaim his carbon."

GENERATION NEMESIS

The Executioner tugged at the rope and the skip-knot binding Porter's ankles came undone. He plunged into the mine shaft in silence, then a thud echoed up from the blackness. The quite terrifying growls of the miner people followed as they began to feast on the fresh body.

Mines, with mercy, meant that one was dropped head first into the shaft. One's neck was broken by the fall, which was merciful. The last seconds of terror during the fall were no mercy at all, but then it was meant to be a punishment. The cover of the shaft was put back in place and locked, and the procession moved on.

Alette came over to me as I stood staring at the covered shaft and experiencing a waking nightmare about what was happening to Porter's body, far below our feet.

"He might not have been very good for the Earth, but he was one of us," she said.

"There was never any hope for him," I replied, trying to reassure myself. "Sorry to be so brutal."

"Dash fash was the monster, not Mark."

"Still, he had a responsibility to stop and think before he opened the cage."

"Don't we all? Now remember, you're invited to a party at Recycling Tent 15, tonight."

"What time?"

"Oscar Wilde once said that important people arrive late, so arrive late."

"Should I bring anything?"

"Just style."

#

That evening people were preparing wheelchairs for a race in Entertainment Field, and a large crowd was gath-

156

ering to watch. Chaz told me that the race was a high-value event, and not to be missed, but I was actually there on first-aid duty. An announcer presided, using a cardboard megaphone painted with exhaust flames.

"Ladies and gentlemen, welcome to the two hundred and seventy ninth Audit Camp 71 Wheelchair Grand Prix."

The crowd cheered enthusiastically. I watched, but neither smiled nor cheered. The Retributor's agents were sure to be there, scanning the audience for people like me showing signs of recidivism.

"I don't mind telling you all that tonight just might be history in the making. Nine hundred and ninety eight pushers and drivers have died in this proud event. Going on averages, we just might crack a thousand tonight."

The crowd cheered again. Until that moment I had thought that I was beyond being shocked.

"If that happens, we'll be the first audit camp *ever* whose grand prix made four-figure deaths."

Names of famous models of cars were written on the backs and sides of the wheelchairs, along with brand names of long-defunct sponsors. Cardboard clappers were attached to make engine noises against the spokes. The wheelchairs lined up for the start. For each vehicle there was one small person to drive and someone considerably bigger and stronger to push.

"Ready! Wait for it ..."

The announcer's walking stick slammed against a length of iron pipe, and the clang was the signal for the race to start. The tippers and borderlines cheered as fifteen wheelchairs surged forward along the improvised track of red sand, raising clouds of dust. There were pit stops for pusher changes, paramedic crews for crashes, and cheer squads of elderly women in tattered, skimpy plastic costumes.

As the wheelchair pack rattled past me, a pusher collapsed in the dust. We paramedics dragged the body off the track, then there was a loud cheer from the crowd as Dr Gibson raised his fist, his thumb pointing down.

After several more circuits another man fell, and the wheelchair that he had been pushing crashed into two others, overturning them. We dragged several men off the track, and Dr Gibson signaled that two of them were dead. This raised a prolonged cheer. Audit Camp 71's grand prix had passed a thousand deaths. By now there were two more circuits for the wheelchair pack to complete. Dusk had almost faded in the western sky, and the field had to rely on moonlight to complete the race.

"I never thought I'd see death celebrated like this," I said to one of my fans, who was also in the first-aid squad.

"If you gotta go, go happy!" she babbled.

The race ended, but not before one of the cheer squad went into cardiac arrest and died. The winners, place-getters and dead entrants were carried shoulder high by the crowd to a podium. First, second and third were presented with double rations of water in old champagne bottles. This they splashed on each other, the onlookers and the bodies in a defiant show of trivial squandering.

The announcement of the deaths tally had to be postponed, because the officials were not able to agree on whether or not the dead member of the cheer squad should be counted as a casualty of the race. The precedent of a first-aider run down and killed two years earlier was cited, and his death had been counted. Based on this decision, the death of the cheer squad woman was added in.

"Now what?" I asked Chaz.

"There's a concert of Jan and Dean driving and surfing songs."

"Tell me you're joking."

"It's true! There are some great singers in this camp, and the best humming rock band anywhere."

"Next you'll be telling me there are surfing championships here as well."

"But there are."

I bent over, scooped up a handful of sand and let it fall between my fingers.

"Isn't water a problem?"

"Nah, we use planks towed through the sand by teams of tippers. Not as many deaths as in the grand prix, but it's still exciting."

I left. Alette's party was not really my scene, but it was preferable to a concert of retro squander songs.

#

Recycling Tent 15 was Alette's private kingdom, and even the wardens did not dare to interfere with her work. Fashion shared some of the guilt for what had happened to the Earth, and she had solutions. Her solutions showed a stunning degree of lateral thinking, and were based on the fact that a baseline wardrobe could be used to produce many, many combinations of styles. One did not have to constantly go out and buy new clothes, and to junk older clothes to make room. Certain styles were timeless, and fashion could be based on what one did with them.

My very first party of truly cool people turned out better than I had feared. Even though I was the least cool person there, I was made welcome, not sneered at, and never neglected. Water and locally brewed vodka were the drinks of choice, and the snacks were just Refectory Field rations that people had saved up for the occasion.

"White powders and green leaves are available if that sort of thing interests you," said Alette as she poured me a seaweed-flavored vodka.

"Never my style," I replied.

My glass was half a small bottle, neatly split in two by thermal stress, corked, and inverted. It was not very steady when put down, but who puts a glass down unless it is empty?

"Tippers smuggle drugs all the way across the desert, only to find that there is not much of a market for them in Audit Camp 71," she said.

"Probably because those who have managed to survive in this place are healthy, intelligent types, who are less inclined to trash themselves with drugs."

"Like myself and yourself."

Charm glowed from Alette. There had never been anyone like her in my background, so naturally I was not sure what to say - while being particularly anxious not to make a fool of myself.

"I see that you wear the Green Man symbol," I said to her, which seemed safe enough as comments go.

"It tells people that I believe in renewal. It also gives men an excuse to look at my cleavage."

"Oh! Sorry, I never -"

"Stop that, I was only teasing! Now tell me, Jason, do we deserve to survive as a species? Are the Anthrophobes right, and we humans should all kill ourselves before we kill the planet?"

"We need to be more aware, Ms Borden -"

"I also need to be Alette, and you need to be Jason, can we agree on that first?"

"Oh. Er, yes. Whatever you say."

"Go on."

"We can no longer afford to do anything without thinking about the consequences, the Earth is way too small. Mark Porter did not take that into account when he thought of dash fash. We must."

"There we agree. Now tell me, Jason, how old do you think I am?"

"I've seen women in their thirties who don't look as good as you."

"Well done, those were flattering but subtle words. I was born in the same year as you, but I'm a month older."

"You're eighty-five?" I gasped.

"Yes."

"I'm stunned. Do you have ... special secret treatments?"

"No. I just eat sparingly, stay out of the sun, exercise moderately, don't use toxic chemicals for recreation and had hormone and nanotech implants while they were available. I could never see the point of eating a lot more than I needed, then wasting years of my life exercising and dieting the fat away. Always being thin is also a good way to avoid stretch marks and sag bags in later life."

"So you don't find sugar tempting?"

"Of course I do, I just think of it as a very occasional treat."

"How was your carbon footprint, back before the tipping point year?"

"Not as small as yours, but still smaller than GV average. I lived in a lot of cities, rather than having one home."

"So minimal carbon footprint from commuting?"

"Yes. I had quite a nice Mercedes van to carry my worldly goods, and people always wanted me as a house guest."

"Perks of fame."

"Quite so."

At this point she took me by the arm and escorted me around the gathering, introducing me to people. I soon learned that quite a lot of the improvised clothing in Audit Camp 71 had come from Alette and those who worked for her. Their clients still wore rags, but there was a certain elegance to them. Alette should have been running the design department in a fabrication factory, while educating other designers. She could have saved millions of tons of clothing resources worldwide, yet here she was in Audit Camp 71, with borderline status. Presently I realized that I had met everyone who truly mattered.

"So, er, should I let you get on with it? Silvy said I shouldn't try to monopolize people at ultra-cool parties."

"Did she? Silvy is a very dangerous woman, Jason. She has killed nine people with her own hands and caused a lot more deaths indirectly."

"The Auditor General said it was only five."

"I'm not surprised. Even when justice is not blind, it is often a little nearsighted."

I swallowed. Thanks to my daughter I was aware that Silvy had a past, but the raw statistics still proved to be something of a shock.

"I know she had a career in espionage."

"And assassination, and she still does. Be useful to her, Jason, but be her lover at your peril."

"I already have. Once."

"Only once?"

"I have a delicate libido. Knowing that one's lover is a dangerous killer makes it run away and hide."

"Indeed? I've never killed anyone, but don't get ideas. Not yet, anyway. Getting back to social protocols, ignore Silvy's advice, just this once. I only organized this party so that I could talk to you."

"You did? Why?"

"Jason, Jason, that was a stupid thing to say. Very sweet, but still stupid. I listened to your exchange with Mark at dinner last night, and you both got me thinking. Dreamers really can be taken a lot more seriously if they present themselves with a bit more style. That's not a very nice thing to say, but it's true. I'm not a qualified ecologist, but did you know that I managed to get some very wealthy women dressing more elegantly for a hundredth as much money, and a thousandth as much carbon added to the atmosphere?"

"You're joking!" I exclaimed, probably a lot louder than was cool.

"Like you, I keep records and statistics."

"What a pity we didn't meet up in the 1970s," I said. "We might have changed the world together."

"We have met now. Join forces with me, and we can put some style into the science that will heal the world."

Is she making a move on me? flashed through my mind. *Probably not. I'm just a resource, to everyone.*

"I could get shot off the perch at my very next audit," was all that I could think to say. "Team up with me and you could be dragged down."

"But if the auditors think I like you, they might also treat you with more sympathy. Come along, Jason. Let's watch some of the best stylists in Audit Camp 71 at work."

With that she kissed me on the cheek, then took me by the arm and guided me over to a group of men and women who were discussing a sun cape that was being modeled by the party's warden monitor. It was just a very ordinary blanket with three pins made of stiff wire to hold the folds in place, but as design it was brilliant. All the while I was wondering why I really, really wanted to impress Alette.

163

DAY 8: BURNING WOOD

Humanity still reached into space, in spite of the wretched state of the planet and the fact that what survived of heavy industry was mostly focused on urgent projects such as building carbon extraction farms. Spaceflight was actually classed as a green industry, because the World Resource Council's policy was to move damaging but necessary industries off the planet. All but a thousandth of the Earth's surface was now designated as national parks, and therefore off-limits to settlement, industry, and even farming.

Today Overwatch 21 was being prepared for launch on the other side of the planet, at Mount Chimborazo, on the equator in Ecuador. The mountain was two miles high, but another eight miles was cut from each rocket's journey into space by three immense hydrogen balloons. These were tethered above the mountain, and they supported the corners of a carbon fiber triangle whose sides were a mile in length yet weighed only a few tons. Put in terms of a simple one-liner, it was a launch pad a tenth of the distance to low Earth orbit.

It was evening at the launch site, but the morning sun was still well below the horizon at Audit Camp 71. I stopped to watch the launch preparations on the large screen at the entrance to Dormitory Field. Powered by solar cells coating the balloons, electric winches had hauled the rocket and its five ton payload up to the triangle. From there, only ninety miles remained of the journey to free itself of the troubled surface of our planet. From low Earth orbit, clipper tugs with solar sails wider than most of the abandoned cities would slowly ease the supply satellite into a higher orbit and ultimately tow it to the moon. The fuel tanks and rocket engines of the second stage would be dissolved and fabricated into spare parts for other machines in the lunar factories. Nothing was wasted. Absolutely nothing.

The Overwatch 21 satellite contained no humans; crews were flown into space separately, in small winged shuttles but not one flight in a hundred had anything living aboard. Very few humans lived in space. Nine were on the moon, according to the news feeds, overseeing the building of solar power arrays so large that they could be seen from Earth with a small telescope. These powered experimental fabrication factories, mining machines and exploration drones.

It was a worthy experiment, and so far it was working: why not move the grubby tasks of manufacturing away from our precious and unique biosphere? Why not indeed? Why had nobody asked that question in the 1970s, when we already had the technology to get there? Perhaps someone had. If so, why had nobody paid attention? The answer was, of course, that that payoff would take longer than the time to the next budget, election, or funding review.

Now the plan was for all manufacturing to take place on the moon, where there is no biosphere to pollute. So far the projects were all proof-of-concept rather than real industrial ventures, yet useful products were already being returned to Earth. Lunar industry was expanding with the slow, relentless labor of robots and nanotech vats, but there were serious bottlenecks. Rare earths and highly specialized equipment still needed to be shipped from Earth, but most of the payload on Overwatch 21 was pure carbon. In spite of all the grief that carbon from fossil fuels had inflicted upon the Earth's atmosphere, that element was very rare on the moon.

Oxygen and hydrogen came from the ice mined from the polar craters, and there was no shortage of silicone in the lunar surface. A fair proportion of the lunar regolith was also made up of iron, aluminum, calcium and magnesium, and all this was fed into the hungry fabrication vats to build the parts for yet more machines. Even orbiting space junk was being harvested from Earth orbit, and the Twentieth-Century lunar probes and landers had been collected and dissolved for raw materials.

Silicon polymers were used in every lunar structure, but they have nothing like the strength of carbon chains and lattices. Because only one lunar atom in two hundred thousand was carbon, tightly packed blocks of carbon were aboard every flight from Earth. That was nowhere near what was needed for lunar industry, so far away, in deep space, an array of ion engines was nudging a burned-out but carbon-rich comet nucleus toward lunar orbit. It would not arrive for decades, however, so meantime the lunar factories were operating on starvation rations - as were humans, back on Earth.

#

Refectory Field was already crowded with people eating breakfast as I entered, and the announcements screen was showing the rocket being winched the last few yards to the launch triangle. The broadcast was a statement, and that statement said that spaceflight was carbon neutral. The rocket fuel was hydrogen and oxygen, all supplied by the electrolytic breakdown of water by solar power. The booster rocket would be recovered and used again. Not a single fossil carbon atom was to be released into the atmosphere.

"It's a pity we couldn't do this back in the 1990s," said Chaz.

"We could have," I replied.

"Okay, I'll bite. Why didn't we?"

"Nobody could be bothered spending money on the slow, efficient, resource-neutral path into space. Now we have no choice."

"The Anthrophobes reckon the moon should be left like it is."

"The Anthrophobes also think the human race should go extinct, because civilization is destroying the biosphere."

"What do you think?"

"I think that biospheres are the most precious things in the universe, so the Earth must be protected. Industry on airless worlds is something else entirely. It causes no harm."

"I thought you were against high tech."

"I'm against stupidity, and killing everyone to save the planet definitely qualifies as stupidity."

#

We were still in Refectory Field when the public address speakers announced that Overwatch 21 was about to ignite. Chaz and I watched the communal screen as the rocket slowly rose out of the support ring at the center of the triangle. Hydrogen and oxygen burn without sooty smoke, so the engines trailed only an exhaust plume of steam as the rocket lifted free. The flame beneath it was so clear that the rocket seemed to be levitating.

"Boring," said Chaz.

"So you're disappointed?" I asked.

"Well, yeah."

"Would you prefer it to trail a cloud of poisonous muck?"

"Suppose not."

"Well then, you're stuck with a nice clean exhaust of water vapor."

"I had a bet with Pearce the Book that the exhaust would burn one of the balloons as it went up."

"In a hundred launches over ten years there has never been an accident."

"So the National Audit tells us."

"Every launch has been broadcast live."

"What if they use CGI for the broadcasts?"

"What if I'm an elf from Middle-Earth? What of the Auditor General is really a brain-eating alien from Alpha Centauri?"

"Be serious, Jaz."

"I am being serious. You can make up a conspiracy theory for anything you like, but eventually you have to start believing in something."

"No you don't."

"Okay then, I think that our seaweed biscuits have got a chemical in them that makes your testicles shrink."

"What? Bullshit! My balls haven't shrunk."

"Think so? When did you last measure them?"

We were watching the screen as we conducted our meaningless argument, and a camera on Overwatch 21 was showing the three giant balloons dwindling far below. The launch had taken place at sunset, and the Andes Mountains were already in darkness. The three balloons were tethered so high that they still gleamed brightly, like three half moons.

"Well that's five seaweed biscuits lost," muttered Chaz. "I hope they really do shrink his balls. What now?"

"In another hour the cargo satellite will be tethered to a Sun Clipper and be on its way to the moon."

"Just as easy to make all that lunar factory stuff here on Earth."

"Just as easy to shit on your kitchen table, but I bet you never did it."

"What's that meant to mean?" Chaz exclaimed.

"Cooking and eating's for the kitchen, the toilet is for crapping, and the workshop is for building things. The moon is humanity's new workshop."

"I still reckon it's more trouble than it's worth."

"I'll have a word to the Retributor and he can have you audited for -"

"Okay, okay, don't yank my chain. Anyway, who cares what I think?"

"The Retributor, he wants your carbon reclaimed. Learn to like the new way that things are done, Chaz."

"They've taken all the fun out of spaceflight," sighed Chaz. "*Star Trek* would have flopped if it had been like this."

That much was true. Visiting space had become about as exciting as visiting a factory, but was that a bad thing?

#

I stayed within view of a screen outside the Audit Arena as the halflight brightened with dawn's approach. Just as Warden Olivia arrived to escort me inside, a brilliant streak of fire on a black background appeared on the screen.

"Man, that looks bad," said Olivia fearfully.

"It's just the winged booster, descending over the west coast of Africa," I said. "No problem, all good. Haven't you watched other launches?"

"I never bother watching after the rocket goes up."

"The Overwatch booster has to be recovered. There are only five of them, and they have to be used dozens, hundreds, even thousands of times over. This is the new face of human progress, with nothing wasted and the pace slow and sure."

"Dr Fitness, stuff always sounds sort of inspiring when you talk about it. No wonder you're a celeb."

"I've spent my whole life trying to inspire people, so I must be getting good at it by now."

"Time for the day's audit. Ready, willing and able?"

"As always. That's why I'm still alive."

The auditors arrived, but they paused to stare at the night-vision view of the Overwatch booster glowing green with its own heat as it descended beneath a parasail.

"Technically the auditors are guilty of squandering time by watching the landing," I said, softly enough so that only Olivia could hear.

"You gonna tell them that?"

"Maybe not."

"So they make stuff on the moon to keep the Earth clean, but how does it get sent back here? More rockets?"

"There's a rail gun powered by solar electricity on the moon, and it fires canisters back to Earth. Some of what we see streaking through the sky like meteorites are those canisters, glowing white hot. Have you ever seen a rail gun grenade launcher?"

"The RGGLs? Yeah, I'm even qualified to shoot them."

"Same principle, a magnetic field accelerates the projectile. The difference is that the one on the moon is as tall as a mountain."

"Sounds fantastic. What stuff is built up there?"

"Your night-vision goggles, for a start."

"No shit? You mean I'm wearing a bit of the moon when I'm on night patrol?"

"That's one way of putting it."

"Wish I could go there one day."

"Why? Do you want to visit China, just because your assault rifle was built there?"

"Dr Fitness, sometimes you're just no fun at all."

On the screen the Overwatch booster extended skids and touched down smoothly on a runway in Gabon, trailing the huge parasail behind it. The auditors clapped at the screen.

"Show's over," I said.

"Another show's starting, Dr Fitness, and you're the star. Let's go."

#

Some activities looked trivial on the face of it, yet they contributed a lot to greenhouse warming. Others looked like the most blatant of climate crimes, but were perfectly innocent. As my seventh audit got under way, I discovered that my defense was going to be a very hard sell, and I was facing Rising Sea Levels, with mercy.

"The accused burned wood in his fireplace for heating during the winter," declared the Retributor, looking very smug as he spoke.

He would call upon Renny to testify if I questioned the validity of the charge, and this was bound to be his hidden agenda. I had used the testimony of my granddaughter against him the day before, so now it was his turn - or so he thought.

"Do you wish to dispute the charge, Dr Hall?" asked the Auditor General.

"I dispute that burning wood the way that I did was a climate crime," I replied.

"This will sound like an oxymoron to many of those on the audit bench, Dr Hall," she replied. "Please explain."

"I only burned wood that was being attacked by fungi or insects. The breakdown of wood by such agents leads to the release of methane, which is about twenty times more potent as a greenhouse gas than carbon dioxide. Every kilo of rotting wood I burned was preventing twenty times as much greenhouse-induced warming, which would have resulted if it had been left to decompose. Burning also destroyed the insects and spores in the wood."

The argument wandered into trivia at this point. The Retributor said that I should have used solar heating and effective insulation to keep warm in winter. I pointed out that I did do that, but also collected and burned wood with infestations that produced methane. I also fed more power from the solar cells on my roof back into the grid when I was burning wood.

"This helped lower the demand for coal-fired power stations in this country by a very small fraction," I concluded. "Enough of these small fractions put together, and we might have avoided the climate catastrophe that is now upon us."

"It is inconceivable that anyone could burn wood yet claim to be keeping carbon dioxide out of the atmosphere," exclaimed the Retributor.

"There are more greenhouse gases than carbon dioxide."

"But carbon dioxide is a very robust gas. Methane breaks down naturally over time."

"In the meantime, methane is warming the Earth much faster."

"Where are your figures?"

"I can provide figures. Can you understand them?"

SEAN MCMULLEN

"Order!" called the Auditor General. "This is a properly constituted audit, not a bar room brawl. Clerk of the Bench, can you do a Unipedia or crowd request for information on this subject?"

"I already have, your honor. Methane is definitely a more potent greenhouse gas, but opinion is divided about how long it takes for natural processes to remove it from the atmosphere. 81% of the authorities say that a combination of burning the infested wood plus feeding unused solar cell electricity back into the grid would cause marginal but definite net cooling relative to letting wood rot in landfill."

"Have you any comment on that, Retributor?"

"Only that we have no proof that the accused burned only infested wood."

"Objection!" called the Advocate. "We do have a potential witness with a very high degree of integrity and reliability."

"Very well, call your witness," sighed the Auditor General, clasping her hands on her desk and shaking her head.

"I call the Auditor General."

"Please, proceed with your questions."

"When you were staying with your grandfather in winter, were you called upon to feed wood into the fire?"

"I was."

"Did the wood smell of mold, or show evidence of termites or borers?"

"It did."

"All of it?"

"All that I handled."

"The defense rests, your honor," the Advocate concluded.

"Any further comments, Dr Hall?"

"Only that I bought carbon credits for the weight of wood that I burned."

"Make a note of that, Clerk of the Bench. Members of the audit bench, because of my involvement, I shall allow you to determine both the finding and the confirmatory vote. A clear majority will decide. Fellow victims, is the accused guilty on this charge?"

Three hands were raised.

"Not guilty?"

This time four hands went up.

"Does anyone wish to abstain?"

One auditor raised her hand.

"Dr Hall, you are found innocent on this particularly difficult charge. Should you wish to continue your audit tomorrow, you will face death by Rising Sea Levels, without mercy."

"I choose to continue, your honor."

"Then we shall see you again tomorrow morning. Next case, Clerk of the Bench?"

Tomorrow's audit would also be something to do with releasing greenhouse gases and rising sea levels, I was fairly sure of that. The Retributor liked the irony of the climate crime punishing the perpetrator.

#

Today the carbon reclaimings were particularly upsetting for me. At first they looked as normal as something so atrocious could ever be. I was stationed at the tipping point gallows, and the Auditor General was giving her usual declaration.

"Liam Cormack, you have been found guilty of neglect, and have been sentenced to Class Six Death, with mercy. Have you any last words?"

"I lived in the society I was born into," said Cormack. "I lived a moderate, responsible life, never committed a crime,

174

never did drugs, fathered only one child and contributed to Greenpeace. I was a good and honest human being, yet this is how you treat me."

"The world was full of good and honest people who lived with unsustainable carbon footprints," the Auditor General replied. "You donated two hundred retro dollars per year to Greenpeace, but spent three thousand retro dollars on health insurance in the same period - and claimed it on tax. If you had not valued your body's health to be fifteen times greater than that of the Earth's, I might have given you the option of becoming a borderline, but you are part of a vast pool of apathy that cannot be allowed to survive into the future. Executioner, reclaim his carbon."

The first lump of coal had not been removed from the barrel holding down the plank when Cormack kissed the female warden escorting him. I thought nothing of it, but perhaps I should have. I had seen prisoners weep, scream, struggle, curse or just stand quietly and wait for the end, but never had any of them kissed their escorting warden. The plank teetered as the barrel of coal was emptied, then it tipped. The Executioner hurried over to the body and checked for a pulse.

"He has surrendered his carbon," he reported.

The escorting warden unslung her assault rifle, pressed the barrel under her chin and squeezed the trigger! The sound of the shot was followed by gasps of surprise and dismay, and one of those gasps was mine. Screams followed, now that people had drawn breath to scream.

Naturally there was a pause in executions. Dr Gibson inspected the warden's body, then it was carried down the scaffold steps and stretchered out of sight. The Clerk of the Audit set up his portable desk to conduct an investigation. As I expected, Chaz came over to tell me the result before the Clerk reported back to the Auditor General. Half a dozen borderlines were still cleaning the blood and brains off the gallows.

"The warden escorting Cormack was his wife," Chaz said. "He was born in 1998, she was born in 2001."

"The auditors look worried."

"They are. The audit bench doesn't like emo events like this. It makes them look cruel."

Every execution is cruel to someone. These had been a pair of good people who represented hundreds of millions of other good people. They should not have died.

"They're like Romeo and Juliet, caught on different sides of the political fence," I said. "If Shakespeare were alive today he would write a tragedy about them."

"I saw a Shakespeare play once, when I was at school," said Chaz. "Julius Caesar."

"Ah yes, an excellent demonstration of how fickle public opinion can be."

"Like that friends, Romans, countrymen speech?"

"Yes. The National Audit fears only one thing more than climate change, and that's public opinion."

"People aren't going to riot against the National Audit over a suicide."

"Any symbol can start a riot, Chaz, and a riot can easily become a movement. If real money still existed, I'd bet there will be no announcement about what just happened."

"No bet. Hey, did you only volunteer for an audit so you would get to say all your reform stuff in front of a world-wide Cloudcast audience?"

"If I had ever admitted something like that, the National Audit would have locked the Cloudcast down so tight that you could have counted those watching on the fingers of one hand."

"So you did?"

"Chaz, piss off."

A few minutes later the Clerk reported back to the Auditor General. By then the tipping point gallows was free of the mess left from the warden's suicide, so the next prisoner was led up the steps. This execution was rather more routine, although her last words were "Meow! Meow!"

#

As strange as it may sound, Audit Camp 71 had a particularly strong sense of community. Because most of the borderlines were in sound health, there was the ongoing threat that boredom would make subversive work for idle hands. Thus the camp authorities encouraged activities, like the wheelchair races, that tired the prisoners out yet did not consume energy or resources.

Every second week a bush dance was held, so that the sexes had a chance to mingle, socialize and pair up. This led to romances, and even marriages and divorces, although property settlements and the custody of children were never an issue. And where there were romances, there was the potential for sex. There was a booming trade in the Viagra rations, indeed the little blue pills had become something of a currency in Audit Camp 71. Anyone making counterfeit versions of this particular currency did not last long if discovered.

Some particularly skilled borderlines had actually built guitars and fiddles out of scrap wood, and it was rumored that the gut strings had been donated by tippers whose carbon had been reclaimed. Flutes were a lot easier. One just found some plastic pipe of the right diameter and bored holes at the right distances. For percussion there were plenty of empty barrels lying about, and the combination of a barrel, pole and string provided something that sounded vaguely like a double bass.

Most of the songs that people danced to dated back to the Nineteenth Century, and involved shearing sheep, herding cattle, and drinking yourself senseless after shearing sheep or herding cattle.

"I've been a wild rover for many a year,

Spent all my money on whiskey and beer,

But now I'm returning with gold in great store,

And never I'll be a wild rover no more."

A large, loud chorus was doing the singing, because voices were in more plentiful supply than instruments, and the music had to be heard over quite a wide area. I knew this waltz from my days as a university undergraduate in the 1970s. I was told that the first number was always a waltz, so that the dancers could stretch out properly, and not tear aged ligaments.

"Here we are in New South Wales,

Shearing sheep as big as whales,

With leather necks and daggy tails,

Fleece as tough as rusty nails."

Quite probably none of the singers had ever touched a sheep, except on kindergarten animal experience days. Besides, the vast herds of grazing animals that had farted gigaliters of methane had been done away with. Mutton was grown in vats of nutrient, cell by cell, and woolsynth was produced by bacteria and extruded as interlock cloth. Both those processes were carbon neutral.

The bush dances usually resulted in more deaths than the nightclubs events, due to the greater exertion needed for the dances themselves. Alette went along as my partner, and once I had shown her the basic steps she fitted right in. There were only five deaths that night, but all of them were greeted with cheers. Cheating the Executioner and the Retributor of their prey was a very popular way to die, and it seemed to me that nearly everyone aspired to go out that way.

Alette and I did not go on to Dating Field afterwards. Quite apart from the political dangers, sleeping with someone did not involve getting much sleep, and my life depended on being alert in the morning.

#

The Auditor General arrived as I lay looking up at the stars and thinking about how quickly human values had changed. As always, she stood over me like a victorious warrior contemplating a fallen enemy.

"You have questions about this morning," she said.

"I know all the answers. The warden was married to the prisoner, but she was GV and he was GT. They lived identical lives, but he got death."

"The borderlines' espionage system is astonishingly effective," she said, almost approvingly.

"Bad look for the National Audit."

"Not this time. We have a time delay of three seconds built into the transmissions. Security caught the suicide images before they went worldwide. A communications dropout was arranged."

"Sounds like it happens pretty often."

"More often than I would prefer. This is like a civil war between generations, grandfather. Civil wars unite some families and divide others."

This was all too true. At first the elderly members of Generation Tipper could not believe that their children could be so cruel to their own parents and grandparents, but reality began to sink in rapidly, highlighted by the remorseless worsening of the climate. Why share scarce food with those who had caused the famine? Why provide new retirement housing to those whose beachfront homes were being washed away by the rising seas and fiercer storms? Why even recognize the trillions of meaningless retro dollars that had made the tippers wealthy and given them power?

What really intrigued me was the way that most of the GT people actually agreed that the earlier generations had been greedy, lazy and filthy. I say most. There were a few conspiracy theorists who tried to argue that aliens had been strip-mining resources and burning coal, but climatically incorrect and unsubstantiated rumors were classed as treason and would get you escorted onto a plank with a noose around your neck. The party had been going on for centuries, but now the children who had inherited the future were asking who had maxed out the planet's credit card, and why they now had to count out the seaweed flakes at breakfast.

"I suppose you are angry," said Renny.

"Everyone is angry. The young are angry because their inheritance has been squandered. The old are angry because everything they worked for has been taken away."

"Taken away? Shared out equally! Everyone is living hard, grandfather. The people who caused this catastrophe cannot be supported at the planet's expense."

"Why must people born only three years apart be treated so very differently?"

"Have you heard of the Titanic Precedent?"

"Too many passengers, not enough lifeboats?"

"Yes. Those in charge must decide who gets to live, and on what criteria. One of those people is me."

That was not an easy point to argue against, and I did not try.

"So, all ready for the Retributor tomorrow?" Renny asked, after the silence between us had lengthened uncomfortably.

"More ready than most of those born before the first day of the new millennium."

"We had to draw the line somewhere. Give the National Audit a good reason to draw it somewhere else, and we may listen."

She left. For some reason, perhaps because I was angry, I found myself thinking about Generation Tipper's positive contributions to the world. There were not many legacies from the old economy that were not being demolished or deleted. Unaudited tippers had to help dismantle the coal, oil and gas fired power stations, generally with nothing more than sledgehammers, shovels and wheelbarrows. Their generation had built them, so now they had to pull them apart. This was in case future generations forgot the lessons of history and decided on an economic quick fix for some power shortage. Oil refineries, aluminum smelters and steel works were suffering the same fate, because they were all considered to be temples for the worship of squander.

Freeways were being left as they were. They made very convenient bicycle paths, and were great sites for strip-towns. Build houses and shops on the outer lanes of the old freeways and you only had to wheel your bicycle out of your front door to be on a high quality road to somewhere. So, should Generation Victim be grateful for freeways? In reality, freeways were just useful rubbish.

A totally new economy had been built out of mining the past, as it was called. Glass panes were carefully removed from high rise buildings and stockpiled for reuse. Steel was collected in rusty mountains built from cars, girders and bits of factories that used to build things using raw force instead of enzyme vats and layer precipitation fabrication. Above all, everything that contained solid carbon was stored or buried if it did not have an immediate use.

I concluded that Generation Victim had inherited nothing to be truly grateful for from Generation Tipper. We had just left them with rubbish, even though some of it could be re-purposed.

#

DAY 9: RIDING TO THE FIREWORKS

There are some quite trivial charges that are very hard to beat. This morning, facing a sentence of Rising Sea Levels without mercy, I listened with dismay as the Retributor declared a charge that was actually valid.

"The accused is charged with using a motorcycle for recreation, specifically to take his son on a sixteen kilometer round trip to watch fireworks on 31 December 1989."

I really had taken Albert to watch the fireworks on this particular night, and had done so on my motorcycle. What was worse was the fact that Albert had often complained later that the only time I had ever taken him to watch fireworks had been on that night. He had probably even told Renny. I could try to deny the charge, but the Retributor was sure to have a testimony or diary entry that he could produce.

"Dr Hall?" asked the Auditor General after a moment.

"I would like to see the evidence that I did this," I responded.

"I call upon the accused's granddaughter, Renelda Kylie Hall," said the Retributor.

The Auditor General raised her hand.

"Consider me to have taken the stand," she said.

"Your honor, can you confirm that Albert Hall mentioned being taken to the fireworks on the accused's motorcycle, and on the occasion specified?" asked the Retributor.

"I can confirm that. My father was very bitter about only being taken to watch the New Year's Eve fireworks once in his entire childhood, and that was at the end of 1989."

"Dr Hall, do you dispute the testimony of the Auditor General?"

"I do not."

"Then you admit that you are guilty as charged."

"I do not. If I had taken Albert on the train to watch the fireworks there would be no charge."

"Your action destroys the credibility of your testimony on your second and third audits. It shows that you were capable of using a motorcycle for recreation on one occasion, and thus would have probably done so on others. I put it to the audit bench that Dr Hall is not innocent of any climate crimes, and is highly skilled at covering up those very crimes."

The issue here was one of obsessiveness. I had already shown that I was particularly obsessive when it came to environmental responsibility. My problem was that the Retributor was even more obsessive, and I could tell by the haggard look on his face that he had probably been up all night researching this particular charge.

"Do you have a response, Dr Hall?" prompted the Auditor General.

I did not. I had indeed taken Albert to watch the fireworks, joining the crowds at Southbank, beside the river. We had then gone home, and for once Albert had nothing to complain about. I had squandered half a liter of petrol on the trip. While this was hardly an atrocity against the future of the planet, it was proof that I was capable of doing it at all. How many other half liters had I squandered? Quite a few, if one included occasional dates and parties. On the other hand, the Retributor was unlikely to have evidence about all that or he would have cited it.

I looked at Renny. "Tell me, your honor, as a blood relative, would you say that I am something of an obsessive?" I asked.

"Definitely."

"Obsessive enough to cut up a motorcycle to keep it out of the carbon economy?"

"That was established in the sixth audit."

"So how likely is it that I would have made a journey without using it to contribute to the welfare of the planet?"

"Highly unlikely."

"And would you say that the top of the Weather Bureau's high-rise building in the Central Business District was both a perfect vantage to watch fireworks and to monitor atmospheric phenomena?"

"Definitely."

"Clerk of the Bench, can you confirm that I had perfected a laser backscattering monitor in 1989, a device to measure the amount of smoke in the atmosphere at night?"

The Clerk typed in the relevant keywords.

"Confirmed."

"Your honor, I put it to you that I am sufficiently obsessive to have performed an experiment involving the effect of firework smoke on global warming on the 31st of December 1989."

"Objection, your honor!" called the Retributor. "The experiment cited is ludicrously trivial."

"Objection overruled. You have only offered your own opinion, and it is not the opinion of an expert witness. Dr Hall, can you elaborate on your experiment?"

"A colleague of mine, Dr Albrecht, liked to propose wild theories about human influences on climate change. For example, he said that if the entire population of the planet farted half as much, greenhouse warming could be significantly impacted. I calculated that this could keep six billion liters of greenhouse gas out of the atmosphere per day."

Laughter burst from the gallery like water from a collapsing dam, and the Auditor General did not even bother to bang the mace on her desk. The wardens fired their assault rifles into the air in an attempt to restore silence.

"Order!" called the Auditor General once it was again quiet enough to be heard. "Confine your explanation to the New Year's Eve fireworks of 1989, Dr Hall."

"Dr Albrecht also suggested that if the global population took up fireworks as a hobby, the gases and pollutants released would cool the planet by reflecting more heat back into space. By shining my laser through the clouds generated by fireworks I was able to refute his argument. I conducted the experiment on that particular night because I knew there would be a fireworks display. I took my son along because he was always pestering me to take him to see fireworks."

"Enough. I am satisfied that you conducted a legitimate but trivial climatological experiment on this occasion. Fellow victims, do you agree?"

Four hands were raised in favor of my innocence, and four against. The Auditor General raised her hand in my favor. Again she had come to my rescue. Her credibility would suffer if she did this too often.

"Retributor, do you have further charges?" she asked.

"I do, your honor," he said calmly, although his face was pale with fury.

"Dr Hall, do you wish to continue the audit tomorrow and face the Finite Resources Exchange, with mercy?"

"Yes, your honor."

"Try to present a less trivial charge tomorrow, Retributor. Next audit?"

Guilt does not manifest in a unique facial expression, or I would have been found guilty and sentenced to Rising Sea Levels without mercy at that very moment. I had not gone to the Weather Bureau's head office and conducted that experiment, but the only witness was dead and there was no proof to the contrary. I had had the right pass keys to enter the building and get onto the roof, and I had indeed built equipment to measure the density of smoke with a laser beam. I could have done it, perhaps I should have done it, but I had not.

At that moment I felt as if I had let the entire world down by squandering a half liter of petrol, yet I had rehabilitated myself. I represented all Generation Tipper people who had pioneered climate change activism and could still make a vital contribution to the planet's welfare, but the audit bench of Audit Camp 71 was only concerned with lapses. I had to be a climate saint if I were to beat the audit, yet beneath my cloak of innocence I was merely a demon with good intentions.

\#

Although by now I had worked in three of the carbon reclamation fields, being confronted with the reality of the executions was something I had not learned to cope with. Carbon Dioxide Field was for those sentenced to die a Class Five Death. The prisoners were tied to chairs and gas masks fastened over their faces. Plastic bags inflated and deflated as they exhaled and inhaled the same air until they passed out and died. Dr Gibson was waiting for me, and for some reason he looked more haggard than usual.

"Welcome to Class Five Death," he said as I got out of my harnesses.

"I'm already past this one in the audits," I replied.

"It's the best way to go. No pain, just fear from being aware that you're about to slip away."

"How long does it take?"

"I've never seen anyone last over twenty minutes."

"This is not a merciful death."

"No execution is merciful, but it's resource neutral."

"They're all resource neutral. Why do you bother to work as a doctor in this slaughterhouse?"

"I'm a bonus. The camp is only supposed to have five paramedics and a dozen nurses, but sometimes a real doctor is needed. Two years ago an auditor needed an appendix removed in a hurry, and I did the job."

"So in return they keep you well down on the re-audit list?"

"I believe I'm at the very bottom."

While we were speaking, the bag attached to one of the figures ceased to inflate and deflate. It was definitely not a violent death, but the knowledge that every breath taken was another step toward fading out forever made it worse as far as I was concerned.

"Talk to me about something else," I said. "Anything. Why were the Rocky Horror people allowed to suicide, but not Peggy-Anne?"

"She was high profile, very visible and proud of it. The Rockies were nobodies. Wasting bullets on them was not climatically correct, but it's allowed when quotas are falling behind."

"Why didn't Peggy-Anne join them? She must have known she would get death."

"She liked to be the star of her own show."

"She certainly managed that."

"Your friend Chaz said she was a lot of fun."

"I'm sure the Retributor's father thought so too. Nine decades of being a party girl! It must have seemed like being immortal."

"I mean she put the hard word on Chaz the night before."

"You can't be serious!" I gasped.

"That's what he told me. He said she wanted one for the road."

"So did he manage to, er ..."

"Presumably. I gave him one of the blue pills in exchange for some not entirely legal drugs."

"Oh. Er, so you're an addict?"

"Of course not, but legal drugs are in short supply and operations are easier if the patient thinks he's floating on a cloud of warm sugar floss. Getting back to Peggy-Anne, lots of old ladies want to do it before they get audited. They get ideas about having a heart attack during orgasm."

"Amazing. Does it happen?"

"Yes, occasionally."

"Nice way to go."

"Now with men it happens about five times more often."

"I appreciate the warning."

I looked back to the rows of prisoners tied to chairs. By now none of the plastic bags attached to the masks were inflating and deflating.

"Well, time to check for pulses."

"Us?"

"Just you. Go ahead."

"Please, can you do it? I couldn't stand to touch their bodies."

"I have other duties, and you have to work somewhere."

"I'll do another field."

"Okay. Warden! I've got spare help here."

#

Warden Olivia escorted me to Rising Sea Levels Field. Here I saw rows of large aquariums with bound and weighted tippers inside. The water was up to just under their nostrils, and they had plastic tubes in their mouths. This led to a reservoir above the tank, whose water was slowly dribbling down.

"This is Class Three Death," said Warden Olivia. "As long as they can squirt water up the tube, they can breathe. Once they get tired, they're blowing bubbles."

I had escaped this sentence, but that did not make it any easier to look at those fighting for an hour or so of additional life against the remorseless rise of the water. Had this morning's audit not been judged in my favor, I would already be in one of those tanks.

"What am I to do?" I asked, fearing the worst.

"The strong ones last long enough for the sun to evaporate some water, so they can breathe without squirting. That means you have to top up the water."

I fell to my knees, nausea wrenching at my stomach.

"No, please, no, not that," I said once I had finished throwing up. "What else can I do?"

"There's Class Two Death. Come on."

190

\#

She took me into another field, where people were bound to chairs at a circle of desks, each with a laptop. Red tubes connected them.

"This is Finite Resources Field, it's mainly for industry, mining and stock exchange tippers."

"Those tubes!" I exclaimed. "Is that their blood?"

"You got it. They're all connected, the tubes have electronic valves, and they have to trade on a sort of blood exchange. Look here."

In the middle of the circle of desks was an electronic switching unit and a beaker containing a reservoir of blood. The red tubes converged on this assembly.

"But what about blood type incompatibility?" I asked.

"What about it?"

They were ominous words, but I had not yet realized what they implied. The blood traders paid us no attention at all. There was a familiar metallic tang on the air.

"They pull some seriously clever tricks to outsmart each other," Olivia continued.

"And what does the winner get?"

"Maybe fifteen minutes extra."

"What do you mean? There will be nobody else competing for the blood."

She led me between the desks and around the switching unit. Now I saw a large vat, half filled with blood. A steady stream was pouring into it from a single tube.

"The blood still drains away, even when there's only one left."

I squeezed my eyes shut, bent over and tried to throw up again. I failed because my stomach was empty, but my body kept dry reaching until I toppled sideways with exhaustion. Olivia lifted me from the sand, slung me over her shoulder and carried me clear of the blood exchange. Until then I had not realized how strong she was.

"So, I reckon there's not much point telling you what your work would be here," she said as I sat taking deep breaths and trying to keep my mind blank.

"What's the point of this nightmare?" I managed to gasp.

"It shows that resource depletion screws everyone, winners included."

Slowly, and very unsteadily, I got to my feet.

"Take me back to Carbon Dioxide Field, I'd rather check bodies for pulses that aren't there."

"Are you okay to walk, Dr Fitness? It was sort of romantic, like, first time I ever carried a guy who'se still alive."

"If I collapse again, feel free."

#

This had not been a good day, and I was looking forward to the show being advertised for Entertainment Field. It was an episode from the original 1960s *Star Trek* science fiction series. Some members of the audience were wearing improvised starship crew costumes, and even pointed ears.

While no more than a casual science fiction enthusiast, I have always had a soft spot for *Star Trek*. At a time when the world's superpowers were threatening to annihilate life on Earth with a catastrophic and pointless nuclear war, the series suggested that we would survive into the future, prosper, and travel out into space. Here we would have glorious adventures without causing any more damage to the planet, and our society would be just and humane.

Alette went with me. She said that she wanted to experience entertainments that were not considered to be cool, yet might have been treated unfairly by the cool people. The episode was 'A Taste of Armageddon,' which I did not remember seeing. It seemed to be a great favorite with the borderlines, and the host for the night said it was being acted with no departures from the original script.

The starship *Enterprise* visits a planet at war with its neighbor, and the war has been going on for a very long time. There is no evidence of the chaos and destruction that war involves, however. Computers make simulated attacks on the cities of both planets without damaging anything real - except for real people. They are selected by the computers, then executed as if enemy missiles really had taken their lives.

This was government-mandated slaughter of its own citizens, and it resonated powerfully with the inmates of Audit Camp 71. People died so that civilization in general and property in particular would remain unharmed. Nobody in the audience laughed or whistled for the entire performance; this was clearly some sort of sacred ceremony for the borderlines.

There was, of course, a happy ending. The stars of the show destroy one of the disintegration chambers where citizens meekly go to their deaths, and execution quotas fall behind. Faced with the prospect of a very messy and unpleasant real war breaking out, the governments of the two planets decide that maybe ending the virtual war might be a better idea. Negotiations are beginning as the episode ends.

"What did you think of it?" asked Alette as the audience left the field.

"I feel as if I am trapped in that episode," I replied, "except there are no heroes to save us."

"There's you."

193

"I don't have pointed ears or a starship."

"But you have eight wins in the Audit Arena, and that has never happened until now. If you can beat a few more charges, the audit bench will have to make a decision about what to do when someone from Generation Tipper genuinely deserves pardoning. That will open the door to allow other tippers and borderlines of good will to be pardoned. The National Audit will not like that."

"True, Alette. Killing people is always easier than dealing with problems intelligently."

"Some executions can be hard to justify. I pioneered fashion without waste, and I got borderlined because sentencing me to death would have been squandering."

"So ... are you asking me to accept borderline status rather than risking my life and squandering my skills?"

"No. I support you, even though my support may put my own life at risk. We are in the same situation as the aliens in that *Star Trek* episode and we must try to break out, even if the risks are appalling."

That was an enormous boost to my morale.

As with most other aspects of life in Audit Camp 71, there were traditions associated with the night's entertainment. Some of the more enthusiastic members of the audience were dressed in the costumes of the original 1960s television series, while others had dressed as if they were from the subsequent series, *Star Trek: The Next Generation*. Alette and I watched as the fans of the two series proceeded to shout insults and beat each other with walking sticks that had little warp drive engines attached. This was apparently a way of lightening the mood, but nevertheless there were two deaths.

"I wish I had worked in costuming for the original shows," said Alette as we kissed each other on the cheek at the entrance to Dormitory Field. "I could have given science fiction such an elegant look."

DAY 10: RECREATIONAL TRAIN BY PROXY

"The three tipper escapees have been on the run for six days now," the Auditor General announced at the start of the morning's proceedings. "They are weakening and running low on supplies, so in the interests of climate justice, they will now be audited."

This came as quite a surprise for me. The three men had traveled a hundred and twenty miles since they had escaped, but by now they were covering only three miles per day - or perhaps that should be per night. They were still traveling in darkness and sleeping under their sun blankets while the sun was up. The main display screen in the Audit Arena showed them digging a distillation pit and filling it with whatever vegetation they had been able to collect, which was not much. During the day the sun would evaporate whatever water was in the plant material, and it would condense out on the plastic. They were even adding their own urine to distill for drinkable water.

"Clerk of the Bench, tell the operator to fly the drone to within hailing distance," the Auditor General ordered.

The drone descended, then a microphone was lowered on a thin cable. The escapees had already rigged their blankets on poles to keep the direct sunlight off themselves for the day. We could not see their faces as the drone began to broadcast to them.

"Clerk of the Bench, next case?" called the Auditor General.

"William Fitzgibbon, charged with squander, display and eco-vandalism."

"Retributor?"

"The accused made a practice of taking extended holidays in the desert in a sports utility vehicle and 'living off the land', as he described it. He did this for two decades."

A head appeared from beneath one of the shelters.

"Where the fuck are you?" croaked the voice of someone who sounded very feeble.

"Do you have anything to say in your defense?" asked the Auditor General.

"We need water and food."

"Clerk of the Bench, enter a refusal to plead. Fellow victims, who votes guilty?"

All eight auditors raised their hands.

"William Fitzgibbon, you are sentenced to Class One Death, and at my discretion this will be accomplished by Release instead of Mines."

"Stop this bullshit!" called whichever of the three was talking. "We're dying. We need help."

"Next audit?"

"Bruce Nagal, also charged with squander, display and eco-vandalism."

"Retributor?"

"As before."

SEAN MCMULLEN

"Anything to say in your defense, Mr Nagal?"

"Piss off, bitch shit-face!" called a much weaker voice.

"Stop this fuck shit comedy," shouted the original voice. "We're dying!"

"Do you wish that to be your comment?"

"We need water, damn you!"

"Two decades ago there was water and game where you are now, but global warming has roasted all that away," said the Auditor General. "Did you really think that nothing had changed?"

"Yeah, okay, okay. Now we need help."

"When you escaped, you were in denial about how badly the desert's ecosystem has been damaged. Now you realize that the desert can no longer support you."

"Yeah, yeah, now help us. We'll plant trees for the rest of our lives if you want."

"Oh no. You must cope with the consequences of your denial."

"We were wrong, okay? We're saying it."

"That is gratifying, but it is far too late."

"Stop this political bullshit and help us! We're convinced we were wrong, okay?"

"I don't believe you. You still think that driving your recreation vehicle had nothing to do with global warming. You blame anything else but yourself, whether it's sunspots, aliens, or bad fairies."

"We don't have time for this! Me mate's just died. Bruce and I are hangin' on by our fingernails."

"Honorable victims, who votes guilty?" asked the Auditor General, apparently unmoved.

All the auditors raised their hands.

197

"Bruce Nagal, you are sentenced to Class One Death, and by Release, at my discretion."

One of the men crawled clear of the shelters on his knees, pointed his assault rifle at the drone and opened fire. The screen went blank, but a moment later I realized that the microphone unit was still working, and transmitting to a nearby relay drone. That drone was still high above, and its camera now presented a more distant view of the shelters.

"I hit the fucker!" called the first voice.

"Nice one," the other replied.

"Too bad Leacher didn't live to see that."

"Harrison Leach was the third guy," said someone behind me.

"Clerk of the Bench, note that Harrison Leach surrendered his carbon prior to being audited," said the Auditor General.

"The fuckin' drone's still live!" shouted Fitzgibbon.

The second drone showed a figure stumble from the shelters and search for the remains of the first drone. The microphone picked up the crunch of sandals on sand, then a burst of gunfire. Only now was the sound cut off.

"Game bastards," said the borderline behind me.

"Game and tough," said another.

"But stupid."

"Still, you have to admire them."

The Auditor General banged her mace on her desk, and the conversation ceased.

"Clerk of the Bench, arrange for a medical drone to examine the body of Harrison Leach after the other two have moved on. If he is indeed dead, use its scalpels to flay his skin open for desiccation."

"And if he's still alive?"

"We shall conduct an audit."

The audit of the escapees had been brutal in the extreme. They had a strong grasp of bush craft, just as I did, and in their position I would be doing nothing differently. Their problem was that their skills were obsolete. The climate had changed, so the desert had changed - changed into a landscape that could no longer support humans traveling across it. Those who did not carry their own supplies died because nobody could now live off the land. I should not have felt sympathy for them, yet I did. They were tough, resourceful, confident men, yet they were in denial about what was going on all around them and in plain sight. The world had no place for their type, and they could contribute nothing but damage to our long-suffering planet.

#

I was next. On first impressions, my ninth audit was for a reason that seemed as trivial as the eighth.

"The accused is charged with allowing his son to travel on a recreational train whose engine was powered by coal," the Retributor declared, then he called up a 1992 photograph of Albert and the rest of an excursion group from his school leaning out of the windows of the Puffing Billy heritage steam train.

There was a certain amount of hypocrisy in this charge. Everyone who had used electricity before the Tipping Point Year had made use of power that had been at least partly generated by burning coal. That meant everyone who had ever watched television had been squandering fossil fuels and pumping carbon dioxide into the atmosphere for entertainment. This was dangerous territory for Generation Victim, however, because coal-fired power stations had still been in use after the Tipping Point Year. Was everyone guilty

199

of climate crimes and deserving of execution? Members of the Anthrophobe movement actually said yes.

My problem was more immediate. If the unavoidable use of climatically incorrect power could be pardoned, the whole of Generation Victim was technically guilty but potentially eligible for pardon. Burning coal in a recreational vehicle was a different matter, however. It was in the same class as burning petrol in a motorcycle for no purpose other than fun. If you were Generation Victim, it would get you a lengthy sentence of service. Were you Generation Tipper? Sorry, you have to give your carbon back. For me, this would be by means of Finite Resources Field, which meant a painless but horrifying death.

"Do you deny the charge?" asked the Auditor General.

"I do. This trip was signed off by my wife, and we had separated by 1992."

"You should have vetoed it," said The Retributor.

"I did complain to the school that it was a bad example for the children. I was laughed at."

"Have you proof that you protested?"

"Have you proof that I did not?"

"Order!" called the Auditor General. "The accused will not answer questions with more questions."

It was a respite of only seconds, but that was enough for me to get my thoughts sorted.

"Your honor, I believe that my previous eight audits demonstrate that I always thought through the climatic impact of all of my actions and decisions. True, I only protested verbally about this recreational trip, so I have no proof. On the other hand, the audit bench accepted in my sixth audit that I went to a great deal of trouble to dispose of a climatically inefficient motorcycle. If I went to so much trouble in that case, why should I not bother to pick up the phone and complain about a recreational trip on a coal-burning train?"

The Auditor General sat back and folded her arms, then shook her head. This was yet again a very bad moment for me, and I noticed the Retributor allow himself the trace of a smile.

"I accept the accused's argument," she said, and right on cue there were cheers, whistles and cries of "Meow! Meow!" from the gallery. The Auditor General called for order, then turned to the Retributor.

"Retributor, I need to point out that your last two charges skirted the boundaries of the trivial, and as such could be considered to be low-level squander. There are three audit days left to Dr Hall, after which we shall have to make a unilateral decision on whether or not to pardon him. This is because the law states that the penalty escalates from Class Six death, with mercy, through to Class One death, without mercy, for difficult audits. Once there is no longer scope for escalation, there can be no further audits. That clause is in the National Audit's constitution to prevent open ended litigation that squanders resources for years. Do I make myself clear?"

"You do, your honor. Please accept my apologies."

"Honorable victims, who votes that the charge has been answered?"

Four hands were raised.

"Against?"

The other four auditors voted against me.

"Clerk of the Audit, note that my casting vote is in favor of the accused. Dr Hall, I assume you will agree to continuing tomorrow, with your sentence upgraded to Finite Resources Field, without mercy."

"You assume correctly, your honor."

This had been my closest call so far. Would my granddaughter's credibility survive another casting vote in my favor?

Alette was in the gallery tiers, and gave me a wave as I was led back to my seat. She was definitely paying me special attention. What was I to make of that? Did she want a liaison with a fellow celeb or was there another motive? I'd had several partners when younger, but genuine romance was a blank spot in my life.

#

"Clerk of the Bench, what is the next case?" asked the Auditor General.

"Eustace Lee."

"Retributor?"

"Lee is charged with building and burning a small-scale Trojan horse using a hundred thousand live matches."

I had heard about this case, and although I consider myself to be a liberal, I definitely felt anger boil up within me as I walked back to my seat. My granddaughter seemed to agree.

"I am tempted to pass a Class Four Death sentence now, but a note on my screen says that this was meant as a symbolic act of protest," she said. "Retributor?"

"This is clearly a gross act of squandering, and representative of many other climate crimes the accused has committed. There can be no possible justification."

The Auditor General turned back to the accused.

"Throwing a rock through the plate glass window of a coal mining company could technically be classed as an act of squander, yet the action might have been intended to benefit the planet. Mr Lee, speak in your own defense. How do you justify squandering two thousand boxes of matches?"

The man was young enough to be a GV, and so had grown up amid quite urgent warnings about climate change and resource depletion. Some of those warnings had come from me.

"The Trojan horse was allegorical, it was meant to symbolize fossil fuels infiltrating our civilization from within, then destroying it by causing climate change."

His manner was confident, but he struck me as just a little cocky rather than sincere. That would count against him with the auditors.

"The YouTube video had several million viewings," said the Advocate. "If the act was meant to be a warning, it was very widely viewed."

"Retributor?" asked the Auditor General.

"There was no reference to climate change or greenhouse warming in any of the annotating texts associated with this act of gross squander. The accused also built thirty-seven other match-head models, including the *Titanic*, *Death Star*, the mushroom cloud of a nuclear bomb and Arnold Schwarzenegger as the Terminator, riding a petroleum tanker. All this consumed 74,000 boxes of matches and 5,000 tubes of glue."

"Mr Lee, how do you respond?"

"I was using popular culture to make people aware of the role of fire and burning in entertainment."

"To achieve what?"

"To raise awareness about everything heating up."

"Yet you did not mention this in any interview or publicity release."

"I wanted to keep the message subtle, so people would have debates and think about why I was building and burning the models."

"Advocate?"

"Quite a lot of debate was generated in social media, your honor."

"About climate change?"

"Some of it, yes."

"Retributor?"

"Just 14% of the debate related to climate change, your honor. I must also point out that if the matchboxes involved were stacked up, they would stand a hundred meters high."

"Objection," said the Advocate. "This is an emotive comparison."

"Objection sustained. Eustace Lee, while I am inclined to believe that your models were merely designed to generate popularity on social media, and thus amounted to display, they did contribute to a raised awareness of climate change. You may have your audit adjourned, and you may join the borderlines pool. Do you consent to this?"

"Yes, your honor."

"Next audit?"

Lee had been very, very lucky, but would his luck hold out? He looked fit, so he might live another fifty years. If I had been an auditor, I would have given him a verdict of guilty, along with a Class Two Death sentence. Was the borderlines pool so large that the Audit would not return to him before he died of natural causes? Possibly.

#

For the rest of that day I was swamped by people wishing me well and offering to do my duties so that I could either rest or prepare for whatever the following morning would bring. The Retributor's reputation was clearly taking damage, because Eustace Lee had been made a borderline in spite of quite convincing evidence of climate crimes. That meant the Retributor would be either desperate or dangerous tomorrow. Desperate was better for me, because desperate people make mistakes.

#

People were entering Refectory Field for dinner when Warden Olivia took me aside. I had been with Silvy and her fifteen Owl Academy experts in the crowd streaming through the gates. Several of the Owls gathered around me protectively. Silvy and the others did not seem to notice, and continued along with the crowd.

"We got a date with the armory, Dr Fitness," Olivia said. "Dinner's on hold for you."

"Is there a problem?" I asked.

"The problem's you, doc. You just walked away from your ninth audit alive, and the Auditor General's worried that someone might try to blow you away."

"I don't understand. It's the Auditor General who is trying to kill me."

"No, she just wants you audited. Trouble is, if someone else offs you, it looks like the National Audit is a bad loser and had you killed when they thought you might beat the climate crime charges."

"So what now?"

"We get body armor."

"We?"

"Just you and me, I've been made your official minder."

"But why the rush? I'm hungry."

"Comms has caught an encrypted string of text from a hacked router that decodes as OWL-71-GO."

"What is that meant to mean?"

"I don't know, neither does anyone else, and that worries the AG. You're one of the Owls and this is Audit Camp 71. You can bet your balls that it's a signal for someone to do something bad involving you."

"So all good, Dr Hall?" asked Gibson, who was not officially an Owl but hung out with us.

Before I could reply I heard a woman shouting "Viva Perfecti! Viva Perfecti!" then there was an explosion like a thunderclap so loud that you felt it rather than heard the noise. We were perhaps fifty yards away, and shielded by quite a thick press of borderlines in front of us.

The chaos was immediate, fueled by terror and panic, as everyone tried to flee the blast site. Olivia herded us over to the entrance of the administration building before the crowd could trample us. Soon the area was swarming with wardens, and as safe as could be expected. I offered my services as a first-aid volunteer, even though Olivia insisted that I had probably been the target of the bomber. Twenty-four borderlines and two wardens had been killed, and another three dozen had injuries so severe that they died before the stretchers arrived. Then and there it was not apparent to anyone what had happened, as the closest witnesses were all dead. I set about trying to control the bleeding of several survivors.

"Dr Fitness is being a real doctor tonight," Olivia said as she directed Dr Gibson my way. "I'll radio for stretchers. How many are needed, do you reckon?"

"All of them, probably," I guessed.

Dr Gibson got to work, allocating all the straightforward work to me. Presently I had the worst of the bleeding stopped in the victims in my care.

"Any idea what happened?" I asked Gibson.

"A bomb ticks all the boxes."

"I worked that out for myself."

"I've been told not to comment on anything not medical."

"If it was a suicide bomber the body parts will be part of the shrapnel. That's medically relevant, because infection might be an issue."

"What does it matter, this is death in a death camp."

"You must know something."

"Okay, okay, but keep this to yourself, right?"

"Yes."

"I was briefed by a warden from the video room. He saw a borderline charge the wardens out of the crowd, waving what looked like a pistol, but was probably a lashup. One of the wardens tasered her, and that set off her bomb."

"Her?"

"Apparently."

"But why attack the wardens with a fake gun when she could just detonate her bomb in the middle of the crowd?"

"To kill the wardens?"

"But I heard her shouting 'Viva Perfecti!' just before the explosion," I said. "That's an Anthrophobe slogan, and they don't care who they kill."

"An Anthro slogan? Are you sure?"

"Yes! Why target the wardens? The bomber could have killed twice as many by staying in the crowd."

"Wait a tick, she might have needed the jolt from the taser to set off her bomb."

"Possibly. How do you think she got the bomb into the camp?"

"I would say she didn't," sighed Gibson. "Explosives are depressingly easy to make. She probably worked in the farm fields, where she had access to fertilizer chemicals that can act as oxidants, and any type of sugar will do for fuel. Mix them together and boom."

"So easy?"

"Oh yes. The borderlines distill their own liquor without getting caught, where do you think my medicinal alcohol comes from?"

Eight of the dead were from Silvy's Owl Academy. I found this particularly harrowing, because they were not just strangers having their carbon reclaimed. Worse, their very formidable skills had been lost. By the time the last of the bodies had been stretchered away, some tippers and border-lines were forming lines to collect their dinner rations. I tried to join them, but Olivia took me by the arm.

"Time to get us that body armor, Dr Fitness," she called.

"Would it have been any help against a bomb?" I said, because I was particularly tired and very hungry.

"Probably not, but orders are orders. Come on, it's not far to the armory."

"Do you know if this happens often?" I asked as we set off.

"Killing people facing a death sentence? Yeah, sometimes. The Anthrophobes like publicity, so anyone high profile can be a target."

"First Anthrophobe attack here?"

"Yeah. We thought it could never happen."

"As in too hard to smuggle weapons or bombs all the way here?"

"Yeah, it's quite a trek. Besides, anyone with Anthro connections would be taken aside and shot for treason before they even joined a caravan. That lady just might have been a loner who knew some chemistry."

#

Our body armor turned out to be vests made of agamid fabric and steel plate. Olivia took her shirt off, shook her breasts in my direction, then slipped into her vest and pressed the Velcro down.

"I'll need your autograph in the register, Doc Hall," said the stores warden. "Bet you wish you were wearing this thing a couple of hours back."

"Everything helps," I said, although not really convinced.

"Hey Brad, any word on the bomber yet?" asked Olivia.

"Haven't you heard?"

"Me, hear anything but the bang? In this place I could shoot a tipper gone feral and still be the last to hear about it."

"It was Doc Hall's friend, Rossica."

"Silvy!" I exclaimed.

"Yeah - hey, but you didn't hear it from me."

"Why choose the dinner queue to detonate?" asked Olivia.

"Some detonators need a jolt from a taser, others can be touched off by the shockwave of a bullet. She must have had a taser type, and the guards at Refectory Field always carry tasers."

They might have said more, but my mind went into overload and blanked out. Silvy. She had told me she wanted the Owl Academy together for dinner, she was going to propose that I be made a member. All the while she knew that she was only minutes from oblivion, and that she would pass through Death's portal before she reached the archway of Refectory Field.

She had intended to kill us all, but luckily she did not notice that some of us had left her group. Perhaps when death is so very close one becomes absolutely focused on one's last tasks: waving her fake gun, shouting to draw attention to herself, charging the wardens, getting herself tasered. She had been my friend and even lover, but clearly I had been no friend of hers. Had she been planning to kill me even back when we had sex in Dating Field?

#

I finally got a serving of dinner, escorted by Olivia. I doubt that there would have been anything else but the bombing being discussed, right across Audit Camp 71. A glance across to the announcement screens told me nothing, of course. The best way to deal with an attack on any high-profile target is to pretend that it did not happen. The screen was displaying a news feed about the expansion of Antarctic kelp farms.

As I ate whatever I had been served, I tried to think like an Anthrophobe. Why target Refectory Field, apart from needing to be tasered? Crowds, of course. An explosion during the dinner rush would inflict the maximum number of casualties. A lone believer would take a simple approach like that, yet Silvy was more sophisticated.

She had formed the Owl Academy in the fist place. Why? Because we were sixteen scientists and engineers who might really make a difference in the efforts to heal the planet and save humanity. If I beat the audit, the other fifteen might be pardoned and be put to work instead of being punished for just being old. It was only through blind chance that eight of us had dropped behind and survived.

Security was sure to be tightened as a result of the bombing. Everything in the camp that could act as an oxidant or fuel would be monitored and audited far more closely, and the armory would get an extra warden or two.

"Anyone home?" asked Elver Lyn, waving a hand before my eyes.

I had not even noticed that she had joined me and Olivia.

"Just thinking about the attack," I said. "If it had not been for Olivia we would have been blood and body parts by now. Getting to sleep after that sort of close call is not going to be easy."

"Why not come along to the Owl Academy and talk it out? We're having a meeting tonight."

"But eight of you are in Desiccation Field, waiting to be slashed and staked."

"Seven are still breathing, and you make eight."

"Will it get us charged with conspiracy?" I asked, turning to Olivia.

"Not if you got a warden present as monitor," she replied. "The trick is to get someone sympathetic."

"Are you sympathetic?"

"Yeah, I reckon. With some wardens it's like inviting the pope to a condom factory, but I'm okay."

"We also need to talk through the bombing, or it's PTSD all round," added Elver.

#

The Owl Academy met whenever the members felt like it, generally after something important had happened in the camp or been reported on the news feeds. The bombing definitely counted as important. Warden Olivia managed to get us into the Audit Arena, so it was here that we assembled by the light of a single security lantern.

Sitting on the audit bench was suggested, but that was too much for Olivia.

"The AG would think it's screwing the dignity of the place," was how she put it.

Instead, we gathered at the bottom of the audience gallery. Because I had been doing first aid at the crime scene,

I was expected to have the big picture. Thus I was first to speak, after I had been voted in as a member.

"As we are all too well aware, Refectory Field was bombed by a lone Anthrophobe shouting a Neo-Cathar slogan this evening. That Anthrophobe was Silvy Rossica, who had apparently been a sleeper here for years. She got herself tasered to set off a bomb wrapped in ceramic chips."

"But why?" asked Elver. "She founded the Owl Academy."

"The Owls' meetings got sixteen highly qualified and valuable experts together. Killing us all would have been a big step along the road to human extinction. It sounds weird but we were lucky that only eight of us Owls died."

"Seven," said a professor of engineering named Dermot Hughes. "Rossica was never really one of us."

That killed the thread of the conversation for a moment.

"Warden Olivia, how do you feel about us discussing the Anthrophobes?" I asked, just to keep the talk moving.

"Whatever the National Audit likes, I do too."

"I'm sure that nobody here dislikes the Anthrophobes any less than the members of the National Audit."

"Is anyone an expert on the Anthrophobes," asked Elver, who had been the Owls' most recent recruit before me.

I raised my hand. "They tried to kill me a few times."

"That's close enough."

"Okay, let's do Anthrophobes versus National Audit 101," I said. "It is not often that genocides take place on the basis of age. King Herod's slaughter of the innocents is what probably springs to mind for most people, but condemning the entire previous generation to death is something new, even for creatures as inventive as humans, and that's the National Audit. The Anthrophobes have gone one step more extreme. Their leaders have condemned the entire human species to oblivion."

Nobody said anything. I already knew that the Owls all had an unshakable belief in progress, and the Anthrophobes only believed in annihilation. This meant that my audience was totally unsympathetic to the Anthrophobe outlook.

"What most people don't realize is that the Anthrophobes consider themselves to follow the principles of a medieval religious sect known as the Cathars. This evening's suicide bomber shouted 'Viva Perfecti!' before she blew up, and the Perfecti were something like saints to the Cathars. Who wants some background on the Cathars?"

Seven shadowy hands were raised in the solar lantern's bluish light.

"You don't, Warden Olivia?"

"Just checking with the National Audit regs database," she said, tapping at her phone. "All good, go ahead."

"They came to Southern France from Eastern Europe, nine hundred years ago. They were nominally Christian, but they believed in a dual deity. For them, the material world was created and ruled by the god of darkness, while the god of light looked after spiritual things like souls. Thus they thought the extinction of living humans was a good thing, and that we should all strive to become pure and unblemished spirits, instead of being trapped in material bodies."

"That's a bleak sort of belief," said Hughes.

"It works for some people. The Cathar faithful were encouraged to not have children, because that just brought more humans into the world of the dark god, where they were condemned to suffer."

"What happened to them?" asked Elver.

"Around 1200 the Catholic Church decided that they had to go. The original Cathars were quite humane, they provided free health care and gave women rights that were unheard of elsewhere in the Christian world. The pope of the time took a pretty dim view of their beliefs, however, and

213

once it became clear that they were not going to listen to his envoys, a crusade was sent. The fighting lasted for nearly half a century, and the last of the Cathars were not hunted down until just after 1300. Cities were torched by the papal crusaders, and captured Cathars who did not recant were burned at the stake by the Inquisition. The movement was annihilated, and what little we know about them today only comes from Inquisition records."

"So who are these modern Cathar dudes?" asked Olivia.

"The Neo-Cathars are probably revivalists, who read up on what the Inquisition wrote about the originals. The Neos are quite a bit more extreme than the medieval faithful, and believe in human extinction. They are what we call the Anthrophobes. The National Audit has the Green Man and Mother Earth, and the Neo-Cathars have the gods of light and darkness."

"They make even the National Audit look good," called someone.

"Were the Cathars really wiped out?" asked Olivia. "Like, they might have gone underground and only just resurfaced."

"After what the Inquisition and crusade did to them? Definitely possible. After all, some pre-Columbian religions in Central and South America lay low for nearly five hundred years, then came back into the open when the power of the Catholic Church took a nosedive last century."

"But I just can't see the attraction of species suicide," said Hughes. "They had no sense of progress."

"Is progress meant to be good?" I asked.

"What sort of question is that? If course it is."

"Progress is something that's sorted by trial and error. Good sanitation, nutrition and medical advances all sound great, but they allowed the global human population to expand catastrophically. Then advances in chemistry and yet more medical research gave us reliable contraception to limit population increase. That gave us slower population growth and a lot more recreational sex. How does progress fit with that?"

"Sounds good, if you're young enough," called another of the men.

"Progress means a better quality of life," said Hughes. "Back in the stone age we used to spend all our time feeding ourselves and fighting off those who wanted to steal our food. By the Twentieth Century we had the leisure and wealth to do things like study, read for fun and go on holidays in comfortable trains and ships."

"So that's progress?" I exclaimed. "Burn tons of jet fuel to fly to Egypt, tour the pyramids, say 'Fuck, look at that!' then burn more fossil fuel to fly home?"

"That's the means, not the principle," said Hughes. "People used to travel on sailing ships, and they were carbon neutral."

"And now we've returned to wind power. Most of today's ships are wind or solar electric. I'm not seeing any progress."

"So you're saying jet aircraft were a big mistake?" asked Hughes. "They were not real progress?"

"Maybe not," I said. "Would you agree, Warden Olivia?"

"The National Audit's got hard words out about jet engines, so they're not on my list of who to invite to a party."

"Back in the Middle Ages people used to go on pilgrimages, walking," I pointed out. "Pilgrims were the first tourists, but they had a minuscule carbon footprint. Who really needs an overseas holiday every year? Maybe holidays should be a once-in-a-lifetime experience. If you want to go see more of the world, get a job on a ship."

Half a century ago, when I was thirty-five, very few people would have had a conversation like this - except in university staff clubs, in front of cheery wood fires, while drinking good scotch. Were the Cathars right, all those centuries ago? Were humans inherently bad, and was progress something to be kept in a cage and only let out on a very strong chain?

I tried to put myself in the position of an Anthrophobe. Was there an allure to the idea of the last humans being elderly, sterile hunters patrolling the overgrown ruins of cities, on the lookout for young people to kill? In a way it was the ultimate revenge on the National Audit. The young wipe out the old, who had ruined the Earth for fun and profit. The young then get old and wipe out the young of the next generation. Some might even call that progress, at least as far as the other surviving species on Earth were concerned.

"This has gotta sound like a silly question, but are the Anthrophobes carbon neutral?" asked Warden Olivia.

"They don't have an official policy on the subject, but get rid of humans and the world will be on the road to recovery in a thousand years and fully recovered in maybe a million."

"What does the National Audit say?" she asked.

"Policy is that the Earth can be restored way faster if we humans tackle climate damage actively and intelligently."

"Sounds good to me."

For no reason in particular, this sent me over the edge.

"Don't you have any opinions of your own, Warden Olivia?" I asked, exasperated.

"Oh yeah, but I don't agree with them."

What was really going on in her head? Was she typical of those who were being called Generation Victim?

"Who do you think will win, Dr Hall?" asked Elver. "Like, the Anthros or the Auditors?"

"The Audit movement, without a doubt. The Neo-Cathars are not nearly as well organized, and the only new weapons are built by Audit movement factories."

SEAN MCMULLEN

"One conspiracy theory is that the Anthros are actually supported by the Audit movement, to get the human population down to a supportable level faster, and with fewer audits," said Hughes.

"Want to field that one, Olivia?" I asked.

"The Auditors would never do that," she said at once. "Everyone gets a fair audit, it's policy."

The truth was probably rather more murky than that. A third of the tippers had died on the trek that had brought me to Audit Camp 71. Did the auditors care? Kill a fellow borderline for snoring and the wardens would not conduct a crime scene investigation. Dead borderlines and tippers were just resources saved, but nobody discussed it.

It had taken the whole of the Thirteenth Century to suppress the original Cathars, so had the Catholics dragged their feet for some political agenda? The Audit movement had a definite interest in keeping the Anthrophobe Neo-Cathars active. They were more extreme, but they trimmed away inconvenient tippers who were cluttering up the Earth. Everyone was supposed to get an audit, but if the Anthrophobes got to a few of us first, no real harm done.

The meeting broke up after some more climatically correct discussion, but Olivia raised another fear as she, Elver and myself were walking to Dormitory Field, some distance behind the others.

"The Greenhands are the religion of the Audit movement, right?" Elver asked.

"Yes, but the cult of the Green Man is more of a collection of gentle beliefs than a religion," I said.

"Then the Anthrophobes are guaranteed to win," said Elver. "They're a superior type of monster. That's depressing."

"Would you say the teachings of Christ are humane and gentle?" I asked.

217

"I suppose. Yes."

"Then may I draw your attention to the words of the papal legate during the sack of the Cathar city of Beziers in 1209, when twenty thousand were killed by the pope's crusaders? When told there were Catholics mixed in among the Cathars, he said 'Kill them all, God will know his own.' Members of some of the most humane religions have been among the worst monsters to walk the planet. The Anthrophobes have no edge over the members of the Audit movement."

So who was there to save the Earth? Monsters. Who was leading us into the future? Monsters. Who was fighting the monsters? Worse monsters. Who was standing between the competing monsters? Me. Both groups of monsters wanted me dead, yet one of them was willing to listen to me first. My granddaughter. I was never more grateful to scoop the sand out of my sleeping trench and climb in.

#

DAY 11: RETIREMENT FUND

The next day's audit began with a very strange case. An online link was established to a data farm on Macquarie Island, where a coal mining billionaire had been found in hiding. This may seem unlikely, because the island is just a speck of land in the Southern Ocean, halfway between Australia and Antarctica. It is, however, superbly placed for wind generators and is geologically stable, so one of the world's largest data farms is located there. Within this data farm Herbert Trollar had been found by a hunter-stalker algorithm.

"First audit of the day, that of the fourteenth image of Herbert Trollar," declared the Clerk of the Bench.

Trollar had been somewhat more savvy than most of his peers, and had used eShadow technology to generate a core image of his mind in two petabytes of data storage. He had then made multiple copies of his image and scattered them across the databases of the world before suiciding. Two petabytes of storage space is two thousand terabytes, however, and not easy to disguise.

His most impressive grasp at immortality had been to shoot one of the images into space, aboard a capsule designed to return to Earth in five centuries. He was probably hoping that the fury over Generation Tipper's climate crimes would have died down by then, and that the damage to the Earth's ecosystems would have been repaired.

He had not counted on the International Audit Movement sending a missile with a hunter auton in pursuit of him, armed with a fusion bomb. His capsule had not even reached the orbit of Mars when a flash so bright that it was visible from Earth reduced his two petabytes of storage to a cloud of radioactive gas. There were complaints about squander from some auditors, but it was argued that the exercise also tested technology that might be needed to deal with an asteroid on a collision course with Earth.

"Herbert Trollar and I have met before," declared the Auditor General to her audit bench. "I have presided over three of his thirteen trials."

"Twelve trials, your honor," said the Clerk. "One of his images was shot while trying to escape."

"My apologies, you are correct, although being vaporized by a hydrogen bomb is stretching the term *shot* beyond reasonable usage. Can I have the accused online?"

"Online now, your honor."

"Trollar Fourteen, I do believe this is the last of your copies that we will have to deal with," she said to the laptop screen before her.

"I made millions of copies of my image," replied a voice after the usual communications delay.

"You made only sixty-three copies, because you did not want to share the world with vast numbers of yourself."

"Some of the copies are buried in capsules. You will never find them."

"There are forty-nine of them, and we have all their locations thanks to defectors among your staff. They are being recovered at this very moment. If this audit goes against you, they will all be destroyed in acid vats, because they are guilty of the same crimes as yourself. Retributor, have you prepared charges against Trollar that attract the death penalty?"

"Yes, your honor."

"How many?"

"Billions."

"Select one."

"In the category of Greed, Herbert Trollar did actively deny overwhelming evidence of climate change due to human activity for financial gain, resulting in the release of such large quantities of carbon dioxide into the atmosphere that the Tipping Point Year arrived well before previous projections."

"Fellow victims, who votes guilty?"

The vote was unanimous. The Auditor General clasped her hands and stared at the screen of her laptop.

"Herbert John Trollar, you are sentenced to Class One Death, without mercy. Have you anything to say for yourself?"

"You think you've won, don't you?"

"Not at all. You won."

This was not the answer that Trollar was expecting. The delay in his response was a lot longer than the light-speed interval from the satellite link between Macquarie Island and Audit Camp 71.

"I should have expected you to have some clever-dick comeback ready," he managed.

"Clever, yes I am, and that is why I am auditor general in this camp. Dick, no, I do not have one. As for comebacks, this is an audit, not a debating contest. Your system and colleagues won, just like an Ebola virus infection beating a patient's immune system. Now the International Audit Movement is trying to save both humanity and the world as they teeter on the edge of death."

"You greenies can do what you like. The human race will always go back to the free market economy because humans are free market animals. When it does, some image of me will be revived, and I'll be a hero."

"There are doomsday viruses patrolling the WorldCloud, and they have your image profile, among others. Doomsday viruses cannot be deactivated, that is their nature. They have no trapdoor access or kill switches. Any image of yourself that is *ever* activated will not last long."

"There are others like me, you can't catch them all."

"Thirty-one other eShadows of climate criminals were created, and seven of them were Generation Victim. Five of those survived their audits, but all the others have been deleted."

"You can't stop progress."

"Of course not. The National Audit has an active eShadow research program, and it is possible that eShadows will eventually become a new, resource-efficient form of humanity that can inhabit Luna, Mars or the Jovian moons. Earth is actually quite a hostile environment for electronics."

"The system I represent was the most successful the world has ever known."

"From the 1950s to the 1990s your system was ready, willing and able to sterilize the world with a thermonuclear war to save it from communism. The communists were no less guilty or wasteful, but they did have the edge on you for stupidity, I will concede that."

"Yeah? Well you also have an edge on me for dumb bitchery."

"Retributor, do you have anything to add?"

"No, your honor."

"Herbert John Trollar, what are we to do with you?" the Auditor General asked the image on the other end of the link. "Your other images were merely deleted, yet I can't help thinking that deletion is not enough. Clerk of the Bench, what is two petabytes divided by seven billion deaths?"

"Just a moment ... 222,222 bytes per death, your honor."

"Delete as many bytes of storage per second, and it will take how long?"

"Roughly 285 years, your honor."

"Too long, make that a hundred deaths per second, so that it takes ... nearly three years for him to be deleted. Trollar, you will be kept operational while your datasets are deleted in units of a hundred, totaling the seven billion deaths you contributed to causing. Your higher cognitive functions will be kept operational for as long as possible, so that you can witness yourself being obliterated."

"This is nothing but blatant sadism and genocide!" said Trollar's eShadow in what was probably meant to be an angry shout, except that a volume control app spoiled the effect.

"I was not instrumental in ending seven billion lives for profit. I have heard 11,394 audits, resulting in 9,120 carbon reclaimings. In terms of shared responsibility per death per person, you have helped kill nearly a million times more people than me. We are not about revenge, we are demonstrating that mindlessly chewing up the Earth and shitting it into the gutter has terrible consequences and will never again be tolerated. Clerk of the Bench, contact the alpha system administrator at Macquarie Island and authorize deletion of eTrollar-14 at the specified rate immediately."

"The entire world was behind me!" shouted Trollar in what we heard as a very soft, peevish voice. "Real justice would mean executing everyone, including yourself!"

"If the entire world had been behind you, you had a responsibility to not lead them straight into hell," replied the Auditor General, then she tapped the mute key on her laptop. "Clerk of the Bench, announce the next audit."

"Continuation of the audit of Dr Jason Hall, climatologist."

#

I was facing Class Two Death, which was Finite Resources Field, without mercy. This means that the blood was drained away slower, and the tipper was able to compete with other condemned tippers for food and water rations as well as blood. Why is slow death considered more cruel? I cannot say, perhaps it is a GV thing.

"The accused is charged with being in a retirement fund that invested in climatically damaging companies and schemes," said the Retributor.

I was tempted to laugh. The Auditor General's warning had obviously rattled the Retributor, so the charge he had selected was a standard, safe climate crime with plenty of verifiable evidence available.

"I have your retirement fund records on the screen, Dr Hall," said the Auditor General. "You definitely were a member of this fund, and it definitely invested in some climatically irresponsible companies."

"I was not aware of this at the time, your honor."

"So, you admit to not checking what was being done with your money?" asked the Retributor at once.

"Golden Sunset Financials presented themselves as ethical investors while secretly diverting funds to higher yielding companies and regimes that their investors would definitely not approve of. There was a class action against them, which I joined."

"You joined but did not initiate. I put it to you that neglect and greed motivated you in the management of your retirement funds. You were happy to accept a good return, and you had no interest in doing background checks."

"So I am being accused of neglect and greed?"

"Yes."

"Together?"

"Of course!"

"I lost $300,000 when Golden Sunset Financials went bankrupt during the Global Financial Crisis of 2008 and 2009. Were you aware of that?"

"The audit does not require -"

"In other words, you did not bother to check. The company had invested in the so-called NINJA housing loans without its investors or shareholders being aware of what was going on. If greed had been motivating me, I would have done enough research to learn of this practice. Instead, I lost over a quarter of a million retro dollars. That's sixty thousand coffee allocations today."

"There is still the charge of neglect. You did not do sufficient research into the company's investment practices."

"I did as much research into the financial viability of the investments as I did into the ethical credentials of those investments. If I had had the slightest idea that I would lose so much money, I would have switched funds. They concealed their investments in fossil fuels and Third World exploitation equally well."

"In short, the accused put his money where his mouth is," said the Advocate, finally catching on.

The Auditor General banged her desk with her mace.

"I am satisfied that Dr Hall has answered this quite involved and difficult charge," she said. "Honorable victims, who agrees?"

Five auditors raised their hands. The three auditors who were more radical in outlook voted against me, but five votes were enough to keep me alive.

"Dr Hall, will you face an eleventh audit tomorrow, and its mandatory sentence of Mines, with mercy?"

"I will, your honor."

#

Thinking about it, I doubt that the Retributor expected to win with that charge. Most people are more concerned with doing their job and getting on with their lives than they are with uncovering fraud in large organizations. In that sense he could have argued that I had been guilty of sloth, yet there was a deep pitfall hidden beneath that path.

If I had done an excessive amount of research into my investment funds, I could have been accused of neglecting my climatology work for self-interest - greed, in short. However, he would have had to argue that retirement funds were more important than climate research, and that would have put him on the path to the tipping point gallows.

There was applause as I returned to my seat, but not wild cheering. The charge was too convoluted and difficult to generate excitement. I had beaten it, but the Retributor had not been humiliated or ridiculed. It was not even an important milestone, because I still had two more audits to survive. Tomorrow's audit would be a different matter entirely. It would be the beginning of the end.

#

At lunchtime, the announcements screens showed the death of one of the remaining escapees, Bruce Nagal. One day after his audit, he could go no further. The camp's public screens showed him lie out on the sand, cut his wrists and bleed into their distillation pit. I had to look away. It was Chaz who told me that he was dead.

"I reckon Bruce gave his mate at least a couple of pints of drinkable water before he faded out," he said.

"Does Fitzgibbon know?"

"Not yet. The guy will go apeshit when he finds out his mate killed himself to give him a bit of water."

I volunteered to shovel out the privy pits that afternoon, because it gave me time away from the screens. I could not afford to let anything tire or upset me, now that the prospect of winning was almost within my grasp. Entertainment Field was only doing *Science of Stupid* stunt reenactments, with the participants occasionally killing themselves. I was not at all tempted to watch, so I went to my place in Dormitory Field early.

#

DAY 12: DOCTOR, DOCTOR

I was up at halflight, as usual, but all through my morning routine a bleak and confronting thought kept slipping into my mind: even if I won again, the dawn that I was about to see might well be my second last.

If I had to die for political convenience, my death would be arranged. I had been given body armor, but it would not protect me from a head shot or poison. Convicting me was the perfect solution. Dealing with a genuinely innocent tipper was messy, but an assassination that could be blamed on Anthrophobes would clean that mess away.

"Your honor, I have records proving that the accused squandered the resources of the Earth to take out a second doctorate," said the Retributor.

"Objection," said the Advocate almost casually. "Education and research are not climate crimes."

"Objection sustained," said the Auditor General. "Expand on the charge, Retributor."

"I maintain that he took his second PhD for sheer vanity, and for no other reason. He is thus guilty of display and squandering."

"Dr Hall, you may respond to the charge."

"Your honor, I did my second doctorate in history -"

"History has no relevance here!" interjected the Retributor.

"Objection!" called the Advocate. "The accused has not been given a chance to explain himself."

"Objection sustained. Retributor, one more outburst like that, and I shall have you audited for display."

"I apologize, your honor."

"Apologize to the accused."

"I apologize for having an excess of zeal in my defense of the Earth, Dr Hall."

"Do you accept that, Dr Hall?" said the Auditor General.

This was a very delicate moment. My only defense was to seem reasonable whenever the Retributor lost it and ranted.

"As long as it was only in defense of the Earth, yes," I replied.

"Continue, Dr Hall."

"I did my second PhD in order to put credibility behind my warnings about climate change. It was not display or squandering."

"Credibility? In what sense?" asked the Auditor General.

"I was studying links between a climatic event called the Little Ice Age and the witch burnings that took place in Europe from the Fifteenth to the Eighteenth Centuries."

A buzz of speculation rippled through the tiers of tippers and borderlines in the gallery. Even the auditors whispered among themselves.

"Ridiculous," said the Retributor. "The topic is frivolous."

"Not so. My research showed close parallels between the witch burnings and the National Audit."

This really was treading on the sleeping tiger's tail. I felt a drop of sweat trickle from an armpit and run down my ribs.

"Please, explain further," said the Auditor General, sitting forward and giving me her undivided attention.

"When the Little Ice Age became really severe in Europe, the number of witch trials and burnings increased. Witches were said to call up storms and cause frosts."

"Point of clarification," said the Auditor General. "Are you suggesting that witches caused the Little Ice Age?"

"Absolutely not, but records show that many people believed them to be responsible."

"Point taken. Proceed."

"When the cold weather caused crop failures and famines, people wanted someone to blame. Witches were plausible and vulnerable targets."

"Are you suggesting that this audit, here, today, is a witch trial?"

"Not at all."

"I'm sure we are all very relieved to hear that. Proceed."

"As I said, I did my second PhD to get credibility. As an expert in both history and climatology I thought my warnings about the consequences of climate change would be taken more seriously."

"You were warning the world about climate change as early as the 1980s," said the Retributor. "Why bother with the PhD after three decades of warnings?"

"Because I had spent three decades being ignored! By then I had to resort to warning the polluters and squanderers that young people might want revenge when human-induced climate change started to really take hold and affect economies and lifestyles."

"Young people, as in Generation Victim?"

"Yes. There would be whole generations of old tippers still alive to provide guilty and vulnerable targets. I published papers to this effect."

"I have the accused's papers on this subject available," said the Advocate. "To quote one keytag: 'Nuremberg-style trials of entire generations accused of crimes against the climate are entirely possible.'"

"Order! If the accused wishes to cite these papers, he must do so himself."

"That will not be necessary, your honor," I said.

"Dr Hall, the National Audit is secular, and sponsored by all victim citizens born in the new millennium. The Christian church initiated the witch trials, did it not?"

"Not so, your honor. Most witch trials were secular, and at the village level."

"Then what are you suggesting?"

"I am only relating history, and drawing parallels with the current situation. Popular anger has revived, this time due to human induced climate change."

"Is this a warning?"

"It's too late for warnings. The apocalypse is already happening."

"Enough, enough. You have demonstrated to my satisfaction that your second doctorate was in defense of the ecosphere. Honorable victims, who agrees?"

Eight hands were raised.

"Retributor, do you have any further accusations?"

"Yes, your honor."

"Dr Hall, you have just completed an eleventh successful defense of yourself, while consuming over an order of magnitude more of the audit bench's time and resources than is usual. Will you subject yourself to a twelfth and final audit tomorrow? The mandatory sentence will be Mines, without mercy, but the audit bench may also be forced to decide what to do with an audit that strays so far beyond the existing guidelines. Should you be designated a lifetime borderline, or should you be executed for squandering the resources of the audit bench? Our decision may not be fair or just, because we have a duty not to squander resources, even at the expense of someone like yourself."

"I want a twelfth audit, your honor."

"Then you shall have it, and face the mandatory sentence. Next audit?"

I was escorted back to the gallery by Warden Olivia, then hoisted shoulder high and carried to the top tier by a crowd of cheering borderlines. I could see the Auditor General banging her mace on her desk and shouting for order, but her voice was inaudible.

#

Nathan Buckley was brought in by two wardens. This was not because he was dangerous, but because of who he was. He was wearing a suit made from plastic garbage bags pinned into shape by scrap wire, and he maintained the bearing and authority of a politician in a national government.

"Nathan Buckley, former Minister for Mines," said the Clerk of the Bench.

"Retributor?" said the Auditor General.

"There is a very long list of primary charges, your honor. Should I squander resources with a reading of them?"

"No, just put them on our screens."

"Members of the audit bench, fellow victims," said the Retributor. "You are doubtless all familiar with the accused's notorious quote, which is on public record: *'Renewable energy has made coal so cheap that it would be economic madness not to utilize it in a new generation of coal-fired green power stations.'*"

"Response, Mr Buckley?" asked the Auditor General.

"My statement has been taken out of context."

"Clerk of the Bench, put the quote, in context, on our screens."

"*'The jury is still out on the link between climate change and human industrial activity,*" the Retributor read aloud. "*Until we have absolute scientific proof of such a link, we have a duty to support business as usual. Renewable energy -*"

"I was speaking in good faith!" protested Buckley.

"Order. Dr Jason Hall, you are hereby summoned as a technical witness," said the Auditor General. "Come forward and stand before the audit bench."

I stood, then had to walk all the way down from the ninth tier of the gallery. At last I reached the audit bench.

"Dr Hall, speaking as a scientist, would you say that absolute scientific proof is ever possible?" asked the Auditor General.

"No. The whole idea of the scientific method is to propose theories that fit your observations, then try to disprove them."

"Nathan Buckley, did you employ a qualified scientist to vet your speeches?"

"My speech writers worked to a brief attuned to the realities of -"

"In short, no. Members of the Audit, a show of hands for guilty? Guilty as charged. Nathan Buckley, I sentence you to Death, Class One, without mercy."

Buckley fell to his knees.

"I was only doing my job!" he cried. "The economy was in a negative growth situation."

His two wardens hauled him back to his feet.

"You were ignoring the plight of the ecosphere for personal and political advantage. Next audit?"

#

This was the first time I had seen an execution by Mines, without mercy. A tipping point board had been rigged over the mouth of a vertical mine shaft. Buckley sat on the end of the board while wardens filed past the tub holding down the other end, removing lumps of coal. Buckley was clutching a rope and was screaming incoherently. Chaz, Olivia and myself looked on, along with quite a large audience of wardens, tippers and borderlines.

"This is a really big day," said Olivia. "Not often we get to see a former minister sentenced to Mines, without mercy."

"I was once on a renewable energy committee with him," I recalled.

"Did he do much for the environment?" asked Gibson, who was the observing medical officer.

"No."

"The last politician to get Mines without mercy was a former prime minister. That was two years ago."

"So you don't get many?" asked Olivia.

"We used to, but hardly any are left. This audit was quite long compared to the others, who - There he goes!"

The board tipped and Buckley slipped off. He was still clutching the rope, but the weight of his body soon defeated his grip and he began to slide down the rope and into the pit. He continued screaming until after he was lost to sight. The babble of strange growls from deeper in the pit grew louder. His screaming intensified as he came within reach of the grasping hands at the bottom of the pit.

"Why don't they hurry up and kill him?" I asked, fighting back the nausea.

"They don't get much fresh meat, unless they eat each other," said Dr Gibson. "They might make him last a couple of hours."

Olivia nudged me playfully.

"Hey, they'll have you tomorrow if the audit bench says you're guilty. Bet you never thought you'd end up as main course."

This was not a good moment. Buckley's fate would indeed be mine if the judgment went against me. The wardens hauled at the rope - and it was immediately obvious that someone was clutching it. My first thought was that Buckley was still holding on, but as the rope was drawn up I saw that a pale, skeletal, naked man with long, straggly hair was clinging to it. He grimaced at me, showing teeth that had been filed into sharp points, perfect for tearing raw flesh. A shot from one of the wardens blew out the side of his head, and the body plunged back into the darkness. Growling and weakening screams continued to rise from the bottom of the pit.

"Come on, Dr Fitness," said Olivia. "Got to pick up the coal and bolt the hatch back over that shaft or the miners might climb out tonight and make a free supermarket of this place."

#

I was having lunch in the refectory field when the escapee Fitzgibbon finally gave up. He had struggled a further five miles after his companion suicided, but he was still not even a quarter of the way to the coast and the carbon dioxide extraction farms. Even if he had made it, he would have been collected by a patrol and put with the next caravan heading back for Audit Camp 71.

The announcements screen suddenly switched from general schedules and timetables to an overhead view of Fitzgibbon collapsed on the sand and lying still. I thought he was dead. So did the operator of the medi-drone, but as it descended the runaway tipper rolled on his back and sprayed it with a burst from his assault rifle. The picture was lost, but as before, the microphone survived.

"Got you, little fucker!" he called triumphantly. "If those chinless shits in green bowler hats want to watch me die, they can pay for broadcast rights."

"Unless he dies in the next thirty seconds, he's going to be a media star whether the Audit likes it or not," said Olivia, who had stopped beside me. "I bet the reserve drone is already moving in -"

The microphone picked up a single shot.

"- about now."

The backup drone did indeed arrive a few seconds later. It showed Fitzgibbon lying dead with the barrel of his rifle pressed beneath his chin and the top of his head blown away.

"He sure gave up his carbon the hard way," said Olivia.

"But he died free," I said.

"Does that make a difference?"

"To him, probably. Still, there's no place on the planet for his kind."

Have you ever watched as someone you dislike intensely goes into some sporting event against impossible odds, performs heroically, but is totally outclassed? That is how I felt. Fitzgibbon and his companions were everything that I despised and I wanted them defeated by the very landscape they had helped to create. Now they were dead, but it gave me no satisfaction.

On the screen the medi-drone had deployed sand grapples and was slashing Fitzgibbon's body open to desiccate in the sun. Very few of us were watching. That sort of thing happened every day in Audit camp 71, except that we prisoners did the slashing.

Had Fitzgibbon watched webcasts of my early audits, as I battled the Retributor and won? Had he wished me well, even though he despised me for what I am? For some perverse reason I wished he could have known if I beat the National Audit, but it was too late for him to know anything.

#

Later that afternoon Chelsea Garden died. Her real name was Chelsea Whyte, but to everyone except the auditors she was Garden. Chelsea was about eighty, and wore the backpack in which she carried what was supposed to be a forest where the spirit of the Green Man could shelter. The small bushes helped shelter her from the sun, and were the only greenery within the camp that was growing in soil.

People donated part of their water ration to keep the camp's biggest private garden alive, and one of those people was me. One did not go for a walk in the garden, one walked with the garden when one visited Chelsea.

Lawrence Payne was another walking garden. He wore an air plant called old man's beard woven into his real beard. Most remarkable of all was the borderline named Hanna who had waterweeds growing in bottles strapped to her belt.

Why were these fantastically resourceful people not in charge of Farm Field or working in the Antarctic universities, lecturing to young people about how to grow things in the most difficult of circumstances? If ever there was squander to be seen, it was the waste of these people on maintenance duties in Audit Camp 71.

Chelsea had been collecting desiccation stakes when she just pitched forward and collapsed without any warning symptoms or cries of distress. I was working nearby and was called over to help, but I could feel no pulse. Removing her garden pack and performing CPR did not produce any response. Dr Gibson arrived, pronounced her dead, and made an entry on his slate for the auditors.

"Massive coronary rupture," he guessed, "but we'll need an autopsy to be sure."

"Is anybody in authority going to care?" I asked.

"You know auditors, they like records better than they like people."

Word soon spread, and members of the Hands of the Green Man arrived to claim the portable garden. Its members said that the anarchic organization dated back to the end of the last ice age, and although I thought that a charming story, the scientist in me kept an open and very skeptical mind. The Greenhands each wore a wooden disk bearing the face of a bearded man framed by branches and leaves.

I was now surprised to discover that Gibson was actually some type of priest for the Greenhands. He carried a razor sharp chip of quartz, and with this he cut open one of Chelsea's fingers and squeezed a few drops of blood into the soil of her backpack garden. To mark the place, her wooden disk was cut from the cord around her neck and pressed into the soil. I counted eleven other disks in the soil of the backpack.

"Is my imagination out of control, or is that backpack a portable graveyard?" I asked Gibson.

"More of a shrine," he replied. "There's about two hundred Hands of the Green Man in the camp, and we need to maintain a garden to keep our lives in balance."

"So you Greenhands are a religion?"

"Yes and no. We have no gods and don't believe in souls, but a commitment to rebirth and renewal unites us."

He reached into his shirt and drew out a wooden disk on a whiskery string. Perhaps because of Fitzgibbon's death earlier that day, I was feeling particularly vulnerable. Fitzgibbon had been a fighter, like me. The National Audit had beaten him, and even though I would have voted for his death had I been an auditor, I still identified with him. Chelsea was entirely different, she was the sort of person who would try to keep a snowflake from melting in hell if there were a good enough reason. Gibson was the sort who would actually succeed.

I aspired to be like Dr Gibson, yet the idea that I was more like Fitzgibbon worried me. I had the absurd feeling that his troubled soul was traveling back to Audit Camp 71, even though I do not believe in souls. Would his malevolent shade paralyze my voice at the audit tomorrow, then chill my fingers until they lost strength as I clung to a rope dangling into the mine shaft?

I finally had to admit to myself that I could no longer go on alone, and I was indeed alone, even though I was a celeb and always the center of attention. Warden Olivia treated me as a well-fed cat might toy with a mouse under her paw. Chaz just wanted me around because working for a celeb had benefits. Alette charmed me, but I had the feeling that she could charm anyone if it suited her agenda, whatever that was. For Renny, the planet always came first. Gibson and the Greenhands were something entirely different. There was a chance that they might let me do what I always, desperately, wanted to: belong.

#

That night I approached Dr Gibson in Refectory Field.
"So what do I do to join up?" I asked.
"Join up?"

"Become a Hand of the Green Man."

"You are quite welcome to join now. You were spreading the words of climate truth long before Overshoot Day and the Tipping Point Year. Some of the Greenhands say that *you* really are the Green Man."

"That's going a bit far," I said, taking care to keep a straight face. "I don't worship anything, woodland spirits included. I'm certainly not one myself."

"Dr Hall, none of us worship, we just believe. That's enough."

"Believe in what?"

"Believe in renewal. Believe that our touch on the face of the Earth should be as soft as that of a falling leaf in autumn. Believe in the importance of giving back more than we take."

"I already believe in all that."

"Then you are already one of us."

"Who are us?"

"Two hundred borderlines, along with some wardens and the auditors."

"The *Auditors*?"

"Every one."

"Yet they audited you and made you a borderline?"

"Yes, and some Greenhands have even had their carbon reclaimed."

"That's terrible!"

"Why? Christian judges have been sentencing Christian felons to death for centuries."

Put that way, it very nearly made sense. Gibson reached into a coat pocket and drew out a wooden disk dangling from a loop of string. It was about the size of a retro dollar coin.

"Wear this, if you wish to identify yourself as one of us," he said.

I was so very, very tired of being alone. Although I am an agnostic, this was a group that had everything in common with my beliefs.

"Is there some sort of ceremony?" I asked.

"No. Just wear his face so people can see that you believe."

"Very well," I said, and reached for the disk.

There was scattered applause from the Greenhands nearby as I fastened the string around my neck, but that was as close as my initiation came to being a ceremony. A man named Jorge was now wearing the garden backpack, and I was permitted to touch the leaves of the little bushes to remind myself to fight for renewal.

"Why did you become a Greenhand, Dr Gibson?" I asked later, as we were leaving Refectory Field.

"Please, just Adam. In this place it is my job to see death all the time. Thinking of death as just one stage in a great cycle of renewal makes it easier to keep working."

#

"So what's this, then?" asked Chaz, pointing at my disk as I joined him in Entertainment Field.

"I've just joined an eleven-thousand-year-old cult," I said.

"You've become a Greenhand?"

"That's right."

"Why?"

"Because I've been a Greenhand for eighty-five years without knowing it."

"The Retributor might say it's just a stunt to get sympathy from the auditors."

"Then the Retributor can go screw himself."

Chaz laughed and nudged me with his elbow.

"He probably does."

The night's entertainment was an adapted episode of the television series *Blackadder,* but set in Audit Camp 71. The desperate gallows humor of the show was particularly popular with the audience. Edmund Blackadder was facing the auditors on a squander charge, for using too much toothpaste when he brushed his teeth. Baldrick was charged with neglect, for using too little. Both were sentenced to Mines, without mercy.

All through the performance I sat with a hand clasped over my little wooden image of the Green Man's face. For no rational reason at all it gave me a lot of comfort. Imagine an agnostic cowering in a graveyard and grasping a crucifix because there might be a vampire nearby. That was how I felt. The wooden disk connected me to people like Chelsea, Jorge and Gibson, who were the sorts of fighters and warriors that the Earth really needed. It reminded me that I was no longer alone, and that I had a duty to others.

Stand alone before overwhelming odds, and you feel like dead meat that's not yet dead. Stand between the enemy and those who are important to you, and you really do become stronger. I needed to be strong, because my final audit was only hours away.

#

DAY 13: NOT EEXTREME ENOUGH

Facing a sentence of Mines, without mercy, is not a good way to start any day. Worse, all of the wardens who escorted me from Refectory Field to the Audit Arena were new, apart from Olivia. They had arrived with the previous day's caravan, and while friendly in a general sort of way, they did not fit in. Even their assault rifles were different. What did this remind me of? My entire life, so far. For once I found myself relieved to be with Warden Olivia, in spite of her annoying humor about climatically correct death.

"Not the usual weapons," Olivia remarked to the squad leader as we walked.

"Just standard AK-47s," he replied.

"They have hundred-round drums."

"Seven times more shots, so less need to change magazines in a riot."

"You're expecting a riot?"

"Could be. Dr Hall is popular. If he gets audited guilty, it would make a lot of people very angry."

243

This was nothing like a casual conversation. His replies were fast, precise and monotonal, it was as if he were reciting dot points. Had there recently been a riot somewhere in the world where the wardens had been massacred? News of that would not have been put on the camp's news feeds. Were these wardens survivors from that massacre? If that were so, they would not be kindly disposed to someone like me.

The stands were jammed with borderlines, and they screamed my name as we entered the Audit Arena. Six of the women had dressed in identical and minimal electric blue rags and were waving bunches of blue plastic ribbons. I actually had a cheer squad:

"Doctor Hall!

Beat them all!

Rah! Rah!

Doctor Hall!"

True, the chant was nothing intellectual, but then what chant ever is?

"Order!" shouted the Auditor General, banging her mace on the top of her desk, to which a metal plate had been attached so that it would not splinter further. "First audit, Clerk of the Bench?"

It's as if she's pretending that the most significant audit in the history of the camp is just routine, I thought, and very nearly laughed.

"Twelfth audit of Dr Jason Hall, climatologist," said the Clerk.

There was renewed cheering and waving of ribbons as I was collected by Warden Olivia and marched to stand before the bench.

"Doctor Hall!

Save us all!

Rah! Rah!

Doctor Hall.!"

"Retributor, declare a charge," said the Auditor General once order had been restored.

"The accused is charged with being aware of the plight of the environment before the Tipping Point Year, yet not taking sufficiently extreme actions to raise public awareness."

"Dr Hall?" the Auditor General asked.

I turned to the Retributor.

"Extreme relative to what?"

"Extreme as in driving spikes into logs to be wood chipped, sabotaging oil rigs, smashing SUV windscreens, or spraying oil on auto race tracks."

"I believed that such extreme actions alienated the public, and so discredited the message of climate change."

"So you chose to neglect your duty to perform such actions?"

"Absolutely not," I said firmly.

"Then what did you do?"

"I lived an environmentally correct lifestyle that everyone else could and should have adopted."

"Please, tell us more."

"I turned off my television, DVD, microwave, stereo, and computer at the wall sockets when I was not using them. I installed energy efficient lights, used solar panels and rechargeable batteries, had two minute showers, washed my clothes in shower water, then used the same water to flush the toilet."

"And this was meant to save the world?"

"If everyone had lived like me, resource use would have plunged by sixty percent in industrialized nations. Apart from the solar panels, even people on low incomes could have done what I was doing,"

"That would not have saved the Earth."

"Not by itself, but it would have postponed the Tipping Point Year. That would have given us a realistic chance of developing and adopting technologies to save the planet."

"You should have publicized what you were doing."

"I did, whenever I spoke in conferences or to the media."

"We have the relevant records, your honor," said the Advocate. "Do you wish to see them?"

"Not necessary. Fellow victims, because this is the Twelfth Audit of Dr Hall, I am compelled to order a departure from our usual procedures. Clerk of the Bench, call up the relevant procedural regulation file and read out the details, if you please."

#

I was saved by some problem that the Clerk of the Bench had with the file. As I stood with Warden Olivia I noticed that all five of the new wardens who had escorted me were putting on ski masks.

"How long since there's been snow in Australia?" I asked, just as one of the wardens pointed his assault rifle at us.

I felt a massive blow, as if I had been struck with a mallet. Olivia collapsed across me. We lay still as gunfire erupted.

"You alive, Dr Fitness?" hissed Olivia.

"Sort of."

"Lie still, they don't know we got body armor. You hurt?"

"Ribs feel broken."

"Just think happy thoughts. Pretend we're having rec sex."

The five wardens turned on the audience of tippers and borderlines and opened fire together. The chatter of gunshots was almost continual, but I became aware that the sounds were growing fainter. That was strange, because the rogue wardens were not moving away. Then I remembered that in an extreme emergency the human body tends to shut down senses that are not needed. Eyesight? Vital! My vision was as sharp as you could imagine. Hearing? Who needs it when the people who are meant to be standing guard are doing the shooting? Touch? If you've been shot, live with it or die. Need to smell anything? Get real! Genuine wardens arrived at that moment and the attackers engaged them.

The auditors were out of sight, crouched behind overturned desks. The wardens at the entrance to the Arena were falling, but none of the attackers seemed to be getting hit. *Body armor*, I thought. *They've also got agamid fabric sewn into their uniforms, like my vest. Five times stronger than steel.* Except for Olivia, the wardens of Audit Camp 71 were not wearing armor, and the magazines of their assault rifles only held fifteen rounds.

With two attackers guarding the entrance, the three others climbed the tiers of the gallery, finishing off wounded borderlines as others leaped over the back tier. I saw members of my cheer squad dash up the steps and jump together. Although in their fifties and sixties, they were a lot fitter than most of the other borderlines in the gallery. Presently there was nobody moving in the Audit Arena, and the attackers made for the entrance. After a minute of listening to departing gunfire, I realized that I just might survive, and my body started winding down from hyper-survival mode. A quavering voice called out from somewhere nearby.

"Should we move?"

"Play dead, they're Anthrophobes!" called Warden Olivia. "They think we're all dead here."

Anthophobes. They were sure to be in Audit Camp 71 because of me. By now my audit was being Cloudcast to seventeen million viewers worldwide. Maximum coverage and maximum casualties, it made perfect sense. It was surprising that those in charge of security had not anticipated it.

Real wardens now streamed into the Audit Arena, and these were wearing sand-red body armor suits. It was not until they actually checked the auditors that I realized none of them had been killed. We were herded together.

"Anthrophobes, and they have body armor!" someone called, but that was already obvious.

It was soon decided that the Audit Arena was actually the safest place for us. The place was like a citadel within a fortress, and its single entrance was easily defended. As the only person present with medical experience, I was sent to the gallery to check for any who were still alive. The body of a member of my cheer squad was lying face down in the sand, and it suddenly filled my entire universe. She had put about 98% of her body on display and waved a couple of bunches of blue ribbons because she thought I was worth supporting. Now she was dead, her body covered by more of her blood than her bikini. I was furious because I wanted to thank her, yet she was dead.

After all the dead bodies that I had seen and handled, why should the sight of a dead woman in a ragged blue bikini have very nearly shut down my mind with grief? Perhaps it was because she had been one of *my* people, someone who had never met me but did not want me to feel alone. She had been shot in the back three times, and one of the wounds was level with her heart. She would have been frightened for a few seconds, then died instantly.

I managed to pull myself together and check a few more corpses. Most appeared to have been brought down by a disabling shot, then finished off with a bullet to the head. Elver Lyn was still sitting where she had been watching the audit, staring straight ahead, her eyes open. The bullet that had killed her had struck her forehead dead-center, and I remember thinking that the Anthrophobe who had killed her had probably been very proud of that particular shot.

I must have blacked out about then, because I was lying on the sand near the auditors and senior wardens when I came to my senses again.

"Those guys have armor and automatics," someone was shouting.

"We have weapons and armor for our people in case of attacks from outside," someone else replied. "Red gear is good, don't shoot at red. "

I sat up, and saw that Dr Gibson was there. He told me that I had been shaking Elver's body and screaming at her to wake up, but I did not remember that. He said that everyone who was still alive only had only minor injuries, and that I should stay with the auditors. I glanced toward the gallery, caught sight of the body in the blue bikini, and looked away so fast that my neck clicked.

Images from wardens' drone cameras were displayed on the auditors' laptop screens, and I watched the drones monitoring the camp's wardens as they tracked down the attackers. Both sides poured bullets into each other, apparently with no effect. In the midst of the exchange, a warden arrived with a combat shotgun. He knew how to use it to best effect, and aimed it at the head of an Anthrophobe. The agamid ski mask might have been strong enough to stop the lead, but not the shockwave of the impact. The man went down, but before he even hit the ground the warden fired again, hitting another in the head.

Standing over the two fallen attackers, the other three formed a shoulder to shoulder triangle which turned slowly, covering every approach to them. They concentrated their fire on the warden with the combat shotgun. He was unarmored, and quickly collapsed.

More of the genuine wardens arrived, and soon there were three or four dozen wardens for every surviving attacker. Some of the torrent of assault rifle fire struck one of the Anthrophobes in the head, and he fell. Olivia appeared on the screen, dashing across the sand and snatching up the combat shotgun without breaking stride. I screamed at the screen for her to take cover - then the two surviving Anthrophobes exploded! At first I thought that one of them had been wearing a suicide bomb, then I saw a real warden carrying a rail gun grenade launcher. Very slowly the camp's wardens advanced on the dead attackers. As I huddled with the auditors, a warden officer hurried through the Arena's gate.

"Thirty-seven dead in Refectory Field, your honor," he reported. "Three wardens, the rest borderlines, cleaning up after breakfast."

"In here there's at least three hundred tippers and borderlines dead, and eleven wardens," said the Auditor General.

"How did they get their weapons and armor in? Surely the other wardens in the convoy would have noticed?"

"If *all* wardens in the convoy were Anthrophobes, then nobody would have checked."

"There were twenty-five of them!"

"And ninety tippers. Some or all of the tippers may have been Anthros as well. The five from the Audit Arena took the weapons from the wardens they killed, and why bother doing that when their own weapons were so much better?"

"To arm their tippers, and any sleepers in the camp?" said Renny.

"Most likely, your honor, and we don't know how many of those there are. And there's one more issue."

"Tell me."

"Some Anthro hacked the comms server. The kill switch to the web feed was disabled."

"You mean the world is still watching?"

"Yes, your honor. Shall I have the cameras shot out?"

"No. We're going to win, and the rest of the world must see us win. Leave the cameras on until every last Anthrophobe is dead or captured."

At least a hundred and ten Anthrophobes were still loose in Audit Camp 71, and they would try to kill anyone showing signs of movement. The Oversight Warden and three of his staff arrived with iPads linked to drones, and these showed that four groups of five Anthrophobe wardens were working their way through the fields, killing whoever they encountered. A general alert was issued: any tipper with a weapon was liable to be shot on sight, along with any warden using a drum-feed magazine.

One screen showed an Anthrophobe group shooting out the locks over a mine shaft. One of them heaved a small cylinder into the pit, then the cover was hauled back into place.

"Probably sarin gas or some such," said the Oversight Warden. "The miners will be dead in a few minutes."

The Warden Commander joined us, running crouched over to our wagon-fortress.

"Reports coming in from the armory, they're under attack, but holding," he reported.

"Three paramedics and five nurses dead. They're trying to make sure that anyone who gets shot does not recover," said the Oversight Warden.

"Broadcast to all wardens," said the Warden Commander. "Repeat the order to target the heads of anyone with a drum-feed magazine."

I really wish I had not seen what happened next. Jorge, the man who had taken over Chelsea's backpack garden, blundered into view. I screamed at the screen for him to go back, but a stream of bullets from some Anthrophobe's automatic weapon shredded the portable garden as well as the man. Then and there, I would have cheerfully picked up a gun and shot every Anthrophobe in the entire camp. Had I become a religious fanatic for a few moments? I still wonder about that.

The Anthrophobes had a good tactical plan. Two attack cells out of five were moving on the armory, and behind them were several dozen tippers, probably from the previous day's convoy. The attack cells were meant to take the armory, which was guarded by just two wardens and their octant major. They would then arm the Anthrophobe tippers, who would spread out through the camp, killing whoever they found. There was just one flaw with this plan, which soon became apparent on our drone camera overview.

The two attack cells were moving on the armory, their ten assault rifles spraying as many as six thousand rounds per minute at the defenders. Suddenly they were obliterated in a cloud of red dust. As it cleared I saw that all of the Anthrophobes had been knocked off their feet. Some were still conscious, however, and I watched as they regrouped. Another explosion blotted them out again. One of our wardens had a rail gun grenade launcher.

"RGGL," said the Oversight Warden. "Body armor can stop some of the blast from a grenade, but you still feel rubber ducked."

"Language, warden," said the Auditor General.

A single figure walked out of the armory, and the Oversight Warden zoomed onto him. He was carrying a pistol.

"Duty octant major," said the Oversight Warden.

We watched as he calmly went from body to body, shooting the fallen Anthrophobes in the eye. After three shots he was cut down by a burst of assault rifle fire. Now the Anthrophobe tippers charged, at least two dozen of them armed with pistols and assault rifles from dead wardens. They wore no armor fabric, however, and were methodically killed by fire from the armory.

Incredibly, three of the Anthrophobe wardens from the first group survived, and they got to their feet and rallied their tippers for another charge. Even more incredibly, they had not yet learned that armored attackers in a tight group were a perfect target for someone armed with a rail gun grenade launcher. The third grenade from the armory hit the middle Anthrophobe, and they were wiped out.

It might sound like the wardens in the armory had all the advantages, but this was not the case at all. There were only two of them, one with an AK-47, the other with an RGGL. If the tippers had made a truly suicidal charge they could have overwhelmed the two defenders, but when the attack cell was blown apart they wavered. Another grenade fired into their midst broke the charge. Those with the guns were in front and were the first to die. The rest fled.

"Two Anthro cells still shooting," said the Oversight Warden. "Greenhouse Field and Farms."

"Issue coordinates to our people," said the Warden Commander. "Pin them down until we can get RGGLs from the armory."

Why was I allowed to remain in what had become a makeshift command center? Most likely because I was not in the way and nobody could be spared to remove me. It soon became apparent that even the unarmed Anthrophobe tippers were dangerous. They broke into seven attack cells of five each and went about cornering borderlines, holding them down and breaking their necks.

Orders were put out on the camp's public address system that all borderlines and tippers were to stay where they were and not move. This quickly identified the Anthrophobe cells. The drones hovered above them, marking them for the squads of real wardens. Two drones were shot out of the sky, but the camp had plenty more. In a way it was good tactics to have the enemy shooting at the drones. Hovering at a thousand feet they were difficult targets, and they made the Anthrophobes waste ammunition.

The cell in Greenhouse Field was wiped out next. The field was flat and without cover, and the Anthrophobes were working their way down the rows of glass tents, shooting those staked out inside - whether they were alive or dead. A squad of wardens arrived escorting three with RGGLs, but the Anthrophobes here were already spread out. It took thirty grenades to kill or disable them, and by then the glass panes of nine out of every ten greenhouse tents had been shattered.

The last of the cells could well have been the worst of all. They were in Farm Field because this was where a third of the camp's borderlines had been working. They could have killed more than all the other cells put together, but unlike Greenhouse Field, there were tanks, vats, storage sheds, pipes, carts and pumps to provide cover. Thus the borderlines were able to hide and dodge about, forcing the Anthrophobes to separate to hunt them down. Two Anthrophobes were mobbed by borderlines and beaten to death. Had the other three decided to use their weapons on the food production equipment, Audit Camp 71 would have been crippled, but their aim was only to kill as many people as possible. Our borderlines armed themselves with two captured AK-47s and pinned down one of the Anthrophobes in a storage shed.

"Give them a weapons exemption," said the Auditor General, who had been watching the screens as the wardens regained control of the camp.

"But they disobeyed a directive, your honor," replied the Warden Commander.

"If I pick up a gun and shoot at an Anthrophobe, would you have me shot?" she demanded.

"No, but -"

"Those borderlines are giving themselves and others a chance to be audited for climate crimes, commander. This is a prison, not a slaughterhouse. Remember that."

"As you will, your honor."

Over in Farm Field, at the nutrient ponds, another of the Anthrophobes found himself facing a warden with a combat shotgun. There was a brief but deadly exchange of fire that ended when a shotgun blast caught the attacker full in the face. I later heard that five of the pellets entered his mask's eyeholes.

By now the last two Anthrophobes were pinned down by the wardens. One was well barricaded behind a pile of pipes, and had realized that although he could not kill anyone else, he could put bullets into storage tanks and equipment. I watched as a drone was positioned directly above him, then something small and round fell from the drone, dwindling as it dropped. A cloud of fire and dust obliterated the scene, and once the smoke from the grenade's explosion cleared I saw that the Anthrophobe was held together only by his body armor.

A curious alliance developed between the borderlines and wardens at the siege of the storage shed where the single remaining Anthrophobe was holed up. After a standoff lasting an hour, the borderlines asked to be given body armor and shotguns to make what was sure to be a suicidal charge across open ground. Permission to do this had to come all the way from the Auditor General, and after another half hour they were ready to go. Gunfire from thirty wardens kept the Anthrophobe behind cover as the borderlines charged, lead by a warden with a combat shotgun. The screen display identified the warden as Olivia. They entered the shed, and I counted six shotgun blasts before all went silent.

A drone descended, and showed that the Anthrophobe and two borderlines were down. I later heard that the borderlines had shot each other in the confusion. The Anthrophobe was lying dazed on the floor, and I watched as Olivia pressed the barrel of her shotgun against an eye hole. Blood and brains poured out of the other eyehole when she pulled trigger. I turned away and tried to be sick, but there was nothing left in my stomach.

Bear in mind that it was not yet 9 am when the last Anthrophobe died. My very first act once the guns had fallen silent was to collect the bodies of the cheer squad woman and Elver, and I refused to let anyone else near them until Gibson fetched the other women from the cheer squad to tend them.

The borderlines and tippers of the camp were more than cooperative when it came to identifying the twenty-eight Anthrophobe tippers who had survived. Several had been long-term sleepers from within the camp. By noon the bodies had been collected and tagged, and weapons were being returned to the armory. All up, the hundred and twenty Anthrophobes had killed nineteen wardens and roughly six hundred tippers and borderlines. I say roughly, because the number of condemned tippers in the mines who were killed by sarin gas could only be estimated.

#

A special sitting of the audit bench was convened at noon. I had no interest in attending, but the Auditor General wanted people in the gallery for the sake of the drone cameras. Thus I was one of only a couple of dozen tippers and borderlines who were rounded up and made to watch. The surviving Anthrophobes were brought in by the camp's wardens, their wrists and ankles shackled. Olivia was one of the guards, and she was still carrying the combat shotgun. Her right leg was spattered with the dead Anthrophobe's blood and brains.

"Pick a representative," said the Auditor General.

"I am next in the chain of command, so I speak for all of us," said a small but wiry looking woman of about fifty as she stepped forward.

I recognized her as Vera, a borderline from the camp. Naturally I tried to remember whether Silvy and Vera had been friends, but I had never seen them together. Perhaps they had been working independently, but then I had never seen Silvy with any of the surviving Anthrophobes gathered here. In a camp holding eleven thousand tippers and border-lines this should not have been significant ... yet had she been deliberately avoiding them? Almost certainly, I decided.

"My name is Vera Laravis," the woman declared.

"Clerk of the Bench?" said the Auditor General.

"Verified, your honor. Been in the camp two years, borderlined on a charge of squander. All twenty-eight of these tippers have been identified as fighting with the An-throphobes. Twenty-three are from the caravan that arrived yesterday. The other five were sleepers from the camp."

"Charges, Retributor?"

"The accused are charged with first degree murder to obstruct the dispensation of climate justice to an estimated six hundred people accused of climate crimes, and being ac-cessories in the murder of nineteen wardens of the National Audit. All are also charged with high treason in support of espionage. I can produce video drone camera evidence."

"Advocate?"

"I have reviewed the video evidence, and am satisfied that the charges are indefensible, your honor."

"Laravis, how do you respond to the charges and video evidence?"

"Your honor, before the tipping year I was a solicitor -"

"Order!" barked the Auditor General, striking her desk with the mace. "Respond to the charges and video evidence with the words guilty or not guilty, or remain silent."

"Not guilty, your honor."

"In the face of clear video evidence that every one of your people participated in the fighting?"

"We are prisoners of war, and as such we are entitled to be held in accordance with the terms of the Geneva Convention."

"I am inclined to think that this was an act of terrorism. Comments, Retributor?"

"There is no doubt that all of those assembled here participated in the fighting," said the Retributor. "Not a single member of the caravan failed to assemble for the attacks, nor did any of them report suspicious activity to the camp's wardens. This suggests that the entire caravan was complicit."

"We do not need further convincing on that matter, Retributor. What of the borderlines who stand before us?"

"A review of the fixed camera record of this morning shows five borderlines of the camp taking the newly arrived convoy wardens on what turned out to be a tour of choice targets. There is a strong case for these five to be charged with high treason against the International Audit Movement."

"I am inclined to agree," said the Auditor General.

"We are warriors of the Neo-Cathar Alliance, which is at war with the National Audit!" Laravis shouted.

"Nobody is disputing that you are members of the Alliance," said the Auditor General. "The question is one of status. Is the Alliance an alternative government or a foreign power?"

"The Alliance is a revolutionary religious movement."

"You will have to do better than that. The distinction between guerilla organizations, revolutionary movements, gratuitous terrorism and blatant nihilism has become blurred since the mid-Twentieth Century."

"The Alliance is a revolutionary movement dedicated to the extinction of the human species for the welfare of the planet. The attack on Audit Camp 71 was in accordance with our aim of easing the burden on the ecosphere by reducing the number of humans."

"Which is at odds with the International Audit Movement, whose aim is to bring climate criminals to justice, while easing the burden on the ecosphere."

"We are not concerned with justice!" Laravis shouted.

"Order!" cried the Auditor General, striking her desk with the mace. "This is a legally constituted audit, not a consciousness-raising rally. As a lawyer you should know that."

"I will not apologize for being passionate on this subject. We conducted this attack in support of our faith. Remember, we used sarin gas in the mineshafts only, and did not release it into the biosphere where it might harm other species."

"Your concern for other species surprises me. Your group has claimed responsibility for the attacks that resulted in the extinction of gorillas, chimpanzees, bonobos and all tool-using monkeys. You also waged quite a determined campaign against crows, parrots and dolphins, but they were too dispersed and numerous to be wiped out."

"We of the Alliance believe that intelligence and tool use is evil by its very nature. Apes have been shown to wage war, and dolphins have been observed practicing pack rape, just as humans do."

"Domestic cats and dogs hunt for sport, male lions practice infanticide on the cubs of defeated alpha males, and even ants keep slaves. Do you propose to kill them all for doing what a minority of humans did?"

"There is no doubt that humans are by far the worst offenders when it comes to crimes and atrocities. Intelligence combined with tool use must be wiped out. Our perfecti teach that some behaviors mimicking human behaviors that are not a product of intelligence can be overlooked. They do not endanger the planet."

The Auditor General now sat back with her arms folded and stared at the screen of her laptop. All around the world other auditors were watching, listening and providing opinions that were streaming into her earpiece and scrolling across her screen. I sat in silence, thinking how disturbingly similar Vera was to Silvy.

"There are divergent approaches to common problems at work here," the Auditor General said presently. "The Neo-Cathar Alliance cannot stop ants keeping slaves, except by wiping out specific species of ants. The National Audit cannot eliminate the desire of some humans to accumulate wealth and display it to other people - otherwise known as the climate crimes of greed, display and squander. The difference between us is that we consider those behaviors to be criminal acts, to be kept under control, while you consider all intelligence to be criminal. Our two ideologies are at war, although both have the welfare of the planet as the objective."

"Intelligence will destroy the biosphere!" insisted Laravis.

"Order! An asteroid strike could destroy the biosphere as just effectively, but science has never found any evidence that asteroids are intelligent nihilists. Intelligent humans built the Skywatch telescope system and maintain an arsenal of fifty missiles armed with hydrogen bombs that can deflect or destroy any asteroids that threaten the planet. How do you respond to that?"

"Asteroid strike is a natural process."

"As natural as ants keeping slaves or lions killing the cubs of rival males? No matter, this is not a forum for ideological debate. I am satisfied that this morning's attack on Audit Camp 71 was an act of terrorism. As such, it involved the mass slaughter of civilians, but with no military objective. This fits the definition of a war crime."

"We had an objective -"

"Order!" shouted the Auditor General, striking her desk plate several times. "One more outburst like that and I will order you gagged. You had an ideological objective, just as the Nazis did when they slaughtered Jews and gypsies last century. Murder for ideological or religious motives is still a crime in the eyes of the International Audit Movement, even though it is not a climate crime.

"I am also satisfied that the self-declared Anthrophobe warriors were not engaged in a recognized act of war, but intended to kill every inhabitant of Audit Camp 71 while a very high profile audit was being Cloudcast to the entire world. This constitutes obstruction of climate justice. We of the audit bench are not here to commit mass murder. *Everyone* must be audited against what are legally considered to be climate or civil crimes. Honorable members of the audit bench, fellow victims, who finds the charge of high treason for obstructing climate crime justice upheld?"

Every auditor's hand rose.

"Espionage, where it applies?"

Again, the verdict of the auditors was unanimous, and that verdict was guilty.

"The Neo-Cathar Alliance does not recognize -" began Laravis.

"Gag her!" ordered the Auditor General.

Three wardens converged on the Anthrophobe leader, while the other wardens trained their weapons on the rest of the group. The gag was a plastic ball encased in a strip of cheesecloth.

"On the six hundred charges of first degree murder, who finds guilty?"

Again, all auditors raised their hands.

"The sentence for all those crimes is death, but espionage and obstructing justice are not climate crimes," the Auditor General now declared. "According to my interpretation of the guidelines for reclaiming carbon, if the crimes are not climate crimes, they cannot be punished by such devices as Greenhouse Tents or Rising Sea Level tanks. The guidelines only specify that executions must have a minimum impact on the environment.

"At my discretion the five borderlines from this camp who spied for the Anthrophobe Alliance are sentenced to death by hanging on a traditional gallows. The surviving wardens and tippers from yesterday's convoy are deemed to be enemy combatants who engaged in war crimes, and are hereby sentenced to death by firing squad. Bullets and shell casings will be recovered for refurbishment and re-use. The sentences will be carried out directly after the rising of the audit bench. Clerk of the Bench, is there any more business to be conducted today?"

"There is the matter of the borderlines of the Camp who took up arms in defiance of an order from the Warden Commander," said the Clerk of the Bench. "There are thirty-one individuals involved."

"Move the Anthrophobes clear and bring the borderlines before the bench."

It would be fair to say that the borderlines looked anxious as they were herded forward by the wardens. There was a lengthy pause as the Retributor, Advocate and Clerk of the Bench conferred.

"Your honor, this case involves a breach of regulations," the Retributor declared once they had returned to their positions. "A clear directive had been issued forbidding tippers and borderlines to take up arms, and the borderlines assembled here can be proved to have done so by video evidence. The prescribed sentence for this charge is death."

My impression was that although he was pressing for the death sentence, the Retributor's heart was not in his words.

"Advocate?" said the Auditor General.

"They did not commit a climate, civil or military crime," she said with a great deal more conviction. Had she learned defiance from me? "If the borderlines who stand before the audit bench had killed Anthrophobes with their bare hands they would have been honored as heroes. Several of them were wounded, and fifteen others gave their lives in the fighting. Video evidence shows none of the accused assembled here shooting at wardens, and I put it to you that the two borderlines who were killed by fellow borderlines lost their lives in what is termed the fog of war."

"Clerk of the Bench?"

"I have a petition from a witness who wishes to speak on behalf of the accused."

"Proceed."

Nobody was really surprised when the Warden Commander walked forward to stand before the audit bench.

"Your honor, I wish to expand upon the intent and execution of my orders," he said. "Is this permissible?"

"Go on."

"Three borderlines not engaged in combat activities were mistakenly shot by my wardens this morning. Enquiries about the circumstances have been conducted, and the wardens cleared of any charges involving the obstruction of climate justice. Mistakes can be made in what you have rightly described as the fog of war."

"Accepted."

"In the same way, I maintain that I made an error by issuing a blanket prohibition against any borderlines and tippers taking up arms against the Anthrophobe attackers. It was a confused situation and I issued a simple but flawed order. If these borderlines are given the ultimate sentence for doing what they did, then I too should be charged, found guilty and have my carbon reclaimed."

"Thank you, Warden Commander, but charges are the province of the Retributor," said the Auditor General. "The audit bench hands down the verdict and I do the sentencing. I would like to add, however, that there does not seem to be a precedent for borderlines coming to the assistance of wardens in direct violation of orders. My feeling is that their actions should have been described as aiding wardens in direct violation of an order. Members of the bench, honorable victims, do you agree?"

Six hands were raised in agreement, two auditors abstained.

"My finding is that there is no charge to answer. Further, these borderlines have clearly fought for climate justice, and should be rewarded for what they did. Clerk of the Bench, reassign their names to the bottom of the register for re-auditing. The audit bench is hereby adjourned in order to witness the executions that have just been passed."

As we dispersed, I was suddenly filled with optimism. This latest verdict actually supported my own audit. If borderlines could be rewarded after fighting for climate justice, there might be other legal bolt holes through which more people of good will could escape.

#

There was a delay of two hours while the tipping point gallows was modified so that a trapdoor that could be released by a lever operated by the Warden Commander. This was because the condemned prisoners were considered to be members of a military force engaged in acts of terrorism, and the Executioner was only licensed for climate justice. I had little to do for most of that time, and I was hard put to keep Silvy out of my mind. She had seduced me, yet all the while she had intended to kill me. Try as I might, I could not come to terms with that.

I was assigned to help haul a pushcart with the five bodies of those who had been hanged. Kate, a woman from my cheer squad who had been a dance teacher, was on the other side of the harness, and was still in her cheer squad bikini. As can be imagined, Desiccation Field was crowded with borderlines staking out the dead. There was a distant blast of gunfire as we lifted Vera Lavaris's body from the cart. Kate cringed down by the cart at once.

"The military executions must be by firing squad," I said. "That is, if you can call three wardens a firing squad."

"Why so few?"

"They're using hollow point bullets, so even three is over-kill."

"Will anyone take it up with the Auditor General?" Kate said, shaking her head. "Will someone be charged with climate crimes for squander?"

More gunshots echoed across to us.

"Hanging is for treason, but a firing squad must be used to off war criminals or terrorists," I explained. "Inventive variations on climate change consequences can only be used to reclaim the carbon from everyone else."

I turned away and hammered stakes into the sand as Kate stripped the rags from Lavaris's body. There was an informal, unspoken convention that men stripped the bodies of male corpses, and women attended to those of women. Shots from the distant executions continued in the distance. We dragged Lavaris between the stakes and spread eagled her, then I left Kate to slash the skin open.

"Sixty-nine bullets to execute twenty-three people," she said as she worked. "That means forty-six bullets wasted. I thought Generation Victim people were against waste."

"The idea with firing squads is to share responsibility among the shooters. The death must be due to the squad, not an individual."

We pulled the next body off the cart. The man had been heavily built for a borderline, and we struggled to move him. The sound of another execution reached us as I removed his clothes.

"Ejaculated," said Kate as I handed her the trousers. "I hate it when they do that."

"Some people just don't think."

Cutting people open still gave me the creeps, even after the long trip there through the desert and a fortnight in the camp.

"Careful what you're doing with that knife," said Kate. "It looks like you're doing it with your eyes closed."

"I am."

She sighed and reached out a hand.

"Give it here."

I stood back with considerable relief and let her work. We were staking out the third body when the sound of the tenth execution reached us.

"We're going to be late for the firing squad bodies," I said. "Dump the other two so we can take the cart back for another load,"

"We're supposed to stake all of them out first."

"We can do that later, they're not going anywhere."

#

As we pulled the cart past one of the mine shafts we saw a wooden crane on wheels being pushed up to the head of the pit by several dozen borderlines. Dangling from the crane was a makeshift plug that was to be lowered to seal the shaft, keeping the sarin and decomposition gases out of the atmosphere. This was probably the same crane that had been used to stack the cars that made up Audit Camp 71's wall, towers and Entertainment Field stands.

"Hey there, Dr Fitness, you must be relieved that both the mines are being sealed," called Warden Olivia, who was standing guard with her assault rifle.

"They'll think of something as bad, or worse," I replied.

"In the other camps you get Release, without mercy. That's when -"

"The prisoner gets released outside the camp without food, water or weapons."

"Too cool, you know already. Hey, and next time I get an excuse to jump on you, make sure you got your clothes off."

Kate and I tramped on with the empty cart.

"Have you ever, like, with her?"

"Do I look suicidal?"

She laughed.

"Some say Release is worse than Mines," she said. "If there's any insects where you collapse, they begin eating your body before you die."

"And generating greenhouse gases as they digest you," I replied. "Should they be audited for climate crimes?"

"What is Release *with* mercy?"

"That's when you get given a phial of poison that you can drink at any time."

"Works for me."

"It's not as humane as you think. The poison is an acid that hurts like hell for the half hour it takes to kill you."

"I knew there'd be a catch. Speaking of suffering, did you hear about the Auditor General?"

"What about her?"

"Caught a bullet in the arm. She tried to keep it to herself so she could stay in charge, but one of the wardens saw blood dripping from her when the executions started and called Dr Gibson. The Warden Commander took over from her."

I felt as if I were floating on air as Kate and I continued on with the cart. My granddaughter, concealing a gunshot wound so that she could keep doing her duty. Why couldn't she have been *my* daughter? In spite of who she was and what she was doing, I was so proud of Renny.

I heard the shots that announced the eighteenth death as we approached the sand mound and post where the executions were taking place. As Kate had said, the Auditor General was not there.

We began loading bodies into the cart as the nineteenth Anthrophobe was being tied to the post. All of the bodies we were loading had two shots to the head and one to the heart. The wardens stood only ten paces from those being executed, because bullets were not to be squandered. A paramedic was with them to certify the deaths. I looked up as the Auditor General and Dr Gibson appeared in the distance, walking toward us.

"Present arms!"

That was the Warden Commander, raising a sword that had probably been part of some senior officer's parade ground uniform in the distant past.

"Take aim!"

"That girl just can't delegate," I began as Kate and I heaved another body onto the cart.

"Fire!"

The rifles fired as the sword swept down, and the body of the man tied to the post exploded with a blast that merged with the collective rattle of gunshots. Even though we were more than fifty yards away from the explosion, we were knocked off our feet. A moment later one of the wardens got up. Apparently he thought that one of the remaining four Anthrophobes had something to do with the explosion. As he sprayed them with a burst from his AK-47 there was a second explosion. The dust settled to reveal a scatter of body parts and shreds of clothing.

#

My first thought was for Renny, but she was nowhere to be seen. The wardens of her escort had apparently hurried her to safety after the first explosion. It did not take long to establish that there was nobody alive who had been anywhere near the execution post. Kate had been shielded from sprays of ceramic shards by the cart, but I stopped two of them with my body armor. As we stood about awaiting orders, Dr Gibson arrived, assessed the scene and inspected what was left of the bodies. The camp was now down to one properly qualified paramedic, so because I knew first aid I was delegated acting paramedic status and put to work.

"Seven wardens and five Anthrophobe prisoners killed in two blasts," Gibson explained. "Metal detectors picked up nothing when the prisoners arrived, so I would guess that Semtex with a ceramic shockwave detonator and ceramic fletchettes had been surgically implanted in place of the left lung. The shockwave from a bullet striking the explosive would set off the detonator, killing everyone within about ten yards."

"The Warden Commander was at ground zero for the first explosion," I reported.

"Then someone gets a promotion, Dr Hall, but it will not be either of us. Collect the bits and try to sort them into warden and Anthro piles."

The bodies and body parts of the wardens were stretchered away to Cemetery Field, which was reserved for camp staff. After being desiccated and sealed in plastic, they would be buried there and even get a small headstone and a metal plaque. It took five trips for us to transport the remains of the Anthrophobes to Desiccation Field.

"You can bet that from now on firing squads will be using AK-47s with telescopic sights at four hundred yards," I said as we collected the last load.

Gibson had us reconstruct the bodies in Desiccation Field. The fragments of those who had harbored plastic explosive bombs were scattered about on the sand to dry, while the ceramic fletchettes had flayed the other three so badly that we did not even need to slice their skin to let their body fluids evaporate. The sun was low in the sky before we were finished. The pile of ragged, bloodstained clothing in the cart was almost as heavy as a load of bodies as we hauled it along to Recycling for Alette's attention.

#

The bugler played "Goodnight Irene," but on this day work did not stop with sunset. The camp was a mess, so restoring such facilities as food production and waste disposal was given priority. Although there were six hundred dead, there were a further fifteen hundred with wounds of varying severity, and the camp was not set up to handle mass

SEAN MCMULLEN

casualties. In Recycling, unused clothing was being boiled, dried and cut up for bandages. The supply of antiseptics and antibiotics quickly ran out, and even bottles of bootleg spirits, distilled in secret by the borderlines, were donated and pressed into service while more supplies were being flown in.

While attacks on audit camps were not unknown, Audit Camp 71 was one of the most remote on the planet, so it was unexpected. Even reaching the place with a credible force required a major effort, so the possibility of conflict between the wardens and well-armed, trained infiltrators had never been considered. Dating Field was renamed Infirmary Field, but there were only enough trained staff to cope with thirty wounded at any one time. Most people with any formal medical training were dead, and there were fifteen hundred patients laid out on blankets and groaning, so anyone who had ever done a course in basic first aid was made a nurse.

There was a bright side for the auditors in the wake of the massacre and battle. Audit Camp 71 was now three weeks ahead of quota for executions, carbon reclaimings, mass murder, easing the burden on the biosphere, or whatever you feel like calling violent and brutal death in that place.

We paused to look up as parachutes marked by flares descended. Twelve hours after the attack, the first of the slow but carbon-neutral solar aircraft had arrived with medical supplies, food concentrate, spare parts, tools, engineers, wardens and paramedics. It went without saying that there was no event in Entertainment Field that night, and it was past midnight before I climbed into my trench in Dormitory Field.

#

I had ideas about falling asleep within a seconds of lying down, but on this night there was a background clatter and babble as damage was repaired and rubble was cleared away.

271

There were also groans and screams from the direction of Infirmary Field, and occasional shots as some borderlines lost patience with wardens, argued the point when given orders, and were functionally stabilized in a prompt and efficient manner.

I could tell when the Auditor General was approaching even in the dimly lit gloom of Dormitory Field at night. The wardens patrolled singly or in pairs, but she was always escorted by two guards. She held up a hand and the guards stopped, then she walked on until she was standing before me.

"Will this take long?" I asked.

"I'm afraid so."

"I've been working in the sun all day."

"The Earth has been in the sun all day, as have I. Come along."

I got up and walked with her, stiff and aching from my nineteen hour day. She led me between the dimly lit sleepers, while her guards followed at a distance.

"I heard you were shot," I said as we walked.

"He was probably aiming at the bagpiper. I was told you were not hurt in the explosions."

"Just bruised ribs from where my armor stopped two fletchettes. I continue to be lucky, just as I am in the Audit Arena."

"That's good, because we are going there."

From what I could see by the light of the solar security lanterns, the place had been put back in order - although there were quite a few bullet holes in the gallery seats and auditors' desks. All seemed ready for sunrise and the first audit, which would be mine.

"What's the occasion?" I asked. "Tea, cakes and old family photos?"

"No."

"Then why bring me here?"

"This is related to your audit. Think back two weeks. How would you have sentenced James Harrington?"

"Meteor Man? He was just a fool who never checked his carbon footprint."

"But how would you have sentenced him?"

"Service, Second Class, in wilderness restoration."

"Really? He chose to ignore the plight of the wilderness he loved. He was like a doctor fondling a woman's breast, yet not telling her she has breast cancer."

That image was rather confronting. I folded my arms and looked down at the sand, which seemed black in the dim light.

"Are you saying there was no hope for him?" I asked.

"I am saying he was indulgent, and would have always put his own pleasure and interests first if he had lived. I ask again, how would you sentence him?"

"Death, I suppose, but only Class Six, Tipping Point Gallows, with mercy."

"Which was my sentence. What of Sara Robbins, the woman who followed him onto the tipping gallows?"

"I don't remember her case."

"She built a fourteen-room house just to impress her friends, and vacationed on cruise ships three months out of every twelve."

"Guilty, for aggravated display and squandering."

"And your sentence?"

"Service, first class. Half a lifetime of healing the environment as punishment for half a lifetime of screwing it."

"She would have taken all day to plant a single tree, and probably need help to even do that. What would be better for the Earth?"

"Class Six Death, with mercy," I sighed.

"I agree. She was an idiot who never stopped to think or look around at the real world. No need for her to suffer."

And so it went. Hundreds of people had faced the Audit since I had arrived, but only a dozen cases had been adjourned as borderlines. My amazing, ruthless granddaughter remembered every name, crime and sentence.

"What about Craig Brand? He built super-tuned engines for street racers and was a paid-up member of the Climate Change Deniers Party."

"Guilty. Death, Class Four, with mercy."

"Death by being force fed motor oil, then put in a greenhouse? That's strict, for you."

"Fools I can forgive. Vindictive psychopaths deserve what they get."

"And yourself, Jason Hall?"

"Innocent."

"There is no such verdict."

"Then I should be pardoned for being born when I was, and into the society of the time"

"You are less severe than the audit bench. Out of all the cases I presented, your first preference was death for only three of them."

"I feel more compassion for tippers than you auditors."

"Why?"

"Most were fools, not monsters."

"Fools caused more damage than monsters before the Tipping Point Year. Most monsters got caught and locked up. The fools were left free to do more damage."

"True, but some fools were harmless. The Audit Camp 71's bench has a perfect record, it's always death or borderlining for tippers."

"Is this bad?"

"Yes! Some fools just deserve service, branding, or even a pardon."

"Many audits are adjourned. Remember the borderlines?"

"The borderlines live in slavery, and do nothing to repair their own damage to the climate."

"They're performing services, not living in slavery."

"Same thing."

"Would you abolish the National Audit?"

"No, but you auditors must be seen to have good will or you will look like a pack of Nazis."

"We like to think of ourselves as more like the judges in the Nuremberg trials, holding Denialist Climate Nazis to account."

"You're not real judges. To you, everyone born before 2000 is a denialist, guilty of climate crimes."

"That may well be true."

"Prove it."

"Very well, and you can be my shadow auditor. If you can beat the Audit, I shall judge all the borderlines accordingly."

#

DAY 14: SQUANDER BY INACTION

Warden Olivia woke me at halflight.

"Dr Fitness, rise and shine!"

"If the sun's not shining, I don't have to."

"Don't be like that. This is the first day of the rest of your life."

"And the last."

"Yeah, but if the Anthros hadn't attacked yesterday, you might have had your carbon reclaimed already. Look on the bright side, you're ahead by one day."

Alette met me in Refectory Field.

"Here, you might need these," she said softly.

She handed me three small black spheres.

"Illicit drugs?" I asked.

"Genuine chocolate coffee beans, to get your mind fired up. They are more potent than the watery mud that passes for coffee here. These three are worth a thousand neo dollars, I got them for five Viagra coupons."

"Thank you."

"Not just me, Dr Gibson chipped in."

I crunched and swallowed the three beans, then started on the rest of my breakfast.

"You didn't offer me these yesterday."

"You had not been deprived of sleep yesterday. The attack has really shaken up the auditors. Three of them were wounded, and two more took bullets through their cloaks. That's five close calls, and it might work in your favor."

"Why so?"

"Some borderlines fought for the camp, and a few of those were killed. That's good symbolism, it shows that tippers of good will can really support the National Audit and contribute to climate justice. Hold together, Jason, the rest of your life is only an hour away."

#

If one did not look too closely, the damage from the massacre the day before did not really stand out in the halflight, yet the mood of the camp was entirely different. Rumors were spreading that the attack had been launched to stop my audit, because the Anthrophobes had something to lose if even one Generation Tipper was found worthy of a pardon. Why was this? I heard several theories from Alette while I was eating my breakfast, but none of them made any sense.

People like a good show, especially after a close encounter with death, so the gallery of the Audit Arena was again packed and people were sitting on the steps. I was not surprised to see upwards of fifty heavily armed and armored wardens standing guard - and risking heatstroke. There was the usual procession of auditors, and my cheer squad was back. Each of the survivors was wearing a black armband.

"Doctor Hall,

One last goal,

Score! Score!

Doctor Hall."

The Auditor General did not call on the Clerk of the Bench to announce the first audit, and for the first time she remained standing when she reached her desk.

"I need not remind anyone present about what happened yesterday," she began, her left arm now in a sling and her right hand still holding her mace. "At last count the total number of deaths had risen above eight hundred, and the doctor estimates that deaths directly resulting from the attack will reach a thousand once the weaker patients die."

She paused to let this sink in. The massacre had done the impossible by making the audit bench look reasonable.

"Canisters of sarin gas were dropped into both of the mine shafts being used for the disposal of desiccated bodies," she continued after letting us think on the sheer magnitude of the figures. "This means that all those sentenced to Mines are dead. It also means that the mines are inaccessible because they have been sealed off while detoxification equipment is flown in. For this reason I have adopted the default Class One punishment of many other audit camps sited in deserts. Death by Mines will become Death by Release. Clerk of the Bench, please explain."

"Death by Release with mercy means you are turned out of the camp with no supplies or equipment other than a phial of poison. Release without mercy means no poison. All outposts and camps within a five hundred mile radius will be alerted to not assist you in any way, and you will be tracked by solar drones."

"Thank you, Clerk of the Bench. First audit of the day?"

"Continuation of the twelfth audit of Dr Jason Hall, climatologist, who is now facing a sentence of Release, without mercy."

SEAN MCMULLEN

Whatever was in store for me over the next few minutes had to be an anti-climax after what had happened the day before, yet there was still a strong atmosphere of anticipation and interest. I walked up to my assigned place with Warden Olivia beside me, backed by enthusiastic cheering.

"This continues the twelfth hearing of your audit, Dr Hall," said the Auditor General. "You have broken all records for survival, but consumed many times your share of National Audit resources."

"With respect, your honor, the audit bench has consumed the resources," I pointed out.

"Not so. You were in a reserved occupation, so your audit would have been postponed indefinitely. In the time taken to audit you we could have sentenced a hundred less difficult tippers to have their carbon reclaimed."

"I believe that my audit is an important precedent, your honor."

"Believe what you will, this audit has gone on long enough. Your default sentence is currently Class One Death, without mercy. However, to prevent further squandering of the Audit's time I will allow you to accept borderline status here and now."

"I choose to continue."

"Very well. Retributor, please proceed."

"When the Anthrophobes attacked, we were about to view the regulations regarding procedures for a tipper beating twelve charges. The members of the audit bench discussed that file after the attack on the camp, so we can now proceed with a vote for guilt or dismissal. The accused is charged with being aware of the plight of the environment before the Tipping Point Year, yet not taking sufficiently extreme actions to raise public awareness."

"Members of the audit bench, fellow victims, who votes to dismiss the charge?"

279

Four hands were raised.

"Guilt?"

The four other hands went up.

"Clerk of the Audit, I place my casting vote for dismissal."

The cheering that erupted in the gallery was quickly taken up by the borderlines in the rest of the camp, and the ladies of my cheer squad jumped and gyrated through their routine until they slumped to the sand with exhaustion.

"Doctor Hall

Beat them all!

Twelve goals!

Doctor Hall."

The cheering outside the Audit Arena was still going on when the Auditor General and wardens finally managed to restore order.

"Retributor, have you any comment?" she asked.

"It is my position that the accused's entire generation is guilty, so he must be guilty."

"Objection," called the Advocate. "The accused is being audited, not his generation."

"Objection sustained. Retributor, if the accused's entire generation were being audited, there would have been just one audit and several million carbon reclaimings. Have you anything else to say?"

"Your honor, I could bring thousands more charges against the accused, but I cannot because of audit regulations to prevent squander. My current position is unprecedented, because technically I am in conflict with existing law. I wish to appeal to you for advice on how to proceed."

"What advice can I give? If the accused has endured twelve audit hearings, no further charges can be brought against him."

"I maintain that the accused must not be pardoned, and remains guilty."

"Indeed? Explain yourself."

"Nobody from the accused's generation has ever demonstrated grounds for a pardon."

"That is not proof of individual guilt."

"I believe that they all are guilty."

"Belief is not evidence."

"That is my honest belief, your honor."

"Your concerns and dilemmas are noted, and shall be taken into account. Anything else?"

"Only this. The easy solution would be to declare the accused a borderline."

"He cannot be declared a borderline without his explicit consent, that is also the law. Dr Hall, do you give that consent? The resources put into this audit must not be squandered."

"I do not, your honor," I replied.

"Advocate, any comments?"

"Your honor, Dr Hall must be audited, not his generation. That audit must be decided on the merits of the evidence."

"Noted," declared the Auditor General. "Auditors of the bench, after the carbon reclaimings this afternoon we shall discuss the proposition that Dr Hall is currently committing squander by inaction before this very audit bench. This might amount to a new climate crime, committed over the fortnight past, and it most certainly can be audited within existing law. We shall deliver our verdict tomorrow at dawn."

For a moment she stared into space from behind her sunshades, as if she thought there was something still hanging in the air. I felt as if a huge rock had been lowered onto my shoulders. So this had been their plan all along. In order to beat the audit, I had to commit a climate crime! Did I look crushed? I certainly felt that way.

"Dr Hall, the law states that the sentence must be escalated to the next most severe level in the event of an adjourned audit," she continued. "You are currently at the most severe level, so I cannot escalate your sentence. This means I cannot adjourn your audit. Tomorrow I will deliver a verdict, and the mandatory sentence is death by Release, without mercy. For the very last time, will you accept borderline status?"

I might have been crushed, but I was also very angry. Anger is an excellent fuel when all one's other resources are gone.

"I will not, your honor."

"Audit adjourned until tomorrow. Clerk of the Bench, please note a suspension of standard procedures, then stand ready."

#

My audit was over, but there was no result. I had not anticipated this, and neither had anyone else. The feeling of frustration was almost strong enough to force tears from my eyes as I was walked back to my seat, and although I was cheered, the cheering lacked conviction. People patted me on the shoulder, called "Well done!" and offered me their water rations, but all I could do was sit there with my face in my hands.

No verdict! My mind dropped into a sort of panic mode. Would the auditors postpone their verdict indefinitely? I might become a sort of default borderline, with the verdict postponed every day for the rest of my life because laws covering squander prevented the audit bench from spending any more time on my case. All my work, all that suffering, would have been for nothing.

My eight and a half decades were now pressing down on me very, very heavily. Was one of those hands patting me on the shoulder that of Death?

"There are five more audits pending this morning, but first there is an announcement that is to be broadcast to all of Audit Camp 71," said the Auditor General. "Clerk of the Bench, please switch me through to the public address network of the camp."

I looked up.

"Attend the Auditor General!" called the Clerk of the Bench through the PA system.

"Generation Victims and Generation Tippers of Audit Camp 71, I wish to inform you that the Anthrophobe Alliance has launched coordinated attacks on audit camps across the continent. Seventy other camps have reported massacres, apparently signaled by the attack on this audit camp yesterday. As you may know, the Anthrophobes have killed considerably more people in earlier attacks over the years, but the attack on this camp gave them far better media coverage. Apparently the idea was to spread the message that human extinction is a good thing. The National Audit may seem harsh, but it is not about murder. Everyone gets an audit, so everyone has a chance."

I had no sympathy at all for the Anthrophobes. To become an Anthrophobe you just had to be sterilized and to perform at least one killing in the cause of human extinction. You then qualified to be hidden and protected as long as you performed one killing every week, on average. This made membership attractive to anyone with homicidal tendencies. It also meant that even speaking in favor of Anthrophobe practices was liable to get you shot on sight by the wardens of the National Audit.

The Auditor General read out figures. Six thousand had been killed during the day just past. That was over eighty-six per camp, at the cost of two thousand Anthrophobe lives. This would have disappointed the Anthrophobe leaders, because it was a very low kill ratio. Of course it was possible that the National Audit was falsifying the figures, but how to tell? Actually I was inclined to believe the National Audit, because auditors like to be precise about statistics. On the other hand, they are also skilled at manipulating statistics to get the outcomes desired, so where was the truth to be found?

The Anthrophobes' model was quite a simple one: they would kill everyone who was not an Anthrophobe, and the survivors would then live out their lives patrolling the Earth and - most importantly - not reproducing. If you liked the idea of other people dying so that the planet would be saved, the movement had a lot going for it. They were not normally as suicidal as those who had ripped through our camp; the idea was to stay alive and keep killing.

"Only three wardens, borderlines or tippers died for every Anthrophobe killed," the Auditor General concluded. "In short, their attacks were a failure."

These were the nationwide figures, of course, but most people only listened to headlines. On the other hand, this headline held a subtle message: wardens, borderlines and tippers were being grouped together as allies.

The audits for the day were resumed, and all five of them resulted in the accused being declared borderline. I had the feeling that things were being postponed, and that nobody wanted to make any important decisions. Why?

Overall, the National Audit's response to the attacks was to carry on as if they had been just a minor inconvenience. I stopped to scan the bulletin screen on the way to my assigned tasks for the day. Sure enough, the audit of Dr Jason Hall was the only real news as far as the news streams were concerned.

\#

Because my views and standards had been considered a bit extreme for most of my life, I had tended not to make many friends. Now I had gone from being an extremist in the eyes of Generation Tipper to conservative status as far as Generation Victim was concerned. To be a conservative was to be an execution waiting to happen, yet I was a conservative whose record was clean and sharp enough for brain surgery. In other words, I had fans and enemies on both sides of politics.

Chaz was different to my other fans. He was one of those people who used to be called gofors. Famous and rich people once had entourages of followers to go for whatever took their fancy, hence the name. This was Chaz, but he was more than just a glorified fan. Even the greatest warrior needs someone to mind his back, and that's what Chaz did for me. He was not famous, notorious, talented, skilled or important, but he hung out with me and that brought him credibility - which seemed to be worth something. There was plenty for me in our relationship. I had been in Audit Camp 71 for only fourteen days, while he had lived there for years. He knew everything about everything, and that made my life a lot easier.

"So how are you feeling about tomorrow?" he asked as we sat having lunch in Refectory Field.

"As nervous as ever," I replied, truthfully enough.

"Bet you were more nervous when the Anthros attacked."

"I hung out with the auditors, safest place to be. How about you?"

"I got bolt holes all over the camp. The people who don't have a disaster plan are the ones who get splattered. I figured that the only dudes who would attack this place were the Anthros, and they would be looking for maximum kill stats. I made sure that I got into a place that was too much like hard work to search, so they would walk on by. "

"So where were you?"

"Desiccation field, under a pile of dried bodies."

"Clever."

"Reckon I was in less danger than you. Like, the auditors had a load of wardens protecting them, but they were higher-value targets."

"Wrong call, Chaz. They were surrounded by wardens and seriously hard targets. The Anthros would have put them way down on their list."

"You may be right, good thinking. Hey, the routines are in a mess, don't you think? Only six audits this morning and no executions."

Executions, the magic word. Carbon reclaimings were what climatically correct people called the killing of tippers. Chaz was flagging that more subversive words were on the way.

"So there's something I need to know?" I asked, because I was tired of small talk and circumlocutions.

"Look around," he replied. "What do you see?"

"Confusion, mainly. People trying to learn new jobs because the folk who used to do them are dead. Many understudies are dead too, because they were working with their mentors when the Anthros dashed in and started shooting."

"Security's taken a hit."

"What are you building up to?"

"There's total focus on keeping people out of the camp, Jaz. Think about it."

He gave me a knowing smirk, then left. One did not have to be a genius to work out that he had been talking about escaping. Without transport, however, that option was in the *Don't Even Think About It* file.

#

Greenhouse Field had taken the worst of the damage from the Anthrophobes. One bullet, fired along a line of glass tents, could - and often did - shatter dozens of glass plates. Only a half dozen glass tents were still usable, and these were well and truly booked up. Plate glass windows were in abundant supply in the deserted cities, but it would be months before they could be cut up into tent-sized rectangles and triangles, and dragged out here on SUV caravans.

I was put to work in Greenhouse Field, working amid the shattered glass tents to find the rectangles and triangles that were intact, or at least usable. My survey showed that enough panels could be collected for another five greenhouse tents to be assembled. The resin that held them together was there for the taking, we only had to heat the glass fragments in a solar vat and that resin would melt and flow out through a filter. Next I hauled a cartload of clothing to Recycling Field.

"Has anyone approached you about escaping?" Alette asked when I arrived and began unloading.

"You have to be joking."

"I am not. Perimeter security has weakened because of the attack."

"And?"

"That is all."

"It's hardly evidence of a conspiracy."

"Quite true, but some people keep talking about security having more holes in it than Jarlsberg cheese."

"I remember Jarlsberg cheese."

"Don't joke about it."

"I'm not. Alette, I know that there's hundreds of miles of desert to cross, as well as drone patrols every few hours. The whole camp saw what happened to those three tipper escapees, and they were well armed and knew their bush craft."

"The remote patrol drones are down, apparently. The controlling server was damaged."

"The chip system is still up. Miss the daily scan for the ID chip in your arm and an alarm goes off."

"Jason, even I could hack holes in the chip register."

"You're not serious, are you?"

"I just wondered if you had heard rumors about anyone planning a breakout."

"Why leave?" I said, genuinely baffled. "Most borderlines are safe enough here."

"The camp has few creature comforts."

"It's way ahead of being dead, and not much different to life on the run. Besides, we're hated by the Generation Victim people back in what's left of the cities. Out here we are a lot safer."

"The living is more civilized in the Antarctic settlements."

"There's an ocean in the way, and security is even tighter than here. I know, I used to work there. Why even think about escaping?"

"I am not. I was just worried that you might have associated with the wrong people."

"So you are trying to warn me not to try it?"

"Yes."

"Thanks, but I volunteered to come here for a reason. Escape is so far away from my agenda that you couldn't see it with a telephoto lens."

Everyone had an agenda, but mine was genuine and open to public scrutiny. Was Alette spying on me? After what Silvy did, I was ready to believe anything. Chaz was a little dodgy in much the same way that the desert is a little sandy, but he was more of a petty criminal than a secret agent. Alette's innermost thoughts were definitely not on display, so she was probably dangerous.

#

It seemed that everyone wanted a piece of my time that evening. Alette made a point of having dinner with me, and she actually took an interest in how I had become the way I am. Until now I had just been a person of value to be seen with. Now the subject matter was getting just a little personal.

"Nobody ever mentions your sexuality," she said as I dipped my seaweed biscuit in the protein concentrate stew. "Are there things somewhat dark or unusual in your background?"

"No. I'm hetro, with one dead son, one dead wife, and four consecutive sexual partners, two of whom are also dead."

"Four partners? How long were you with them?"

"Seven years was the longest liaison."

"With your environmental standards, I suppose you are quite a handful to live with."

"All too true."

"How did you become so environmentally responsible, so long before it was fashionable?"

"I put it down to Christmas presents."

"No, seriously."

"I'm absolutely serious."

"So your parents gave you climatically correct presents?"

"No, just the usual Sixties crap. Plastic ray guns that squirted water, cowboy suits, that sort of thing. The difference was that other kids were given their presents when they got out of bed on Christmas morning, but I had to wait. My friends would ask what I'd got, and I had to tell them I was still waiting. My sisters got the same treatment. My parents used to say 'The longer you wait, the better it will be.' On my seventh birthday I was not given my toy telescope until one minute to midnight."

"Weird."

"It was the following Christmas that pushed me over the edge. I asked for a plastic model of the Vostok spacecraft that took the first man into space. Dad said 'Well, a Russian toy can only be given to you at Russian Christmas.'"

"Which is January 7th."

"Right. He and mum thought that was hilarious. When they finally gave it to me, even Twelfth Night was already over and the Christmas decorations had been put away. There was a very lonely but brightly wrapped present locked in the crystal cabinet when I got up in the morning. My mother was wearing the key around her neck."

"So they made you wait until just before midnight?"

"Worse. They said I would have to wait until midnight Moscow time, which was 7 am the next morning."

"That borders on child abuse."

"In the Sixties it was called building character. The next morning I was given the key to the crystal cabinet after breakfast. I took it to the bathroom and flushed it down the toilet."

Alette actually laughed.

"And you were only seven? I am impressed."

"Dad took his belt off and thrashed me until my bottom was cherry red, then he had to get a locksmith in to open the cabinet and make another key. He took my present out and dumped it on the floor in my room. I put it in the garbage bin. That earned me another thrashing, but I still left it there. The next Easter, I refused to go hunting for my chocolate eggs, and mum and dad began to wonder if they might have been a bit too cute with the character building. When I turned eight my birthday presents were on the breakfast table when I got up, but I ignored them. The next Christmas there was a big family lunch, but I left my presents under the tree, untouched."

"And all the relatives noticed?"

"Oh yeah. My folks were emotional idiots, but they taught me that a kid could wield a lot of power by not wanting loads of material crap. They panicked about then. Me and my sisters were given our Christmas presents on Christmas Eve from then on."

"As in Christmas on the International Date Line?"

"You catch on fast, Alette. In the years that followed I was given bicycles, guitars, surfboards, and even my own television, but they all stayed in the wrapping until they were handed on to my sisters. By the time I was a teenager I had cast iron self control, no interest in material goods and manically sharp focus. Then I learned about climate change, and I realized where my life had to go."

"And you did that as a kid?" She giggled. "No wonder everything the Retributor throws at you bounces off. I ..."

"Yes?"

"Either you're telling me a clever story so I'll drag you off to Dating Field before it's too late, or it's already too late."

"Dating Field is full of wounded borderlines. And it is too late."

The conversation had wandered back to the subject of sex, like an escaping tipper wandering into a minefield.

"I have bad incidents and people in my past as well," she said guardedly.

"I don't need to know."

This was unexpected, as far as she was concerned. I was supposed to be interested. Talk sex, and very soon you are having sex. That's the nightclub protocol, as Chaz called it. She decided to force the issue and tell me anyway.

"Rich but sleazy men kept expecting me to be an easy lay just because they were the gatekeepers to a lot of money and influence," she said. "It is usually the way with beautiful women."

"Do you mind if we close down the topic?" I asked.

If she wanted to, Alette could always make you feel like there was nothing more important to her in the entire world than your opinion. You got all her attention, and she said little about herself. She was not used to this sort of reaction.

"Have I offended you?" she asked.

"No."

"Then why so cool?"

"The problem with getting old is that I've learned to spot when women are too good at being wonderful. *You* are truly wonderful."

I expected a slapped face. Instead she turned away and just sat there, staring down at the sand between her feet. All her best social weapons now had their safety catches engaged. She was not looking me in the face, smiling, or even trying to persuade me to say more about myself.

"You think I'm doing what your parents used to do," she said. "Dangling sex just out of your reach and making you want it so much that you would do anything for me."

"Like I said, I think we should close down the topic."

"Oh rubbish, Jason, I am not playing games! Just make a move on me and my answer is already yes. Happy?"

"I do appreciate the gesture, but no."

"Do you need the little blue pills? I have coupons."

"Believe it or not, I'm still functional."

"Ah yes, silly of me. You managed it with the suicide bomber,."

"That was a mistake, and she went out of her way to seduce me."

"I am genuinely jealous, and I have not felt that way for decades. Remember, hell has no fury like a woman scorned."

"You're not being scorned, I'm trying to protect you! Just trust me, close down the sex talk, and see what tomorrow brings."

The truth was that after what Silvy had tried to do to me, nobody was above suspicion as far as I was concerned. To say that would have hurt Alette's feelings, however, so she did not need to know.

#

A feature-length performance of the 1984 movie *The Terminator* was staged that evening. You could never imagine a more scrawny Terminator than the lead performer, but he was greeted with near-hysterical cries of approval by the audience. The car chases were improvised on wheelchairs and the bullets were origami packets filled with sand. Gunshot sounds were made by hitting pipes against each other.

I could have been excused for not attending; after all, I had a another very important day looming. On the other hand, I wanted to be seen. Alette and I attended together, on a sort of platonic date. It probably looked as if I were enjoying myself on my last night alive.

The police station shootout was hilarious. The actors were dressed in improvised warden costumes, and the cheers were deafening as the arthritic Terminator mowed them down with packets of red sand. Can you imagine a petrol tanker consisting of a large plastic pipe lashed between two wheelchairs and towed by six old men? Stage hands flung sand to suggest that it had exploded and caught fire.

At the end of the performance I was called down to the stage by the Terminator actor himself. The man did quite a credible sort of Arnie-style accent, if you can imagine Arnold Schwarzenegger with a reedy, quavering voice.

"Hey all you people, I want you to meet our very own Terminator!" he declared, holding up my arm.

The cheering that erupted lasted longer than that for the show.

"Everything that those fuckers fired at Dr Hall for the last twelve days has bounced off, and even the Anthros couldn't kill him with real bullets and bombs. Come tomorrow, he gets a chance to become the Terminator who survived."

This set off more cheers and applause, and as it died down he pushed me forward to say a few words.

"Best not to get too excited, because I might not make it," I said, absolutely unrehearsed. "Still, over the past fortnight I think I managed to make an important point. We Generation Tippers caused the mess that the world's become, but denying tippers of good will the chance to help clean up that mess is a serious crime of squander, and maybe even neglect. If I don't make it through tomorrow, keep that message alive."

Now the Terminator actor stepped up beside me again.

"He'll be back," he said as he held my arm high.

The applause and cheers might have gone on all night, but Alette steered me away from the well wishers.

"Someone with your sort of willpower and discipline is not going to have a change of heart about finding a quiet corner tonight, yes?" she asked.

"Afraid so."

"Then what about a kiss for good luck?"

A kiss. In public. That meant she wanted to declare for me, even without sex. I was genuinely touched.

"Be my lady Fortune," I replied.

I then experienced my first kiss on the lips since that night with Silvy in Dating Field. To be perfectly honest, I was not keeping my distance from Alette entirely out of fear of being betrayed or from concern for her safety. When you perform a sex act in company, you always surrender a little control, and make yourself a little vulnerable. While isolated, I was in total control. If I hooked up with someone else, other agendas kicked in.

True, I had declared myself as a Hand of the Green Man, but all the Greenhands required was belief, and in return they gave me a sense of belonging. The Retributor might have been building a case that I was challenging the National Audit for fame and notoriety - display, in other words. Sex with another admirer might be held up as evidence of that. Would I be tempted to plead guilty on the condition that Alette was spared? I did not know, and I did not want to know. I was so very tired of walking through minefields of hidden agendas.

#

I was still digging out my bed trench when my granddaughter arrived with her escort of wardens. Because I had just denied myself the chance to participate in one last sex act, I was feeling particularly scratchy.

"What?" I said after glancing up.

"This may be our last personal time together, and all you can say is *what*?"

"Renny, I am forty years older than you and very tired. You are probably going to keep me awake for another ninety minutes, and I will be so wretched tomorrow that I will probably say something stupid and get a death sentence. Do you think I am happy about that?"

"Actually, judgment has already been passed on your audit. Tomorrow it will be announced, that's all. You will not have to do anything."

"Let me guess. If the news were good, you would not come past. That means the news is bad, so you are here to say goodbye. Very well, goodbye."

"I just wanted to say -"

"I know what you want to say! All we tippers are guilty, so even if some of us lived with a smaller footprint than the best of Generation Victim, we must still be guilty. Why audit us? It's only because you don't want to look like a lot of Nazis, just killing people because of what they are."

"This is not fair!" she protested, sounding genuinely hurt. "I can't tell you the verdict."

"I know the verdict. Pardon me and you look weak and stay in Audit Camp 71 as a very minor auditor general. You're already in a bad position for using your casting vote to tip the verdict my way so many times."

"I used my casting vote in your favor because I believed they were the right decisions! That was my integrity at work. I came here to speak with you because … because I wish we had spent more time together."

"Meaning that there will be no chance to do so after my audit because I am sure to be convicted."

"You know I can't respond to that."

"You don't have to. Convict me, and you win the hardest audit in history, and go to the front of the queue to become the next Presiding Auditor of the National Audit."

Auditors are trained to keep their feelings on a very short leash. Renny's training was good, although she had let a few faint signs of affection slip out.

"You're right, maybe I should just say goodbye," she said, aware that her mask was beginning to crack.

Before I could reply she glided back through the darkness to her escort and was lost to my sight. I finished scooping out my trench, padded my bowl with my scrap of toweling to keep my head warm, and settled down under my blanket.

#

DAY 14: – CONTINUED

Chaz must have been lurking in a nearby trench belonging to someone killed in the Anthrophobe attack. It was darker than usual because the moon was old, and had not yet risen. Most of the security lights had been damaged in the fighting.

"That could have gone better," he whispered as he reached me.

"Whatever you want, Chaz, make it quick," I muttered.

"Reckon your chances are bad for tomorrow?"

"If real money still existed, I'd not put any on myself."

"Way I see it, the woodlands near the coast been gettin' back to normal," he said.

"They were national parks before the tipping year," I replied. "I spent a lot of time working in them."

"Full of game, as I hear."

"That would be due to the ban on hunting, with Class One Death for anyone that the wardens catch."

"You know, I saw this coming."

"Me too. I wrote a lot of articles about the consequences of climate change. They were ignored, mostly."

"No, I mean I prepared. I buried some guns and three thousand rounds in the woods, all wrapped in grease and plastic. Old M16, a couple of Glock pistols, and a great hunting rifle."

"In a thousand years some archeologist will find them fascinating."

"I figure we could live pretty well in the woods, hunting game."

"That sort of talk will get you staked down in a greenhouse tent if the wrong people heard."

"So you're not in?"

"I've heard nothing."

"But you heard the AG just now. You're a dead man walking. "

"They'd hunt us down in a day. Probably less. Worse, they might ignore us."

"Hey, I'm a bushman, and you're more savvy with wilderness living than any other tipper or borderline in this camp. They'd never find us."

"How are you going to get there, Chaz? Bush craft is no help when there's no bush. We're in a bleeding desert, hundreds of miles from the coast. We all saw what happened to those three guys who tried to escape."

"But I've got a suncycle."

A suncycle. They were made from carbon fiber, had mesh wheels, and could carry three. With night-vision goggles you could ride all night, then lay out solar cell fabric in the morning to recharge the batteries while sleeping through the worst of the day's heat. Traveling cross country at highway speeds, Chaz had pretty good prospects of reaching what was left of some national park within two or three days.

"Where the hell did you get it?" I asked. "They don't even allow them in the camp in case some clown tries to steal one and do a runner."

"Yeah, but there's a few hidden out in the desert, in case the wardens need fast transport in emergencies."

"The satellites will spot you."

"Satellites have to be told to do a search, and camp security has fallen on its face. How are they going to tell we're not a patrol?"

"Because all patrols are registered on a grid. You will be an anomaly, and they'll send ranger wardens after you. They ride suncycles too, and they have rifles, image enhancers, acoustic scopes, geopositioning, solar sleeper drones and satellite feed."

"Those greenie ferals don't cut it."

"Feral animals are great hunters, and they have a nasty bite. Generation V people still launch satellites and build weapons, remember? They just use renewable tech, and that tech will find you very quickly."

"I'm serious, and I'm armed. Remember, I got those LR 22 rounds from the gun nut, I keep 'em up my arse during inspections. With all the metal scrap around here it was a no-brainer to rig up a zip gun and silencer. I've even cut ID chips from dead wardens. The satellites and drones would scan us as a legit patrol."

"I'm staying."

"Listen, this isn't a fag proposition. I got a girl coming with me, that warden with the brand."

"Olivia? The cheerful psycho?"

"She's got the right attitude."

For a moment I felt a pang of jealousy, which was quite a puzzle. Olivia was less than half my age and way too confronting to be my type.

"My answer's still no."

"Why not? They'll give you Class One Death tomorrow, and make sure you die slowly."

"I want to beat the Audit."

"That's shit, nobody's beaten it. You'll get nailed for squandering the audit's time and being born on the wrong side of the Year 2000."

"Nobody's escaped from here, Chaz."

"I got friends in high places -"

"I don't care if you have friends in the lunar factories. You fight in your way, and I'll fight in mine."

"Is that your final word?"

"Yes!"

#

I do not remember hearing the shot or seeing the flash from Chaz's improvised gun. I returned to consciousness quite some time later, and consciousness brought with it a very impressive headache. Dr Gibson, who was attending me, ran through a few standard tests and questions to determine whether I had sustained brain damage. Apparently my brain was fine, but it still felt damaged. Word was sent to the Auditor General that I was awake, and she entered the infirmary tent within a few minutes.

"Just why do you wear a metal helmet in bed?" she asked.

"Hello Renny, I'm glad to see that you're alive, too."

"Answer my question, grandfather. The Retributor says you planned to escape with Chaz Cherveril, who shot you when you got cold feet."

"The Retributor? Try this for a conspiracy, then. The Retributor bribes Chaz to trick me into an escape attempt.

I don't want to go because I came here to do a job, so why escape? Chaz drops back to Plan B, which involves me being shot by persons unknown. He doesn't realize that I wear the bowl on my head to keep the sand out of my hair."

The Auditor General stood with her arms folded for some moments, staring down at the sand. Finally she nodded.

"I accept that. So, you decided not to escape with Cherveril?"

"There was never any question of it. I did not volunteer to come to Audit Camp 71 so that I could escape. I'm here to beat the Audit."

"The Advocate did point that out. You do have some people on your side."

She reached under her cloak and drew out a tube that looked like a long, old-style torch with some sort of mechanism powered by elastic bands at one end.

"Believe it or not, this is a crude pistol. It fires 22 caliber cartridges, but takes about as long to reload as a flintlock from the Napoleonic Wars."

"They were called zip guns back last century."

"Before my time. You were saved because the bullet was very light, the gun was not accurate, and the bullet did not fit the barrel very well. You are also alive because the relatively slow, light bullet glanced off the side of the bowl on your head."

"Lucky me. What will you do with Chaz?"

"Nothing. He's dead."

I gasped, then sat up. My head blazed with pain, and I lay back again, slowly.

"With so much death in this place, I shouldn't be surprised." I sighed. "Did he get far?"

"Only Desiccation Field."

"Makes sense as an escape route. Nobody alive, so no wardens on patrol."

"Did you know that he had a companion?"

"Would it make any difference if I did?"

"Well fielded. The warden he chose to escape with played along with him, then cut his throat."

Warden Olivia, I thought as I closed my eyes. *All fun and frolics until her blade slices through your carotid artery.*

"She has been commended for preventing an escape without squandering a bullet."

"How climatically correct."

"So you had no chance to report either of them before you were shot?"

"Yes."

"The Retributor will be disappointed."

The Retributor, disappointed? That was highly significant. Were I already sentenced to being stripped naked and released out into the desert, he would not care. That meant the verdict had gone in my favor! Renny had a mind like a chess champion, so she would have chosen those last five words with exquisite care.

"Can I ask a sensitive question?" I said.

"Ask. I'll try to give a sensitive answer."

"Tomorrow is the verdict on my audit."

"Yes."

"Why permit two weeks to be spent auditing me? You squandered a lot of resources on my case, and some of the charges were marginal enough to go either way."

"It was not squander. We were getting your life and work on the public record."

"All that is already on the public record."

"That was the old public record, full of movie stars and fashionistas with no detectable intelligence, real estate sharks with the conscience of a COVID-19 virus, and politicians who couldn't say 'Good morning' without a speechwriter to help. You are on *our* records now, and that's what really matters."

"This is leading up to something, isn't it?"

"Of course."

"Not death, I suspect."

"Well done."

"Not at all. For someone facing certain death, I'm being given a lot of medical attention. That tells me all I need to know."

"Unfortunately not. My decision can be vetoed by the National Audit Congress, and a veto -"

"Automatically triggers the sentence outstanding, yeah, yeah, I know the law too."

#

DAY 15: SENTENCE

It was not a good night, even though I spent it on a padded bunk under blankets. I might have slept, but it felt as if I were just lying awake with my temple throbbing. At my age, any heavy blow to the head brings with it the risk of a stroke because one's blood vessels are fairly brittle. On the other hand, I had been living pretty clean, so maybe my body was in better shape than the medical average for eighty-five.

At halflight I got up and managed to shamble about, with Gibson hovering close by in case I collapsed. He kept offering me tablets for the pain, but the last thing I needed was a chemical fog in my mind when I stood before the audit bench. Breakfast was grilled vat-grown cheese on seaweed biscuits, washed down by mango-flavored soy milk. I would have enjoyed it, except that it felt like I was being given my last meal before Class One Death, without mercy. Why was I fearful? Perhaps it was the fear that winning my audit might change nothing.

Another surprise was being given a tepid bath in water from Farm Field. When my rags were returned to me, they had been washed and dried. A gleaming white bandage was applied to the lurid bruise where Chaz's bullet had nearly ended my life, and the tangles were combed out of my hair and beard. This made me feel as if I were being groomed for military honors. The cameras would be sending the verdict on my twelfth audit to the entire world, and it would not be a good look for a hero to resemble an improvised toilet brush ... not that there were any toilet bowls in Audit Camp 71. A wooden pole laid above a pit of turds and piss did not need brushing. Was I a hero? Whose hero? There were certainly subversives among the medical staff. Did the Auditor General know I was being cleaned up? Was someone trying to antagonize the Retributor? Again?

Olivia had already received her medal and had been promoted to octant warden by the time she arrived to take me to the Audit Arena. Octant was a bit like the old rank of sergeant, and as the name implies, she was now leader of a squad of eight wardens.

"Dr Fitness, you look mighty fine for someone who just got shot!" she exclaimed as she caught sight of me.

I showed her the dent in the side of my food bowl.

"Trust me, I don't feel fine. Getting shot is never a load of laughs."

"That was mean of Chaz, don't you think?" she said.

"As mean as cutting his throat?"

"Hey, brighten up. If I'd turned him in, he would have got audited for intent to squander. I was being humane."

Humane? What were those seconds like, between his throat being cut and him fading out forever? Chaz had known death was closing in, at least for a very short time. More immediately, how was I meant to reply to Olivia?

"Time to go?" I asked.

"Don't be like that. I think of you as Gen V who was just born on the wrong side of 2000. I'm a big fan of yours."

"I've got a fan? I must be a celeb."

"You've been a celeb for two weeks, Dr Fitness. It's gonna be party time like you never imagined if you get off."

She had been working for the Retributor, I was convinced of that. The Retributor had almost certainly arranged for Chaz to escape with Olivia, taking me with them. Chaz was to shoot me if I said no. Olivia had apparently been a double agent, however, and she would then kill Chaz. Had I said yes, she would have killed both Chaz and myself. As long as I were dead, it was a good result for the Retributor. I was still alive, however, and this gave him a very bad result.

#

With an escort of an octant, her eight armed wardens and a nurse, I was marched out to the Audit Arena. We must have been an impressive sight, led by Olivia wearing her medal and me with my conspicuously bandaged head. Tippers and borderlines lined the path as we passed, cheering and reaching out to touch me. I was the first good news in Audit Camp 71 for a very long time, and probably ever.

What really surprised me was that many wardens who were stationed along the route also smiled and gave me the thumbs up when I came into view. I had proved that a tipper could also be Generation Victim, and hardly a GV anywhere could match my credentials when it came to trying to save the world. It was 2045, after all, and everyone was desperate to declare themselves in favor of saving the world.

The entrance to the Audit Arena was so packed with borderlines that we had to wait while a path was cleared. The camp's authorities had gone to some trouble to make this day's audit seem just like any other, but that was pretty pointless. The Arena was surrounded by a crowd of tippers and borderlines at least fifty deep.

I was marched into the Audit Arena and put in the accused's queue with everyone else - although I was first in line. The gallery was jammed solid with spectators, and of course my cheer squad of borderline women was there, decked out in their blue cheesecloth and plastic bikinis and high heel sandals, waving even bigger bunches of ribbons made from shredded plastic bags. They were shouting:

"Doctor Hall!

"Invinci-ble!

"Rah! Rah!

"Doctor Hall!"

The auditors arrived in their usual procession, except that there were twice as many wardens escorting them. They all looked as if they had bathed and dressed in fresh robes. Had they used the recycled water before or after I had? For some reason the idea worried me, but I could not say why. The Auditor General seated herself, then the other auditors took their places on the bench. We tippers and borderlines remained standing until the auditors were settled.

"Clerk of the Bench?" said the Auditor General.

"The first audit of the day continues that of Jason Hall, climatologist," he said, without looking at his screen.

That set off my cheer squad again, but their performance was tolerated. Once silence had returned, the Auditor General read something on her screen, rested her uninjured arm on her desk and looked across to me.

"There can be no doubt that this has been the most difficult audit I have ever presided over," she began. "Quite probably no auditor general has ever had a case like this. Tippers are usually easy to audit, because their life histories are filled with self-delusion, laziness, greed, short-sightedness, indulgence, neglect and gratuitous display. How many Generation Tipper people ever bought and buried coal to offset the petrol that they burned while commuting to work, or ordered chicken instead of beef at a restaurant because chicken meat has a smaller carbon footprint? Jason Hall, you did things like that, and from a remarkably young age."

She paused to let her audience think about that. How many GVs could match my record? Until recently only dedicated believers such as the Auditor General and Advocate might have approached it. Possibly the Retributor as well, although I suspected that he had some sort of guilt psychosis, probably related to the lifestyle of his parents.

"We auditors must factor justice into our decisions. Should we distinguish between a tipper and a GV who have identical records? Is it just to condemn a tipper who has lived more responsibly than a GV, just because of his year of birth? Conventional wisdom is that people of Generation Victim are innocent of minor lifestyle infringements because those infringements are due to the crimes of their parents and grandparents. If they prove themselves incapable of meeting the standards of Generation Victim, we do punish them."

She gestured to the Cloudcast drone, as if acknowledging the worldwide audience of around sixty million behind it.

"This audit bench has been endorsed by the International Audit Movement, and I sit in the National Audit Congress of Australia. Thus our decisions may be viewed as decisions endorsed by the highest authorities. I communicated our decision regarding Dr Hall to the National Audit Congress last night. This morning I was informed whether or not there would be a veto."

The Retributor shook his head, but remained silent. Was it because I had been pardoned, or because he had been involved with last night's assassination attempt and had been discovered? I was convinced that he had bribed Chaz into trying to involve me in the escape attempt. Chaz's interest in escaping had come straight out of left field, because normally the man was as wary as a rat checking out a piece of cheese. He would not have made his hopeless bid for freedom unless he thought all the odds were in his favor. Warden Olivia was still alive, and could provide the truth, but she now had a promotion, a medal and her own squad, so she would be naming no names.

It can still go either way, I told myself.

If Chaz had killed me, no controversial verdict of guilt would have had to be announced. Audit regulations specified that proceedings be halted immediately upon the death of the accused, in order to avoid squander. The issue of squandering the talents of Generation Tipper borderlines could be referred to a committee, and that committee could argue about what to do until the last member of Generation Tipper had died. Could the audit bench be forced to ignore the logic of my defense and execute me anyway?

"Doctor Jason Hall, you are found pardoned of all charges," declared the Auditor General with no preamble at all.

Everyone was caught by surprise, most of all myself. For a moment there was no sound at all, then there was a huge, collective gasp for air from the gallery. A mighty cheer thundered out at the auditors, over the wall, across the Farm Field, and on into the desert. Everyone crowded outside the Audit Arena caught on and began cheering as well, and my cheer squad leaped from their seats with agility that never failed to surprise me and launched into their routine while the tippers and borderlines continued to cheer.

"Doctor Hall!

"Beat them all!

"Live forever!

"Doctor Hall!"

The wardens did not even try to maintain order. Headbands, coffee packets, false teeth, Viagra coupons, walking sticks, spectacles, improvised erotic underwear and even a hemorrhoid cushion rained down from the gallery, and I was mobbed by admiring tippers and borderlines - even though I represented everything that they were not. The wardens who were standing between the crowd and the auditors saluted me, but the auditors themselves did a great job of looking absolutely impassive. After allowing several minutes of jubilation, the wardens herded the tippers and borderlines back to their seats.

"Retributor, you have the right of appeal," said the Auditor General, as if nothing had happened since she had pronounced me pardoned.

"I defer to your verdict, your honor," said the Retributor. "I shall not squander resources by appealing."

This drew yet more cheering from the gallery. *Not anxious to draw attention to himself*, I noted. Now it was my turn, and it was a very delicate moment. Any evidence of the wrong sort of attitude would earn me a charge of display. What to say? I had already said everything that I wanted or needed to. I bowed to the auditors on the bench, then stood in silence, waiting to be dismissed.

"Do you have nothing to declare to us?" asked the Auditor General.

"My life has been my declaration," I said. "This audit has established that it is possible for a Generation Tipper to be no more guilty or innocent than a Generation Victim. I have nothing more to add."

Even saying those words was dangerous, but I had been fielding danger for two weeks and had a fairly good feel for what I could get away with. This was display, but it was climatically correct display. The Retributor himself was guilty of worse. What about my granddaughter? She had killed her parents and her three brothers. She was like a legal serial killer, and very dangerous to have in one's family.

"Doctor Hall, you are too modest," she responded. "You are the standard that every civilization should have lived by.

Had everyone else behaved as you did and shared your values, the world could have been pulled back from the Tipping Point Year."

She turned to the eight other auditors.

"Members of the audit bench, fellow victims, those of you in favor of appointing Doctor Jason Hall to the bench in the new position of Precedent Auditor, be upstanding."

There are no words to describe quite how astounded I felt, there and then. The Auditor General got to her feet. To her right and left the other members of the Audit bench stood up as well.

"Doctor Hall, the audit bench has voted unanimously in favor of admitting you."

There were no cheers from my cheer squad or the gallery. I don't think anyone was angry, they were just as perplexed as I was.

"But, but surely others are more worthy," I said. "Many environmental activists were far more extreme, militant, effective or influential than me."

"Not a single one has volunteered to be audited. All chose to live as tippers in reserved occupations for fear of some little lapse in their past being exposed. You have now set the standard for everyone who has been or will be brought before any audit."

"But what about my climatology work? The Earth is burning up, surely we need climatologists more than auditors."

"The Earth needs both, but there are now many climatologists. You are the only precedent for pardoning auditees from Generation Tipper. If you refuse, you will be guilty of squandering a non-renewable resource. Yourself."

I closed my eyes, and felt myself sag a little inside. Out of all the tippers I had heard audited over the fortnight past, none had come anywhere near my standards. It is very difficult to think clearly in such circumstances. *Will it make any difference if you refuse?* The thought flashed through my mind out of nowhere. The standard had already been set, and would be used whether I was an auditor or not. On the other hand, if I were an auditor, I could argue and vote.

"I am honored to accept," I replied.

"Splendid. Clerk of the Bench, have you finished checking the precedents established in this audit against all those in the National Borderline Database?"

"I have, your honor."

"Give us a summary of the results."

"Sentences of carbon reclamation in all classes of climate crime have been returned in ninety-nine and three quarters of a percent of borderlines."

Suddenly it was as if the great weight had returned to press down on my shoulders yet again. They had judged the entire borderline backlog against the standards I had set!

"Auditor Hall, remember what I said some days ago?" said the Auditor General. "You are indeed a hard act to follow."

"Your honor, this is mass murder, not justice!" I protested.

"This is indeed justice, but not the old justice. This is justice with very high standards and no loopholes. The precedent that you established will be written into climate law, but as an auditor you are now in a position to help interpret the national and international standards you set."

"You mean you're allowing me to save a handful of lives out of thousands?"

"Would you prefer them to die?"

"No, damn you."

"No, damn you, *your honor*," said the Clerk of the Bench.

"Well?" asked the Auditor General.

"I still accept, your honor," I muttered.

"Welcome to the audit bench, Dr Hall. In honor of this appointment, all further audits for today are postponed for one hour."

#

The audit bench led the procession to Entertainment Field, where the entire encampment assembled to watch my appointment as Auditor Precedent. This time there was no cheer squad, only silence and eyes. Many borderlines now glared at me with undisguised hatred, while others seemed to plead with me to treat them with mercy when their turn came to be re-audited. Renny walked beside me. Perhaps she had anticipated that I had words for her.

"Instead of giving borderline tippers a proper hearing, you will just check if they measure up to me from now on," I said, staring straight ahead.

"What is wrong with that?"

"Thousands, millions of borderlines who would have died of natural causes will now be executed."

"The climatically correct term is -"

"Don't talk bullshit words, Renny. They're slated to be killed."

"But some will just get service, branding or pardoning. Then they will be free."

"Dozens out of thousands. Thousands out of millions. I only volunteered for an audit because I wanted to give hope to tippers of good will."

"You did that."

"I never realized there were so very few. My standards were too high."

"No they were not. Everyone could and should have lived as you did."

"Don't think that I will not fight this."

"I expect nothing less from the man who beat the National Audit."

While everyone watched, my hair and beard were trimmed short, then I was stripped of the rags that had been my clothes. There was little sense of modesty in Audit Camp 71, so the sight of my scrawny, naked body caused neither shock nor mirth. I was just an old guy with wrinkles and stringy looking muscles, built for endurance rather than speed or strength, and I was certainly no warrior. I was wearing a bandage, however, reminding everyone that a borderline had already tried to kill me.

"Beneath our robes we are all humans," said the Auditor General. "Auditors, wardens, borderlines and tippers, all that separates us is the date of our birth, and the way we have led our lives."

Alette entered, leading a parade of people from Recycling, each carrying an item of clothing. The eight auditors dressed me in the robes of a fellow auditor. The cloth was as close to new as anything since the Tipping Point Year could have been considered new. The rags of dead tippers would have been fed into enzyme vats and been extruded as fiber interlock cloth. All of it had once covered the bodies of the dead, so it was not a good feeling to have that against my skin.

Now came something right outside of my experience. The wardens formed a guard of honor, and the six most senior people in Audit Camp 71 lined up before me. First the Inspector of Wardens and Acting Commander strode forward, went down on one knee and presented me with a pair of red leather gloves on his upturned palms.

"From this day, the blood of the guilty will be on your hands," he said.

He spoke clearly, and the microphone on his lapel picked up his words and carried them to the speaker poles for the entire assembly to hear. Quite obviously he was addressing the camp as much as he was me.

Next the Retributor stood before me, bowed, and gave me a pair of green sunshades.

"From this day, any frailty, pity or mercy in your eyes will be masked," was his declaration.

At that particular moment I suddenly understood what was happening. I was being set apart from the tippers and borderlines, even though I had been born before Year 2000. The old Jason Hall was being killed.

The Advocate followed, and put a green staff into my hand.

"From this day, you must strike down the guilty but spare those tippers who are in truth victims," she said, and her words chilled me no less than those of the Retributor.

The Clerk of the Bench bustled up. He was brisk and efficient, yet self-effacing, someone who looked after tiresome details so that others could get on with the high profile work. Two hundred years ago he might have been tending the machinery of a factory with an oil can. He handed a laptop to me. The auditors used old-style laptops in audits to demonstrate that they rejected planned obsolescence.

"Use this to examine the details of lives before you decide whether or not to end them," he said, then put a hand over his lapel microphone and whispered, "See me later about the password and a charging panel."

Even though I now knew that I was not on the Executioner's list of things to attend to, I still trembled slightly as he approached me. All the other auditors wore a cloak pin in the form of a blue enamel star, symbolizing that they defended the Earth. As a gesture against squander and display, the pins also doubled as lapel microphones. The star that the Executioner used to fasten my cloak was white.

"Your cloak pin symbolizes the planet Venus, where greenhouse warming is rampant. May this remind everyone that your generation threatened Earth with this fate. As you sit among the other auditors, one white star among the blue, may this also remind people that it is important to speak out for what you believe in, even when no others share your opinion."

His words were clear but softly spoken. He too was alone; he understood how I had felt for most of my life.

Last of all, the Auditor General glided down between the two rows of my guard of honor. She presented me with an Auditor's green bowler hat.

"From this day until your death you are an auditor, shielded from the sun because you are without blame for its ravages," she said, as if handing down a life sentence.

She then took me by the arm and led me through my guard of honor to join the other auditors. Standing between us and the crowd of tippers and borderlines, she addressed them.

"Tippers and borderlines of Audit Camp 71, you now have a representative of your own generations on the audit bench. He is sure to judge you with more sympathy than the rest of us, but he is a minority of one. Auditor Hall will now address you."

Me? Give an address? Her words were followed by the most frantic five seconds of creativity of my entire life.

"Borderlines, tippers, wardens and auditors, take a good look at me, because you are looking at the only Generation Tipper auditor in the entire world."

This was an opening designed to get their attention, but I already had their attention. Some people can be a bit thick, however, so it is not always inappropriate to state the bleeding obvious.

"I grew up, then grew old, fighting to warn people that time was running out for the old lifestyles. Now time really has run out, so everyone is listening. How very human of you."

This was not what the borderlines wanted to hear, but I was angry.

"I have proved that it was possible to predict climate change, to work out what to do about it, and to live so that it could be stopped and reversed. Don't get me wrong, I am not after revenge on people who did not listen to me in the bad old days. I was only one of a very few voices. However, what cannot be forgiven is the way that the warnings of the overwhelming majority of qualified scientists and researchers were later ignored, even when houses were being washed into the sea and temperature records were being exceeded every year.

"When the flowers in your garden bloomed in early winter instead of early spring, did you think to yourself that maybe you should buy solar panels for your roof instead of having that annual holiday in Europe? Mostly, no. Did you buy a hybrid car when you needed to upgrade? You probably bought a big SUV with a petrol engine, then argued that you wanted to feel safer in case you crashed, or that you might want to go off-road on your next holiday. That was all squander, neglect, display and greed, the four motorcyclists of the new apocalypse.

"Yes, the National Audit is handing out terrible punishments, but terrible things have been done to our planet. You people have to be reminded about what happened, why it happened, and why you are being held to account. Future generations must be taught what happened to you, so that they never again repeat your mistakes."

If the Generation Victim people were feeling smug, they were about to get an unpleasant shock. Standing alone and telling people on both sides of the political fence that they were fools is in my job statement.

"Generation Victim, you are all guilty of squandering the skills of tippers. Yes, justice has to be done and climate crimes need to be punished, but when a patient is in danger of dying you don't shoot the doctor for being born on the wrong day. We need everyone who can be mustered to plant forests where they will still grow, and to build and operate carbon precipitators everywhere else. Generation Tipper experts of good will must be sent wherever they are most needed, their skills must never again be squandered in the borderline backlogs of Audit Camps.

"What about the hard cases, the blatantly lazy and greedy? My audit has established standards that they will be assessed by. Many of you will be executed, and will curse me with your dying breath. Spare a thought for me, however. I shall be on the audit bench, alone, speaking up for anyone who at least tried to do something about climate change before the Tipping Point Year, or who walked with a soft tread on the face of the Earth and still wants to help.

"Auditors, listen carefully. I can and will bring charges of squander, neglect and display against you if you condemn people of good will to death and deny them a chance to heal what is left of the Earth's biosphere. Check the constitution of the National Audit. Any auditor may press climate crime charges against anyone else, including other auditors, retributors and auditor generals.

"I am eighty-five, and probably don't have many more years left to annoy people. While I do live, I promise to make life very interesting for all of you. The audit bench will now return to the Audit Arena, where eight high-priority audits of highly skilled borderlines will be conducted."

I stood back, and let my granddaughter take my place. If she was angry about what I had just forced the audit bench to do, she did not show it.

"The other audits scheduled for today will be heard tomorrow," she said. "Wardens, tippers and borderlines of Audit Camp 71, return to your normal duties."

We set off for the Audit Arena in silence. I knew how committees worked. That night, over dinner and seaweed vodka, the auditors would try to befriend me, lobby me to take a slow and cautious approach to pardoning borderlines, explain political realities to me, and warn me that I was just one voice against eight. They hoped that by the following morning most of my power and momentum would be gone, but I was not going to let that happen. This was my chance to seize the day, and I was not going to squander that chance.

What reactions to my speech are taking place elsewhere in the country? I wondered. Perhaps junior auditors were thinking about whether slightly more senior auditors could be shot off the perch to make way for them. Perhaps the senior auditors were wondering whether a few pardons might be good for the climate, thus winning over voters, and enhancing their own career prospects.

#

The Clerk of the Bench gave me a crash course in using my laptop, but the system was no great challenge. The other auditors shook my hand and gave me their congratulations, but they were clearly a little uneasy about working with me. That was only to be expected. I now walked clear of the others and held up my hand for silence.

"Wardens, out!" I said.

The Auditor General waved her hand in the direction of the entrance, and the wardens left.

"Before anyone tries to explain that I am exceeding my authority, let me ask this question," I continued, free of the need to be diplomatic, my tone cold, my voice firm. "How can the audit bench justify squandering the skills of eight borderlines worthy of pardon for even a single day? Clerk of the Audit, I am about to call out the names of eight border-lines who symbolize the thousands, perhaps millions, of those who deserve pardoning and can contribute to healing the biosphere. All eight will be pardoned and released today. If any clown among you dares to vote guilty, I shall have him or her audited, convicted and executed on a charge of squander."

"You can't talk to us like -" began the Retributor.

"Fuck you."

That may have been the first time he had ever been addressed with those words by one of his peers. He turned very pale, and did not reply.

"If you can vote to execute a man for the misuse of a leaf blower, I can find a charge to execute each and every one of you. Think carefully. Somewhere in the WorldCloud there will be a video of you drinking coffee from an unrecyclable polystyrene cup, sitting in an SUV or wearing a disposable costume at a Halloween party. Vote guilty in any of the next eight audits, and I *will* come after you. Our duty is to stop the ship sinking, and I will not tolerate anyone squandering time with arguments about what to do with the deck chairs."

That was all I had to say, and I stood back to let the Auditor General do her worst. Her response was nothing like what I had been expecting.

"Dr Hall has exceeded his authority, but he is right," she said. "The National Audit has been placed in a delicate political position by his audit. So has the International Audit Movement. Any hint of us squandering resources needed to heal the biosphere could lead to other national audits withdrawing affiliation. We must make a display of good will now, while the world is watching."

That secured their absolute and undivided attention. I dictated eight names to the Clerk of the Audit. The wardens were called back into the arena, and the chosen borderlines were summoned. Dr Gibson was first to be granted a pardon. The six surviving members of the Owl Academy were next. Their audits took a minute each, and all were pardoned. There is a subtle look of relief that people often have when Death sweeps past them without laying a cold, firm hand on their shoulder. When Alette was pardoned she just straightened slightly, her eyes closed, then her shoulders sagged as she exhaled. She elected to stay at Audit Camp 71, explaining that she could work as well from here as anywhere else, and that travel would amount to squander.

"Clerk of the Bench, who is next?" asked the Auditor General.

"There is nobody else on Auditor Hall's list, your honor."

"A sunwing has already been diverted to pick the newly pardoned and take them to the Antarctic research farms and academies. Make sure that a Cloudcast goes out to Auditor Hall's three hundred million fans, enemies, trolls and other followers, showing them being released and taken aboard. This is a symbolic act to show that we are not squandering in the name of revenge for petty climate infringements. Auditor Hall, do you agree that normal audit procedures must now be resumed, but under Hall Precedent Standards?"

"You have my reluctant agreement," I replied. "However, heed this warning, members of the audit bench and fellow victims. Vote guilty - or innocent - for any reason other than it being your honest and considered judgment, and I will go into the WorldCloud and hunt down your deviations from climatic innocence, no matter how trivial. I endured the worst that you could throw at me. Can any of you do as well?"

I had seized the day, but although I was now releasing it, I had signaled that I was still holding its leash.

"This might be a good time to adjourn," said the Auditor General, and some of the sighs of relief were audible.

I wanted to leave the bench and hug Alette, but I was now an auditor and any display of affection on my part might have compromised her pardon. Might have. How long would I have to wait before I could be more than a colleague to her? Would it be longer than we could reasonably expect to live?

#

The sunwing's arrival the next morning was a truly major event. I had seen these aircraft before and had even flown in one as part of my climatological work, but you never get used to the sheer size of the things. Its single wing—all solar fabric cells powering a hundred electric fan-props—had an area greater than that of Entertainment Field. Most of the space within the airfoil was filled with hydrogen, providing extra lift.

Sunwing stratoliners were slow when compared to the old-style jets, but they could reach the other side of the world within four or five days without using any fuel at all. The central cabin was about the size of a railway carriage and made of carbon fiber composite. Oxygen and water were recycled, so the only limit on how far they could fly untended was the weight of the food for the crew and passengers.

The sunwing was visible for an hour before it arrived over Audit Camp 71, catching the sunlight long before dawn at ground level. It did not land. Ten of its fans tilted upwards, and together with the hydrogen in its structure that was enough to allow it to hover. Harnesses were lowered on cables, and the pardoned members of the Owl Academy were winched aboard. They had no luggage, apart from what they wore or carried.

As I stood watching, I could not help thinking that humanity had returned to the lifestyle pioneered by Homo Habilis two million years earlier. Those hominids owned nothing that they could not carry, which meant a few stone tools and perhaps an animal skin for clothing. Their skills were in their minds, to be passed down to the next generation. How different were the scientists and engineers being drawn up into the sunwing? True, we had machines, vehicles, farms, ships and even satellites, but nobody truly owned them any more. Nobody dared to. Material possessions and traditional wealth were now considered to be evidence of greed, squander and display, and those charges could get a person into a lot of trouble.

Along with the entire camp, the other auditors paused to watch the sunwing taking its passengers aboard. For the first time I stood with the members of the audit bench informally, as a peer. Most had removed their hats and sunshades, as if they needed a rest from deciding who would live and whose carbon would be reclaimed.

"This break from our duties might be considered squander," said the Retributor.

The others just groaned and flung sand at him. So, they actually had a sense of fun. It was a side of life as an auditor that I had neither seen nor even guessed at.

"Remember that the law does not concern itself with trifles," said the Advocate.

"Thousands of trifles put together are thousands of hours squandered," he countered.

"Squander can only be committed if resources that can be used to heal the Earth are wasted," said the Advocate, who had become a lot more assertive over the fortnight past. "Apart from punishing tippers, Audit Camp 71 has no function and is carbon neutral, so this pause in routines is definitely not squander."

"Not so. The camp removes carbon from the biosphere with every body interred."

"That process will not go any faster or slower if we stand about, looking at the sunwing."

"The sunwing is an important symbol," I added, because they were missing a very important point. "It's the most advanced aircraft ever built."

"The builders of the Concorde, 747, Airbus and SR-71 would disagree, were they still alive," said the Clerk of the Bench.

"Could any of those fly for years at a time with no fuel or maintenance?" I asked. "Sunwings are the safest form of air transport ever built. They have a hundred percent safety record, and the only danger from flying in them is from cosmic ray exposure."

"And boredom," said the Technology Assessment Auditor.

"My point is that the sunwing demonstrates that civilization has not collapsed, it has just changed direction and grown up," I concluded. "People need to be reminded of that. It gives them hope, and hope gives them a reason to carry on."

As I was speaking, a crate was winched down from the underhatch of the sunwing.

"That will be the catalytic converter to neutralize the sarin in the mine shafts," said the Clerk of the Bench.

"How long will that take?" asked the Retributor.

"A week for each shaft. Meantime, bodies can be left in Desiccation Field."

"Dr Gibson volunteered to stay here until another medical officer can be brought in," said the Clerk of the Bench. "If I had been him, I couldn't get away from here fast enough."

"Your friend Alette decided to stay as well, Dr Hall," said the Retributor. "Might she have a romantic interest in you?"

"She has a pardon, she may do as she wishes."

The last of the passengers were winched up into the sunwing, and the doors of the underside hatch were closed. I heard distant cheering from all points of the compass. The first inmates of Audit Camp 71 were actually going free. Apart from the symbolism, this was entertainment as sheer spectacle, and far more significant than the bizarre performances, races and other events in Entertainment Field. Very slowly the immense but almost insubstantial wing ascended a few hundred feet, then rotated to face south and powered up its remaining ninety engines and moved away, slowly ascending.

"Next stop Antarctica," said the Clerk of the Bench.

That was where nearly all the research stations, university villages and experimental farms now operated. Industry was based in the old cities, where resources could be mined from the ruins and landfill pits, but living there was hot, unpleasant, unhealthy and dangerous.

The sunwing meant a lot to me. Although designed to last at least a century, at that time it was almost new. It showed that the world in general and humanity in particular were not plunging headlong into decay and ruin, and that a promising future was already taking shape. It was a strange and unfamiliar future with a very light touch, but then all futures are alien for those who have grown up with something else.

\#

There were no executions that day. All of the borderlines who were re-audited were sentenced to Service of one sort or another. These were people with a combination of very useful skills and relatively minor climate crimes. None were pardoned, all got *never to be released* appended to the sentence of Service. Compared to a death sentence, this was a big advance. Some would stay at Audit Camp 71, training other borderlines. Most would be sent to the old coastal cities to collect and recycle useful materials, or to the carbon dioxide extraction farms.

Later in the afternoon the Auditor General called the audit bench to a policy meeting.

"As you may have seen on the news feeds, we have come in for quite a lot of criticism over the audit of Dr Hall," she explained. "The climate fundamentalists are furious, and have declared an assassination vendetta on him. I have arranged for additional security for all of us."

That was the first I had heard of it, but I had expected something along those lines.

"Now then, how do we go about dispensing climate justice? We now have a precedent for pardoning tippers, and an obligation not to squander the skills of Generation Tipper people who can genuinely contribute to the restoration of the biosphere. This is not popular with many Generation Victim citizens, and there is quite a real danger that we could be de-registered as auditors for not dispensing climate justice."

"Would it help if I resigned?" I asked, and there was some uneasy laughter.

"Nice try, Auditor Hall, but no. We have to manage a very delicate balance between punishing those responsible for Hothouse Earth, and not squandering the skills of those born before Year 2000. All the Audit Camps across the entire continent will be monitoring our daily audits from now on. Do we reclaim the carbon from all but one quarter of one percent of the borderlines in this camp? Take away those who have left on the sunwing, and barely a dozen of our borderlines get a full pardon."

She paused to let us think about that.

"Generation Tipper people must be seen to be punished," said the Executioner. "Does it matter how they are punished?"

"Yes, unfortunately," said the Auditor General. "We Generation Victim people have inherited a world that has been described as a dumpster with a fire burning inside. If we forgive and forget, what is to stop those of some future generation committing the same climate crimes in a restored world?"

#

At sunset I had my second meal with the auditors. They had been made auditors because they were well balanced and stable people, but I doubted that they were absolute saints when it came to climate crimes. They now seemed too anxious to prove that they were not monsters, and nothing else but guilt could have been behind that. Even the Retributor confessed that he admired the way I had stood alone against most of my generation back in the 70s and 80s. Much of the talk was about a new direction for the National Audit, one with more emphasis on restoration than revenge.

Yes, everyone born before Year 2000 was guilty, but not all of those people needed to die. Valuable skills could easily be squandered in the name of climate justice, but were vital for the recovery of the planet. Who wanted to be guilty of squander? We held a mock court, in which we tried each other for minor climate crimes and paid fines with squares of seaweed biscuit.

At the end of the meal we were free to do whatever we wished. Auditors did not go to Entertainment Field, but could watch the performances, games and races on television security monitors. Entertainment Field feeds turned out to be surprisingly popular with some of them. Dr Gibson called past to check on the wounded auditors, of which I was now one.

"Any advice for me, Adam?" I asked.

"Advice?"

"As a Green Man vicar, or whatever I'm supposed to call you?"

"We don't have titles. As for advice, try to think of your new duties as putting people through the cycle of rebirth."

"It's still murder!"

"I know, but you asked for advice. If you can't suspend disbelief, just keep busy and don't think about it. That's what I do."

Once he was gone I took the opportunity to catch up with international news on my laptop. I was listening to a North American Alliance politician denouncing Australia for being too lenient when the concierge entered my tent.

"Honorable pardoned victim, one of the borderlines is petitioning for an audience," he said.

"What does that mean?" I asked. "Do I give audiences?"

"If someone who can prove an association wishes to speak with you, they can petition for an audience. She has already had a weapons search."

I had left Renny in the communal tent, watching the antics in Entertainment Field and making notes. I had no other living relatives, so if it were a woman who could prove an association, it had to be Alette or one of my cheer squad.

"I really wondered if I would see tonight's sunset when I was called back for re-audit," Alette said as I waved my warden escort out of earshot.

"It's in the job statement at our age," I replied.

"Congratulations on your win. The National Audit has been out of control for too long."

329

"You call today a win? Borderline audits will be easier and faster from now on. Thousands more people will die in those obscenely cruel climate justice machines instead of just fading away in the borderline queue."

"I wanted to talk to you about that. Shall we walk?"

We walked slowly, but I kept my arms firmly folded. Two wardens trailed behind us, their weapons held ready. I was a high value target for assassins, and they would have preferred to keep me safely in my tent.

"Did you have much to do with my pardon?" Alette asked.

"I influenced it," I said, truthfully enough. "I'd rather not say how."

I had established that blind, vindictive punishment was not always good for the planet. The scientists and engineers that Silvy had gathered together were a valuable resource, and their climate crimes had been trivial. Alette's case had been no different, because fashion can save or squander resources as effectively as any engineering project.

"So, is there anything I can do for you?" she asked.

"When I need a new outfit, you will be top of my list."

"And all is good at a personal level?"

"We're friends, but I dare not let us be anything more. Not for a while, anyway."

"A while is better than never. I owe you what remains of my life, Jason, so I shall wait here. I can do my work anywhere in the world as long as I have communications and a laptop."

From nearby came the roar of the crowd watching a Tippers versus Borderlines football match.

"I talk to people a lot," Alette continued. "Do you know what the long term borderlines say?"

"Surprise me."

"They are happier here than they have ever been."

"I'm surprised," I said, although that was not entirely true.

Life in Audit Camp 71 was unpleasant and brutal, and for some it was very, very short. Unless it were a matter of duty, I would not have chosen to live there.

"A lot of us think we have a real sense of community," Alette continued. "We have jobs, people care about each other, and because nobody has very much, nobody makes a big deal about wealth and status goods."

"All true. There must be a lesson in that."

"There is. People don't need mansions crammed with luxury rubbish to live well and have a wonderful time, that's what I have learned here. I am going to be teaching that to people for the rest of my life, but that's not why I came to see you. You're Dr Hall, who beat them all, yet you only won half the battle."

"Alette, I can't stop the executions. I'm not even sure I want to stop some of them."

"Then find a middle path. You're bright, and there are a lot of good people facing death for living what used to be normal lives. Help them, Jason. Start now."

Up ahead of us, watched over by two more wardens with assault rifles, were the women who had been in my cheer squad. They were again dressed in their minimal costumes, and were not doing a very good job of disguising their excitement.

"I arranged for them to be here," Alette explained. "I thought they deserved to meet you."

#

Predictably, I was expected to sign breasts and buttocks with an indelible marker pen that Alette had smuggled out of the laundry tent. I was then escorted to the execution fields, where they had set up a little party on the tipping point gallows. Even though I had attended hundreds of conference banquets and sat alongside royalty, nothing touched me quite so much as this little revel.

Petra had been a hairdresser, and had been borderlined for squander. While her industry was hardly at the forefront of those trying to save the planet, she had never gone on holidays, always rode a bicycle to work, and was a single mother who had raised two children.

"I haven't had much of an education, but I always tried to do the right thing," she told me. "I took my kids on those rubbish cleanup days and tree planting drives, and once I realized what was going on with climate change I joined the Greens and helped hand out how-to-vote cards at elections. I suppose that wasn't much, but I never owned a car, so it's a bit rich to charge me with squander."

"So you did the hair and makeup for the cheer squad?" I asked.

"Yeah. You liked it?"

"Oh yes, you were the sexiest, bravest ladies imaginable."

I was enfolded by more bare flesh than I had been in contact with since my night with Silvy.

Arlene was next. She was Chinese-Australian, and a former office manager. She had actually won a company award for introducing energy-efficient practices, and that had probably got her borderlined instead of executed.

"Between you and me, I think the company was just pleased because I dropped their power bill by a third," she told me.

"An award by any other name is still an award," I replied.

"And now I'm on the carbon reclamation list. In a few days or weeks I'll be standing on this plank with a noose around my neck."

"But now you have a friend on the audit bench. Don't give up hope, the rules changed today."

Kate sat on my lap and placed a wax and ochre kiss on my cheek. Apart from being a former dancer and dance teacher, she had once been in a real cheer squad for some municipal football team, and had done the training and routines for this one.

"Watching you ladies perform reminded me that I wasn't alone and gave me the strength to go on," I told her.

"You mean we really made a difference?"

"You certainly did."

For that I got a kiss on my lips.

Lia was a third generation Vietnamese-Australian dress-maker who had improvised the electric blue costumes out of plastic rubbish and cheesecloth. She had little consistent material to work with, but this resulted in more exposed flesh. Much of that flesh was wrinkled, but I was eighty-five and rather partial to wrinkles.

Vikki had been a personal trainer, and taught the others to do their routines without tearing muscles or ligaments.

Kylie had been the woman shot by the Anthrophobes, and the others told me that she had been a professional football-er. After years of being cheered on by cheer squads, she had joined one to cheer for me. I still wished that I had been able to thank her while she was alive.

These were the sorts of people I was fighting for, people who had been born into a society and economy that was un-sustainable. They had no say in that, but now that the plight of the world was patently obvious, they just wanted to help. All had lost partners, children, parents, friends and relatives to the audits, famines and plagues, yet they had dressed in undignified blue scraps and waved bunches of ribbons to support their champion - me - in front of a worldwide audience. Now they were staging a party for my benefit, yet I should have been doing it for them.

Any of them would have been happy to spend a night in my new tent, but that could never happen. Very soon I would be one of their auditors and their lives would depend on my vote not being disqualified.

"Ladies, I have to warn you that you all face execution," I said once they had toasted me with vodka fermented from something that nobody wanted to talk about. "That is not the end of the story, however. I shall make sure that you all go so far down the priority list that your executioner is sure to be old age."

"Or an orgasm!" called Kate.

Of course this was favoritism, but they had held my battered morale together during the last of the audits and I do not abandon my friends once they cease to be useful. Although they were under sentence of death for climate crimes, they still wanted to work for the planet's welfare and they certainly could be useful. I took Alette aside.

"Go over to Ryan, my duty warden," I said. "Ask him to fetch the audit laptop from my tent. I need to do a spreadsheet for these five ladies."

#

Around midnight I emerged from my new tent in the dormitory field, unable to sleep. As I paced around the tent Olivia came over.

"Hey there, Dr Auditor, are you okay?" she asked.

"I can't sleep in a tent," I explained. "I've slept in the open for too long."

"I can call a counselor."

"Don't bother, someone might charge me with squander. I'll just sleep outside."

"All good, then?"

"All good."

All was clearly not good, and she was not going to let it go.

"Are you worried about me?" she asked.

"Why should I be?"

"I killed Chaz."

"So you did."

"He was your friend."

"So he was."

"I only offed him because he planned to violate the wilderness."

"Justifiably so."

"Today you chose me and my warden squad as your personal security team."

"True."

"Lucky I like older men. Your tent or mine?"

Olivia put a hand into my robes and began rubbing her leg against me. What do you do when you get cruised by a woman who would not have hesitated to kill you two nights earlier? She was another Silvy, and she was far too close. I seized my libido by the collar, marched it down to a cage in the depths of my brain and slammed the door shut.

"Octant Olivia, you were my choice because I know where I stand with you," I said as I gently disengaged her. "I like you and you're fun to be with, but I know that you can't be trusted, and I shall never, never drop my guard near you."

"Oh. I - er ..."

"Don't feel bad about it."

"So what am I supposed to do? I'm meant to, like, look after you. Personally. Very personally, if you like."

"No, I want you to be a very dangerous person who is very close to me. That will keep me sharp. Now go to bed. Better still, go to someone else's bed."

#

Olivia walked away into the darkness. She was probably offended, but that was unavoidable. Neither of us had noticed the figure standing nearby.

"Hello grandfather."

"So, what's it to be?" I asked. "Quality family time, or saving the world?"

"Saving the world, I'm afraid. Come along, the Audit Arena is clear, open space without hidden ears."

She led me away through the lamp lit gloom, trailed by her wardens and mine. Presently we were standing in the Audit Arena.

"So, do you understand yet?" she asked.

"Yes," I sighed. "It was not just me being audited. It was all borderlines."

"All too true, and Death will sit among the Auditors on the bench tomorrow. You are Death."

"I can already see millions of frightened, desperate, pleading eyes staring at me."

"I see those eyes every day. Welcome to the future."

"Damn you and damn your future."

She shook her head.

"Grandfather, your problem is that you think people are merely misguided. You think that if they learn the truth, they will do whatever is right."

"I don't just think that, I know it."

"Wrong. Humanity is just one vast swamp of apathy, reaching right around the world and washing up against your heels. There are some solid bits here and there, but they are oh so very small."

"I suppose you think the duty of the National Audit is to drain that swamp?"

"Oh no, swamps are wonderful ecosystems, and apathy is a valuable resource."

"I don't follow."

"We are the new park wardens, managing the swamp, and putting human apathy to work in defense of the Earth."

"I still don't follow."

"When it was easy to commute by car, everyone drove. Now apathetic people ride bicycles or walk because it's easier."

"But most people are not apathetic. Progress is part of human nature."

"Progress? What is progress?"

"Bettering the human condition."

"People once thought progress meant spending money they did not have, to buy things they did not need, to impress people they didn't care about, and who didn't care about them."

"Stay on topic!" I said, rather more sharply than was probably necessary. "The borderlines should be kept alive until they have undone their acts of squander and neglect. That betters the human condition. That's progress. My qualifications include numeric modeling. I could write an algorithm to balance length of required service against projected lifespan, tailored to each borderline. It could put estimated lifespan ahead of service required, yet ensure that the prisoners will probably die before that service has ended."

"That sounds like a contradiction."

"It will require some very careful tuning. You can call the sentence Death After Restorational Service."

DARS, the acronym rolled off the tongue easily and did not sound at all sinister. She took her time to reply, which was good. It meant she was impressed by what I was proposing.

"Granddad, I truly admire you," she said presently.

"Weasel words for *I don't agree.*"

"Not true, but I do have to keep the weasels happy."

"So you'll consider my proposal?"

"Yes, yes, all right," she said, nodding reluctantly. "If everyone had lived like you, we could have started saving the future half a century ago, but they didn't. Now we have been forced into drastic action."

"Mass slaughter?"

"If you think of a better way, let me know."

"Weren't you listening? I suggested sentencing people to Death After Restorational Service."

"The audit bench would not like that."

"Then start with the trivial cases or I'll point out that your eight other auditors are squandering the talents of people who committed trivial crimes of omission. No auditor wants to be audited for squandering resources vital to the recovery of the planet. Happy?"

"No, because if I seem too lenient I can be demoted to bench auditor."

"Then attack! Accuse anyone who supports a mandatory death penalty of squander. Intersperse clear cut death sentences among those of Death After Restorational Service. I've stood alone against the world and won. Can you?"

There was more silence, meaning that I had got through to her.

"Granddad, during your trial ... I realized something. I could not have lived to your standards last century. I was just lucky to be born in April 2000."

"Yet you still preside over the audit bench?"

"Yes. I have often thought about resigning, but the work must go on. Future generations need to know the high price of taking more than they replace from the planet. Maybe I don't meet your standards, maybe I am guilty of display because I want to remain as Auditor General, but I do have duties."

She turned away from me and took a few steps toward the entrance.

"Renny!" I called after her.

She stopped and turned.

"Yes granddad?"

"I admire you, too."

She hesitated, then returned and kissed me on the cheek.

"We were both being audited over the past fortnight," she said. "Do I get a pardon?"

"Only if you fight for what is worthwhile. If you really believe in killing all GTs who don't measure up to my standards, then you are putting revenge ahead of survival, and humanity really is doomed."

"Strong words."

"Strong words are my specialty."

"Audit Camp 71 is famous now, and your audit is being called the audit of the century."

"Fame is only worthwhile if it's used for something worthwhile."

"Then use it. Did you know that auditors have always been allowed to speak about the cases and evidence before I take the vote and pass judgment?"

"No. Why don't they?"

"Perhaps they don't want to cause delays, or are frightened of the Retributor. Maybe some are even frightened of me. You fear nobody, so speak out, it may make a difference."

Again she turned to go, but I took her by the arm.

"Earlier tonight I was given a little party by my cheer squad."

"The ladies dressed in tiny blue offcuts? They were a lot of fun. If they were not under sentence of death, I'd be tempted to offer them a job, cheering those who get pardons."

"I asked them about their lifestyles, drew up a spreadsheet and estimated how much carbon they put into the atmosphere, using one of the International Audit Movement algorithms. All five of those women could work for less than their projected lifetime in the carbon extraction farms and actually repay their environmental damage debt. I told them as much, and the funny thing is that they thought that was a great idea. They even said they would keep working after that, and work on until they fell dead to save the Earth for their grandchildren and great grandchildren."

"You're getting ready to pitch a scheme to me."

"Oh I am indeed. If a tipper or borderline has squandered so very much that they can never repay their carbon debt, then reclaim their carbon. If they have left a lighter touch on the Earth, sentence them to work until they have repaid their debt."

"And then reclaim their carbon? Delayed execution is still execution, with all its cruelties and terrors."

Now it was my turn to weave my way through the lethal maze of laws that ruled the continent. There had to be a lateral solution to the mandatory death sentence ... and there was! It was a court case that had been conducted on the other side of the Earth, a few years before I was born.

"Are you familiar with the trial of the computing pioneer, Alan Turing?"

"Yes. It was an important precedent for pardoning a person legally convicted under a law that was subsequently repealed. He was convicted of homosexual activity in 1952 and he suicided two years later, while serving a sentence of chemical castration."

"As you said, the law was later repealed, and in 2013 he was granted a posthumous royal pardon. If he had made it to 1967 he would not even have been arrested for what he did."

"What has this to do with reclaiming the carbon of convicted climate criminals?"

"Public sentiment changes, Renny, so laws do as well. Today Generation Victim is boiling over with fury and hatred for what the tipper generations did to the planet. In twenty years the next generation might decide that many of those who were executed were environmental pioneers who tried to warn the world but were ignored. That generation might even want revenge against people like you."

"But I must enforce the law as it stands."

"Then execute the ladies of my cheer squad tomorrow," I snapped, angry because my own granddaughter was not standing up for what she clearly believed. "I'm sure they will appreciate getting a posthumous pardon twenty years from now."

"Vikki Windling is fifty," she said after some moments of thought. "Tell me about her."

"My model says that thirty-five years of restoration service would balance out her climate crimes."

"So at the end of that she would be eighty-five, and still be under sentence of death. Should she be executed?"

"She would have had thirty-five years of life, with a chance that the public's hatred for everyone from her generation will have softened by then. After all, without those tippers who left a lighter touch on the world, we would already be beyond hope by now."

"Well played. No wonder you beat the Retributor."

"Damn the Retributor! Did I convince you?"

"That is between me and my conscience, grandfather. Time for us to get some sleep now. Lives are in our hands, so we can't afford to be tired and clumsy."

#

EPILOGUE DAY

With dawn only minutes away, Octant Olivia helped me adjust the unfamiliar robes I was now wearing as the auditors assembled for their procession. I walked at the end, proudly escorted by Olivia. We auditors bowed to the Auditor General, then seated ourselves on her cue.

"We are entering a new era, one in which the backlog of borderlines can be cleared," she began. "There are eleven thousand of them in this camp, but I have been convinced that applying the Hall Precedents blindly might lead to squander. Everyone must get a fair re-audit. Any objections?"

There was surprise on every face, mine included most likely, but nobody protested.

"Splendid, let's make a start," said Renny. "First borderline, Clerk of the Bench?"

"Vikki Windling, your honor. Under the Hall Precedents, she has been assessed as guilty."

Vikki looked very frightened as she was brought forward to stand before the audit bench, and all of her cheer squad enthusiasm was gone. She was just dressed in her mundane rags, and her eyes kept flicking in my direction, probably for reassurance.

"Honorable victims, who votes guilty?" asked the Auditor General.

Eight hands were raised. Vikki's face contorted with terror.

"Victoria Windling, our models estimate that thirty-five years of service will remove from the atmosphere the fossil carbon that your life caused to be released. Do you have genuine concerns about your legacy to the climate?"

"Yeah, your honor. That is, yes."

"Then are you willing to perform thirty-five years of service before the carbon of your own body is reclaimed?"

Vikki took a moment to think through the offer.

"Er, what if I don't last thirty-five years?"

"You win."

"Oh, er, then yeah," Vikki managed, suddenly too confused to be terrified. "That is, yes, your honor."

The Auditor General struck her desk plate again.

"Victoria Windling, you are sentenced to thirty-five years service in the Carbon Dioxide Extraction Farm Kappa-12, followed by Class Six Death on the Tipping Point Gallows - with mercy."

The other four surviving women of my cheer squad did not have a chant ready, so they just jumped up and down, screamed Vikki's name and clapped while those in the gallery cheered.

"Order!" called the Auditor General. "Clerk of the Bench, can we have a tipper audit this time?"

The first tipper of the day was walked across the Audit Arena to the dais. He wore an old, ragged scarf and cap in his football team's colors. His warden snatched the cap from his head as he stood before the bench.

"First audit of the day, Raymond Carter," said the Clerk of the Bench.

"He is accused of flying interstate as often twice a month to watch his football team play," said the Retributor. "There are numerous other charges, but in the interests of not squandering the bench's time I am only presenting the most blatant of his climate crimes."

"The accused has a very substantial carbon footprint," said the Auditor General, staring at her screen. "Comments, fellow victims?"

The man was frightened and bewildered. He had done nothing wrong a quarter of a century ago, but now he was on trial for his life. He was what used to be called a good bloke: fun company at the pub, probably a tolerable husband, and perhaps even a passably good father ... yet good fathers should look after their children's future.

"Mr Carter, why did you do it?" I asked. "If you had watched the football matches on television, a ten thousandth as much carbon would have been burned."

"But I couldn't let the Pies face them interstate teams without a friendly voice to cheer 'em on," he replied with absolute, unshakable sincerity.

"Even at the price of the planet's future?"

"I didn't know about that," he said, now mumbling.

"I find that hard to believe. Did you at least buy carbon credits?"

"Er, yeah."

"He did not," said the Retributor. "I have the records here."

"Clerk of the Bench, add perjury to his charge list, not that we need bother hearing that one," said the Auditor General. "Advocate?"

"I could not defend him without committing an act of squander," she replied.

"Have you any comments, Precedent Auditor?"

"No, your honor," I replied, forcing the words out.

"Honorable victims, who audits guilty?" asked the Auditor General.

I closed my eyes, took a deep breath, then slowly raised my hand.

"Guilty as charged. Class Four Death, with mercy."

"Death?" Carter exclaimed. "But can't I work, doin' Service?"

"Clerk of the Audit, do you have an estimate of how long he would have to live, working in a carbon extraction farm, to repay his lifetime carbon debt?"

"Three hundred and five years, your honor," he replied after running my algorithm.

"My understanding of the law is that in order to qualify for Service before execution, you must have a realistic prospect of living long enough to make up for what you have squandered. You are currently sixty-one. Your prospects of living to three hundred and sixty-six are zero. Next audit?"

The bewildered, terrified football fan was led away by his warden as another warden brought Kate forward to stand before the bench, cowering in her sun blanket. I checked the statistics on my screen. She was the same age as Carter, but her carbon footprint was only a tenth of his. Having spent a lifetime in dance she was in good health, so technically she could reach her nineties or beyond before facing execution. Her audit took no longer than that of Vikki, and the outcome was the same.

"Katherine McCormak, you are sentenced to thirty years service in the Carbon Dioxide Extraction Farm Kappa-12, followed by Class Six Death, with mercy," declared the Auditor General.

To our astonishment Kate flung off her sun blanket, revealing her cheer squad bikini beneath, then performed the squad's routine alone while those in the gallery cheered. The Auditor General watched in silence, then reached for her mace and listlessly banged it on her desk plate and called for order.

"Make that another five years for contempt of audit," she said. "Do try to stay alive until you are ninety-six in the interests of climate justice. Next audit?"

I felt relief dissolving the tension inside me. Unlike Carter, Kate would see dawn tomorrow. She might well see over thirteen thousand more dawns and tomorrows, and surely by then the National Audit would have decided that the early punishments for climate crimes had been a bit excessive. Pardons would be handed out to those who were still alive, and one of those would be Kate. Lia, Petra and Arlene were also sentenced to death, but only after a few decades of service in Carbon Dioxide Extraction Farm Kappa-12.

Assuming one hundred years of age as a realistic average maximum for those tough enough to survive in Audit Camp 71, one borderline in ten qualified to do between twenty and fifty years of service before facing execution. Only one out of four hundred borderlines would have escaped death under the Hall Precedent, set during my audit, but now the figure was one in ten. That was still appalling, but Generation Victim still wanted revenge, and Service for everyone found guilty was not sufficiently harsh.

So this was my future, saving one out of ten, and participating in the executions of the other nine. I had thought that I could just beat the National Audit and walk away, leaving others to apply the precedents I had set. I had not realized that anyone who could beat the National Audit was a valuable resource, and in our new and perilous world, squandering a resource carried the death penalty.

I have become Death, yet I am trying to save people's lives, floated into my mind for no apparent reason. The thought was so absurd that I had to stifle a snigger. My lapel microphone betrayed me.

"Order," called the Auditor General, striking her mace on the desk. "Next audit, Clerk of the Bench?"

#

SEAN MCMULLEN

ACKNOWLEDGMENTS

My many friends in meteorology and climatology, who patiently answered my technical questions while I was developing *Generation Nemesis*.

My daughter Catherine, who has more drive than the Roman Empire and often puts it behind me.

My partner Zoya, who alerted me to the impact of fashion on the environment, long before it was fashionable.

My agent Paul Collins, who does not understand the meaning of the words 'give up,' unless they are preceded by 'Never'.

Gordon Van Gelder and John Joseph Adams for giving the original novelette, The Precedent, a chance to frighten people, and Cheryl Morgan for doing likewise with *Generation Nemesis*.

ABOUT THE AUTHOR

Sean McMullen has had twenty-seven books and over a hundred stories published professionally in Australia and internationally. His work has been translated into fourteen languages, he has won over two dozen awards, and he was runner up in the 2011 Hugo Awards.

Sean spent three decades in computer management and planning with the Australian Bureau of Meteorology, while running a parallel career as a science fiction author. In 2008 he gained a PhD from the University of Melbourne, where he is still the deputy chief instructor at the university karate club.

His daughter is the award winning SF and horror screen-writer, Catherine S. McMullen.

Online, Sean is at https://seanmcmullen.net.au

Printed in Australia
AUHW021518251122
371765AU00010B/10

9 781913 892449